THE LAST OF THE MOHICANS

JAMES FENIMORE COOPER

SANAGE
PUBLISHING HOUSE

Paperback: 978-811909049-5

Printed by: Manipal Technologies Limited, Manipal
Sanage Publishing House LLP
Mumbai, India

sanagepublishing@gmail.com

James Fenimore Cooper was an American writer of the first half of the 19th century, whose historical romances depicting colonial and indigenous characters from the 17th to the 19th centuries brought him fame and fortune. He attended Yale College until he was expelled for bad behavior. He served in the U.S. Navy, resigning in 1811 to get married. With his story The Pilot (1823), Cooper set the style for a new genre of sea fiction. His most famous novels are the Leather-Stocking Tales including The Pioneers (1823), The Last of the Mohicans (1826), The Prairie (1827), The Pathfinder (1840), and The Deerslayer (1841), featuring the quintessential American hero Natty Bumppo. Cooper, a keen social critic, wrote several well-regarded naval histories.

CONTENTS

INTRODUCTION

It is believed that the scene of this tale, and most of the information necessary to understand its allusions, are rendered sufficiently obvious to the reader in the text itself, or in the accompanying notes. Still there is so much obscurity in the Indian traditions, and so much confusion in the Indian names, as to render some explanation useful.

Few men exhibit greater diversity, or, if we may so express it, greater antithesis of character, than the native warrior of North America. In war, he is daring, boastful, cunning, ruthless, self-denying, and self-devoted, in peace, just, generous, hospitable, revengeful, superstitious, modest, and commonly chaste. These are qualities, it is true, which do not distinguish all alike; but they are so far, the predominating traits of these remarkable people as to be characteristic.

It is generally believed that the Aborigines of the American continent have an Asiatic origin. There are many physical as well as moral facts which corroborate this opinion, and some few that would seem to weigh against it.

The color of the Indian, the writer believes, is peculiar to himself, and while his cheek bones have a very striking indication of a Tartar origin, his eyes have not. Climate may have had great influence on the former, but it is difficult to see how it can have produced the substantial difference which exists in the latter. The imagery of the Indian, both in his poetry and in his oratory, is oriental; chastened, and perhaps improved, by the limited range of his practical knowledge. He draws his metaphors from the clouds, the seasons, the birds, the beasts, and the vegetable world. In this, perhaps, he does no more than any other energetic and imaginative race would do, being compelled to set bounds to fancy by experience; but the North American Indian clothes his ideas in a dress which is different from that of the African and is oriental in itself. His language has the richness and sententious fullness of the Chinese. He will express a phrase in a word, and he will qualify the meaning of an entire sentence by a syllable; he will even convey different significations by the simplest inflections of the voice.

Philologists have said that there are but two or three languages, properly speaking, among all the numerous tribes which formerly occupied the country that now composes the United States. They ascribe the known difficulty one people have to understand another to corruptions and dialects. The writer remembers to have been present at an interview between two chiefs of the Great Prairies west of the Mississippi, and when an interpreter was in attendance who spoke both their languages. The warriors appeared to be on the friendliest terms, and seemingly conversed much together; yet, according to the account of the interpreter, each was absolutely ignorant of what the other said. They were of hostile tribes, brought together by the influence of the American government; and it is worthy of remark, that a common policy led them both to adopt the same subject. They mutually exhorted each other to be of use in the event of the chances of war throwing either of the parties into the hands of his enemies. Whatever may be the truth, as respects the root and the genius of the Indian tongues, it is quite certain they are now so distinct in their words as to possess most of the disadvantages of strange languages; hence much of the embarrassment that has arisen in learning their histories, and most of the uncertainty which exists in their traditions.

Like nations of higher pretensions, the American Indian gives a very different account of his own tribe or race from that which is given by other people. He is much addicted to overestimating his own perfections, and to undervaluing those of his rival or his enemy; a trait which may possibly be thought corroborative of the Mosaic account of the creation.

The whites have assisted greatly in rendering the traditions of the Aborigines more obscure by their own manner of corrupting names. Thus, the term used in the title of this book has undergone the changes of Mahicanni, Mohicans, and Mohegans; the latter being the word commonly used by the whites. When it is remembered that the Dutch (who first settled New York), the English, and the French, all gave appellations to the tribes that dwelt within the country which is the scene of this story, and that the Indians not only gave different names to their enemies, but frequently to themselves, the cause of the confusion will be understood.

In these pages, Lenni-Lenape, Lenope, Delawares, Wapanachki, and Mohicans, all mean the same people, or tribes of the same stock. The Mengwe, the Maquas, the Mingoes, and the Iroquois, though not all strictly the same, are identified frequently by the speakers, being politically confederated and opposed to those just named. Mingo was a term of peculiar reproach, as were Mengwe and Maqua in a less degree.

The Mohicans were the possessors of the country first occupied by the Europeans in this portion of the continent. They were, consequently, the first dispossessed; and the seemingly inevitable fate of all these people, who disappear before the advances, or it might be termed the inroads, of civilization, as the verdure of their native forests falls before the nipping frosts, is represented as having already befallen them. There is sufficient historical truth in the picture to justify the use that has been made of it.

In point of fact, the country which is the scene of the following tale has undergone as little change, since the historical events alluded to had place, as almost any other district of equal extent within the whole limits of the United States. There are fashionable and well-attended watering-places at and near the spring where Hawkeye halted to drink, and roads traverse the forests where he and his friends were compelled to journey without even a path. Glens has a large village; and while William Henry, and even a fortress of later date, are only to be traced as ruins, there is another village on the shores of the Horican. But, beyond this, the enterprise and energy of a people who have done so much in other places have done little here. The whole of that wilderness, in which the latter incidents of the legend occurred, is nearly a wilderness still, though the red man has entirely deserted this part of the state. Of all the tribes named in these pages, there exist only a few half-civilized beings of the Oneidas, on the reservations of their people in New York. The rest have disappeared, either from the regions in which their fathers dwelt, or altogether from the earth.

There is one point on which we would wish to say a word before closing this preface. Hawkeye calls the Lac du Saint Sacrement, the "Horican." As we believe this to be an appropriation of the name that has its origin with ourselves, the time has arrived, perhaps, when the fact should be frankly admitted. While writing this book, fully a quarter of a century since, it occurred to us that the French name of this lake was too complicated, the American too commonplace, and the Indian too unpronounceable for either to be used familiarly in a work of fiction. Looking over an ancient map, it was ascertained that a tribe of Indians, called "Les Horicans" by the French, existed in the neighborhood of this beautiful sheet of water. As every word uttered by Natty Bumppo was not to be received as rigid truth, we took the liberty of putting the "Horican" into his mouth, as the substitute for "Lake George." The name has appeared to find favor, and all things considered, it may possibly be quite as well to let it stand, instead of going back to the House of Hanover for the appellation of our finest sheet of water. We believe our conscience by the confession, at all events leaving it to exercise its authority as it may see fit.

CHAPTER I.

"Mine ear is open, and my heart prepared:
The worst is wordly loss thou canst unfold;
Say, is my kingdom lost?"—Shakespeare

It was a feature peculiar to the colonial wars of North America, that the toils and dangers of the wilderness were to be encountered before the adverse hosts could meet. A wide and apparently an impervious boundary of forests severed the possessions of the hostile provinces of France and England. The hardy colonist, and the trained European who fought at his side, frequently expended months in struggling against the rapids of the streams, or in effecting the rugged passes of the mountains, in quest of an opportunity to exhibit their courage in a more martial conflict. But, emulating the patience and self-denial of the practiced native warriors, they learned to overcome every difficulty; and it would seem that, in time, there was no recess of the woods so dark, nor any secret place so lovely, that it might claim exemption from the inroads of those who had pledged their blood to satiate their vengeance, or to uphold the cold and selfish policy of the distant monarchs of Europe.

Perhaps no district throughout the wide extent of the intermediate frontiers can furnish a livelier picture of the cruelty and fierceness of the savage warfare of those periods than the country which lies between the head waters of the Hudson and the adjacent lakes.

The facilities which nature had there offered to the march of the combatants were too obvious to be neglected. The lengthened sheet of the Champlain stretched from the frontiers of Canada, deep within the borders of the neighboring province of New York, forming a natural passage across half the distance that the French were compelled to master in order to strike their enemies. Near its southern termination, it received the contributions of another lake, whose waters were so limpid as to have been exclusively selected by the Jesuit missionaries to perform the typical purification of baptism, and to obtain for it the title of lake "du Saint Sacrement." The less zealous English thought they conferred a sufficient honor on its unsullied fountains, when they bestowed the name of their reigning prince, the second of the house of Hanover. The two united to rob the untutored possessors of its wooded scenery of their native right to perpetuate its original appellation of "Horican."[1]

Winding its way among countless islands, and imbedded in mountains, the "holy lake" extended a dozen leagues still further to the south. With the high plain that there interposed itself to the further passage of the water, commenced a portage of as many miles, which conducted the adventurer to the banks of the Hudson, at a point where, with the usual obstructions of the rapids, or rifts, as they were then termed in the language of the country, the river became navigable to the tide.

While, in the pursuit of their daring plans of annoyance, the restless enterprise of the French even attempted the distant and difficult gorges of the Alleghany, it may easily be imagined that their proverbial acuteness would not overlook the natural advantages of the district we have just described. It became, emphatically, the bloody arena, in which most of the battles for the mastery of the colonies were contested. Forts were erected at the different

[1] As each nation of the Indians had its language or its dialect, they usually gave different names to the same places, though nearly all of their appellations were descriptive of the object. Thus, a literal translation of the name of this beautiful sheet of water, used by the tribe that dwelt on its banks, would be "The Tail of the Lake." Lake George, as it is vulgarly, and now, indeed, legally, called, forms a sort of tail to Lake Champlain, when viewed on the map. Hence, the name.

points that commanded the facilities of the route, and were taken and retaken, razed and rebuilt, as victory alighted on the hostile banners. While the husbandman shrank back from the dangerous passes, within the safer boundaries of the more ancient settlements, armies larger than those that had often disposed of the scepters of the mother countries, were seen to bury themselves in these forests, whence they rarely returned but in skeleton bands, that were haggard with care or dejected by defeat. Though the arts of peace were unknown to this fatal region, its forests were alive with men; its shades and glens rang with the sounds of martial music, and the echoes of its mountains threw back the laugh, or repeated the wanton cry, of many a gallant and reckless youth, as he hurried by them, in the noontide of his spirits, to slumber in a long night of forgetfulness.

It was in this scene of strife and bloodshed that the incidents we shall attempt to relate occurred, during the third year of the war which England and France last waged for the possession of a country that neither was destined to retain.

The imbecility of her military leaders abroad, and the fatal want of energy in her councils at home, had lowered the character of Great Britain from the proud elevation on which it had been placed by the talents and enterprise of her former warriors and statesmen. No longer dreaded by her enemies, her servants were fast losing the confidence of self-respect. In this mortifying abasement, the colonists, though innocent of her imbecility, and too humble to be the agents of her blunders, were but the natural participators. They had recently seen a chosen army from that country, which, reverencing as a mother, they had blindly believed invincible an army led by a chief who had been selected from a crowd of trained warriors, for his rare military endowments, disgracefully routed by a handful of French and Indians, and only saved from annihilation by the coolness and spirit of a Virginian boy, whose riper fame has since diffused itself, with the steady influence of moral truth, to the uttermost confines of Christendom.[2] A wide frontier had been laid naked by this unexpected disaster, and more substantial evils were preceded by a thousand fanciful and imaginary dangers. The alarmed colonists believed that the yells of the savages mingled with every fitful gust of wind that issued from the interminable forests of the west. The terrific character of their merciless enemies increased immeasurably the natural horrors of warfare. Numberless recent massacres were still vivid in their recollections; nor was there any ear in the provinces so deaf as not to have drunk in with avidity the narrative of some fearful tale of midnight murder, in which the natives of the forests were the principal and barbarous actors. As the credulous and excited traveler related the hazardous chances of the wilderness, the blood of the timid curdled with terror, and mothers cast anxious glances even at those children which slumbered within the security of the largest towns. In short, the magnifying influence of fear began to set at naught the calculations of reason, and to render those who should have remembered their manhood, the slaves of the basest passions. Even the most confident and the stoutest hearts began to think the issue of the contest was becoming doubtful; and that abject class was hourly increasing in numbers, who thought they foresaw all the possessions of the English crown in America subdued by their Christian foes, or laid waste by the inroads of their relentless allies.

When, therefore, intelligence was received at the fort which covered the southern termination of the portage between the Hudson and the lakes, that Montcalm had been seen moving up the Champlain, with an army "numerous as the leaves on the trees," its truth was admitted with more of the craven reluctance of fear than with the stern joy that a warrior should feel, in finding an enemy within reach of his blow. The news had been brought, toward the decline of a

[2] Washington, who, after uselessly admonishing the European general of the danger into which he was heedlessly running, saved the remnants of the British army, on this occasion, by his decision and courage. The reputation earned by Washington in this battle was the principal cause of his being selected to command the American armies at a later day. It is a circumstance worthy of observation, that while all America rang with his well-merited reputation, his name does not occur in any European account of the battle; at least the author has searched for it without success. In this manner does the mother country absorb even the fame, under that system of rule.

day in midsummer, by an Indian runner, who also bore an urgent request from Munro, the commander of a work on the shore of the "holy lake," for a speedy and powerful reinforcement. It has already been mentioned that the distance between these two posts was less than five leagues. The rude path, which originally formed their line of communication, had been widened for the passage of wagons; so that the distance which had been traveled by the son of the forest in two hours, might easily be affected by a detachment of troops, with their necessary baggage, between the rising and setting of a summer sun. The loyal servants of the British crown had given to one of these forest-fastnesses the name of William Henry, and to the other that of Fort Edward, calling each after a favorite prince of the reigning family. The veteran Scotchman just named held the first, with a regiment of regulars and a few provincials; a force really by far too small to make head against the formidable power that Montcalm was leading to the foot of his earthen mounds. At the latter, however, lay General Webb, who commanded the armies of the king in the northern provinces, with a body of more than five thousand men. By uniting the several detachments of his command, this officer might have arrayed nearly double that number of combatants against the enterprising Frenchman, who had ventured so far from his reinforcements, with an army but little superior in numbers.

But under the influence of their degraded fortunes, both officers and men appeared better disposed to await the approach of their formidable antagonists, within their works, than to resist the progress of their march, by emulating the successful example of the French at Fort du Quesne and striking a blow on their advance.

After the first surprise of the intelligence had a little abated, a rumor was spread through the entrenched camp, which stretched along the margin of the Hudson, forming a chain of outworks to the body of the fort itself, that a chosen detachment of fifteen hundred men was to depart, with the dawn, for William Henry, the post at the northern extremity of the portage. That which at first was only rumor, soon became certainty, as orders passed from the quarters of the commander-in-chief to the several corps he had selected for this service, to prepare for their speedy departure. All doubts as to the intention of Webb now vanished, and an hour or two of hurried footsteps and anxious faces succeeded. The novice in the military art flew from point to point, retarding his own preparations by the excess of his violent and somewhat distempered zeal; while the more practiced veteran made his arrangements with a deliberation that scorned every appearance of haste, though his sober lineaments and anxious eye sufficiently betrayed that he had no very strong professional relish for the as yet untried and dreaded warfare of the wilderness. At length the sun set in a flood of glory, behind the distant western hills, and as darkness drew its veil around the secluded spot the sounds of preparation diminished; the last light finally disappeared from the log cabin of some officer; the trees cast their deeper shadows over the mounds and the rippling stream, and a silence soon pervaded the camp, as deep as that which reigned in the vast forest by which it was environed.

According to the orders of the preceding night, the heavy sleep of the army was broken by the rolling of the warning drums, whose rattling echoes were heard issuing, on the damp morning air, out of every vista of the woods, just as day began to draw the shaggy outlines of some tall pines of the vicinity, on the opening brightness of a soft and cloudless eastern sky. In an instant the whole camp was in motion; the meanest soldier arousing from his lair to witness the departure of his comrades, and to share in the excitement and incidents of the hour. The simple array of the chosen band was soon completed. While the regular and trained hirelings of the king marched with haughtiness to the right of the line, the less pretending colonists took their humbler position on its left, with a docility that long practice had rendered easy. The scouts departed; strong guards preceded and followed the lumbering vehicles that bore the baggage; and before the gray light of the morning was mellowed by the rays of the sun, the main body of the combatants wheeled into column, and left the encampment with a show of high military bearing, that served to drown the slumbering apprehensions of many a novice, who was now about to make his first essay in arms. While in view of their admiring comrades, the same proud front and ordered array was observed, until the notes of their fifes growing fainter in distance, the forest at length appeared to swallow up the living mass which had slowly entered its bosom.

The deepest sounds of the retiring and invisible column had ceased to be borne on the breeze to the listeners, and the latest straggler had already disappeared in pursuit; but there still remained the signs of another departure, before a log cabin of unusual size and accommodations, in front of which those sentinels paced their rounds, who were known to guard the person of the English general. At this spot were gathered some half dozen horses, caparisoned in a manner which showed that two, at least, were destined to bear the persons of females, of a rank that it was not usual to meet so far in the wilds of the country. A third wore trappings and arms of an officer of the staff; while the rest, from the plainness of the housings, and the traveling mails with which they were encumbered, were evidently fitted for the reception of as many menials, who were, seemingly, already waiting the pleasure of those they served. At a respectful distance from this unusual show, were gathered divers' groups of curious idlers; some admiring the blood and bone of the high-mettled military charger, and others gazing at the preparations, with the dull wonder of vulgar curiosity. There was one man, however, who, by his countenance and actions, formed a marked exception to those who composed the latter class of spectators, being neither idle, nor seemingly very ignorant.

The person of this individual was to the last degree ungainly, without being in any particular manner deformed. He had all the bones and joints of other men, without any of their proportions. Erect, his stature surpassed that of his fellows; though seated, he appeared reduced within the ordinary limits of the race. The same contrariety in his members seemed to exist throughout the whole man. His head was large; his shoulders narrow; his arms long and dangling; while his hands were small, if not delicate. His legs and thighs were thin, nearly to emaciation, but of extraordinary length; and his knees would have been considered tremendous, had they not been outdone by the broader foundations on which this false superstructure of blended human orders was so profanely reared. The ill-assorted and injudicious attire of the individual only served to render his awkwardness more conspicuous. A sky-blue coat, with short and broad skirts and low cape, exposed a long, thin neck, and longer and thinner legs, to the worst animadversions of the evil disposed. His nether garment was a yellow nankeen, closely fitted to the shape, and tied at his bunches of knees by large knots of white ribbon, a good deal sullied by use. Clouded cotton stockings, and shoes, on one of the latter of which was a plated spur, completed the costume of the lower extremity of this figure, no curve or angle of which was concealed, but, on the other hand, studiously exhibited, through the vanity or simplicity of its owner.

From beneath the flap of an enormous pocket of a soiled vest of embossed silk, heavily ornamented with tarnished silver lace, projected an instrument, which, from being seen in such martial company, might have been easily mistaken for some mischievous and unknown implement of war. Small as it was, this uncommon engine had excited the curiosity of most of the Europeans in the camp, though several of the provincials were seen to handle it, not only without fear, but with the utmost familiarity. A large, civil cocked hat, like those worn by clergymen within the last thirty years, surmounted the whole, furnishing dignity to a good-natured and somewhat vacant countenance, that apparently needed such artificial aid, to support the gravity of some high and extraordinary trust.

While the common herd stood aloof, in deference to the quarters of Webb, the figure we have described stalked into the center of the domestics, freely expressing his censures or commendations on the merits of the horses, as by chance they displeased or satisfied his judgment.

"This beast, I rather conclude, friend, is not of home raising, but is from foreign lands, or perhaps from the little island itself over the blue water?" he said, in a voice as remarkable for the softness and sweetness of its tones, as was his person for its rare proportions; "I may speak of these things, and be no braggart; for I have been down at both havens; that which is situate at the mouth of Thames, and is named after the capital of Old England, and that which is called 'Haven', with the addition of the word 'New'; and have seen the scows and brigantines collecting their droves, like the gathering to the ark, being outward bound to the Island of Jamaica, for the purpose of barter and traffic in four-footed animals; but never before have I beheld a beast which verified the true scripture war-horse like this: 'He pawed in the valley, and rejoiced in his strength; he goeth on to meet the armed men. He saith among the trumpets, Ha, ha; and he smelled the battle afar off, the thunder of the captains, and the shouting.' It would seem that the stock of the horse of Israel had descended to our own time; would it not, friend?"

Receiving no reply to this extraordinary appeal, which in truth, as it was delivered with the vigor of full and sonorous tones, merited some sort of notice, he who had thus sung forth the language of the holy book turned to the silent figure to whom he had unwittingly addressed himself, and found a new and more powerful subject of admiration in the object that encountered his gaze. His eyes fell on the still, upright, and rigid form of the "Indian runner," who had borne to the camp the unwelcome tidings of the preceding evening. Although in a state of perfect repose, and apparently disregarding, with characteristic stoicism, the excitement and bustle around him, there was a sullen fierceness mingled with the quiet of the savage, that was likely to arrest the attention of much more experienced eyes than those which now scanned him, in unconcealed amazement.

The native bore both the tomahawk and knife of his tribe; and yet his appearance was not altogether that of a warrior. On the contrary, there was an air of neglect about his person, like that which might have proceeded from great and recent exertion, which he had not yet found leisure to repair. The colors of the war-paint had blended in dark confusion about his fierce countenance and rendered his swarthy lineaments still more savage and repulsive than if art had attempted an effect which had been thus produced by chance. His eye, alone, which glistened like a fiery star amid lowering clouds, was to be seen in its state of native wildness. For a single instant his searching and yet wary glance met the wondering look of the other, and then changing its direction, partly in cunning, and partly in disdain, it remained fixed, as if penetrating the distant air.

It is impossible to say what unlooked-for remark this short and silent communication, between two such singular men, might have elicited from the white man, had not his active curiosity been again drawn to other objects. A general movement among the domestics, and a low sound of gentle voices, announced the approach of those whose presence alone was wanted to enable the cavalcade to move. The simple admirer of the war-horse instantly fell back to a low, gaunt, switch-tailed mare, that was unconsciously gleaning the faded herbage of the camp nigh by; where, leaning with one elbow on the blanket that concealed an apology for a saddle, he became a spectator of the departure, while a foal was quietly making its morning repast, on the opposite side of the same animal.

A young man, in the dress of an officer, conducted to their steeds two females, who, as it was apparent by their dresses, were prepared to encounter the fatigues of a journey in the woods. One, and she was the more juvenile in her appearance, though both were young, permitted glimpses of her dazzling complexion, fair golden hair, and bright blue eyes, to be caught, as she artlessly suffered the morning air to blow aside the green veil which descended low from her beaver.

The flush which still lingered above the pines in the western sky was not brighter nor delicate than the bloom on her cheek; nor was the opening day more cheering than the animated smile which she bestowed on the youth, as he assisted her into the saddle. The other, who appeared to share equally in the attention of the young officer, concealed her charms from the gaze of the soldiery with a care that seemed better fitted to the experience of four or five additional years. It could be seen, however, that her person, though molded with the same exquisite proportions, of which none of the graces were lost by the traveling dress she wore, was rather fuller and more mature than that of her companion.

No sooner were these females seated, than their attendant sprang lightly into the saddle of the war-horse, when the whole three bowed to Webb, who in courtesy, awaited their parting on the threshold of his cabin and turning their horses' heads, they proceeded at a slow amble, followed by their train, toward the northern entrance of the encampment. As they traversed that short distance, not a voice was heard among them; but a slight exclamation proceeded from the younger of the females, as the Indian runner glided by her, unexpectedly, and led the way along the military road in her front. Though this sudden and startling movement of the Indian produced no sound from the other, in the surprise her veil also was allowed to open its folds, and betrayed an indescribable look of pity, admiration, and horror, as her dark eye followed the easy motions of the savage. The tresses of this lady were shining and black, like the plumage of the raven. Her complexion was not brown, but it rather appeared charged with the color of the rich blood, that seemed ready to burst its bounds. And yet there was neither coarseness nor want of shadowing in a countenance that was exquisitely regular and dignified and surpassingly beautiful. She smiled, as if in pity at her own momentary forgetfulness, discovering by the act a row of teeth that would have shamed the purest ivory; when, replacing the veil, she bowed her face, and rode in silence, like one whose thoughts were abstracted from the scene around her.

CHAPTER II.

Sola, sola, wo ha, ho, sola!"

—Shakespeare

While one of the lovely beings we have so cursorily presented to the reader was thus lost in thought, the other quickly recovered from the alarm which induced the exclamation, and, laughing at her own weakness, she inquired of the youth who rode by her side:

"Are such specters frequent in the woods, Heyward, or is this sight an especial entertainment ordered on our behalf? If the latter, gratitude must close our mouths; but if the former, both Cora and I shall have need to draw largely on that stock of hereditary courage which we boast, even before we are made to encounter the redoubtable Montcalm."

"Yon Indian is a 'runner' of the army; and, after the fashion of his people, he may be accounted a hero," returned the officer. "He has volunteered to guide us to the lake, by a path but little known, sooner than if we followed the tardy movements of the column; and, by consequence, more agreeably."

"I like him not," said the lady, shuddering, partly in assumed, yet more in real terror. "You know him, Duncan, or you would not trust yourself so freely to his keeping?"

"Say, rather, Alice, that I would not trust you. I do know him, or he would not have my confidence, and least of all at this moment. He is said to be a Canadian too and yet he served with our friends the Mohawks, who, as you know, are one of the six allied nations. He was brought among us, as I have heard, by some strange accident in which your father was interested, and in which the savage was rigidly dealt by; but I forget the idle tale, it is enough, that he is now our friend."

"If he has been my father's enemy, I like him still less!" exclaimed the now really anxious girl. "Will you not speak to him, Major Heyward, that I may hear his tones? Foolish though it may be, you have often heard me avow my faith in the tones of the human voice!"

"It would be in vain and answered, most probably, by an ejaculation. Though he may understand it, he affects, like most of his people, to be ignorant of the English; and least of all will he condescend to speak it now that the war demands the utmost exercise of his dignity. But he stops; the private path by which we are to journey is, doubtless, at hand."

The conjecture of Major Heyward was true. When they reached the spot where the Indian stood, pointing into the thicket that fringed the military road; a narrow and blind path, which might, with some little inconvenience, receive one person at a time, became visible.

"Here, then, lies our way," said the young man, in a low voice. "Manifest no distrust, or you may invite the danger you appear to apprehend."

"Cora, what think you?" asked the reluctant fair one. "If we journey with the troops, though we may find their presence irksome, shall we not feel better assurance of our safety?"

"Being little accustomed to the practices of the savages, Alice, you mistake the place of real danger," said Heyward. "If enemies have reached the portage at all, a thing by no means probable, as our scouts are abroad, they will surely be found skirting the column, where scalps abound the most. The route of the detachment is known, while ours, having been determined within the hour, must still be secret."

"Should we distrust the man because his manners are not our manners, and that his skin is dark?" coldly asked Cora.

Alice hesitated no longer; but giving her Narragansett[1] a smart cut of the whip, she was the first to dash aside the slight branches of the bushes, and to follow the runner along the dark and tangled pathway. The young man regarded the last speaker in open admiration, and even permitted her fairer, though certainly not more beautiful companion, to proceed unattended, while he sedulously opened the way himself for the passage of her who has been called Cora. It would seem that the domestics had been previously instructed; for, instead of penetrating the thicket, they followed the route of the column; a measure which Heyward stated had been dictated by the sagacity of their guide, in order to diminish the marks of their trail, if, haply, the Canadian savages should be lurking so far in advance of their army. For many minutes the intricacy of the route admitted of no further dialogue; after which they emerged from the broad border of underbrush which grew along the line of the highway and entered under the high but dark arches of the forest. Here their progress was less interrupted; and the instant the guide perceived that the females could command their steeds, he moved on, at a pace between a trot and a walk, and at a rate which kept the sure-footed and peculiar animals they rode at a fast yet easy amble. The youth had turned to speak to the dark-eyed Cora, when the distant sound of horse's hoofs, clattering over the roots of the broken way in his rear, caused him to check his charger; and, as his companions

[1] In the state of Rhode Island there is a bay called Narragansett, so named after a powerful tribe of Indians, which formerly dwelt on its banks. Accident, or one of those unaccountable freaks which nature sometimes plays in the animal world, gave rise to a breed of horses which were once well known in America, and distinguished by their habit of pacing. Horses of this race were, and are still, in much request as saddle horses, on account of their hardiness and the ease of their movements. As they were also sure of foot, the Narragansetts were greatly sought for by females who were obliged to travel over the roots and holes in the "new countries."

drew their reins at the same instant, the whole party came to a halt, in order to obtain an explanation of the unlooked-for interruption.

In a few moments a colt was seen gliding, like a fallow deer, among the straight trunks of the pines and in another instant, the person of the ungainly man, described in the preceding chapter, came into view, with as much rapidity as he could excite his meager beast to endure without coming to an open rupture. Until now this personage had escaped the observation of the travelers. If he possessed the power to arrest any wandering eye when exhibiting the glories of his altitude on foot, his equestrian graces were still more likely to attract attention.

Notwithstanding a constant application of his one-armed heel to the flanks of the mare, the most confirmed gait that he could establish was a Canterbury gallop with the hind legs, in which those more forward assisted for doubtful moments, though generally content to maintain a loping trot. Perhaps the rapidity of the changes from one of these paces to the other created an optical illusion, which might thus magnify the powers of the beast; for it is certain that Heyward, who possessed a true eye for the merits of a horse, was unable, with his utmost ingenuity, to decide by what sort of movement his pursuer worked his sinuous way on his footsteps with such persevering hardihood.

The industry and movements of the rider were not less remarkable than those of the ridden. At each change in the evolutions of the latter, the former raised his tall person in the stirrups; producing, in this manner, by the undue elongation of his legs, such sudden growths and diminishing's of the stature, as baffled every conjecture that might be made as to his dimensions. If to this be added the fact that, in consequence of the expert application of the spur, one side of the mare appeared to journey faster than the other; and that the aggrieved flank was resolutely indicated by unremitted flourishes of a bushy tail, we finish the picture of both horse and man.

The frown which had gathered around the handsome, open, and manly brow of Heyward, gradually relaxed, and his lips curled into a slight smile, as he regarded the stranger. Alice made no very powerful effort to control her merriment; and even the dark, thoughtful eye of Cora lighted with a humor that it would seem, the habit, rather than the nature, of its mistress repressed.

"Seek you any here?" demanded Heyward, when the other had arrived sufficiently nigh to abate his speed; "I trust you are no messenger of evil tidings?"

"Even so," replied the stranger, making diligent use of his triangular castor, to produce a circulation in the close air of the woods, and leaving his hearers in doubt to which of the young man's questions he responded; when, however, he had cooled his face, and recovered his breath, he continued, "I hear you are riding to William Henry; as I am journeying thitherward myself, I concluded good company would seem consistent to the wishes of both parties."

"You appear to possess the privilege of a casting vote," returned Heyward; "we are three, while you have consulted no one but yourself."

"Even so. The first point to be obtained is to know one's own mind. Once sure of that, and where women are concerned it is not easy, the next is, to act up to the decision. I have endeavored to do both, and here I am."

"If you journey to the lake, you have mistaken your route," said Heyward, haughtily; "the highway thither is at least half a mile behind you."

"Even so," returned the stranger, nothing daunted by this cold reception; "I have tarried at 'Edward' a week, and I should be dumb not to have inquired the road I was to journey; and if dumb there would be an end to my calling." After simpering in a small way, like one whose modesty prohibited a more open expression of his admiration of a witticism that was perfectly unintelligible to his hearers, he continued, "It is not prudent for any one of my profession to be too familiar with those he has to instruct; for which reason I follow not the line of the army; besides which, I conclude that a gentleman of your character has the best judgment in matters of wayfaring; I have, therefore, decided to join company, in order that the ride may be made agreeable, and partake of social communion."

"A most arbitrary, if not a hasty decision!" exclaimed Heyward, undecided whether to give vent to his growing anger, or to laugh in the other's face. "But you speak of instruction, and of a profession; are you an adjunct to the provincial corps, as a master of the noble science of defense and offense; or, perhaps, you are one who draws lines and angles, under the pretense of expounding the mathematics?"

The stranger regarded his interrogator a moment in wonder; and then, losing every mark of self-satisfaction in an expression of solemn humility, he answered:

"Of offense, I hope there is none, to either party: of defense, I make none by God's good mercy, having committed no palpable sin since last entreating his pardoning grace. I understand not your allusions about lines and angles; and I leave expounding to those who have been called and set apart for that holy office. I lay claim to no higher gift than a small insight into the glorious art of petitioning and thanksgiving, as practiced in psalmody."

"The man is, most manifestly, a disciple of Apollo," cried the amused Alice, "and I take him under my own especial protection. Nay, throw aside that frown, Heyward, and in pity to my longing ears, suffer him to journey in our train. Besides," she added, in a low and hurried voice, casting a glance at the distant Cora, who slowly followed the footsteps of their silent, but sullen guide, "it may be a friend added to our strength, in time of need."

"Think you, Alice, that I would trust those I love by this secret path, did I imagine such need could happen?"

"Nay, nay, I think not of it now; but this strange man amuses me; and if he 'hath music in his soul', let us not churlishly reject his company." She pointed persuasively along the path with her riding whip, while their eyes met in a look which the young man lingered a moment to prolong; then, yielding to her gentle influence, he clapped his spurs into his charger, and in a few bounds was again at the side of Cora.

"I am glad to encounter thee, friend," continued the maiden, waving her hand to the stranger to proceed, as she urged her Narragansett to renew its amble. "Partial relatives have almost persuaded me that I am not entirely worthless in a duet myself; and we may enliven our wayfaring by indulging in our favorite pursuit. It might be of signal advantage to one, ignorant as I, to hear the opinions and experience of a master in the art."

"It is refreshing both to the spirits and to the body to indulge in psalmody, in befitting seasons," returned the master of song, unhesitatingly complying with her intimation to follow; "and nothing would relieve the mind more than such a consoling communion. But four parts are altogether necessary to the perfection of melody. You have all the manifestations of a soft and rich treble; I can, by especial aid, carry a full tenor to the highest letter; but we lack counter and bass! Yon officer of the king, who hesitated to admit me to his company, might fill the latter, if one may judge from the intonations of his voice in common dialogue."

"Judge not too rashly from hasty and deceptive appearances," said the lady, smiling; "though Major Heyward can assume such deep notes on occasion, believe me, his natural tones are better fitted for a mellow tenor than the bass you heard."

"Is he, then, much practiced in the art of psalmody?" demanded her simple companion.

Alice felt disposed to laugh, though she succeeded in suppressing her merriment, ere she answered:

"I apprehend that he is rather addicted to profane song. The chances of a soldier's life are but little fitted for the encouragement of more sober inclinations."

"Man's voice is given to him, like his other talents, to be used, and not to be abused. None can say they have ever known me to neglect my gifts! I am thankful that, though my boyhood may be said to have been set apart, like the youth of the royal David, for the purposes of music, no syllable of rude verse has ever profaned my lips."

"You have, then, limited your efforts to sacred song?"

"Even so. As the psalms of David exceed all other language, so does the psalmody that has been fitted to them by the divines and sages of the land, surpass all vain poetry. Happily, I may say that I utter nothing but the thoughts and the wishes of the King of Israel himself; for though the times may call for some slight changes, yet does this version which we use in the colonies of New England so much exceed all other versions, that, by its richness, its exactness, and its spiritual simplicity, it approached, as near as may be, to the great work of the inspired writer. I never abide in any place, sleeping or waking, without an example of this gifted work. 'Tis the six-and-twentieth edition, promulgated at Boston, Anno Domini 1744; and is entitled, 'The Psalms, Hymns, and Spiritual Songs of the Old and New Testaments; faithfully translated into English Metre, for the Use, Edification, and Comfort of the Saints, in Public and Private, especially in New England'."

During this eulogium on the rare production of his native poets, the stranger had drawn the book from his pocket, and fitting a pair of iron-rimmed spectacles to his nose, opened the volume with a care and veneration suited to its sacred purposes. Then, without circumlocution or apology, first pronounced the word "Standish," and placing the unknown engine, already described, to his mouth, from which he drew a high, shrill sound, that was followed by an octave below, from his own voice, he commenced singing the following words, in full, sweet, and melodious tones, that set the music, the poetry and even the uneasy motion of his ill-trained beast at defiance:

"How good it is, O see,
And how it pleaseth well,
Together e'en in unity,
For brethren so to dwell.

It's like the choice ointment,
From the head to the beard did go;
Down Aaron's head, that downward went
His garment's skirts unto."

The delivery of these skillful rhymes was accompanied, on the part of the stranger, by a regular rise and fall of his right hand, which terminated at the descent, by suffering the fingers to dwell a moment on the leaves of the little volume; and on the ascent, by such a flourish of the member as none but the initiated may ever hope to imitate. It would seem long practice had rendered this manual accompaniment necessary; for it did not cease until the preposition which the poet had selected for the close of his verse had been duly delivered like a word of two syllables.

Such an innovation on the silence and retirement of the forest could not fail to enlist the ears of those who journeyed at so short a distance in advance. The Indian muttered a few words in broken English to Heyward, who, in his turn, spoke to the stranger at once interrupting, and, for the time, closing his musical efforts.

"Though we are not in danger, common prudence would teach us to journey through this wilderness in as quiet a manner as possible. You will then, pardon me, Alice, should I diminish your enjoyments, by requesting this gentleman to postpone his chant until a safer opportunity."

"You will diminish them, indeed," returned the arch girl; "for never did I hear a more unworthy conjunction of execution and language than that to which I have been listening; and I was far gone in a learned inquiry into the causes of such an unfitness between sound and sense, when you broke the charm of my musings by that bass of yours, Duncan!"

"I know not what you call my bass," said Heyward, piqued at her remark, "but I know that your safety, and that of Cora, is far dearer to me than could be any orchestra of Handel's music." He paused and turned his head quickly toward a thicket, and then bent his eyes suspiciously on their guide, who continued his steady pace, in undisturbed gravity. The young man smiled to himself, for he believed he had mistaken some shining berry of the woods for the glistening eyeballs of a prowling savage, and he rode forward, continuing the conversation which had been interrupted by the passing thought.

Major Heyward was mistaken only in suffering his youthful and generous pride to suppress his active watchfulness. The cavalcade had not long passed, before the branches of the bushes that formed the thicket were cautiously moved asunder, and a human visage, as fiercely wild as savage art and unbridled passions could make it, peered out on the retiring footsteps of the travelers. A gleam of exultation shot across the darkly-painted lineaments of the inhabitant of the forest, as he traced the route of his intended victims, who rode unconsciously onward, the light and graceful forms of the females waving among the trees, in the curvatures of their path, followed at each bend by the manly figure of Heyward, until, finally, the shapeless person of the singing master was concealed behind the numberless trunks of trees, that rose, in dark lines, in the intermediate space.

CHAPTER III.

"Before these fields were shorn and till'd,
Full to the brim our rivers flow'd;
The melody of waters fill'd
The fresh and boundless wood;
And torrents dash'd, and rivulets play'd,
And fountains spouted in the shade."—Bryant

Leaving the unsuspecting Heyward and his confiding companions to penetrate still deeper into a forest that contained such treacherous inmates, we must use an author's privilege, and shift the scene a few miles to the westward of the place where we have last seen them.

On that day, two men were lingering on the banks of a small but rapid stream, within an hour's journey of the encampment of Webb, like those who awaited the appearance of an absent person, or the approach of some expected event. The vast canopy of woods spread itself to the margin of the river, overhanging the water, and shadowing its dark current with a deeper hue. The rays of the sun were beginning to grow less fierce, and the intense heat of the day was lessened, as the cooler vapors of the springs and fountains rose above their leafy beds and rested in the atmosphere. Still that breathing silence, which marks the drowsy sultriness of an American landscape in July, pervaded the secluded spot, interrupted only by the low voices of the men, the occasional and lazy tap of a woodpecker, the discordant cry of some gaudy jay, or a swelling on the ear, from the dull roar of a distant waterfall. These feeble and broken sounds were, however, too familiar to the foresters to draw their attention from the more interesting matter of their dialogue. While one of these loiterers showed the red skin and wild accouterments of a native of the woods, the other exhibited, through the mask of his rude and nearly savage equipment's, the brighter, though sun-burned and long-faced complexion of one who might claim descent from a European parentage. The former was seated on the end of a mossy log, in a posture that permitted him to heighten the effect of his earnest language, by the calm but expressive gestures of an Indian engaged in debate. His body, which was nearly naked, presented a terrific emblem of death, drawn in intermingled colors of white and black. His closely-shaved head, on which no other hair than the well-known and chivalrous scalping tuft[1] was preserved, was without ornament of any kind, with the exception of a solitary eagle's plume, that crossed his crown, and depended over the left shoulder. A tomahawk and scalping knife, of English manufacture, were in his girdle; while a short military rifle, of that sort with which the policy of the whites armed their savage allies, lay carelessly across his bare and sinewy knee. The expanded chest, full formed limbs, and grave countenance of this warrior would denote that he had reached the vigor of his days, though no symptoms of decay appeared to have yet weakened his manhood.

The frame of the white man, judging by such parts as were not concealed by his clothes, was like that of one who had known hardships and exertion from his earliest youth. His person, though muscular, was rather attenuated than full; but every nerve and muscle appeared strung and indurated by unremitted exposure and toil. He wore a hunting shirt of forest-green, fringed with faded yellow[2],

---

[1] The North American warrior caused the hair to be plucked from his whole body; a small tuft was left on the crown of his head, in order that his enemy might avail himself of it, in wrenching off the scalp in the event of his fall. The scalp was the only admissible trophy of victory. Thus, it was deemed more important to obtain the scalp than to kill the man. Some tribes lay great stress on the honor of striking a dead body. These practices have nearly disappeared among the Indians of the Atlantic states.
[2] The hunting-shirt is a picturesque smock-frock, being shorter, and ornamented with fringes and tassels. The colors are intended to imitate the hues of the wood, with a view to concealment. Many corps of American riflemen have been thus attired, and the dress is one of the most striking of modern times. The hunting-shirt is frequently white.

and a summer cap of skins which had been shorn of their fur. He also bore a knife in a girdle of wampum, like that which confined the scanty garments of the Indian, but no tomahawk. His moccasins were ornamented after the gay fashion of the natives, while the only part of his under dress which appeared below the hunting-frock was a pair of buckskin leggings, that laced at the sides, and which were gartered above the knees, with the sinews of a deer. A pouch and horn completed his personal accouterments, though a rifle of great length[3], which the theory of the more ingenious whites had taught them was the most dangerous of all firearms, leaned against a neighboring sapling. The eye of the hunter, or scout, whichever he might be, was small, quick, keen, and restless, roving while he spoke, on every side of him, as if in quest of game, or distrusting the sudden approach of some lurking enemy. Notwithstanding the symptoms of habitual suspicion, his countenance was not only without guile, but at the moment at which he is introduced, it was charged with an expression of sturdy honesty.

"Even your traditions make the case in my favor, Chingachgook," he said, speaking in the tongue which was known to all the natives who formerly inhabited the country between the Hudson and the Potomac, and of which we shall give a free translation for the benefit of the reader; endeavoring, at the same time, to preserve some of the peculiarities, both of the individual and of the language. "Your fathers came from the setting sun, crossed the big river[4], fought the people of the country, and took the land; and mine came from the red sky of the morning, over the salt lake, and did their work much after the fashion that had been set them by yours; then let God judge the matter between us, and friends spare their words!"

"My father's fought with the naked red man!" returned the Indian, sternly, in the same language. "Is there no difference, Hawkeye,

[3] The rifle of the army is short; that of the hunter is always long.

[4] The Mississippi. The scout alludes to a tradition which is very popular among the tribes of the Atlantic states. Evidence of their Asiatic origin is deduced from the circumstances, though great uncertainty hangs over the whole history of the Indians.

between the stone-headed arrow of the warrior, and the leaden bullet with which you kill?"

"There is reason in an Indian, though nature has made him with a red skin!" said the white man, shaking his head like one on whom such an appeal to his justice was not thrown away. For a moment he appeared to be conscious of having the worst of the argument, then, rallying again, he answered the objection of his antagonist in the best manner his limited information would allow:

"I am no scholar, and I care not who knows it; but, judging from what I have seen, at deer chases and squirrel hunts, of the sparks below, I should think a rifle in the hands of their grandfathers was not so dangerous as a hickory bow and a good flint-head might be, if drawn with Indian judgment, and sent by an Indian eye."

"You have the story told by your fathers," returned the other, coldly waving his hand. "What say your old men? Do they tell the young warriors that the pale faces met the red men, painted for war, and armed with the stone hatchet and wooden gun?"

"I am not a prejudiced man, nor one who vaunts himself on his natural privileges, though the worst enemy I have on earth, and he is an Iroquois, daren't deny that I am genuine white," the scout replied, surveying, with secret satisfaction, the faded color of his bony and sinewy hand, "and I am willing to own that my people have many ways, of which, as an honest man, I can't approve. It is one of their customs to write in books what they have done and seen, instead of telling them in their villages, where the lie can be given to the face of a cowardly boaster, and the brave soldier can call on his comrades to witness for the truth of his words. In consequence of this bad fashion, a man, who is too conscientious to misspend his days among the women, in learning the names of black marks, may never hear of the deeds of his fathers, nor feel a pride in striving to outdo them. For myself, I conclude the Bumppos could shoot, for I have a natural turn with a rifle, which must have been handed down from generation to generation, as, our holy commandments tell us, all good and evil gifts are bestowed; though I should be loath to answer for other people in such a matter. But every story has its two sides, so I ask you, Chingachgook, what passed, according to the traditions of the red men, when our fathers first met?"

A silence of a minute succeeded, during which the Indian sat mute; then, full of the dignity of his office, he commenced his brief tale, with a solemnity that served to heighten its appearance of truth.

"Listen, Hawkeye, and your ear shall drink no lie. 'Tis what my fathers have said, and what the Mohicans have done." He hesitated a single instant, and bending a cautious glance toward his companion, he continued, in a manner that was divided between interrogation and assertion. "Does not this stream at our feet run toward the summer, until its waters grow salt, and the current flows upward?"

"It can't be denied that your traditions tell you true in both these matters," said the white man; "for I have been there, and have seen them, though why water, which is so sweet in the shade, should become bitter in the sun, is an alteration for which I have never been able to account."

"And the current!" demanded the Indian, who expected his reply with that sort of interest that a man feels in the confirmation of testimony, at which he marvels even while he respects it; "the fathers of Chingachgook have not lied!"

"The holy Bible is not truer, and that is the truest thing in nature. They call this up-stream current the tide, which is a thing soon explained, and clear enough. Six hours the waters run in, and six hours they run out, and the reason is this: when there is higher water in the sea than in the river, they run in until the river gets to be highest, and then it runs out again."

"The waters in the woods, and on the great lakes, run downward until they lie like my hand," said the Indian, stretching the limb horizontally before him, "and then they run no more."

"No honest man will deny it," said the scout, a little nettled at the implied distrust of his explanation of the mystery of the tides; "and I grant that it is true on the small scale, and where the land is level. But everything depends on what scale you look at things. Now, on the small scale, the earth is level but on the large scale it is round. In this manner, pools, and ponds, and even the great fresh-water lakes, may be stagnant, as you and I both know they are, having seen them; but when you come to spread water over a great tract, like the sea, where the earth is round, how in reason can the water be quiet? You might as well expect the river to lie still on the brink of those black rocks a mile above us, though your own ears tell you that it is tumbling over them at this very moment."

If unsatisfied by the philosophy of his companion, the Indian was far too dignified to betray his unbelief. He listened like one who was convinced and resumed his narrative in his former solemn manner.

"We came from the place where the sun is hidden at night, over great plains where the buffaloes live, until we reached the big river. There we fought the Alligewi, till the ground was red with their blood. From the banks of the big river to the shores of the Salt Lake, there was none to meet us. The Maquas followed at a distance. We said the country should be ours from the place where the water runs up no longer on this stream, to a river twenty sun's journey toward the summer. We drove the Maquas into the woods with the bears. They only tasted salt at the licks; they drew no fish from the great lake; we threw them the bones."

"All this I have heard and believe," said the white man, observing that the Indian paused; "but it was long before the English came into the country."

"A pine grew then where this chestnut now stands. The first pale faces who came among us spoke no English. They came in a large canoe, when my fathers had buried the tomahawk with the red men around them. Then, Hawkeye," he continued, betraying his deep emotion, only by permitting his voice to fall to those low, guttural tones, which render his language, as spoken at times, so very musical; "then, Hawkeye, we were one people, and we were happy. The Salt Lake gave us its fish, the wood its deer, and the air its birds. We took wives who bore us children; we worshipped the Great Spirit; and we kept the Maquas beyond the sound of our songs of triumph."

"Know you anything of your own family at that time?" demanded the white. "But you are just a man, for an Indian; and as I suppose you hold their gifts, your fathers must have been brave warriors, and wise men at the council-fire."

"My tribe is the grandfather of nations, but I am an unmixed man. The blood of chiefs is in my veins, where it must stay forever. The Dutch landed and gave my people the firewater; they drank until the heavens and the earth seemed to meet, and they foolishly thought they had found the Great Spirit. Then they parted with their land. Foot by foot, they were driven back from the shores, until I, that am a chief and a Sagamore, have never seen the sunshine but through the trees, and have never visited the graves of my fathers."

"Graves bring solemn feelings over the mind," returned the scout, a good deal touched at the calm suffering of his companion; "and they often aid a man in his good intentions; though, for myself, I expect to leave my own bones unburied, to bleach in the woods, or to be torn asunder by the wolves. But where are to be found those of your race who came to their kin in the Delaware country, so many summers since?"

"Where are the blossoms of those summers! fallen, one by one so, all of my family departed, each in his turn, to the land of spirits. I am on the hilltop and must go down into the valley; and when Uncas follows in my footsteps there will no longer be any of the blood of the Sagamores, for my boy is the last of the Mohicans."

"Uncas is here," said another voice, in the same soft, guttural tones, near his elbow; "who speaks to Uncas?"

The white man loosened his knife in his leathern sheath and made an involuntary movement of the hand toward his rifle, at this sudden interruption but the Indian sat composed, and without turning his head at the unexpected sounds.

At the next instant, a youthful warrior passed between them, with a noiseless step, and seated himself on the bank of the rapid stream. No exclamation of surprise escaped the father, nor was any question asked, or reply given, for several minutes; each appearing to await the moment when he might speak, without betraying womanish curiosity or childish impatience. The white man seemed to take counsel from their customs, and, relinquishing his grasp of the rifle, he also remained silent and reserved. At length Chingachgook turned his eyes slowly toward his son, and demanded:

"Do the Maquas dare to leave the print of their moccasins in these woods?"

"I have been on their trail," replied the young Indian, "and know that they number as many as the fingers of my two hands; but they lie hid like cowards."

"The thieves are outlying for scalps and plunder," said the white man, whom we shall call Hawkeye, after the manner of his companions. "That busy Frenchman, Montcalm, will send his spies into our very camp, but he will know what road we travel!"

"'Tis enough," returned the father, glancing his eye toward the setting sun; "they shall be driven like deer from their bushes. Hawkeye, let us eat tonight, and show the Maquas that we are men tomorrow."

"I am as ready to do the one as the other; but to fight the Iroquois 'tis necessary to find the skulkers; and to eat, 'tis necessary to get the game talk of the devil and he will come; there is a pair of the biggest antlers I have seen this season, moving the bushes below the hill! Now, Uncas," he continued, in a half whisper, and laughing with a kind of inward sound, like one who had learned to be watchful, "I will bet my charger three times full of powder, against a foot of wampum, that I take him atwixt the eyes, and nearer to the right than to the left."

"It cannot be!" said the young Indian, springing to his feet with youthful eagerness; "all but the tips of his horns are hiding!"

"He's a boy!" said the white man, shaking his head while he spoke, and addressing the father. "Does he think when a hunter sees a part of the creature', he can't tell where the rest of him should be!"

Adjusting his rifle, he was about to make an exhibition of that skill on which he so much valued himself, when the warrior struck up the piece with his hand, saying:

"Hawkeye! will you fight the Maquas?"

"These Indians know the nature of the woods, as it might be by instinct!" returned the scout, dropping his rifle, and turning away like a man who was convinced of his error. "I must leave the buck to your arrow, Uncas, or we may kill a deer for them thieves, the Iroquois, to eat."

The instant the father seconded this intimation by an expressive gesture of the hand, Uncas threw himself on the ground, and approached the animal with wary movements. When within a few yards of the cover, he fitted an arrow to his bow with the utmost care, while the antlers moved, as if their owner snuffed an enemy in the tainted air. In another moment the twang of the cord was heard, a white streak was seen glancing into the bushes, and the wounded buck plunged from the cover to the very feet of his hidden enemy. Avoiding the horns of the infuriated animal, Uncas darted to his side, and passed his knife across the throat, when bounding to the edge of the river it fell, dyeing the waters with its blood.

"'Twas done with Indian skill," said the scout laughing inwardly, but with vast satisfaction; "and 'twas a pretty sight to behold! Though an arrow is a near shot and needs a knife to finish the work."

"Hugh!" ejaculated his companion, turning quickly, like a hound who scented game.

"By the Lord, there is a drove of them!" exclaimed the scout, whose eyes began to glisten with the ardor of his usual occupation; "if they come within range of a bullet, I will drop one, though the whole Six Nations should be lurking within sound! What do you hear, Chingachgook? for to my ears the woods are dumb."

"There is but one deer, and he is dead," said the Indian, bending his body till his ear nearly touched the earth. "I hear the sounds of feet!"

"Perhaps the wolves have driven the buck to shelter and are following on his trail."

"No. The horses of white men are coming!" returned the other, raising himself with dignity, and resuming his seat on the log with his former composure. "Hawkeye, they are your brothers; speak to them."

"That I will, and in English that the king needn't be ashamed to answer," returned the hunter, speaking in the language of which he boasted; "but I see nothing, nor do I hear the sounds of man or beast; 'tis strange that an Indian should understand white sounds better than a man who, his very enemies will own, has no cross in his blood, although he may have lived with the red skins long enough to be suspected! Ha! there goes something like the cracking of a dry stick, too now I hear the bushes move yes, yes, there is a trampling that I mistook for the falls and but here they come themselves; God keep them from the Iroquois!"

CHAPTER IV.

"Well go thy way: thou shalt not from this grove
Till I torment thee for this injury."—Midsummer Night's Dream.

The words were still in the mouth of the scout, when the leader of the party, whose approaching footsteps had caught the vigilant ear of the Indian, came openly into view. A beaten path, such as those made by the periodical passage of the deer, wound through a little glen at no great distance, and struck the river at the point where the white man and his red companions had posted themselves. Along this track the travelers, who had produced a surprise so unusual in the depths of the forest, advanced slowly toward the hunter, who was in front of his associates, in readiness to receive them.

"Who comes?" demanded the scout, throwing his rifle carelessly across his left arm, and keeping the forefinger of his right hand on the trigger, though he avoided all appearance of menace in the act. "Who comes hither, among the beasts and dangers of the wilderness?"

"Believers in religion, and friends to the law and to the king," returned he who rode foremost. "Men who have journeyed since the rising sun, in the shades of this forest, without nourishment, and are sadly tired of their wayfaring."

"You are, then, lost," interrupted the hunter, "and have found how helpless 'tis not to know whether to take the right hand or the left?"

"Even so; sucking babes are not more dependent on those who guide them than we who are of larger growth, and who may now be said to possess the stature without the knowledge of men. Know you the distance to a post of the crown called William Henry?"

"Hoot!" shouted the scout, who did not spare his open laughter, though instantly checking the dangerous sounds he indulged his merriment at less risk of being overheard by any lurking enemies. "You are as much off the scent as a hound would be, with Horican atwixt him and the deer! William Henry, man! if you are friends to the king and have business with the army, your way would be to follow the river down to Edward, and lay the matter before Webb, who tarries there, instead of pushing into the defiles, and driving this saucy Frenchman back across Champlain, into his den again."

Before the stranger could make any reply to this unexpected proposition, another horseman dashed the bushes aside, and leaped his charger into the pathway, in front of his companion.

"What, then, may be our distance from Fort Edward?" demanded a new speaker; "the place you advise us to seek we left this morning, and our destination is the head of the lake."

"Then you must have lost your eyesight afore losing your way, for the road across the portage is cut to a good two rods, and is as grand a path, I calculate, as any that runs into London, or even before the palace of the king himself."

"We will not dispute concerning the excellence of the passage," returned Heyward, smiling; for, as the reader has anticipated, it was he. "It is enough, for the present, that we trusted to an Indian guide to take us by a nearer, though blinder path, and that we are deceived in his knowledge. In plain words, we know not where we are."

"An Indian lost in the woods!" said the scout, shaking his head doubtingly; "When the sun is scorching the treetops, and the water courses are full; when the moss on every beech he sees will tell him in what quarter the north star will shine at night. The woods are full of deer-paths which run to the streams and licks, places well known to everybody; nor have the geese done their flight to the Canada waters altogether! 'Tis strange that an Indian should be lost atwixt Horican and the bend in the river! Is he a Mohawk?"

"Not by birth, though adopted in that tribe; I think his birthplace was farther north, and he is one of those you call a Huron."

"Hugh!" exclaimed the two companions of the scout, who had continued until this part of the dialogue, seated immovable, and apparently indifferent to what passed, but who now sprang to their feet with an activity and interest that had evidently got the better of their reserve by surprise.

"A Huron!" repeated the sturdy scout, once more shaking his head in open distrust; "they are a thievish race, nor do I care by whom they are adopted; you can never make anything of them but skulks and vagabonds. Since you trusted yourself to the care of one of that nation, I only wonder that you have not fallen in with more."

"Of that there is little danger since William Henry is so many miles in our front. You forget that I have told you our guide is now a Mohawk, and that he serves with our forces as a friend."

"And I tell you that he who is born a Mingo will die a Mingo," returned the other positively. "A Mohawk! No, give me a Delaware or a Mohican for honesty; and when they will fight, which they won't all do, having suffered their cunning enemies, the Maquas, to make them women but when they will fight at all, look to a Delaware, or a Mohican, for a warrior!"

"Enough of this," said Heyward, impatiently; "I wish not to inquire into the character of a man that I know, and to whom you must be a stranger. You have not yet answered my question; what is our distance from the main army at Edward?"

"It seems that may depend on who is your guide. One would think such a horse as that might get over a good deal of ground atwixt sun-up and sun-down."

"I wish no contention of idle words with you, friend," said Heyward, curbing his dissatisfied manner, and speaking in a gentler voice; "if you will tell me the distance to Fort Edward, and conduct me thither, your labor shall not go without its reward."

"And in so doing, how know I that I don't guide an enemy and a spy of Montcalm, to the works of the army? It is not every man who can speak the English tongue that is an honest subject."

"If you serve with the troops, of whom I judge you to be a scout, you should know of such a regiment of the king as the Sixtieth."

"The Sixtieth! you can tell me little of the Royal Americans that I don't know, though I do wear a hunting-shirt instead of a scarlet jacket."

"Well, then, among other things, you may know the name of its major?"

"Its major!" interrupted the hunter, elevating his body like one who was proud of his trust. "If there is a man in the country who knows Major Effingham, he stands before you."

"It is a corps which has many majors; the gentleman you name is the senior, but I speak of the junior of them all; he who commands the companies in garrison at William Henry."

"Yes, yes, I have heard that a young gentleman of vast riches, from one of the provinces far south, has got the place. He is over young, too, to hold such rank, and to be put above men whose heads are beginning to bleach; and yet they say he is a soldier in his knowledge, and a gallant gentleman!"

"Whatever he may be, or however he may be qualified for his rank, he now speaks to you and, of course, can be no enemy to dread."

The scout regarded Heyward in surprise, and then lifting his cap, he answered, in a tone less confident than before though still expressing doubt.

"I have heard a party was to leave the encampment this morning for the lake shore?"

"You have heard the truth, but I preferred a nearer route, trusting to the knowledge of the Indian I mentioned."

"And he deceived you, and then deserted?"

"Neither, as I believe; certainly not the latter, for he is to be found in the rear."

"I should like to look at the creature; if it is a true Iroquois I can tell him by his knavish look, and by his paint," said the scout; stepping past the charger of Heyward and entering the path behind the mare of the singing master, whose foal had taken advantage of the halt to exact the maternal contribution. After shoving aside, the bushes, and proceeding a few paces, he encountered the females, who awaited the result of the conference with anxiety, and not entirely without apprehension. Behind these, the runner leaned against a tree, where he stood the close examination of the scout with an air unmoved, though with a look so dark and savage, that it might in itself excite fear. Satisfied with his scrutiny, the hunter soon left him. As he repassed the females, he paused a moment to gaze upon their beauty, answering to the smile and nod of Alice with a look of open pleasure. Thence he went to the side of the motherly animal and spending a minute in a fruitless inquiry into the character of her rider, he shook his head and returned to Heyward.

"A Mingo is a Mingo, and God having made him so, neither the Mohawks nor any other tribe can alter him," he said, when he had regained his former position. "If we were alone, and you would leave that noble horse at the mercy of the wolves tonight, I could show you the way to Edward myself, within an hour, for it lies only about an hour's journey hence but with such ladies in your company 'tis impossible!"

"And why? They are fatigued, but they are quite equal to a ride of a few more miles."

"'Tis a natural impossibility!" repeated the scout; "I wouldn't walk a mile in these woods after night gets into them, in company with that runner, for the best rifle in the colonies. They are full of outlying Iroquois, and your mongrel Mohawk knows where to find them too well to be my companion."

"Think you so?" said Heyward, leaning forward in the saddle, and dropping his voice nearly to a whisper; "I confess I have not been without my own suspicions, though I have endeavored to conceal them, and affected a confidence I have not always felt, on account of my companions. It was because I suspected him that I would follow no longer; making him, as you see, follow me."

"I knew he was one of the cheats as soon as I laid eyes on him!" returned the scout, placing a finger on his nose, in sign of caution.

"The thief is leaning against the foot of the sugar sapling, that you can see over them bushes; his right leg is in a line with the bark of the tree and," tapping his rifle, "I can take him from where I stand, between the angle and the knee, with a single shot, putting an end to his tramping through the woods, for at least a month to come. If I should go back to him, the cunning varmint would suspect something, and be dodging through the trees like a frightened deer."

"It will not do. He may be innocent, and I dislike the act. Though, if I felt confident of his treachery"

"'Tis a safe thing to calculate on the knavery of an Iroquois," said the scout, throwing his rifle forward, by a sort of instinctive movement.

"Hold!" interrupted Heyward, "it will not do, we must think of some other scheme and yet, I have much reason to believe the rascal has deceived me."

The hunter, who had already abandoned his intention of maiming the runner, mused a moment, and then made a gesture, which instantly brought his two red companions to his side. They spoke together earnestly in the Delaware language, though in an undertone; and by the gestures of the white man, which were frequently directed towards the top of the sapling, it was evident he pointed out the situation of their hidden enemy. His companions were not long in comprehending his wishes, and laying aside their firearms, they parted, taking opposite sides of the path, and burying themselves in the thicket, with such cautious movements, that their steps were inaudible.

"Now, go you back," said the hunter, speaking again to Heyward, "and hold the imp in talk; these Mohicans here will take him without breaking his paint."

"Nay," said Heyward, proudly, "I will seize him myself."

"Hist! what could you do, mounted, against an Indian in the bushes!"

"I will dismount."

"And think you, when he saw one of your feet out of the stirrup, he would wait for the other to be free? Whoever comes into the woods to deal with the natives, must use Indian fashions, if he would wish to prosper in his undertakings. Go, then; talk openly to the miscreant, and seem to believe him the truest friend you have on 'arth."

Heyward prepared to comply, though with strong disgust at the nature of the office he was compelled to execute. Each moment, however, pressed upon him a conviction of the critical situation in which he had suffered his invaluable trust to be involved through his own confidence. The sun had already disappeared, and the woods, suddenly deprived of his light[1], were assuming a dusky hue, which

[1] The scene of this tale was in the 42d degree of latitude, where the twilight is never of long continuation.

keenly reminded him that the hour the savage usually chose for his most barbarous and remorseless acts of vengeance or hostility, was speedily drawing near. Stimulated by apprehension, he left the scout, who immediately entered into a loud conversation with the stranger that had so unceremoniously enlisted himself in the party of travelers that morning. In passing his gentler companions Heyward uttered a few words of encouragement, and was pleased to find that, though fatigued with the exercise of the day, they appeared to entertain no suspicion that their present embarrassment was other than the result of accident. Giving them reason to believe he was merely employed in a consultation concerning the future route, he spurred his charger, and drew the reins again when the animal had carried him within a few yards of the place where the sullen runner still stood, leaning against the tree.

"You may see, Magua," he said, endeavoring to assume an air of freedom and confidence, "that the night is closing around us, and yet we are no nearer to William Henry than when we left the encampment of Webb with the rising sun.

"You have missed the way, nor have I been more fortunate. But happily, we have fallen in with a hunter, he whom you hear talking to the singer, that is acquainted with the deer paths and by-ways of the woods, and who promises to lead us to a place where we may rest securely till the morning."

The Indian riveted his glowing eyes on Heyward as he asked, in his imperfect English, "Is he alone?"

"Alone!" hesitatingly answered Heyward, to whom deception was too new to be assumed without embarrassment. "Oh! not alone, surely, Magua, for you know that we are with him."

"Then Le Renard Subtil will go," returned the runner, coolly raising his little wallet from the place where it had lain at his feet; "and the pale faces will see none but their own color."

"Go! Whom call you Le Renard?"

"'Tis the name his Canada fathers have given to Magua," returned the runner, with an air that manifested his pride at the distinction. "Night is the same as day to Le Subtil, when Munro waits for him."

"And what account will Le Renard give the chief of William Henry concerning his daughters? Will he dare to tell the hot-blooded Scotsman that his children are left without a guide, though Magua promised to be one?"

"Though the gray head has a loud voice, and a long arm, Le Renard will not hear him, nor feel him, in the woods."

"But what will the Mohawks say? They will make him petticoats and bid him stay in the wigwam with the women, for he is no longer to be trusted with the business of a man."

"Le Subtil knows the path to the great lakes, and he can find the bones of his fathers," was the answer of the unmoved runner.

"Enough, Magua," said Heyward; "are we not friends? Why should there be bitter words between us? Munro has promised you a gift for your services when performed, and I shall be your debtor for another. Rest your weary limbs, then, and open your wallet to eat. We have a few moments to spare; let us not waste them in talk like wrangling women. When the ladies are refreshed, we will proceed."

"The pale faces make themselves dogs to their women," muttered the Indian, in his native language, "and when they want to eat, their warriors must lay aside the tomahawk to feed their laziness."

"What say you, Renard?"

"Le Subtil says it is good."

The Indian then fastened his eyes keenly on the open countenance of Heyward, but meeting his glance, he turned them quickly away, and seating himself deliberately on the ground, he drew forth the remnant of some former repast, and began to eat, though not without first bending his looks slowly and cautiously around him.

"This is well," continued Heyward; "and Le Renard will have strength and sight to find the path in the morning"; he paused, for sounds like the snapping of a dried stick, and the rustling of leaves, rose from the adjacent bushes, but recollecting himself instantly, he continued, "we must be moving before the sun is seen, or Montcalm may lie in our path, and shut us out from the fortress."

The hand of Magua dropped from his mouth to his side, and though his eyes were fastened on the ground, his head was turned aside, his nostrils expanded, and his ears seemed even to stand more erect than usual, giving to him the appearance of a statue that was made to represent intense attention.

Heyward, who watched his movements with a vigilant eye, carelessly extricated one of his feet from the stirrup, while he passed a hand toward the bearskin covering of his holsters.

Every effort to detect the point most regarded by the runner was completely frustrated by the tremulous glances of his organs, which seemed not to rest a single instant on any particular object, and which, at the same time, could be hardly said to move. While he hesitated how to proceed, Le Subtil cautiously raised himself to his feet, though with a motion so slow and guarded, that not the slightest noise was produced by the change. Heyward felt it had now become incumbent on him to act. Throwing his leg over the saddle, he dismounted, with a determination to advance and seize his treacherous companion, trusting the result to his own manhood. In order, however, to prevent unnecessary alarm, he still preserved an air of calmness and friendship.

"Le Renard Subtil does not eat," he said, using the appellation he had found most flattering to the vanity of the Indian. "His corn is not well parched, and it seems dry. Let me examine; perhaps something may be found among my own provisions that will help his appetite."

Magua held out the wallet to the proffer of the other. He even suffered their hands to meet, without betraying the least emotion, or varying his riveted attitude of attention. But when he felt the fingers of Heyward moving gently along his own naked arm, he struck up the limb of the young man, and, uttering a piercing cry, he darted beneath it, and plunged, at a single bound, into the opposite thicket. At the next instant the form of Chingachgook appeared from the bushes, looking like a specter in its paint, and glided across the path in swift pursuit. Next followed the shout of Uncas, when the woods were lighted by a sudden flash, that was accompanied by the sharp report of the hunter's rifle.

CHAPTER V.

..."In such a night

Did This be fearfully o'ertrip the dew;

And saw the lion's shadow ere himself."—Merchant of Venice

The suddenness of the flight of his guide and the wild cries of the pursuers caused Heyward to remain fixed, for a few moments, in inactive surprise. Then recollecting the importance of securing the fugitive, he dashed aside the surrounding bushes, and pressed eagerly forward to lend his aid in the chase. Before he had, however, proceeded a hundred yards, he met the three foresters already returning from their unsuccessful pursuit.

"Why so soon disheartened!" he exclaimed; "the scoundrel must be concealed behind some of these trees and may yet be secured. We are not safe while he goes at large."

"Would you set a cloud to chase the wind?" returned the disappointed scout; "I heard the imp brushing over the dry leaves, like a black snake, and blinking a glimpse of him, just over again yon big pine, I pulled as it might be on the scent; but it wouldn't do! and yet for a reasoning aim, if anybody but myself had touched the trigger, I should call it a quick sight; and I may be accounted to have experience in these matters, and one who ought to know. Look at this sumach; its leaves are red, though everybody knows the fruit is in the yellow blossom in the month of July!"

"'Tis the blood of Le Subtil! he is hurt and may yet fall!"

"No, no," returned the scout, in decided disapprobation of this opinion, "I rubbed the bark off a limb, perhaps, but the creature leaped the longer for it. A rifle bullet acts on a running animal, when it barks him, much the same as one of your spurs on a horse; that is, it quickens motion, and puts life into the flesh, instead of taking it away. But when it cuts the ragged hole, after a bound or two, there is, commonly, a stagnation of further leaping, be it Indian or be it deer!"

"We are four able bodies, to one wounded man!"

"Is life grievous to you?" interrupted the scout. "Yonder red devil would draw you within swing of the tomahawks of his comrades, before you were heated in the chase. It was an unthoughtful act in a man who has so often slept with the war-whoop ringing in the air, to let off his piece within sound of an ambushment! But then it was a natural temptation! 'twas very natural! Come, friends, let us move our station, and in such fashion, too, as will throw the cunning of a Mingo on a wrong scent, or our scalps will be drying in the wind in front of Montcalm's marquee, again this hour tomorrow."

This appalling declaration, which the scout uttered with the cool assurance of a man who fully comprehended, while he did not fear to face the danger, served to remind Heyward of the importance of the charge with which he himself had been entrusted. Glancing his eyes around, with a vein effort to pierce the gloom that was thickening beneath the leafy arches of the forest, he felt as if, cut off from human aid, his unresisting companions would soon lie at the entire mercy of those barbarous enemies, who, like beasts of prey, only waited till the gathering darkness might render their blows more fatally certain. His awakened imagination, deluded by the deceptive light, converted each waving bush, or the fragment of some fallen tree, into human forms, and twenty times he fancied he could distinguish the horrid visages of his lurking foes, peering from their hiding places, in never ceasing watchfulness of the movements of his party. Looking upward, he found that the thin fleecy clouds, which evening had painted on the blue sky, were already losing their faintest tints of rose-color, while the imbedded stream, which glided past the spot where he stood, was to be traced only by the dark boundary of its wooded banks.

"What is to be done!" he said, feeling the utter helplessness of doubt in such a pressing strait; "desert me not, for God's sake! remain to defend those I escort, and freely name your own reward!"

His companions, who conversed apart in the language of their tribe, heeded not this sudden and earnest appeal. Though their dialogue was maintained in low and cautious sounds, but little above a whisper, Heyward, who now approached, could easily distinguish the earnest tones of the younger warrior from the more deliberate speeches of his seniors. It was evident that they debated on the propriety of some measure, that nearly concerned the welfare of the travelers. Yielding to his powerful interest in the subject, and impatient of a delay that seemed fraught with so much additional danger, Heyward drew still nigher to the dusky group, with an intention of making his offers of compensation more definite, when the white man, motioning with his hand, as if he conceded the disputed point, turned away, saying in a sort of soliloquy, and in the English tongue:

"Uncas is right! it would not be the act of men to leave such harmless things to their fate, even though it breaks up the harboring place forever. If you would save these tender blossoms from the fangs of the worst of serpents, gentleman, you have neither time to lose nor resolution to throw away!"

"How can such a wish be doubted! Have I not already offered"

"Offer your prayers to Him who can give us wisdom to circumvent the cunning of the devils who fill these woods," calmly interrupted the scout, "but spare your offers of money, which neither you may live to realize, nor I to profit by. These Mohicans and I will do what man's thoughts can invent, to keep such flowers, which, though so sweet, were never made for the wilderness, from harm, and that without hope of any other recompense but such as God always gives to upright dealings. First, you must promise two things, both in your own name and for your friends, or without serving you we shall only injure ourselves!"

"Name them."

"The one is, to be still as these sleeping woods, let what will happen and the other is, to keep the place where we shall take you, forever a secret from all mortal men."

"I will do my utmost to see both these conditions fulfilled."

"Then follow, for we are losing moments that are as precious as the heart's blood to a stricken deer!"

Heyward could distinguish the impatient gesture of the scout, through the increasing shadows of the evening, and he moved in his footsteps, swiftly, toward the place where he had left the remainder of the party. When they rejoined the expecting and anxious females, he briefly acquainted them with the conditions of their new guide, and with the necessity that existed for their hushing every apprehension in instant and serious exertions. Although his alarming communication was not received without much secret terror by the listeners, his earnest and impressive manner, aided perhaps by the nature of the danger, succeeded in bracing their nerves to undergo some unlooked for and unusual trial. Silently, and without a moment's delay, they permitted him to assist them from their saddles, and when they descended quickly to the water's edge, where the scout had collected the rest of the party, more by the agency of expressive gestures than by any use of words.

"What to do with these dumb creatures!" muttered the white man, on whom the sole control of their future movements appeared to devolve; "it would be time lost to cut their throats and cast them into the river; and to leave them here would be to tell the Mingoes that they have not far to seek to find their owners!"

"Then give them their bridles, and let them range the woods," Heyward ventured to suggest.

"No; it would be better to mislead the imps and make them believe they must equal a horse's speed to run down their chase. Ay, ay, that will blind their fireballs of eyes! Chingach, Hist! what stirs the bush?"

"The colt."

"That colt, at least, must die," muttered the scout, grasping at the mane of the nimble beast, which easily eluded his hand; "Uncas, your arrows!"

"Hold!" exclaimed the proprietor of the condemned animal, aloud, without regard to the whispering tones used by the others; "spare the foal of Miriam! it is the comely offspring of a faithful dam and would willingly injure naught."

"When men struggle for the single life God has given them," said the scout, sternly, "even their own kind seem no more than the beasts of the wood. If you speak again, I shall leave you to the mercy of the Maquas! Draw to your arrow's head, Uncas; we have no time for second blows."

The low, muttering sounds of his threatening voice were still audible, when the wounded foal, first rearing on its hinder legs, plunged forward to its knees. It was met by Chingachgook, whose knife passed across its throat quicker than thought, and then precipitating the motions of the struggling victim, he dashed into the river, down whose stream it glided away, gasping audibly for breath with its ebbing life. This deed of apparent cruelty, but of real necessity, fell upon the spirits of the travelers like a terrific warning of the peril in which they stood, heightened as it was by the calm though steady resolution of the actors in the scene. The sisters shuddered and clung closer to each other, while Heyward instinctively laid his hand on one of the pistols he had just drawn from their holsters, as he placed himself between his charge and those dense shadows that seemed to draw an impenetrable veil before the bosom of the forest.

The Indians, however, hesitated not a moment, but taking the bridles, they led the frightened and reluctant horses into the bed of the river.

At a short distance from the shore, they turned and were soon concealed by the projection of the bank, under the brow of which they moved, in a direction opposite to the course of the waters. In the meantime, the scout drew a canoe of bark from its place of concealment beneath some low bushes, whose branches were waving with the eddies of the current, into which he silently motioned for the females to enter. They complied without hesitation, though many a fearful and anxious glance was thrown behind them, toward the thickening gloom, which now lay like a dark barrier along the margin of the stream.

So soon as Cora and Alice were seated, the scout, without regarding the element, directed Heyward to support one side of the frail vessel, and posting himself at the other, they bore it up against the stream, followed by the dejected owner of the dead foal. In this manner they proceeded, for many rods, in a silence that was only interrupted by the rippling of the water, as its eddies played around them, or the low dash made by their own cautious footsteps. Heyward yielded the guidance of the canoe implicitly to the scout, who approached or receded from the shore, to avoid the fragments of rocks, or deeper parts of the river, with a readiness that showed his knowledge of the route they held. Occasionally he would stop; and in the midst of a breathing stillness, that the dull but increasing roar of the waterfall only served to render more impressive, he would listen with painful intenseness, to catch any sounds that might arise from the slumbering forest. When assured that all was still, and unable to detect, even by the aid of his practiced senses, any sign of his approaching foes, he would deliberately resume his slow and guarded progress. At length they reached a point in the river where the roving eye of Heyward became riveted on a cluster of black objects, collected at a spot where the high bank threw a deeper shadow than usual on the dark waters. Hesitating to advance, he pointed out the place to the attention of his companion.

"Ay," returned the composed scout, "the Indians have hid the beasts with the judgment of natives! Water leaves no trail, and an owl's eyes would be blinded by the darkness of such a hole."

The whole party was soon reunited, and another consultation was held between the scout and his new comrades, during which, they, whose fates depended on the faith and ingenuity of these unknown foresters, had a little leisure to observe their situation more minutely.

The river was confined between high and cragged rocks, one of which impended above the spot where the canoe rested. As these, again, were surmounted by tall trees, which appeared to totter on the brows of the precipice, it gave the stream the appearance of running through a deep and narrow dell. All beneath the fantastic limbs and ragged treetops, which were, here and there, dimly painted against the starry zenith, lay alike in shadowed obscurity. Behind them, the curvature of the banks soon bounded the view by the same dark and wooded outline; but in front, and apparently at no great distance, the water seemed piled against the heavens, whence it tumbled into caverns, out of which issued those sullen sounds that had loaded the evening atmosphere. It seemed, in truth, to be a spot devoted to seclusion, and the sisters imbibed a soothing impression of security, as they gazed upon its romantic though not unappalling beauties. A general movement among their conductors, however, soon recalled them from a contemplation of the wild charms that night had assisted to lend the place to a painful sense of their real peril.

The horses had been secured to some scattering shrubs that grew in the fissures of the rocks, where, standing in the water, they were left to pass the night. The scout directed Heyward and his disconsolate fellow travelers to seat themselves in the forward end of the canoe, and took possession of the other himself, as erect and steady as if he floated in a vessel of much firmer materials. The Indians warily retraced their steps toward the place they had left, when the scout, placing his pole against a rock, by a powerful shove, sent his frail bark directly into the turbulent stream. For many minutes the struggle between the light bubble in which they floated, and the swift current was severe and doubtful. Forbidden to stir even a hand, and almost afraid to breath, lest they should expose the frail fabric to the fury of the stream, the passengers watched the glancing waters in feverish suspense. Twenty times they thought the whirling eddies were sweeping them to destruction, when the master-hand of their pilot would bring the bows of the canoe to stem the rapid. A long, a vigorous, and, as it appeared to the females, a desperate effort, closed the struggle. Just as Alice veiled her eyes in horror, under the impression that they were about to be swept within the vortex at the foot of the cataract, the canoe floated, stationary, at the side of a flat rock, that lay on a level with the water.

"Where are we, and what is next to be done!" demanded Heyward, perceiving that the exertions of the scout had ceased.

"You are at the foot of Glenn's," returned the other, speaking aloud, without fear of consequences within the roar of the cataract; "and the next thing is to make a steady landing, lest the canoe upset, and you should go down again the hard road we have traveled faster than you came up; 'tis a hard rift to stem, when the river is a little swelled; and five is an unnatural number to keep dry, in a hurry-skurry, with a little birchen bark and gum. There, go you all on the rock, and I will bring up the Mohicans with the venison. A man had better sleep without his scalp, than famish in the midst of plenty."

His passengers gladly complied with these directions. As the last foot touched the rock, the canoe whirled from its station, when the tall form of the scout was seen, for an instant, gliding above the waters, before it disappeared in the impenetrable darkness that rested on the bed of the river. Left by their guide, the travelers remained a few minutes in helpless ignorance, afraid even to move along the broken rocks, lest a false step should precipitate them down some one of the many deep and roaring caverns, into which the water seemed to tumble, on every side of them. Their suspense, however, was soon relieved; for, aided by the skill of the natives, the canoe shot back into the eddy, and floated again at the side of the low rock before they thought the scout had even time to rejoin his companions.

"We are now fortified, garrisoned, and provisioned," cried Heyward cheerfully, "and may set Montcalm and his allies at defiance. How, now, my vigilant sentinel, can see anything of those you call the Iroquois, on the mainland!"

"I call them Iroquois, because to me every native, who speaks a foreign tongue, is accounted an enemy, though he may pretend to serve the king! If Webb wants faith and honesty in an Indian, let him bring out the tribes of the Delawares, and send these greedy and lying Mohawks and Oneidas, with their six nations of varlets, where in nature they belong, among the French!"

"We should then exchange a warlike for a useless friend! I have heard that the Delawares have laid aside the hatchet and are content to be called women!"

"Aye, shame on the Hollanders and Iroquois, who circumvented them by their deviltries, into such a treaty! But I have known them for twenty years, and I call him liar that says cowardly blood runs in the veins of a Delaware. You have driven their tribes from the seashore, and would now believe what their enemies say, that you may sleep at night upon an easy pillow. No, no; to me, every Indian who speaks a foreign tongue is an Iroquois, whether the castle[1] of his tribe be in Canada, or be in York."

---

[1] The principal villages of the Indians are still called "castles" by the whites of New York. "Oneida castle" is no more than a scattered hamlet; but the name is in general use.

Heyward, perceiving that the stubborn adherence of the scout to the cause of his friends the Delawares, or Mohicans, for they were branches of the same numerous people, was likely to prolong a useless discussion, changed the subject.

"Treaty or no treaty, I know full well that your two companions are brave and cautious warriors! have they heard or seen anything of our enemies?"

"An Indian is a mortal to be felt afore he is seen," returned the scout, ascending the rock, and throwing the deer carelessly down. "I trust to other signs than such as come in at the eye, when I am outlying on the trail of the Mingoes."

"Do your ears tell you that they have traced our retreat?"

"I should be sorry to think they had, though this is a spot that stout courage might hold for a smart scrimmage. I will not deny, however, but the horses cowered when I passed them, as though they scented the wolves; and a wolf is a beast that is apt to hover about an Indian ambushment, craving the offal's of the deer the savages kill."

"You forget the buck at your feet! or, may we not owe their visit to the dead colt? Ha! what noise is that?"

"Poor Miriam!" murmured the stranger; "thy foal was foreordained to become a prey to ravenous beasts!" Then, suddenly lifting up his voice, amid the eternal din of the waters, he sang aloud:

"First born of Egypt, smite did he,
Of Mankind, and of beast also:
O, Egypt! Wonders sent 'midst thee,
On Pharaoh and his servants too!"

"The death of the colt sits heavy on the heart of its owner," said the scout; "but it's a good sign to see a man account upon his dumb friends. He has the religion of the matter, in believing what is to happen will happen and with such a consolation, it won't be long afore he submits to the rationality of killing a four-footed beast to save the lives of human men. It may be as you say," he continued, reverting to the purport of Heyward's last remark; "and the greater the reason why we should cut our steaks, and let the carcass drive down the stream, or we shall have the pack howling along the cliffs, begrudging every mouthful we swallow. Besides, though the Delaware tongue is the same as a book to the Iroquois, the cunning varlets are quick enough at understanding the reason of a wolf's howl."

The scout, while making his remarks, was busied in collecting certain necessary implements; as he concluded, he moved silently by the group of travelers, accompanied by the Mohicans, who seemed to comprehend his intentions with instinctive readiness, when the whole three disappeared in succession, seeming to vanish against the dark face of a perpendicular rock that rose to the height of a few yards, within as many feet of the water's edge.

CHAPTER VI.

"Those strains that once did sweet in Zion glide;
He wales a portion with judicious care;
And 'Let us worship God', he says, with solemn air."—Burns

Heyward and his female companions witnessed this mysterious movement with secret uneasiness; for, though the conduct of the white man had hitherto been above reproach, his rude equipment's, blunt address, and strong antipathies, together with the character of his silent associates, were all causes for exciting distrust in minds that had been so recently alarmed by Indian treachery.

The stranger alone disregarded the passing incidents. He seated himself on a projection of the rocks, whence he gave no other signs of consciousness than by the struggles of his spirit, as manifested in frequent and heavy sighs. Smothered voices were next heard, as though men called to each other in the bowels of the earth, when a sudden light flashed upon those without, and laid bare the much-prized secret of the place.

At the further extremity of a narrow, deep cavern in the rock, whose length appeared much extended by the perspective and the nature of the light by which it was seen, was seated the scout, holding a blazing knot of pine. The strong glare of the fire fell full upon his sturdy, weather-beaten countenance and forest attire, lending an air of romantic wildness to the aspect of an individual, who, seen by the sober light of day, would have exhibited the peculiarities of a man remarkable for the strangeness of his dress, the iron-like inflexibility of his frame, and the singular compound of quick, vigilant sagacity, and of exquisite simplicity, that by turns usurped the possession of his muscular features. At a little distance in advance stood Uncas, his whole person thrown powerfully into view. The travelers anxiously regarded the upright, flexible figure of the young Mohican, graceful and unrestrained in the attitudes and movements of nature. Though his person was more than usually screened by a green and fringed hunting-shirt, like that of the white man, there was no concealment to his dark, glancing, fearless eye, alike terrible and calm; the bold outline of his high, haughty features, pure in their native red; or to the dignified elevation of his receding forehead, together with all the finest proportions of a noble head, bared to the generous scalping tuft. It was the first opportunity possessed by Duncan and his companions to view the marked lineaments of either of their Indian attendants, and each individual of the party felt relieved from a burden of doubt, as the proud and determined, though wild expression of the features of the young warrior forced itself on their notice. They felt it might be a being partially benighted in the value of ignorance, but it could not be one who would willingly devote his rich natural gifts to the purposes of wanton treachery. The ingenuous Alice gazed at his free air and proud carriage, as she would have looked upon some precious relic of the Grecian chisel, to which life had been imparted by the intervention of a miracle; while Heyward, though accustomed to see the perfection of form which abounds among the uncorrupted natives, openly expressed his admiration at such an unblemished specimen of the noblest proportions of man.

"I could sleep in peace," whispered Alice, in reply, "with such a fearless and generous-looking youth for my sentinel. Surely, Duncan, those cruel murders, those terrific scenes of torture, of which we read and hear so much, are never acted in the presence of such as he!"

"This certainly is a rare and brilliant instance of those natural qualities in which these peculiar people are said to excel," he answered. "I agree with you, Alice, in thinking that such a front and eye were formed rather to intimidate than to deceive; but let us not practice a deception upon ourselves, by expecting any other exhibition of what we esteem virtue than according to the fashion of the savage. As bright examples of great qualities are but too uncommon among Christians, so are they singular and solitary with the Indians; though, for the honor of our common nature, neither are incapable of producing them. Let us then hope that this Mohican may not disappoint our wishes, but prove what his looks assert him to be, a brave and constant friend."

"Now Major Heyward speaks as Major Heyward should," said Cora; "who that looks at this creature of nature, remembers the shade of his skin?"

A short and apparently an embarrassed silence succeeded this remark, which was interrupted by the scout calling to them, aloud, to enter.

"This fire begins to show too bright a flame," he continued, as they complied, "and might light the Mingoes to our undoing. Uncas, drop the blanket, and show the knaves its dark side. This is not such a supper as a major of the Royal Americans has a right to expect, but I've known stout detachments of the corps glad to eat their venison raw, and without a relish, too[1]. Here, you see, we have plenty of salt, and can make a quick broil. There's fresh sassafras boughs for the ladies to sit on, which may not be as proud as their my-hog-guinea chairs, but which sends up a sweeter flavor, than the skin of any hog can do, be it of Guinea, or be it of any other land. Come, friend, don't be mournful for the colt; 'twas an innocent thing, and had not seen much hardship. Its death will save the creature many a

[1] In vulgar parlance the condiments of a repast are called by the American "a relish," substituting the thing for its effect. These provincial terms are frequently put in the mouths of the speakers, according to their several conditions in life. Most of them are of local use, and others quite peculiar to the particular class of men to which the character belongs. In the present instance, the scout uses the word with immediate reference to the "salt," with which his own party was so fortunate as to be provided.

sore back and weary foot!"

Uncas did as the other had directed, and when the voice of Hawkeye ceased, the roar of the cataract sounded like the rumbling of distant thunder.

"Are we quite safe in this cavern?" demanded Heyward. "Is there no danger of surprise? A single armed man, at its entrance, would hold us at his mercy."

A spectral-looking figure stalked from out of the darkness behind the scout, and seizing a blazing brand, held it toward the further extremity of their place of retreat. Alice uttered a faint shriek, and even Cora rose to her feet, as this appalling object moved into the light; but a single word from Heyward calmed them, with the assurance it was only their attendant, Chingachgook, who, lifting another blanket, discovered that the cavern had two outlets. Then, holding the brand, he crossed a deep, narrow chasm in the rocks which ran at right angles with the passage they were in, but which, unlike that, was open to the heavens, and entered another cave, answering to the description of the first, in every essential particular.

"Such old foxes as Chingachgook and myself are not often caught in a barrow with one hole," said Hawkeye, laughing; "you can easily see the cunning of the place, the rock is black limestone, which everybody knows is soft; it makes no uncomfortable pillow, where brush and pine wood is scarce; well, the fall was once a few yards below us, and I dare to say was, in its time, as regular and as handsome a sheet of water as any along the Hudson. But old age is a great injury to good looks, as these sweet young ladies have yet to learn! The place is sadly changed! These rocks are full of cracks, and in some places, they are softer than at othersome, and the water has worked out deep hollows for itself, until it has fallen back, ay, some hundred feet, breaking here and wearing there, until the falls have neither shape nor consistency."

"In what part of them are we?" asked Heyward.

"Why, we are nigh the spot that Providence first placed them at, but where, it seems, they were too rebellious to stay. The rock proved softer on each side of us, and so they left the center of the river bare and dry, first working out these two little holes for us to hide in."

"We are then on an island!"

"Ay! there are the falls on two sides of us, and the river above and below. If you had daylight, it would be worth the trouble to step up on the height of this rock and look at the perversity of the water. It falls by no rule at all; sometimes it leaps, sometimes it tumbles; there it skips; here it shoots; in one place 'tis white as snow, and in another 'tis green as grass; hereabouts, it pitches into deep hollows, that rumble and crush the 'arth; and there aways, it ripples and sings like a brook, fashioning whirlpools and gullies in the old stone, as if 'twas no harder than trodden clay. The whole design of the river seems disconcerted. First it runs smoothly, as if meaning to go down the descent as things were ordered; then it angles about and faces the shores; nor are their places wanting where it looks backward, as if unwilling to leave the wilderness, to mingle with the salt. Ay, lady, the fine cobweb-looking cloth you wear at your throat is coarse, and like a fishnet, to little spots I can show you, where the river fabricates all sorts of images, as if having broken loose from order, it would try its hand at everything. And yet what does it amount to! After the water has been suffered so to have its will, for a time, like a headstrong man, it is gathered together by the hand that made it, and a few rods below you may see it all, flowing on steadily toward the sea, as was foreordained from the first foundation of the 'arth!"

While his auditors received a cheering assurance of the security of their place of concealment from this untutored description of Glenn's,[2] they were much inclined to judge differently from

[2] Glenn's Falls are on the Hudson, some forty or fifty miles above the head of tide, or that place where the river becomes navigable for sloops. The description of this picturesque and remarkable little cataract, as given by the scout, is sufficiently correct, though the application of the water to uses of civilized life has materially injured its beauties. The rocky island and the two caverns are known to every traveler, since the former sustains the pier of a bridge, which is now thrown across the river, immediately above the fall. In explanation of the taste of Hawkeye, it should be remembered that men always prize that most which is least enjoyed. Thus, in a new country, the woods, and other objects, which in an old country would be maintained at great cost, are got rid of, simply with a view of "improving" as it is called.

Hawkeye, of its wild beauties. But they were not in a situation to suffer their thoughts to dwell on the charms of natural objects; and, as the scout had not found it necessary to cease his culinary labors while he spoke, unless to point out, with a broken fork, the direction of some particularly obnoxious point in the rebellious stream, they now suffered their attention to be drawn to the necessary though more vulgar consideration of their supper.

The repast, which was greatly aided by the addition of a few delicacies that Heyward had the precaution to bring with him when they left their horses, was exceedingly refreshing to the weary party. Uncas acted as attendant to the females, performing all the little offices within his power, with a mixture of dignity and anxious grace, that served to amuse Heyward, who well knew that it was an utter innovation on the Indian customs, which forbid their warriors to descend to any menial employment, especially in favor of their women. As the rights of hospitality were, however, considered sacred among them, this little departure from the dignity of manhood excited no audible comment. Had there been one there sufficiently disengaged to become a close observer, he might have fancied that the services of the young chief were not entirely impartial. That while he tendered to Alice the gourd of sweet water, and the venison in a trencher, neatly carved from the knot of the pepperidge, with sufficient courtesy, in performing the same offices to her sister, his dark eye lingered on her rich, speaking countenance. Once or twice, he was compelled to speak, to command the attention of those he served. In such cases he made use of English, broken and imperfect, but sufficiently intelligible, and which he rendered so mild and musical, by his deep, guttural voice, that it never failed to cause both ladies to look up in admiration and astonishment. In the course of these civilities, a few sentences were exchanged, that served to establish the appearance of an amicable intercourse between the parties.

In the meanwhile, the gravity of Chingcachgook remained immovable. He had seated himself more within the circle of light, where the frequent, uneasy glances of his guests were better enabled to separate the natural expression of his face from the artificial terrors of the war paint. They found a strong resemblance between father and son, with the difference that might be expected from age and hardships. The fierceness of his countenance now seemed to slumber, and in its place was to be seen the quiet, vacant composure which distinguishes an Indian warrior when his faculties are not required for any of the greater purposes of his existence. It was, however, easy to be seen, by the occasional gleams that shot across his swarthy visage, that it was only necessary to arouse his passions, in order to give full effect to the terrific device which he had adopted to intimidate his enemies. On the other hand, the quick, roving eye of the scout seldom rested. He ate and drank with an appetite that no sense of danger could disturb, but his vigilance seemed never to desert him. Twenty times the gourd or the venison was suspended before his lips, while his head was turned aside, as though he listened to some distant and distrusted sounds, a movement that never failed to recall his guests from regarding the novelties of their situation, to a recollection of the alarming reasons that had driven them to seek it. As these frequent pauses were never followed by any remark, the momentary uneasiness they created quickly passed away, and for a time was forgotten.

"Come, friend," said Hawkeye, drawing out a keg from beneath a cover of leaves, toward the close of the repast, and addressing the stranger who sat at his elbow, doing great justice to his culinary skill, "try a little spruce; 'twill wash away all thoughts of the colt, and quicken the life in your bosom. I drink to our better friendship, hoping that a little horseflesh may leave no heart-burnings atween us. How do you name yourself?"

"Gamut, David Gamut," returned the singing master, preparing to wash down his sorrows in a powerful draught of the woodsman's high-flavored and well-laced compound.

"A very good name, and, I dare say, handed down from honest

forefathers. I'm an admiration of names, though the Christian fashions fall far below savage customs in this particular. The biggest coward I ever knew was called Lyon; and his wife, Patience, would scold you out of hearing in less time than a hunted deer would run a rod. With an Indian 'tis a matter of conscience; what he calls himself, he generally is not that Chingachgook, which signifies Big Sarpent, is really a snake, big or little; but that he understands the windings and turnings of human nature', and is silent, and strikes his enemies when they least expect him. What may be your calling?"

"I am an unworthy instructor in the art of psalmody."

"Anan!"

"I teach singing to the youths of the Connecticut levy."

"You might be better employed. The young hounds go laughing and singing too much already through the woods, when they ought not to breathe louder than a fox in his cover. Can you use the smoothbore, or handle the rifle?"

"Praised be God, I have never had occasion to meddle with murderous implements!"

"Perhaps you understand the compass, and lay down the watercourses and mountains of the wilderness on paper, in order that they who follow may find places by their given names?"

"I practice no such employment."

"You have a pair of legs that might make a long path seem short! you journey sometimes, I fancy, with tidings for the general."

"Never; I follow no other than my own high vocation, which is instruction in sacred music!"

"'Tis a strange calling!" muttered Hawkeye, with an inward laugh, "to go through life, like a catbird, mocking all the ups and downs that may happen to come out of other men's throats. Well, friend, I suppose it is your gift, and mustn't be denied any more than if 'twas shooting, or some other better inclination. Let us hear what you can do in that way; 'twill be a friendly manner of saying good-night, for 'tis time that these ladies should be getting strength for a hard and a long push, in the pride of the morning, afore the Maquas are stirring."

"With joyful pleasure do I consent", said David, adjusting his iron-rimmed spectacles, and producing his beloved little volume, which he immediately tendered to Alice. "What can be more fitting and consolatory, than to offer up evening praise, after a day of such exceeding jeopardy!"

Alice smiled but, regarding Heyward, she blushed and hesitated.

"Indulge yourself," he whispered; "ought not the suggestion of the worthy namesake of the Psalmist to have its weight at such a moment?"

Encouraged by his opinion, Alice did what her pious inclinations, and her keen relish for gentle sounds, had before so strongly urged. The book was open at a hymn not ill adapted to their situation, and in which the poet, no longer goaded by his desire to excel the inspired King of Israel, had discovered some chastened and respectable powers. Cora betrayed a disposition to support her sister, and the sacred song proceeded, after the indispensable preliminaries of the pitchpipe, and the tune had been duly attended to by the methodical David.

The air was solemn and slow. At times it rose to the fullest compass of the rich voices of the females, who hung over their little book in holy excitement, and again it sank so low, that the rushing of the waters ran through their melody, like a hollow accompaniment. The natural taste and true ear of David governed and modified the sounds to suit the confined cavern, every crevice and cranny of which was filled with the thrilling notes of their flexible voices. The Indians riveted their eyes on the rocks and listened with an attention that seemed to turn them into stone. But the scout, who had placed his chin in his hand, with an expression of cold indifference, gradually suffered his rigid features to relax, until, as verse succeeded verse, he felt his iron nature subdued, while his recollection was carried back to boyhood, when his ears had been accustomed to listen to similar sounds of praise, in the settlements of the colony. His roving eyes began to moisten, and before the hymn was ended scalding tears rolled out of fountains that had long seemed dry, and followed each other down those cheeks, that had oftener felt the storms of heaven than any testimonials of weakness. The singers were dwelling on one of those low, dying chords, which the ear devours with such greedy rapture, as if conscious that it is about to lose them, when a cry, that seemed neither human nor earthly, rose in the outward air, penetrating not only the recesses of the cavern, but to the inmost hearts of all who heard it. It was followed by a stillness apparently as deep as if the waters had been checked in their furious progress, at such a horrid and unusual interruption.

"What is it?" murmured Alice, after a few moments of terrible suspense.

"What is it?" murmured Alice, after a few moments of terrible suspense.

"What is it?" repeated Hewyard aloud.

Neither Hawkeye nor the Indians made any reply. They listened, as if expecting the sound would be repeated, with a manner that expressed their own astonishment. At length they spoke together, earnestly, in the Delaware language, when Uncas, passing by the inner and most concealed aperture, cautiously left the cavern. When he had gone, the scout first spoke in English.

"What it is, or what it is not, none here can tell, though two of us have ranged the woods for more than thirty years. I did believe there was no cry that Indian, or beast could make, that my ears had not heard but this has proved that I was only a vain and conceited mortal."

"Was it not, then, the shout the warriors make when they wish to intimidate their enemies?" asked Cora who stood drawing her veil about her person, with a calmness to which her agitated sister was a stranger.

"No, no; this was bad, and shocking, and had a sort of unhuman sound; but when you once hear the war-whoop, you will never mistake it for anything else. Well, Uncas!" speaking in Delaware to the young chief as he re-entered, "what see you? do our lights shine through the blankets?"

The answer was short, and apparently decided, being given in the same tongue.

"There is nothing to be seen without," continued Hawkeye, shaking his head in discontent "and our hiding-place is still in darkness. Pass into the other cave, you that need it, and seek for sleep; we must be afoot long before the sun and make the most of our time to get to Edward, while the Mingoes are taking their morning nap."

Cora set the example of compliance, with a steadiness that taught the timider Alice the necessity of obedience. Before leaving the place, however, she whispered a request to Duncan, that he would follow. Uncas raised the blanket for their passage, and as the sisters turned to thank him for this act of attention, they saw the scout seated again before the dying embers, with his face resting on his hands, in a manner which showed how deeply he brooded on the unaccountable interruption which had broken up their evening devotions.

Heyward took with him a blazing knot, which threw a dim light through the narrow vista of their new apartment. Placing it in a favorable position, he joined the females, who now found themselves alone with him for the first time since they had left the friendly ramparts of Fort Edward.

"Leave us not, Duncan," said Alice: "we cannot sleep in such a place as this, with that horrid cry still ringing in our ears."

"First let us examine into the security of your fortress," he answered, "and then we will speak of rest."

He approached the further end of the cavern, to an outlet, which, like the others, was concealed by blankets; and removing the thick screen, breathed the fresh and reviving air from the cataract. One arm of the river flowed through a deep, narrow ravine, which its current had worn in the soft rock, directly beneath his feet, forming an effectual defense, as he believed, against any danger from that quarter; the water, a few rods above them, plunging, glancing, and sweeping along in its most violent and broken manner.

"Nature has made an impenetrable barrier on this side," he continued, pointing down the perpendicular declivity into the dark current before he dropped the blanket; "and as you know that good men and true are on guard in front, I see no reason why the advice of our honest host should be disregarded. I am certain Cora will join me in saying that sleep is necessary to you both."

"Cora may submit to the justice of your opinion though she cannot put it in practice," returned the elder sister, who had placed herself by the side of Alice, on a couch of sassafras; "there would be other causes to chase away sleep, though we had been spared the shock of this mysterious noise. Ask yourself, Heyward, can daughters forget the anxiety a father must endure, whose children lodge he knows not where or how, in such a wilderness, and in the midst of so many perils?"

"He is a soldier and knows how to estimate the chances of the woods."

"He is a father and cannot deny his nature."

"How kind has he ever been to all my follies, how tender and indulgent to all my wishes!" sobbed Alice. "We have been selfish, sister, in urging our visit at such hazard."

"I may have been rash in pressing his consent in a moment of much embarrassment, but I would have proved to him, that however others might neglect him in his strait his children at least were faithful."

"When he heard of your arrival at Edward," said Heyward, kindly, "there was a powerful struggle in his bosom between fear and love; though the latter, heightened, if possible, by so long a separation, quickly prevailed. 'It is the spirit of my noble-minded Cora that leads them, Duncan', he said, 'and I will not balk it. Would to God, that he who holds the honor of our royal master in his guardianship, would show but half her firmness!'"

"And did he not speak of me, Heyward?" demanded Alice, with jealous affection; "surely, he forgot not altogether his little Elsie?"

"That were impossible," returned the young man; "he called you by a thousand endearing epithets, that I may not presume to use, but to the justice of which, I can warmly testify. Once, indeed, he said"

Duncan ceased speaking; for while his eyes were riveted on those of Alice, who had turned toward him with the eagerness of filial affection, to catch his words, the same strong, horrid cry, as before, filled the air, and rendered him mute. A long, breathless silence succeeded, during which each looked at the others in fearful expectation of hearing the sound repeated. At length, the blanket was slowly raised, and the scout stood in the aperture with a countenance whose firmness evidently began to give way before a mystery that seemed to threaten some danger, against which all his cunning and experience might prove of no avail.

CHAPTER VII.

"They do not sleep,
On yonder cliffs, a grizzly band,
I see them sit."—Gray

"'Twould be neglecting a warning that is given for our good to lie hid any longer," said Hawkeye "when such sounds are raised in the forest. These gentle ones may keep close, but the Mohicans and I will watch upon the rock, where I suppose a major of the Sixtieth would wish to keep us company."

"Is, then, our danger so pressing?" asked Cora.

"He who makes strange sounds, and gives them out for man's information, alone knows our danger. I should think myself wicked, unto rebellion against His will, was I to burrow with such warnings in the air! Even the weak soul who passes his days in singing is stirred by the cry, and, as he says, is 'ready to go forth to the battle' If 'twere only a battle, it would be a thing understood by us all, and easily managed; but I have heard that when such shrieks are atween heaven and 'arth, it betokens another sort of warfare!"

"If all our reasons for fear, my friend, are confined to such as proceed from supernatural causes, we have but little occasion to be alarmed," continued the undisturbed Cora, "are you certain that our enemies have not invented some new and ingenious method to strike us with terror, that their conquest may become easier?"

"Lady," returned the scout, solemnly, "I have listened to all the sounds of the woods for thirty years, as a man will listen whose life and death depend on the quickness of his ears. There is no whine of the panther, no whistle of the catbird, nor any invention of the devilish Mingoes, that can cheat me! I have heard the forest moan like mortal men in their affliction; often, and again, have I listened to the wind playing its music in the branches of the girdled trees; and I have heard the lightning cracking in the air like the snapping of blazing brush as it spitted forth sparks and forked flames; but never have I thought that I heard more than the pleasure of him who sported with the things of his hand. But neither the Mohicans, nor I, who am a white man without a cross, can explain the cry just heard. We, therefore, believe it a sign given for our good."

"It is extraordinary!" said Heyward, taking his pistols from the place where he had laid them on entering; "be it a sign of peace or a signal of war, it must be looked to. Lead the way, my friend; I follow."

On issuing from their place of confinement, the whole party instantly experienced a grateful renovation of spirits, by exchanging the pent air of the hiding-place for the cool and invigorating atmosphere which played around the whirlpools and pitches of the cataract. A heavy evening breeze swept along the surface of the river and seemed to drive the roar of the falls into the recesses of their own cavern, whence it issued heavily and constant, like thunder rumbling beyond the distant hills. The moon had risen, and its light was already glancing here and there on the waters above them; but the extremity of the rock where they stood still lay in shadow. With the exception of the sounds produced by the rushing waters, and an occasional breathing of the air, as it murmured past them in fitful currents, the scene was as still as night and solitude could make it. In vain were the eyes of each individual bent along the opposite shores, in quest of some signs of life, that might explain the nature of the interruption they had heard. Their anxious and eager looks were baffled by the deceptive light, or rested only on naked rocks, and straight and immovable trees.

"Here is nothing to be seen but the gloom and quiet of a lovely evening," whispered Duncan; "how much should we prize such a scene, and all this breathing solitude, at any other moment, Cora! Fancy yourselves in security, and what now, perhaps, increases your terror, may be made conducive to enjoyment"

"Listen!" interrupted Alice.

The caution was unnecessary. Once more the same sound arose, as if from the bed of the river, and having broken out of the narrow bounds of the cliffs, was heard undulating through the forest, in distant and dying cadences.

"Can any here give a name to such a cry?" demanded Hawkeye, when the last echo was lost in the woods; "if so, let him speak; for myself, I judge it not to belong to 'arth!"

"Here, then, is one who can undeceive you," said Duncan; "I know the sound full well, for often have I heard it on the field of battle, and in situations which are frequent in a soldier's life. 'Tis the horrid shriek that a horse will give in his agony; oftener drawn from him in pain, though sometimes in terror. My charger is either a prey to the beasts of the forest, or he sees his danger, without the power to avoid it. The sound might deceive me in the cavern, but in the open air I know it too well to be wrong."

The scout and his companions listened to this simple explanation with the interest of men who imbibe new ideas, at the same time that they get rid of old ones, which had proved disagreeable inmates. The two latter uttered their usual expressive exclamation, "Hugh!" as the truth first glanced upon their minds, while the former, after a short, musing pause, took upon himself to reply.

"I cannot deny your words," he said, "for I am little skilled in horses, though born where they abound. The wolves must be hovering above their heads on the bank, and the timorsome creatures are calling on man for help, in the best manner they are able. Uncas" he spoke in Delaware "Uncas, drop down in the canoe, and whirl a brand among the pack; or fear may do what the wolves can't get at to perform, and leave us without horses in the morning, when we shall have so much need to journey swiftly!"

The young native had already descended to the water to comply, when a long howl was raised on the edge of the river and was borne swiftly off into the depths of the forest, as though the beasts, of their own accord, were abandoning their prey in sudden terror. Uncas, with instinctive quickness, receded, and the three foresters held another of their low, earnest conferences.

"We have been like hunters who have lost the points of the heavens, and from whom the sun has been hid for days," said Hawkeye, turning away from his companions; "now we begin again to know the signs of our course, and the paths are cleared from briers! Seat yourselves in the shade which the moon throws from yonder beech 'tis thicker than that of the pines and let us wait for that which the Lord may choose to send next. Let all your conversation be in whispers; though it would be better, and, perhaps, in the end, wiser, if each one held discourse with his own thoughts, for a time."

The manner of the scout was seriously impressive, though no longer distinguished by any signs of unmanly apprehension. It was evident that his momentary weakness had vanished with the explanation of a mystery which his own experience had not served to fathom; and though he now felt all the realities of their actual condition, that he was prepared to meet them with the energy of his hardy nature. This feeling seemed also common to the natives, who placed themselves in positions which commanded a full view of both shores, while their own persons were effectually concealed from observation. In such circumstances, common prudence dictated that Heyward, and his companions should imitate a caution that proceeded from so intelligent a source. The young man drew a pile of the sassafras from the cave and placing it in the chasm which separated the two caverns, it was occupied by the sisters, who were thus protected by the rocks from any missiles, while their anxiety was relieved by the assurance that no danger could approach without a warning. Heyward himself was posted at hand, so near that he might communicate with his companions without raising his voice to a dangerous elevation; while David, in imitation of the woodsmen, bestowed his person in such a manner among the fissures of the rocks, that his ungainly limbs were no longer offensive to the eye.

In this manner hours passed without further interruption. The moon reached the zenith and shed its mild light perpendicularly on the lovely sight of the sisters slumbering peacefully in each other's arms. Duncan cast the wide shawl of Cora before a spectacle he so much loved to contemplate, and then suffered his own head to seek a pillow on the rock. David began to utter sounds that would have shocked his delicate organs in more wakeful moments; in short, all but Hawkeye and the Mohicans lost every idea of consciousness, in uncontrollable drowsiness. But the watchfulness of these vigilant protectors neither tired nor slumbered. Immovable as that rock, of which each appeared to form a part, they lay, with their eyes roving, without intermission, along the dark margin of trees, that bounded the adjacent shores of the narrow stream. Not a sound escaped them; the most subtle examination could not have told they breathed. It was evident that this excess of caution proceeded from an experience that no subtlety on the part of their enemies could deceive. It was, however, continued without any apparent consequences, until the moon had set, and a pale streak above the treetops, at the bend of the river a little below, announced the approach of day.

Then, for the first time, Hawkeye was seen to stir. He crawled along the rock and shook Duncan from his heavy slumbers.

"Now is the time to journey," he whispered; "awake the gentle ones, and be ready to get into the canoe when I bring it to the landing-place."

"Have you had a quiet night?" said Heyward; "for myself, I believe sleep has got the better of my vigilance."

"All is yet still as midnight. Be silent but be quick."

By this time Duncan was thoroughly awake, and he immediately lifted the shawl from the sleeping females. The motion caused Cora to raise her hand as if to repulse him, while Alice murmured, in her soft, gentle voice, "No, no, dear father, we were not deserted; Duncan was with us!"

"Yes, sweet innocence," whispered the youth; "Duncan is here, and while life continues or danger remains, he will never quit thee. Cora! Alice! awake! The hour has come to move!"

A loud shriek from the younger of the sisters, and the form of the other standing upright before him, in bewildered horror, was the unexpected answer he received.

While the words were still on the lips of Heyward, there had arisen such a tumult of yells and cries as served to drive the swift currents of his own blood back from its bounding course into the fountains of his heart. It seemed, for near a minute, as if the demons of hell had possessed themselves of the air about them and were venting their savage humors in barbarous sounds. The cries came from no particular direction, though it was evident they filled the woods, and, as the appalled listeners easily imagined, the caverns of the falls, the rocks, the bed of the river, and the upper air. David raised his tall person in the midst of the infernal din, with a hand on either ear, exclaiming:

"Whence comes this discord! Has hell broke loose, that man should utter sounds like these!"

The bright flashes and the quick reports of a dozen rifles, from the opposite banks of the stream, followed this incautious exposure of his person, and left the unfortunate singing master senseless on that rock where he had been so long slumbering. The Mohicans boldly sent back the intimidating yell of their enemies, who raised a shout of savage triumph at the fall of Gamut. The flash of rifles was then quick and close between them, but either party was too well skilled to leave even a limb exposed to the hostile aim. Duncan listened with intense anxiety for the strokes of the paddle, believing that flight was now their only refuge. The river glanced by with its ordinary velocity, but the canoe was nowhere to be seen on its dark waters. He had just fancied they were cruelly deserted by their scout, as a stream of flame issued from the rock beneath them, and a fierce yell, blended with a shriek of agony, announced that the messenger of death sent from the fatal weapon of Hawkeye, had found a victim. At this slight repulse the assailants instantly withdrew, and gradually the place became as still as before the sudden tumult.

Duncan seized the favorable moment to spring to the body of Gamut, which he bore within the shelter of the narrow chasm that protected the sisters. In another minute the whole party was collected in this spot of comparative safety.

"The poor fellow has saved his scalp," said Hawkeye, coolly passing his hand over the head of David; "but he is a proof that a man may be born with too long a tongue! 'Twas downright madness to show six feet of flesh and blood, on a naked rock, to the raging savages. I only wonder he has escaped with life."

"Is he not dead?" demanded Cora, in a voice whose husky tones showed how powerfully natural horror struggled with her assumed firmness. "Can we do ought to assist the wretched man?"

"No, no! the life is in his heart yet, and after he has slept awhile, he will come to himself, and be a wiser man for it, till the hour of his real time shall come," returned Hawkeye, casting another oblique glance at the insensible body, while he filled his charger with admirable nicety. "Carry him in, Uncas, and lay him on the sassafras. The longer his nap lasts the better it will be for him, as I doubt whether he can find a proper cover for such a shape on these rocks; and singing won't do any good with the Iroquois."

"You believe, then, the attack will be renewed?" asked Heyward.

"Do I expect a hungry wolf will satisfy his craving with a mouthful! They have lost a man, and 'tis their fashion, when they meet a loss, and fail in the surprise, to fall back; but we shall have them on again, with new expedients to circumvent us, and master our scalps. Our main hope," he continued, raising his rugged countenance, across which a shade of anxiety just then passed like a darkening cloud, "will be to keep the rock until Munro can send a party to our help! God send it may be soon and under a leader that knows the Indian customs!"

"You hear our probable fortunes, Cora," said Duncan, "and you know we have everything to hope from the anxiety and experience of your father. Come, then, with Alice, into this cavern, where you, at least, will be safe from the murderous rifles of our enemies, and where you may bestow a care suited to your gentle natures on our unfortunate comrade."

The sisters followed him into the outer cave, where David was beginning, by his sighs, to give symptoms of returning consciousness, and then commending the wounded man to their attention, he immediately prepared to leave them.

"Duncan!" said the tremulous voice of Cora when he had reached the mouth of the cavern. He turned and beheld the speaker, whose color had changed to a deadly paleness, and whose lips quivered, gazing after him, with an expression of interest which immediately recalled him to her side. "Remember, Duncan, how necessary your safety is to our own, how you bear a father's sacred trust how much depends on your discretion and care in short," she added, while the telltale blood stole over her features, crimsoning her very temples, "how very deservedly dear you are to all of the name of Munro."

"If anything could add to my own base love of life," said Heyward, suffering his unconscious eyes to wander to the youthful form of the silent Alice, "it would be so kind an assurance. As major of the Sixtieth, our honest host will tell you I must take my share of the fray; but our task will be easy; it is merely to keep these bloodhounds at bay for a few hours."

Without waiting for a reply, he tore himself from the presence of the sisters, and joined the scout and his companions, who still lay within the protection of the little chasm between the two caves.

"I tell you, Uncas," said the former, as Heyward joined them, "you are wasteful of your powder, and the kick of the rifle disconcerts your aim! Little powder, light lead, and a long arm, seldom fail of bringing the death screech from a Mingo! At least, such has been my experience with the creature's. Come, friends: let us to our covers, for no man can tell when or where a Maqua[1] will strike his blow."

The Indians silently repaired to their appointed stations, which were fissures in the rocks, whence they could command the approaches to the foot of the falls. In the center of the little island, a few short and stunted pines had found root, forming a thicket, into which Hawkeye darted with the swiftness of a deer, followed by the active Duncan. Here they secured themselves, as well as circumstances would permit, among the shrubs and fragments of stone that were scattered about the place. Above them was a bare, rounded rock, on each side of which the water played its gambols, and plunged into the abysses beneath, in the manner already described. As the day had now dawned, the opposite shores no longer presented a confused outline, but they were able to look into the woods, and distinguish objects beneath a canopy of gloomy pines.

A long and anxious watch succeeded, but without any further evidences of a renewed attack; and Duncan began to hope that

[1] Mingo was the Delaware term of the Five Nations. Maquas was the name given them by the Dutch. The French, from their first intercourse with them, called them Iroquois.

their fire had proved more fatal than was supposed, and that their enemies had been effectually repulsed. When he ventured to utter this impression to his companions, it was met by Hawkeye with an incredulous shake of the head.

"You know not the nature of a Maqua, if you think he is so easily beaten back without a scalp!" he answered. "If there was one of the imps yelling this morning, there were forty! and they know our number and quality too well to give up the chase so soon. Hist! look into the water above, just where it breaks over the rocks. I am no mortal, if the risky devils haven't swum down upon the very pitch, and, as bad luck would have it, they have hit the head of the island. Hist! man, keep close! or the hair will be off your crown in the turning of a knife!"

Heyward lifted his head from the cover and beheld what he justly considered a prodigy of rashness and skill. The river had worn away the edge of the soft rock in such a manner as to render its first pitch less abrupt and perpendicular than is usual at waterfalls. With no other guide than the ripple of the stream where it met the head of the island, a party of their insatiable foes had ventured into the current, and swam down upon this point, knowing the ready access it would give, if successful, to their intended victims.

As Hawkeye ceased speaking, four human heads could be seen peering above a few logs of driftwood that had lodged on these naked rocks, and which had probably suggested the idea of the practicability of the hazardous undertaking. At the next moment, a fifth form was seen floating over the green edge of the fall, a little from the line of the island. The savage struggled powerfully to gain the point of safety and favored by the glancing water, he was already stretching forth an arm to meet the grasp of his companions, when he shot away again with the shirling current, appeared to rise into the air, with uplifted arms and starting eyeballs, and fell, with a sudden plunge, into that deep and yawning abyss over which he hovered. A single, wild, despairing shriek rose from the cavern, and all was hushed again as the grave.

The first generous impulse of Duncan was to rush to the rescue of the hapless wretch; but he felt himself bound to the spot by the iron grasp of the immovable scout.

"Would ye bring certain death upon us, by telling the Mingoes where we lie?" demanded Hawkeye, sternly; "'Tis a charge of powder saved, and ammunition is as precious now as breath to a worried deer! Freshen the priming of your pistols, the midst of the falls is apt to dampen the brimstone and stand firm for a close struggle, while I fire on their rush."

He placed a finger in his mouth, and drew a long, shrill whistle, which was answered from the rocks that were guarded by the Mohicans. Duncan caught glimpses of heads above the scattered driftwood, as this signal rose on the air, but they disappeared again as suddenly as they had glanced upon his sight. A low, rustling sound next drew his attention behind him, and turning his head, he beheld Uncas within a few feet, creeping to his side. Hawkeye spoke to him in Delaware, when the young chief took his position with singular caution and undisturbed coolness. To Heyward this was a moment of feverish and impatient suspense; though the scout saw fit to select it as a fit occasion to read a lecture to his more youthful associates on the art of using firearms with discretion.

"Of all we'pons," he commented, "the long barreled, true-grooved, soft-metaled rifle is the most dangerous in skillful hands, though it wants a strong arm, a quick eye, and great judgment in charging, to put forth all its beauties. The gunsmiths can have but little insight into their trade when they make their fowling-pieces and short horsemen's"

He was interrupted by the low but expressive "hugh" of Uncas.

"I see them, boy, I see them!" continued Hawkeye; "they are gathering for the rush, or they would keep their dingy backs below the logs. Well, let them," he added, examining his flint; "the leading man certainly comes on to his death, though it should be Montcalm himself!"

At that moment the woods were filled with another burst of cries, and at the signal four savages sprang from the cover of the driftwood. Heyward felt a burning desire to rush forward to meet them, so intense was the delirious anxiety of the moment; but he was restrained by the deliberate examples of the scout and Uncas.

When their foes, who had leaped over the black rocks that divided them, with long bounds, uttering the wildest yells, were within a few rods, the rifle of Hawkeye slowly rose among the shrubs, and poured out its fatal contents. The foremost Indian bounded like a stricken deer and fell headlong among the clefts of the island.

"Now, Uncas!" cried the scout, drawing his long knife, while his quick eyes began to flash with ardor, "take the last of the screeching imps; of the other two we are sartain!"

He was obeyed and, but two enemies remained to be overcome. Heyward had given one of his pistols to Hawkeye, and together they rushed down a little declivity toward their foes; they discharged their weapons at the same instant, and equally without success.

"I know'd it! and I said it!" muttered the scout, whirling the despised little implement over the falls with bitter disdain. "Come on, ye bloody minded hell-hounds! ye meet a man without a cross!"

The words were barely uttered, when he encountered a savage of gigantic stature, of the fiercest mien. At the same moment, Duncan found himself engaged with the other, in a similar contest of hand to hand. With ready skill, Hawkeye, and his antagonist each grasped that uplifted arm of the other which held the dangerous knife. For near a minute, they stood looking one another in the eye, and gradually exerting the power of their muscles for the mastery.

At length, the toughened sinews of the white man prevailed over the less practiced limbs of the native. The arm of the latter slowly gave way before the increasing force of the scout, who, suddenly wresting his armed hand from the grasp of the foe, drove the sharp weapon through his naked bosom to the heart. In the meantime, Heyward had been pressed in a more deadly struggle. His slight sword was snapped in the first encounter. As he was destitute of any other means of defense, his safety now depended entirely on bodily strength and resolution. Though deficient in neither of these qualities, he had met an enemy every way his equal. Happily, he soon succeeded in disarming his adversary, whose knife fell on the rock at their feet; and from this moment it became a fierce struggle who should cast the other over the dizzy height into a neighboring cavern of the falls. Every successive struggle brought them nearer to the verge, where Duncan perceived the final and conquering effort must be made. Each of the combatants threw all his energies into that effort, and the result was, that both tottered on the brink of the precipice. Heyward felt the grasp of the other at his throat, and saw the grim smile the savage gave, under the revengeful hope that he hurried his enemy to a fate similar to his own, as he felt his body slowly yielding to a resistless power, and the young man experienced the passing agony of such a moment in all its horrors. At that instant of extreme danger, a dark hand and glancing knife appeared before him; the Indian released his hold, as the blood flowed freely from around the severed tendons of the wrist; and while Duncan was drawn backward by the saving hand of Uncas, his charmed eyes still were riveted on the fierce and disappointed countenance of his foe, who fell sullenly and disappointed down the irrecoverable precipice.

"To cover! to cover!" cried Hawkeye, who just then had dispatched the enemy; "to cover, for your lives! the work is but half ended!"

The young Mohican gave a shout of triumph, and followed by Duncan, he glided up the acclivity they had descended to the combat and sought the friendly shelter of the rocks and shrubs.

CHAPTER VIII.

"They linger yet,
Avengers of their native land."—Gray

The warning call of the scout was not uttered without occasion. During the occurrence of the deadly encounter just related, the roar of the falls was unbroken by any human sound whatever. It would seem that interest in the result had kept the natives on the opposite shores in breathless suspense, while the quick evolutions and swift changes in the positions of the combatants effectually prevented a fire that might prove dangerous alike to friend and enemy. But the moment the struggle was decided, a yell arose as fierce, and savage as wild and revengeful passions could throw into the air. It was followed by the swift flashes of the rifles, which sent their leaden messengers across the rock in volleys, as though the assailants would pour out their impotent fury on the insensible scene of the fatal contest.

A steady, though deliberate return was made from the rifle of Chingachgook, who had maintained his post throughout the fray with unmoved resolution. When the triumphant shout of Uncas was borne to his ears, the gratified father raised his voice in a single responsive cry, after which his busy piece alone proved that he still guarded his pass with unwearied diligence. In this manner many minutes flew by with the swiftness of thought; the rifles of the assailants speaking, at times, in rattling volleys, and at others in occasional, scattering shots. Though the rock, the trees, and the shrubs, were cut and torn in a hundred places around the besieged, their cover was so close, and so rigidly maintained, that, as yet, David had been the only sufferer in their little band.

"Let them burn their powder," said the deliberate scout, while bullet after bullet whizzed by the place where he securely lay; "there will be a fine gathering of lead when it is over, and I fancy the imps will tire of the sport afore these old stones cry out for mercy! Uncas, boy, you waste the kernels by overcharging; and a kicking rifle never carries a true bullet. I told you to take that loping miscreant under the line of white point; now, if your bullet went a hair's breadth it went two inches above it. The life lies low in a Mingo, and humanity teaches us to make a quick end to the sarpents."

A quiet smile lighted the haughty features of the young Mohican, betraying his knowledge of the English language as well as of the other's meaning; but he suffered it to pass away without vindication of reply.

"I cannot permit you to accuse Uncas of want of judgment or of skill," said Duncan; "he saved my life in the coolest and readiest manner, and he has made a friend who never will require to be reminded of the debt he owes."

Uncas partly raised his body and offered his hand to the grasp of Heyward. During this act of friendship, the two young men exchanged looks of intelligence which caused Duncan to forget the character and condition of his wild associate. In the meanwhile, Hawkeye, who looked on this burst of youthful feeling with a cool, but kind regard made the following reply:

"Life is an obligation which friends often owe each other in the wilderness. I dare say I may have served Uncas some such turn myself before now; and I very well remember that he has stood between me and death five different times; three times from the Mingoes, once in crossing Horican, and"

"That bullet was better aimed than common!" exclaimed Duncan, involuntarily shrinking from a shot which struck the rock at his side with a smart rebound.

Hawkeye laid his hand on the shapeless metal, and shook his head, as he examined it, saying, "Falling lead is never flattened, had it come from the clouds this might have happened."

But the rifle of Uncas was deliberately raised toward the heavens, directing the eyes of his companions to a point, where the mystery was immediately explained. A ragged oak grew on the right bank of the river, nearly opposite to their position, which, seeking the freedom of the open space, had inclined so far forward that its upper branches overhung that arm of the stream which flowed nearest to its own shore. Among the topmost leaves, which scantily concealed the gnarled and stunted limbs, a savage was nestled, partly concealed by the trunk of the tree, and partly exposed, as though looking down upon them to ascertain the effect produced by his treacherous aim.

"These devils will scale heaven to circumvent us to our ruin," said Hawkeye; "keep him in play, boy, until I can bring 'killdeer' to bear, when we will try his metal on each side of the tree at once."

Uncas delayed his fire until the scout uttered the word.

The rifles flashed, the leaves and bark of the oak flew into the air, and were scattered by the wind, but the Indian answered their assault by a taunting laugh, sending down upon them another bullet in return, that struck the cap of Hawkeye from his head. Once more the savage yells burst out of the woods, and the leaden hail whistled above the heads of the besieged, as if to confine them to a place where they might become easy victims to the enterprise of the warrior who had mounted the tree.

"This must be looked to," said the scout, glancing about him with an anxious eye. "Uncas, call up your father; we have need of all our we'pons to bring the cunning varmint from his roost."

The signal was instantly given; and, before Hawkeye had reloaded his rifle, they were joined by Chingachgook. When his son pointed out to the experienced warrior the situation of their dangerous enemy, the usual exclamatory "hugh" burst from his lips; after which, no further expression of surprise or alarm was suffered to escape him. Hawkeye and the Mohicans conversed earnestly together in Delaware for a few moments, when each quietly took his post, in order to execute the plan, they had speedily devised.

The warrior in the oak had maintained a quick, though ineffectual fire, from the moment of his discovery. But his aim was interrupted by the vigilance of his enemies, whose rifles instantaneously bore on any part of his person that was left exposed. Still his bullets fell in the center of the crouching party. The clothes of Heyward, which rendered him peculiarly conspicuous, were repeatedly cut, and once blood was drawn from a slight wound in his arm.

At length, emboldened by the long and patient watchfulness of his enemies, the Huron attempted a better and more fatal aim. The quick eyes of the Mohicans caught the dark line of his lower limbs incautiously exposed through the thin foliage, a few inches from the trunk of the tree. Their rifles made a common report, when, sinking on his wounded limb, part of the body of the savage came into view. Swift as thought, Hawkeye seized the advantage, and discharged his fatal weapon into the top of the oak. The leaves were unusually agitated; the dangerous rifle fell from its commanding elevation, and after a few moments of vain struggling, the form of the savage was seen swinging in the wind, while he still grasped a ragged and naked branch of the tree with hands clenched in desperation.

"Give him, in pity, give him the contents of another rifle," cried Duncan, turning away his eyes in horror from the spectacle of a fellow creature in such awful jeopardy.

"Not a karnel!" exclaimed the obdurate Hawkeye; "his death is certain, and we have no powder to spare, for Indian fights sometimes last for days; 'tis their scalps or ours! and God, who made us, has put into our natures the craving to keep the skin on the head."

Against this stern and unyielding morality, supported as it was by such visible policy, there was no appeal. From that moment the yells in the forest once more ceased, the fire was suffered to decline, and all eyes, those of friends as well as enemies, became fixed on the hopeless condition of the wretch who was dangling between heaven and earth. The body yielded to the currents of air, and though no murmur or groan escaped the victim, there were instants when he grimly faced his foes, and the anguish of cold despair might be traced, through the intervening distance, in possession of his swarthy lineaments. Three several times the scout raised his piece in mercy, and as often, prudence getting the better of his intention, it was again silently lowered. At length one hand of the Huron lost its hold and dropped exhausted to his side. A desperate and fruitless struggle to recover the branch succeeded, and then the savage was seen for a fleeting instant, grasping wildly at the empty air. The lightning is not quicker than was the flame from the rifle of Hawkeye; the limbs of the victim trembled and contracted, the head fell to the bosom, and the body parted the foaming waters like lead, when the element closed above it, in its ceaseless velocity, and every vestige of the unhappy Huron was lost forever.

No shout of triumph succeeded this important advantage, but even the Mohicans gazed at each other in silent horror. A single yell burst from the woods, and all was again still. Hawkeye, who alone appeared to reason on the occasion, shook his head at his own momentary weakness, even uttering his self-disapprobation aloud.

"'Twas the last charge in my horn and the last bullet in my pouch, and 'twas the act of a boy!" he said; "what mattered it whether he struck the rock living or dead! feeling would soon be over. Uncas, lad, go down to the canoe, and bring up the big horn; it is all the powder we have left, and we shall need it to the last grain, or I am ignorant of the Mingo nature."

The young Mohican complied, leaving the scout turning over the useless contents of his pouch, and shaking the empty horn with renewed discontent. From this unsatisfactory examination, however, he was soon called by a loud and piercing exclamation from Uncas, that sounded, even to the unpracticed ears of Duncan, as the signal of some new and unexpected calamity. Every thought filled with apprehension for the previous treasure he had concealed in the cavern, the young man started to his feet, totally regardless of the hazard he incurred by such an exposure. As if actuated by a common impulse, his movement was imitated by his companions and together they rushed down the pass to the friendly chasm, with a rapidity that rendered the scattering fire of their enemies perfectly harmless. The unwonted cry had brought the sisters, together with the wounded David, from their place of refuge; and the whole party, at a single glance, was made acquainted with the nature of the disaster that had disturbed even the practiced stoicism of their youthful Indian protector.

At a short distance from the rock, their little bark was to be seen floating across the eddy, toward the swift current of the river, in a manner which proved that its course was directed by some hidden agent. The instant this unwelcome sight caught the eye of the scout, his rifle was leveled as by instinct, but the barrel gave no answer to the bright sparks of the flint.

"'Tis too late, 'tis too late!" Hawkeye exclaimed, dropping the useless piece in bitter disappointment; "the miscreant has struck the rapid; and had we powder, it could hardly send the lead swifter than he now goes!"

The adventurous Huron raised his head above the shelter of the canoe, and, while it glided swiftly down the stream, he waved his hand, and gave forth the shout, which was the known signal of success. His cry was answered by a yell and a laugh from the woods, as tauntingly exulting as if fifty demons were uttering their blasphemies at the fall of some Christian soul.

"Well may you laugh, ye children of the devil!" said the scout, seating himself on a projection of the rock, and suffering his gun to fall neglected at his feet, "for the three quickest and truest rifles in these woods are no better than so many stalks of mullein, or the last year's horns of a buck!"

"What is to be done?" demanded Duncan, losing the first feeling of disappointment in a more manly desire for exertion; "what will become of us?"

Hawkeye made no other reply than by passing his finger around the crown of his head, in a manner so significant, that none who witnessed the action could mistake its meaning.

"Surely, surely, our case is not so desperate!" exclaimed the youth; "the Hurons are not here; we may make good the caverns, we may oppose their landing."

"With what?" coolly demanded the scout. "The arrows of Uncas, or such tears as women shed! No, no; you are young, and rich, and have friends, and at such an age I know it is hard to die! But" glancing his eyes at the Mohicans, "let us remember we are men without a cross and let us teach these natives of the forest that white blood can run as freely as red, when the appointed hour is come."

Duncan turned quickly in the direction indicated by the other's eyes and read a confirmation of his worst apprehensions in the conduct of the Indians. Chingachgook, placing himself in a dignified posture on another fragment of the rock, had already laid aside his knife and tomahawk, and was in the act of taking the eagle's plume from his head, and smoothing the solitary tuft of hair in readiness to perform its last and revolting office. His countenance was composed, though thoughtful, while his dark, gleaming eyes were gradually losing the fierceness of the combat in an expression better suited to the change he expected momentarily to undergo.

"Our case is not, cannot be so hopeless!" said Duncan; "even at this very moment succor may be at hand. I see no enemies! They have sickened of a struggle in which they risk so much with so little prospect of gain!"

"It may be a minute, or it may be an hour, afore the wily sarpents steal upon us, and it is quite in natur' for them to be lying within hearing at this very moment," said Hawkeye; "but come they will, and in such a fashion as will leave us nothing to hope! Chingachgook" he spoke in Delaware "my brother, we have fought our last battle together, and the Maquas will triumph in the death of the sage man of the Mohicans, and of the pale face, whose eyes can make night as day, and level the clouds to the mists of the springs!"

"Let the Mingo women go weep over the slain!" returned the Indian, with characteristic pride and unmoved firmness; "the Great Snake of the Mohicans has coiled himself in their wigwams and has poisoned their triumph with the wailings of children, whose fathers have not returned! Eleven warriors lie hid from the graves of their tribes since the snows have melted, and none will tell where to find them when the tongue of Chingachgook shall be silent! Let them draw the sharpest knife, and whirl the swiftest tomahawk, for their bitterest enemy is in their hands. Uncas, topmost branch of a noble trunk, call on the cowards to hasten, or their hearts will soften, and they will change to women!"

"They look among the fishes for their dead!" returned the low, soft voice of the youthful chieftain; "the Hurons float with the slimy eels! They drop from the oaks like fruit that is ready to be eaten! and the Delawares laugh!"

"Ay, ay," muttered the scout, who had listened to this peculiar burst of the natives with deep attention; "they have warmed their Indian feelings, and they'll soon provoke the Maquas to give them a speedy end. As for me, who am of the whole blood of the whites, it is befitting that I should die as becomes my color, with no words of scoffing in my mouth, and without bitterness at the heart!"

"Why die at all!" said Cora, advancing from the place where natural horror had, until this moment, held her riveted to the rock; "the path is open on every side; fly, then, to the woods, and call on God for succor. Go, brave men, we owe you too much already; let us no longer involve you in our hapless fortunes!"

"You but little know the craft of the Iroquois, lady, if you judge they have left the path open to the woods!" returned Hawkeye, who, however, immediately added in his simplicity, "the downstream current, it is certain, might soon sweep us beyond the reach of their rifles or the sound of their voices."

"Then try the river. Why linger to add to the number of the victims of our merciless enemies?"

"Why," repeated the scout, looking about him proudly; "because it is better for a man to die at peace with himself than to live haunted by an evil conscience! What answer could we give Munro, when he asked us where and how we left his children?"

"Go to him, and say that you left them with a message to hasten to their aid," returned Cora, advancing nigher to the scout in her generous ardor; "that the Hurons bear them into the northern wilds, but that by vigilance and speed they may yet be rescued; and if, after all, it should please heaven that his assistance come too late, bear to him," she continued, her voice gradually lowering, until it seemed nearly choked, "the love, the blessings, the final prayers of his daughters, and bid him not mourn their early fate, but to look forward with humble confidence to the Christian's goal to meet his children." The hard, weather-beaten features of the scout began to work, and when she had ended, he dropped his chin to his hand, like a man musing profoundly on the nature of the proposal.

"There is reason in her words!" at length broke from his compressed and trembling lips; "ay, and they bear the spirit of Christianity; what might be right and proper in a redskin, may be sinful in a man who has not even a cross in blood to plead for his ignorance. Chingachgook!

Uncas! hear you the talk of the dark-eyed woman?"

He now spoke in Delaware to his companions, and his address, though calm and deliberate, seemed very decided. The elder Mohican heard with deep gravity, and appeared to ponder on his words, as though he felt the importance of their import. After a moment of hesitation, he waved his hand in assent, and uttered the English word "Good!" with the peculiar emphasis of his people. Then, replacing his knife and tomahawk in his girdle, the warrior moved silently to the edge of the rock which was most concealed from the banks of the river. Here he paused a moment, pointed significantly to the woods below, and saying a few words in his own language, as if indicating his intended route, he dropped into the water, and sank from before the eyes of the witnesses of his movements.

The scout delayed his departure to speak to the generous girl, whose breathing became lighter as she saw the success of her remonstrance.

"Wisdom is sometimes given to the young, as well as to the old," he said; "and what you have spoken is wise, not to call it by a better word. If you are led into the woods, that is such of you as may be spared for a while, break the twigs on the bushes as you pass, and make the marks of your trail as broad as you can, when, if mortal eyes can see them, depend on having a friend who will follow to the ends of the 'earth afore he departs you."

He gave Cora an affectionate shake of the hand, lifted his rifle, and after regarding it a moment with melancholy solicitude, laid it carefully aside, and descended to the place where Chingachgook had just disappeared. For an instant he hung suspended by the rock, and looking about him, with a countenance of peculiar care, he added bitterly, "Had the powder held out, this disgrace could never have befallen!" then, loosening his hold, the water closed above his head, and he also became lost to view.

All eyes now were turned on Uncas, who stood leaning against the ragged rock, in immovable composure. After waiting a short time,

Cora pointed down the river and said:

"Your friends have not been seen, and are now, most probably, in safety. Is it not time for you to follow?"

"Uncas will stay," the young Mohican calmly answered in English.

"To increase the horror of our capture, and to diminish the chances of our release! Go, generous young man," Cora continued, lowering her eyes under the gaze of the Mohican, and perhaps, with an intuitive consciousness of her power; "go to my father, as I have said, and be the most confidential of my messengers. Tell him to trust you with the means to buy the freedom of his daughters. Go! 'tis my wish, 'tis my prayer, that you will go!"

The settled, calm look of the young chief changed to an expression of gloom, but he no longer hesitated. With a noiseless step he crossed the rock and dropped into the troubled stream. Hardly a breath was drawn by those he left behind, until they caught a glimpse of his head emerging for air, far down the current, when he again sank, and was seen no more.

These sudden and apparently successful experiments had all taken place in a few minutes of that time which had now become so precious. After a last look at Uncas, Cora turned and with a quivering lip, addressed herself to Heyward:

"I have heard of your boasted skill in the water, too, Duncan," she said; "follow, then, the wise example set you by these simple and faithful beings."

"Is such the faith that Cora Munro would exact from her protector?" said the young man, smiling mournfully, but with bitterness.

"This is not a time for idle subtleties and false opinions," she answered, "but a moment when every duty should be equally considered. To us you can be of no further service here, but your precious life may be saved for other and nearer friends."

He made no reply, though his eye fell wistfully on the beautiful form of Alice, who was clinging to his arm with the dependency of an infant.

"Consider," continued Cora, after a pause, during which she seemed to struggle with a pang even more acute than any that her fears had excited, "that the worst to us can be but death; a tribute that all must pay at the good time of God's appointment."

"There are evils worse than death," said Duncan, speaking hoarsely, and as if fretful at her importunity, "but which the presence of one who would die in your behalf may avert."

Cora ceased her entreaties; and veiling her face in her shawl, drew the nearly insensible Alice after her into the deepest recess of the inner cavern.

CHAPTER IX.

"Be gay securely;
Dispel, my fair, with smiles, the tim'rous clouds,
That hang on thy clear brow."—Death of Agrippina

The sudden and almost magical change, from the stirring incidents of the combat to the stillness that now reigned around him, acted on the heated imagination of Heyward like some exciting dream. While all the images and events he had witnessed remained deeply impressed on his memory, he felt a difficulty in persuading him of their truth. Still ignorant of the fate of those who had trusted to the aid of the swift current, he at first listened intently to any signal or sounds of alarm, which might announce the good or evil fortune of their hazardous undertaking. His attention was, however, bestowed in vain; for with the disappearance of Uncas, every sign of the adventurers had been lost, leaving him in total uncertainty of their fate.

In a moment of such painful doubt, Duncan did not hesitate to look around him, without consulting that protection from the rocks which just before had been so necessary to his safety. Every effort, however, to detect the least evidence of the approach of their hidden enemies was as fruitless as the inquiry after his late companions. The wooded banks of the river seemed again deserted by everything possessing animal life. The uproar which had so lately echoed through the vaults of the forest was gone, leaving the rush of the waters to swell and sink on the currents of the air, in the unmingled sweetness of nature. A fish-hawk, which, secure on the topmost branches of a dead pine, had been a distant spectator of the fray, now swooped from his high and ragged perch, and soared, in wide sweeps, above his prey; while a jay, whose noisy voice had been stilled by the hoarser cries of the savages, ventured again to open his discordant throat, as though once more in undisturbed possession of his wild domains. Duncan caught from these natural accompaniments of the solitary scene a glimmering of hope and he began to rally his faculties to renewed exertions, with something like a reviving confidence of success.

"The Hurons are not to be seen," he said, addressing David, who had by no means recovered from the effects of the stunning blow he had received; "let us conceal ourselves in the cavern, and trust the rest to Providence."

"I remember to have united with two comely maidens, in lifting up our voices in praise and thanksgiving," returned the bewildered singing-master; "since which time I have been visited by a heavy judgment for my sins. I have been mocked with the likeness of sleep, while sounds of discord have rent my ears, such as might manifest the fullness of time, and that nature had forgotten her harmony."

"Poor fellow! thine own period was, in truth, near its accomplishment! But arouse and come with me; I will lead you were all other sounds but those of your own psalmody shall be excluded."

"There is melody in the fall of the cataract, and the rushing of many waters is sweet to the senses!" said David, pressing his hand confusedly on his brow. "Is not the air yet filled with shrieks and cries, as though the departed spirits of the damned"

"Not now, not now," interrupted the impatient Heyward, "they have ceased, and they who raised them, I trust in God, they are gone, too! everything but the water is still and at peace; in, then, where you may create those sounds, you love so well to hear."

David smiled sadly, though not without a momentary gleam of pleasure, at this allusion to his beloved vocation. He no longer hesitated to be led to a spot which promised such unalloyed gratification to his wearied senses; and leaning on the arm of his companion, he entered the narrow mouth of the cave. Duncan seized a pile of the sassafras, which he drew before the passage, studiously concealing every appearance of an aperture. Within this fragile barrier he arranged the blankets abandoned by the foresters, darkening the inner extremity of the cavern, while its outer received a chastened light from the narrow ravine, through which one arm of the river rushed to form the junction with its sister branch a few rods below.

"I like not the principle of the natives, which teaches them to submit without a struggle, in emergencies that appear desperate," he said, while busied in this employment; "our own maxim, which says, 'while life remains there is hope', is more consoling, and better suited to a soldier's temperament. To you, Cora, I will urge no words of idle encouragement; your own fortitude and undisturbed reason will teach you all that may become your sex; but cannot we dry the tears of that trembling weeper on your bosom?"

"I am calmer, Duncan," said Alice, raising herself from the arms of her sister, and forcing an appearance of composure through her tears; "much calmer, now. Surely, in this hidden spot we are safe, we are secret, free from injury; we will hope everything from those generous men who have risked so much already in our behalf."

"Now does our gentle Alice speak like a daughter of Munro!" said Heyward, pausing to press her hand as he passed toward the outer entrance of the cavern. "With two such examples of courage before him, a man would be ashamed to prove other than a hero." He then seated himself in the center of the cavern, grasping his remaining pistol with a hand convulsively clenched, while his contracted and frowning eye announced the sullen desperation of his purpose. "The Hurons, if they come, may not gain our position so easily as they think," he slowly muttered; and propping his head back against the rock, he seemed to await the result in patience, though his gaze was unceasingly bent on the open avenue to their place of retreat.

With the last sound of his voice, a deep, a long, and almost breathless silence succeeded. The fresh air of the morning had penetrated the recess, and its influence was gradually felt on the spirits of its inmates. As minute after minute passed by, leaving them in undisturbed security, the insinuating feeling of hope was gradually gaining possession of every bosom, though each one felt reluctant to give utterance to expectations that the next moment might so fearfully destroy.

David alone formed an exception to these varying emotions. A gleam of light from the opening crossed his wan countenance, and fell upon the pages of the little volume, whose leaves he was again occupied in turning, as if searching for some song more fitted to their condition than any that had yet met their eye. He was, most probably, acting all this time under a confused recollection of the promised consolation of Duncan. At length, it would seem, his patient industry found its reward; for, without explanation or apology, he pronounced aloud the words "Isle of Wight," drew a long, sweet sound from his pitchpipe, and then ran through the preliminary modulations of the air whose name he had just mentioned, with the sweeter tones of his own musical voice.

"May not this prove dangerous?" asked Cora, glancing her dark eye at Major Heyward.

"Poor fellow! his voice is too feeble to be heard above the din of the falls," was the answer; "besides, the cavern will prove his friend. Let him indulge his passions since it may be done without hazard."

"Isle of Wight!" repeated David, looking about him with that dignity with which he had long been wont to silence the whispering echoes of his school; "'tis a brave tune, and set to solemn words! let it be sung with meet respect!"

After allowing a moment of stillness to enforce his discipline, the voice of the singer was heard, in low, murmuring syllables, gradually stealing on the ear, until it filled the narrow vault with sounds rendered trebly thrilling by the feeble and tremulous utterance produced by his debility. The melody, which no weakness could destroy, gradually wrought its sweet influence on the senses of those who heard it. It even prevailed over the miserable travesty of the song of David which the singer had selected from a volume of similar effusions and caused the sense to be forgotten in the insinuating harmony of the sounds. Alice unconsciously dried her tears and bent her melting eyes on the pallid features of Gamut, with an expression of chastened delight that she neither affected nor wished to conceal. Cora bestowed an approving smile on the pious efforts of the namesake of the Jewish prince, and Heyward soon turned his steady, stern look from the outlet of the cavern, to fasten it, with a milder character, on the face of David, or to meet the wandering beams which at moments strayed from the humid eyes of Alice. The open sympathy of the listeners stirred the spirit of the votary of music, whose voice regained its richness and volume, without losing that touching softness which proved its secret charm. Exerting his renovated powers to their utmost, he was yet filling the arches of the cave with long and full tones, when a yell burst into the air without, that instantly stilled his pious strains, choking his voice suddenly, as though his heart had literally bounded into the passage of his throat.

"We are lost!" exclaimed Alice, throwing herself into the arms of Cora.

"Not yet, not yet," returned the agitated but undaunted Heyward: "the sound came from the center of the island, and it has been produced by the sight of their dead companions. We are not yet discovered, and there is still hope."

Faint and almost despairing as was the prospect of escape, the words of Duncan were not thrown away, for it awakened the powers of the sisters in such a manner that they awaited the results in silence. A second yell soon followed the first, when a rush of voices was heard pouring down the island, from its upper to its lower extremity, until they reached the naked rock above the caverns, where, after a shout of savage triumph, the air continued full of horrible cries and screams, such as man alone can utter, and he only when in a state of the fiercest barbarity.

The sounds quickly spread around them in every direction. Some called to their fellows from the water's edge and were answered from the heights above. Cries were heard in the startling vicinity of the chasm between the two caves, which mingled with hoarser yells that arose out of the abyss of the deep ravine. In short, so rapidly had the savage sounds diffused themselves over the barren rock, that it was not difficult for the anxious listeners to imagine they could be heard beneath, as in truth they were above on every side of them.

In the midst of this tumult, a triumphant yell was raised within a few yards of the hidden entrance to the cave. Heyward abandoned every hope, with the belief it was the signal that they were discovered. Again, the impression passed away, as he heard the voices collect near the spot where the white man had so reluctantly abandoned his rifle. Amid the jargon of Indian dialects that he now plainly heard, it was easy to distinguish not only words, but sentences, in the patois of the Canadas. A burst of voices had shouted simultaneously, "La Longue Carabine!" causing the opposite woods to re-echo with a name which, Heyward well remembered, had been given by his enemies to a celebrated hunter and scout of the English camp, and who, he now learned for the first time, had been his late companion.

"La Longue Carabine! La Longue Carabine!" passed from mouth to mouth, until the whole band appeared to be collected around a trophy which would seem to announce the death of its formidable owner. After a vociferous consultation, which was, at times, deafened by bursts of savage joy, they again separated, filling the air with the name of a foe, whose body, Heywood could collect from their expressions, they hoped to find concealed in some crevice of the island.

"Now," he whispered to the trembling sisters, "now is the moment of uncertainty! if our place of retreat escape this scrutiny, we are still safe! In every event, we are assured, by what has fallen from our enemies, that our friends have escaped, and in two short hours we may look for succor from Webb."

There were now a few minutes of fearful stillness, during which Heyward well knew that the savages conducted their search with greater vigilance and method. More than once he could distinguish their footsteps, as they brushed the sassafras, causing the faded leaves to rustle, and the branches to snap. At length, the pile yielded a little, a corner of a blanket fell, and a faint ray of light gleamed into the inner part of the cave. Cora folded Alice to her bosom in agony, and Duncan sprang to his feet. A shout was at that moment heard, as if issuing from the center of the rock, announcing that the neighboring cavern had at length been entered. In a minute, the number and loudness of the voices indicated that the whole party was collected in and around that secret place.

As the inner passages to the two caves were so close to each other, Duncan, believing that escape was no longer possible, passed David and the sisters, to place himself between the latter and the first onset of the terrible meeting. Grown desperate by his situation, he drew nigh the slight barrier which separated him only by a few feet from his relentless pursuers, and placing his face to the casual opening, he even looked out with a sort of desperate indifference, on their movements.

Within reach of his arm was the brawny shoulder of a gigantic Indian, whose deep and authoritative voice appeared to give directions to the proceedings of his fellows. Beyond him again, Duncan could look into the vault opposite, which was filled with savages, upturning, and rifling the humble furniture of the scout. The wound of David had dyed the leaves of sassafras with a color that the native well knew as anticipating the season. Over this sign of their success, they sent up a howl, like an opening from so many hounds who had recovered a lost trail. After this yell of victory, they tore up the fragrant bed of the cavern, and bore the branches into the chasm, scattering the boughs, as if they suspected them of concealing the person of the man they had so long hated and feared. One fierce and wild-looking warrior approached the chief, bearing a load of the brush, and pointing exultingly to the deep red stains with which it was sprinkled, uttered his joy in Indian yells, whose meaning Heyward was only enabled to comprehend by the frequent repetition of the name "La Longue Carabine!" When his triumph had ceased, he cast the brush on the slight heap Duncan had made before the entrance of the second cavern and closed the view. His example was followed by others, who, as they drew the branches from the cave of the scout, threw them into one pile, adding, unconsciously, to the security of those they sought. The very slightness of the defense was its chief merit, for no one thought of disturbing a mass of brush, which all of them believed, in that moment of hurry and confusion, had been accidentally raised by the hands of their own party.

As the blankets yielded before the outward pressure, and the branches settled in the fissure of the rock by their own weight, forming a compact body, Duncan once more breathed freely. With a light step and lighter heart, he returned to the center of the cave, and took the place he had left, where he could command a view of the opening next the river. While he was in the act of making this movement, the Indians, as if changing their purpose by a common impulse, broke away from the chasm in a body, and were heard rushing up the island again, toward the point whence they had originally descended. Here another wailing cry betrayed that they were again collected around the bodies of their dead comrades.

Duncan now ventured to look at his companions; for, during the most critical moments of their danger, he had been apprehensive that the anxiety of his countenance might communicate some additional alarm to those who were so little able to sustain it.

"They are gone, Cora!" he whispered; "Alice, they are returned whence they came, and we are saved! To Heaven, that has alone delivered us from the grasp of so merciless an enemy, be all the praise!"

"Then to Heaven will I return my thanks!" exclaimed the younger sister, rising from the encircling arm of Cora, and casting herself with enthusiastic gratitude on the naked rock; "to that Heaven who has spared the tears of a gray-headed father; has saved the lives of those I so much love."

Both Heyward and the more temperate Cora witnessed the act of involuntary emotion with powerful sympathy, the former secretly believing that piety had never worn a form so lovely as it had now assumed in the youthful person of Alice. Her eyes were radiant with the glow of grateful feelings; the flush of her beauty was again seated on her cheeks, and her whole soul seemed ready and anxious to pour out its thanksgivings through the medium of her eloquent features. But when her lips moved, the words they should have uttered appeared frozen by some new and sudden chill. Her bloom gave place to the paleness of death; her soft and melting eyes grew hard, and seemed contracting with horror; while those hands, which she had raised, clasped in each other, toward heaven, dropped in horizontal lines before her, the fingers pointed forward in convulsed motion. Heyward turned the instant she gave a direction to his suspicions and peering just above the ledge which formed the threshold of the open outlet of the cavern, he beheld the malignant, fierce, and savage features of Le Renard Subtill.

In that moment of surprise, the self-possession of Heyward did not desert him. He observed by the vacant expression of the Indian's countenance, that his eye, accustomed to the open air had not yet been able to penetrate the dusky light which pervaded the depth of the cavern. He had even thought of retreating beyond a curvature in the natural wall, which might still conceal him and his companions, when by the sudden gleam of intelligence that shot across the features of the savage, he saw it was too late, and that they were betrayed.

The look of exultation and brutal triumph which announced this terrible truth was irresistibly irritating. Forgetful of everything but the impulses of his hot blood, Duncan leveled his pistol and fired. The report of the weapon made the cavern bellow like an eruption from a volcano; and when the smoke it vomited had been driven away before the current of air which issued from the ravine the place so lately occupied by the features of his treacherous guide was vacant. Rushing to the outlet, Heyward caught a glimpse of his dark figure stealing around a low and narrow ledge, which soon hid him entirely from sight.

Among the savages a frightful stillness succeeded the explosion, which had just been heard bursting from the bowels of the rock. But when Le Renard raised his voice in a long and intelligible whoop, it was answered by a spontaneous yell from the mouth of every Indian within hearing of the sound.

The clamorous noises again rushed down the island; and before Duncan had time to recover from the shock, his feeble barrier of brush was scattered to the winds, the cavern was entered at both its extremities, and he and his companions were dragged from their shelter and borne into the day, where they stood surrounded by the whole band of the triumphant Hurons.

CHAPTER X.

"I fear we shall outsleep the coming morn
As much as we this night have overwatched!"
—Midsummer Night's Dream

The instant the shock of this sudden misfortune had abated, Duncan began to make his observations on the appearance and proceedings of their captors. Contrary to the usages of the natives in the wantonness of their success they had respected, not only the persons of the trembling sisters, but his own. The rich ornaments of his military attire had indeed been repeatedly handled by different individuals of the tribes with eyes expressing a savage longing to possess the baubles; but before the customary violence could be resorted to, a mandate in the authoritative voice of the large warrior, already mentioned, stayed the uplifted hand and convinced Heyward that they were to be reserved for some object of particular moment.

While, however, these manifestations of weakness were exhibited by the young and vain of the party, the more experienced warriors continued their search throughout both caverns, with an activity that denoted they were far from being satisfied with those fruits of their conquest which had already been brought to light. Unable to discover any new victim, these diligent workers of vengeance soon approached their male prisoners, pronouncing the name "La Longue Carabine," with a fierceness that could not be easily mistaken.

Duncan affected not to comprehend the meaning of their repeated and violent interrogatories, while his companion was spared the effort of a similar deception by his ignorance of French. Wearied at length by their importunities, and apprehensive of irritating his captors by too stubborn a silence, the former looked about him in quest of Magua, who might interpret his answers to questions which were at each moment becoming more earnest and threatening.

The conduct of this savage had formed a solitary exception to that of all his fellows. While the others were busily occupied in seeking to gratify their childish passion for finery, by plundering even the miserable effects of the scout, or had been searching with such bloodthirsty vengeance in their looks for their absent owner, Le Renard had stood at a little distance from the prisoners, with a demeanor so quiet and satisfied, as to betray that he had already affected the grand purpose of his treachery. When the eyes of Heyward first met those of his recent guide, he turned them away in horror at the sinister though calm look he encountered. Conquering his disgust, however, he was able, with an averted face, to address his successful enemy.

"Le Renard Subtill is too much of a warrior," said the reluctant Heyward, "to refuse telling an unarmed man what his conquerors say."

"They ask for the hunter who knows the paths through the woods," returned Magua, in his broken English, laying his hand, at the same time, with a ferocious smile, on the bundle of leaves with which a wound on his own shoulder was bandaged. "'La Longue Carabine'! His rifle is good, and his eye never shut; but, like the short gun of the white chief, it is nothing against the life of Le Subtil."

"Le Renard is too brave to remember the hurts received in war, or the hands that gave them."

"Was it war, when the tired Indian rested at the Sugartree to taste his corn! who filled the bushes with creeping enemies! who drew the knife, whose tongue was peace, while his heart was colored with blood! Did Magua say that the hatchet was out of the ground, and that his hand had dug it up?"

As Duncan dared not retort upon his accuser by reminding him of his own premeditated treachery and disdained to deprecate his resentment by any words of apology, he remained silent. Magua seemed also content to rest the controversy as well as all further communication there, for he resumed the leaning attitude against the rock from which, in momentary energy, he had arisen. But the cry of "La Longue Carabine" was renewed the instant the impatient savages perceived that the short dialogue was ended.

"You hear," said Magua, with stubborn indifference: "the red Hurons call for the life of 'The Long Rifle', or they will have the blood of him that keep him hid!"

"He is gone, escaped; he is far beyond their reach."

Renard smiled with cold contempt, as he answered:

"When the white man dies, he thinks he is at peace; but the red men know how to torture even the ghosts of their enemies. Where is his body? Let the Hurons see his scalp."

"He is not dead but escaped."

Magua shook his head incredulously.

"Is he a bird, to spread his wings; or is he a fish, to swim without air! The white chief read in his books, and he believes the Hurons are fools!"

"Though no fish, 'The Long Rifle' can swim. He floated down the stream when the powder was all burned, and when the eyes of the Hurons were behind a cloud."

"And why did the white chief stay?" demanded the still incredulous Indian. "Is he a stone that goes to the bottom, or does the scalp burn his head?"

"That I am not stone, your dead comrade, who fell into the falls, might answer, were the life still in him," said the provoked young man, using, in his anger, that boastful language which was most likely to excite the admiration of an Indian. "The white man thinks none, but cowards desert their women."

Magua muttered a few words, inaudibly, between his teeth, before he continued, aloud:

"Can the Delawares swim, too, as well as crawl in the bushes? Where is 'Le Gros Serpent'?"

Duncan, who perceived by the use of these Canadian appellations, that his late companions were much better known to his enemies than to himself, answered, reluctantly: "He also is gone down with the water."

"'Le Cerf Agile' is not here?"

"I know not whom you call 'The Nimble Deer'," said Duncan gladly profiting by any excuse to create delay.

"Uncas," returned Magua, pronouncing the Delaware name with even greater difficulty than he spoke his English words. "'Bounding Elk' is what the white man says, when he calls to the young Mohican."

"Here is some confusion in names between us, Le Renard," said Duncan, hoping to provoke a discussion. "Daim is the French for deer, and Cerf for stag; elan is the true term, when one would speak of an elk."

"Yes," muttered the Indian, in his native tongue; "the pale faces are prattling women! they have two words for each thing, while a red-skin will make the sound of his voice speak for him." Then, changing his language, he continued, adhering to the imperfect nomenclature of his provincial instructors. "The deer is swift, but weak; the elk is swift, but strong; and the son of 'Le Serpent' is 'Le Cerf Agile.' Has he leaped the river to the woods?"

"If you mean the younger Delaware, he, too, has gone down with the water."

As there was nothing improbable to an Indian in the manner of the escape, Magua admitted the truth of what he had heard, with a readiness that afforded additional evidence how little he would prize such worthless captives. With his companions, however, the feeling was manifestly different.

The Hurons had awaited the result of this short dialogue with characteristic patience, and with a silence that increased until there was a general stillness in the band. When Heyward ceased to speak, they turned their eyes, as one man, on Magua, demanding, in this expressive manner, an explanation of what had been said. Their interpreter pointed to the river, and made them acquainted with the result, as much by the action as by the few words he uttered. When the fact was generally understood, the savages raised a frightful yell, which declared the extent of their disappointment. Some ran furiously to the water's edge, beating the air with frantic gestures, while others spat upon the element, to resent the supposed treason it had committed against their acknowledged rights as conquerors. A few and they are not the least powerful and terrific of the band, threw lowering looks, in which the fiercest passion was only tempered by habitual self-command, at those captives who still remained in their power, while one or two even gave vent to their malignant feelings by the most menacing gestures, against which neither the sex nor the beauty of the sisters was any protection. The young soldier made a desperate but fruitless effort to spring to the side of Alice, when he saw the dark hand of a savage twisted in the rich tresses which were flowing in volumes over her shoulders, while a knife was passed around the head from which they fell, as if to denote the horrid manner in which it was about to be robbed of its beautiful ornament. But his hands were bound; and at the first movement he made, he felt the grasp of the powerful Indian who directed the band, pressing his shoulder like a vise. Immediately conscious how unavailing any struggle against such an overwhelming force must prove, he submitted to his fate, encouraging his gentle companions by a few low and tender assurances, that the natives seldom failed to threaten more than they performed.

But while Duncan resorted to these words of consolation to quiet the apprehensions of the sisters, he was not so weak as to deceive himself. He well knew that the authority of an Indian chief was so little conventional, that it was oftener maintained by physical superiority than by any moral supremacy he might possess. The danger was, therefore, magnified exactly in proportion to the number of the savage spirits by which they were surrounded. The most positive mandate from him who seemed the acknowledged leader, was liable to be violated at each moment by any rash hand that might choose to sacrifice a victim to the manes of some dead friend or relative. While, therefore, he sustained an outward appearance of calmness and fortitude, his heart leaped into his throat, whenever any of their fierce captors drew nearer than common to the helpless sisters, or fastened one of their sullen, wandering looks on those fragile forms which were so little able to resist the slightest assault.

His apprehensions were, however, greatly relieved, when he saw that the leader had summoned his warriors to himself in counsel. Their deliberations were short, and it would seem, by the silence of most of the party, the decision unanimous. By the frequency with which the few speakers pointed in the direction of the encampment of Webb, it was apparent they dreaded the approach of danger from that quarter. This consideration probably hastened their determination and quickened the subsequent movements.

During his short conference, Heyward, finding a respite from his gravest fears, had leisure to admire the cautious manner in which the Hurons had made their approaches, even after hostilities had ceased.

It has already been stated that the upper half of the island was a naked rock, and destitute of any other defenses than a few scattered logs of driftwood. They had selected this point to make their descent, having borne the canoe through the wood around the cataract for that purpose. Placing their arms in the little vessel a dozen men clinging to its sides had trusted themselves to the direction of the canoe, which was controlled by two of the most skillful warriors, in attitudes that enabled them to command a view of the dangerous passage. Favored by this arrangement, they touched the head of the island at that point which had proved so fatal to their first adventurers, but with the advantages of superior numbers, and the possession of firearms. That such had been the manner of their descent was rendered quite apparent to Duncan; for they now bore the light bark from the upper end of the rock, and placed it in the water, near the mouth of the outer cavern. As soon as this change was made, the leader made signs to the prisoners to descend and enter.

As resistance was impossible, and remonstrance useless, Heyward set the example of submission, by leading the way into the canoe, where he was soon seated with the sisters and the still wondering David. Notwithstanding the Hurons were necessarily ignorant of the little channels among the eddies and rapids of the stream, they knew the common signs of such a navigation too well to commit any material blunder. When the pilot chosen for the task of guiding the canoe had taken his station, the whole band plunged again into the river, the vessel glided down the current and in a few moments the captives found themselves on the south bank of the stream, nearly opposite to the point where they had struck it the preceding evening.

Here was held another short but earnest consultation, during which the horses, to whose panic their owners ascribed their heaviest misfortune, were led from the cover of the woods, and brought to the sheltered spot. The band now divided. The great chief, so often mentioned, mounting the charger of Heyward, led the way directly across the river, followed by most of his people, and disappeared in the woods, leaving the prisoners in charge of six savages, at whose head was Le Renard Subtil. Duncan witnessed all their movements with renewed uneasiness.

He had been fond of believing, from the uncommon forbearance of the savages, that he was reserved as a prisoner to be delivered to Montcalm. As the thoughts of those who are in misery seldom slumber, and the invention is never livelier than when it is stimulated by hope, however feeble and remote, he had even imagined that the parental feelings of Munro were to be made instrumental in seducing him from his duty to the king. For though the French commander bore a high character for courage and enterprise, he was also thought to be expert in those political practices which do not always respect the nicer obligations of morality, and which so generally disgraced the European diplomacy of that period.

All those busy and ingenious speculations were now annihilated by the conduct of his captors. That portion of the band who had followed the huge warrior took the route toward the foot of the Horican and no other expectation was left for himself and companions, than that they were to be retained as hopeless captives by their savage conquerors. Anxious to know the worst, and willing, in such an emergency, to try the potency of gold he overcame his reluctance to speak to Magua. Addressing himself to his former guide, who had now assumed the authority and manner of one who was to direct the future movements of the party, he said, in tones as friendly and confiding as he could assume:

"I would speak to Magua, what is fit only for so great a chief to hear."

The Indian turned his eyes on the young soldier scornfully, as he answered:

"Speak; trees have no ears."

"But the red Hurons are not deaf; and counsel that is fit for the great men of a nation would make the young warriors drunk. If Magua will not listen, the officer of the king knows how to be silent."

The savage spoke carelessly to his comrades, who were busied, after their awkward manner, in preparing the horses for the reception of the sisters, and moved a little to one side, whither by a cautious gesture he induced Heyward to follow.

"Now, speak," he said; "if the words are such as Magua should hear."

"Le Renard Subtil has proved himself worthy of the honorable name given to him by his Canada fathers," commenced Heyward; "I see his wisdom, and all that he has done for us, and shall remember it when the hour to reward him arrives. Yes! Renard has proved that he is not only a great chief in council, but one who knows how to deceive his enemies!"

"What has Renard done?" coldly demanded the Indian.

"What! has he not seen that the woods were filled with outlying parties of the enemies, and that the serpent could not steal through them without being seen? Then, did he not lose his path to blind the eyes of the Hurons? Did he not pretend to go back to his tribe, who had treated him ill, and driven him from their wigwams like a dog? And, when we saw what he wished to do, did we not aid him, by making a false face, that the Hurons might think the white man believed that his friend was his enemy? Is not all this true? And when Le Subtil had shut the eyes and stopped the ears of his nation by his wisdom, did they not forget that they had once done him wrong, and forced him to flee to the Mohawks? And did they not leave him on the south side of the river, with their prisoners, while they have gone foolishly on the north? Does not Renard mean to turn like a fox on his footsteps, and to carry to the rich and gray-headed Scotchman his daughters? Yes, Magua, I see it all, and I have already been thinking how so much wisdom and honesty should be repaid. First, the chief of William Henry will give as a great chief should for such a service. The medal[1] of Magua will no longer be of tin, but of beaten gold; his horn will run over with powder; dollars will be as plenty in his pouch as pebbles on the shore of Horican and the deer will lick his hand, for they will know it to be vain to fly from the rifle he will carry! As for myself, I know not how to exceed the gratitude of the Scotchman, but I...yes, I will."

"What will the young chief, who comes from toward the sun, give?"

---

[1] It has long been a practice with the whites to conciliate the important men of the Indians by presenting medals, which are worn in the place of their own rude ornaments. Those given by the English generally bear the impression of the reigning king, and those given by the Americans that of the president.

demanded the Huron, observing that Heyward hesitated in his desire to end the enumeration of benefits with that which might form the climax of an Indian's wishes.

"He will make the fire-water from the islands in the Salt Lake flow before the wigwam of Magua, until the heart of the Indian shall be lighter than the feathers of the humming-bird, and his breath sweeter than the wild honeysuckle."

Le Renard had listened gravely as Heyward slowly proceeded in this subtle speech. When the young man mentioned the artifice, he supposed the Indian to have practiced on his own nation, the countenance of the listener was veiled in an expression of cautious gravity. At the allusion to the injury which Duncan affected to believe had driven the Huron from his native tribe, a gleam of such ungovernable ferocity flashed from the other's eyes, as induced the adventurous speaker to believe he had struck the proper chord. And by the time he reached the part where he so artfully blended the thirst of vengeance with the desire of gain, he had, at least, obtained a command of the deepest attention of the savage. The question put by Le Renard had been calm, and with all the dignity of an Indian; but it was quite apparent, by the thoughtful expression of the listener's countenance, that the answer was most cunningly devised. The Huron mused a few moments, and then laying his hand on the rude bandages of his wounded shoulder, he said, with some energy:

"Do friends make such marks?"

"Would 'La Longue Carbine' cut one so slight on an enemy?"

"Do the Delawares crawl upon those they love like snakes, twisting themselves to strike?"

"Would 'Le Gros Serpent' have been heard by the ears of one he wished to be deaf?"

"Does the white chief burn his powder in the faces of his brothers?"

"Does he ever miss his aim, when seriously bent to kill?" returned Duncan, smiling with well-acted sincerity.

Another long and deliberate pause succeeded these sententious questions and ready replies. Duncan saw that the Indian hesitated. In order to complete his victory, he was in the act of recommencing the enumeration of the rewards, when Magua made an expressive gesture and said:

"Enough; Le Renard is a wise chief, and what he does will be seen. Go, and keep the mouth shut. When Magua speaks, it will be the time to answer."

Heyward, perceiving that the eyes of his companion were warily fastened on the rest of the band, fell back immediately, in order to avoid the appearance of any suspicious confederacy with their leader. Magua approached the horses and affected to be well pleased with the diligence and ingenuity of his comrades. He then signed to Heyward to assist the sisters into the saddles, for he seldom deigned to use the English tongue, unless urged by some motive of more than usual moment.

There was no longer any plausible pretext for delay; and Duncan was obliged, however reluctantly, to comply. As he performed this office, he whispered his reviving hopes in the ears of the trembling females, who, through dread of encountering the savage countenances of their captors, seldom raised their eyes from the ground. The mare of David had been taken with the followers of the large chief; in consequence, its owner, as well as Duncan, was compelled to journey on foot. The latter did not, however, so much regret this circumstance, as it might enable him to retard the speed of the party; for he still turned his longing looks in the direction of Fort Edward, in the vein expectation of catching some sound from that quarter of the forest, which might denote the approach of succor. When all were prepared, Magua made the signal to proceed, advancing in front to lead the party in person. Next followed David, who was gradually coming to a true sense of his condition, as the effects of the wound became less and less apparent. The sisters rode in his rear, with Heyward at their side, while the Indians flanked the party, and brought up the close of the march, with a caution that seemed never to tire.

In this manner they proceeded in uninterrupted silence, except when Heyward addressed some solitary word of comfort to the females, or David gave vent to the moaning's of his spirit, in piteous exclamations, which he intended should express the humility of resignation. Their direction lay toward the south, and in a course nearly opposite to the road to William Henry. Notwithstanding this apparent adherence in Magua to the original determination of his conquerors, Heyward could not believe his tempting bait was so soon forgotten; and he knew the windings of an Indian's path too well to suppose that its apparent course led directly to its object when artifice was at all necessary. Mile after mile was, however, passed through the boundless woods, in this painful manner, without any prospect of a termination to their journey. Heyward watched the sun, as he darted his meridian rays through the branches of the trees and pined for the moment when the policy of Magua should change their route to one more favorable to his hopes. Sometimes he fancied the wary savage, despairing of passing the army of Montcalm in safety, was holding his way toward a well-known border settlement, where a distinguished officer of the crown, and a favored friend of the Six Nations, held his large possessions, as well as his usual residence. To be delivered into the hands of Sir William Johnson was far preferable to being led into the wilds of Canada; but in order to affect even the former, it would be necessary to traverse the forest for many weary leagues, each step of which was carrying him further from the scene of the war, and, consequently, from the post, not only of honor, but of duty.

Cora alone remembered the parting injunctions of the scout, and whenever an opportunity offered, she stretched forth her arm to bend aside the twigs that met her hands. But the vigilance of the

Indians rendered this act of precaution both difficult and dangerous. She was often defeated in her purpose, by encountering their watchful eyes, when it became necessary to feign an alarm she did not feel and occupy the limb by some gesture of feminine apprehension. Once, and once only, was she completely successful; when she broke down the bough of a large sumach, and by a sudden thought, let her glove fall at the same instant. This sign, intended for those that might follow, was observed by one of her conductors, who restored the glove, broke the remaining branches of the bush in such a manner that it appeared to proceed from the struggling of some beast in its branches, and then laid his hand on his tomahawk, with a look so significant, that it put an effectual end to these stolen memorials of their passage.

As there were horses, to leave the prints of their footsteps, in both bands of the Indians, this interruption cut off any probable hopes of assistance being conveyed through the means of their trail.

Heyward would have ventured a remonstrance had there been anything encouraging in the gloomy reserve of Magua. But the savage, during all this time, seldom turned to look at his followers, and never spoke. With the sun for his only guide or aided by such blind marks as are only known to the sagacity of a native, he held his way along the barrens of pine, through occasional little fertile vales, across brooks and rivulets, and over undulating hills, with the accuracy of instinct, and nearly with the directness of a bird. He never seemed to hesitate. Whether the path was hardly distinguishable, whether it disappeared, or whether it lay beaten and plain before him, made no sensible difference in his speed or certainty. It seemed as if fatigue could not affect him. Whenever the eyes of the wearied travelers rose from the decayed leaves over which they trod, his dark form was to be seen glancing among the stems of the trees in front, his head immovably fastened in a forward position, with the light plume on his crest fluttering in a current of air, made solely by the swiftness of his own motion.

But all this diligence and speed were not without an object. After crossing a low vale, through which a gushing brook meandered, he suddenly ascended a hill, so steep and difficult of ascent, that the sisters were compelled to alight in order to follow. When the summit was gained, they found themselves on a level spot, but thinly covered with trees, under one of which Magua had thrown his dark form, as if willing and ready to seek that rest which was so much needed by the whole party.

CHAPTER XI.

"Cursed be my tribe If I forgive him."
—Shylock

The Indian had selected for this desirable purpose one of those steep, pyramidal hills, which bear a strong resemblance to artificial mounds, and which so frequently occur in the valleys of America. The one in question was high and precipitous; its top flattened, as usual; but with one of its sides more than ordinarily irregular. It possessed no other apparent advantage for a resting place, than in its elevation and form, which might render defense easy, and surprise nearly impossible. As Heyward, however, no longer expected that rescue which time and distance now rendered so improbable, he regarded these little peculiarities with an eye devoid of interest, devoting himself entirely to the comfort and condolence of his feebler companions. The Narragansetts were suffered to browse on the branches of the trees and shrubs that were thinly scattered over the summit of the hill, while the remains of their provisions were spread under the shade of a beech, that stretched its horizontal limbs like a canopy above them.

Notwithstanding the swiftness of their flight, one of the Indians had found an opportunity to strike a straggling fawn with an arrow and had borne the more preferable fragments of the victim, patiently on his shoulders, to the stopping place. Without any aid from the science of cookery, he was immediately employed, in common with his fellows, in gorging himself with this digestible sustenance. Magua alone sat apart, without participating in the revolting meal, and apparently buried in the deepest thought.

This abstinence, so remarkable in an Indian, when he possessed the means of satisfying hunger, at length attracted the notice of Heyward. The young man willingly believed that the Huron deliberated on the most eligible manner of eluding the vigilance of his associates. With a view to assist his plans by any suggestion of his own, and to strengthen the temptation, he left the beech, and straggled, as if without an object, to the spot where Le Renard was seated.

"Has not Magua kept the sun in his face long enough to escape all danger from the Canadians?" he asked, as though no longer doubtful of the good intelligence established between them; "and will not the chief of William Henry be better pleased to see his daughters before another night may have hardened his heart to their loss, to make him less liberal in his reward?"

"Do the pale faces love their children less in the morning than at night?" asked the Indian, coldly.

"By no means," returned Heyward, anxious to recall his error, if he had made one; "the white man may, and does often, forget the burial place of his fathers; he sometimes ceases to remember those he should love, and has promised to cherish; but the affection of a parent for his child is never permitted to die."

"And is the heart of the white-headed chief soft, and will he think of the babes that his squaws have given him? He is hard on his warriors and his eyes are made of stone!"

"He is severe to the idle and wicked, but to the sober and deserving he is a leader, both just and humane. I have known many fond and tender parents, but never have I seen a man whose heart was softer toward his child. You have seen the grayhead in front of his warriors, Magua; but I have seen his eyes swimming in water when he spoke of those children who are now in your power!"

Heyward paused, for he knew not how to construe the remarkable expression that gleamed across the swarthy features of the attentive Indian. At first it seemed as if the remembrance of the promised reward grew vivid in his mind, while he listened to the sources of parental feeling which were to assure its possession; but, as Duncan proceeded, the expression of joy became so fiercely malignant that it was impossible not to apprehend it proceeded from some passion more sinister than avarice.

"Go," said the Huron, suppressing the alarming exhibition in an instant, in a death-like calmness of countenance; "go to the dark-haired daughter, and say, 'Magua waits to speak.' The father will remember what the child promises."

Duncan, who interpreted this speech to express a wish for some additional pledge that the promised gifts should not be withheld, slowly and reluctantly repaired to the place where the sisters were now resting from their fatigue, to communicate its purport to Cora.

"You understand the nature of an Indian's wishes," he concluded, as he led her toward the place where she was expected, "and must be prodigal of your offers of powder and blankets. Ardent spirits are, however, the most prized by such as he; nor would it be amiss to add some boon from your own hand, with that grace you so well know how to practice. Remember, Cora, that on your presence of mind and ingenuity, even your life, as well as that of Alice, may in some measure depend."

"Heyward, and yours!"

"Mine is of little moment; it is already sold to my king and is a prize to be seized by any enemy who may possess the power. I have no father to expect me, and but few friends to lament a fate which I have courted with the insatiable longings of youth after distinction. But hush! we approach the Indian. Magua, the lady with whom you wish to speak, is here."

The Indian rose slowly from his seat and stood for near a minute silent and motionless. He then signed with his hand for Heyward to retire, saying, coldly:

"When the Huron talks to the women, his tribe shut their ears."

Duncan, still lingering, as if refusing to comply, Cora said, with a calm smile:

"You hear, Heyward, and delicacy at least should urge you to retire. Go to Alice, and comfort her with our reviving prospects."

She waited until he had departed, and then turning to the native, with the dignity of her sex in her voice and manner, she added: "What would Le Renard say to the daughter of Munro?"

"Listen," said the Indian, laying his hand firmly upon her arm, as if willing to draw her utmost attention to his words; a movement that Cora as firmly but quietly repulsed, by extricating the limb from his grasp: "Magua was born a chief and a warrior among the red Hurons of the lakes; he saw the suns of twenty summers make the snows of twenty winters run off in the streams before he saw a pale face; and he was happy! Then his Canada fathers came into the woods, and taught him to drink the firewater, and he became a rascal. The Hurons drove him from the graves of his fathers, as they would chase the hunted buffalo. He ran down the shores of the lakes and followed their outlet to the 'city of cannon.' There he hunted and fished, till the people chased him again through the woods into the arms of his enemies. The chief, who was born a Huron, was at last a warrior among the Mohawks!"

"Something like this I had heard before," said Cora, observing that he paused to suppress those passions which began to burn with too bright a flame, as he recalled the recollection of his supposed injuries.

"Was it the fault of Le Renard that his head was not made of rock? Who gave him the firewater? who made him a villain? 'Twas the pale faces, the people of your own color."

"And am I answerable that thoughtless and unprincipled men exist, whose shades of countenance may resemble mine?" Cora calmly demanded of the excited savage.

"No; Magua is a man, and not a fool, such as you never open their lips to the burning stream: the Great Spirit has given you wisdom!"

"What, then, have I done to, or say, in the matter of your misfortunes, not to say of your errors?"

"Listen," repeated the Indian, resuming his earnest attitude; "when his English and French fathers dug up the hatchet, Le Renard struck the war-post of the Mohawks, and went out against his own nation. The pale faces have driven the red skins from their hunting grounds, and now when they fight, a white man leads the way. The old chief at Horican, your father, was the great captain of our war-party. He said to the Mohawks do this, and do that, and he was minded. He made a law, that if an Indian swallowed the firewater, and came into the cloth wigwams of his warriors, it should not be forgotten. Magua foolishly opened his mouth, and the hot liquor led him into the cabin of Munro. What did the grayhead? let his daughter say."

"He forgot not his words, and did justice, by punishing the offender," said the undaunted daughter.

"Justice!" repeated the Indian, casting an oblique glance of the most ferocious expression at her unyielding countenance; "is it justice to make evil and then punish for it? Magua was not himself; it was the firewater that spoke and acted for him! but Munro did believe it. The Huron chief was tied up before all the pale-faced warriors and whipped like a dog."

Cora remained silent, for she knew not how to palliate this imprudent severity on the part of her father in a manner to suit the comprehension of an Indian.

"See!" continued Magua, tearing aside the slight calico that very imperfectly concealed his painted breast; "here are scars given by knives and bullets of these a warrior may boast before his nation; but the gray-head has left marks on the back of the Huron chief that he must hide like a squaw, under this painted cloth of the whites."

"I had thought," resumed Cora, "that an Indian warrior was patient, and that his spirit felt not and knew not the pain his body suffered."

"When the Chippewas tied Magua to the stake, and cut this gash," said the other, laying his finger on a deep scar, "the Huron laughed in their faces, and told them, Women struck so light! His spirit was then in the clouds! But when he felt the blows of Munro, his spirit lay under the birch. The spirit of a Huron is never drunk; it remembers forever!"

"But it may be appeased. If my father has done you this injustice, show him how an Indian can forgive an injury, and take back his daughters. You have heard from Major Heyward"

Magua shook his head, forbidding the repetition of offers he so much despised.

"What would you have?" continued Cora, after a most painful pause, while the conviction forced itself on her mind that the too sanguine and generous Duncan had been cruelly deceived by the cunning of the savage.

"What a Huron loves good for good; bad for bad!"

"You would, then, revenge the injury inflicted by Munro on his helpless daughters. Would it not be more like a man to go before his face, and take the satisfaction of a warrior?"

"The arms of the pale faces are long, and their knives sharp!" returned the savage, with a malignant laugh: "why should Le Renard go among the muskets of his warriors, when he holds the spirit of the gray-head in his hand?"

"Name your intention, Magua," said Cora, struggling with herself to speak with steady calmness. "Is it to lead us prisoners to the woods, or do you contemplate even some greater evil? Is there no reward, no means of palliating the injury, and of softening your heart? At least, release my gentle sister, and pour out all your malice on me. Purchase wealth by her safety and satisfy your revenge with a single victim. The loss of both his daughters might bring the aged man to his grave, and where would then be the satisfaction of Le Renard?"

"Listen," said the Indian again. "The light eyes can go back to the Horican and tell the old chief what has been done, if the dark-haired woman will swear by the Great Spirit of her fathers to tell no lie."

"What must I promise?" demanded Cora, still maintaining a secret ascendancy over the fierce native by the collected and feminine dignity of her presence.

"When Magua left his people, his wife was given to another chief; he has now made friends with the Hurons and will go back to the graves of his tribe, on the shores of the great lake. Let the daughter of the English chief follow and live in his wigwam forever."

However, revolting a proposal of such a character might prove to Cora, she retained, notwithstanding her powerful disgust, sufficient self-command to reply, without betraying the weakness.

"And what pleasure would Magua find in sharing his cabin with a wife he did not love; one who would be of a nation and color different from his own? It would be better to take the gold of Munro and buy the heart of some Huron maid with his gifts."

The Indian made no reply for near a minute but bent his fierce looks on the countenance of Cora, in such wavering glances, that her eyes sank with shame, under an impression that for the first time they had encountered an expression that no chaste female might endure. While she was shrinking within herself, in dread of having her ears wounded by some proposal still more shocking than the last, the voice of Magua answered, in its tones of deepest malignancy:

"When the blows scorched the back of the Huron, he would know where to find a woman to feel the smart. The daughter of Munro would draw his water, hoe his corn, and cook his venison. The body of the grayhead would sleep among his cannon, but his heart would lie within reach of the knife of Le Subtil."

"Monster! well dost thou deserve thy treacherous name," cried Cora, in an ungovernable burst of filial indignation. "None but a fiend could meditate such a vengeance. But thou overratest thy power! You shall find it is, in truth, the heart of Munro you hold, and that it will defy your utmost malice!"

The Indian answered this bold defiance by a ghastly smile, that showed an unaltered purpose, while he motioned her away, as if to close the conference forever. Cora, already regretting her precipitation, was obliged to comply, for Magua instantly left the spot, and approached his gluttonous comrades. Heyward flew to the side of the agitated female and demanded the result of a dialogue that he had watched at a distance with so much interest. But, unwilling to alarm the fears of Alice, she evaded a direct reply, betraying only by her anxious looks fastened on the slightest movements of her captors. To the reiterated and earnest questions of her sister concerning their probable destination, she made no other answer than by pointing toward the dark group, with an agitation she could not control, and murmuring as she folded Alice to her bosom.

"There, there; read our fortunes in their faces; we shall see; we shall see!"

The action, and the choked utterance of Cora, spoke more

impressively than any words, and quickly drew the attention of her companions on that spot where her own was riveted with an intenseness that nothing but the importance of the stake could create.

When Magua reached the cluster of lolling savages, who, gorged with their disgusting meal, lay stretched on the earth in brutal indulgence, he commenced speaking with the dignity of an Indian chief. The first syllables he uttered had the effect to cause his listeners to raise themselves in attitudes of respectful attention. As the Huron used his native language, the prisoners, notwithstanding the caution of the natives had kept them within the swing of their tomahawks, could only conjecture the substance of his harangue from the nature of those significant gestures with which an Indian always illustrates his eloquence.

At first, the language, as well as the action of Magua, appeared calm and deliberative. When he had succeeded in sufficiently awakening the attention of his comrades, Heyward fancied, by his pointing so frequently toward the direction of the great lakes, that he spoke of the land of their fathers, and of their distant tribe. Frequent indications of applause escaped the listeners, who, as they uttered the expressive "Hugh!" looked at each other in commendation of the speaker. Le Renard was too skillful to neglect his advantage. He now spoke of the long and painful route by which they had left those spacious grounds and happy villages, to come and battle against the enemies of their Canadian fathers. He enumerated the warriors of the party; their several merits; their frequent services to the nation; their wounds, and the number of the scalps they had taken. Whenever he alluded to any present (and the subtle Indian neglected none), the dark countenance of the flattered individual gleamed with exultation, nor did he even hesitate to assert the truth of the words, by gestures of applause and confirmation. Then the voice of the speaker fell, and lost the loud, animated tones of triumph with which he had enumerated their deeds of success and victory. He described the cataract of Glenn's; the impregnable position of its rocky island, with its caverns and its numerous rapids and whirlpools; he named the name of "La Longue Carabine," and paused until the forest beneath them had sent up the last echo of a loud and long yell, with which the hated appellation was received. He pointed toward the youthful military captive, and described the death of a favorite warrior, who had been precipitated into the deep ravine by his hand. He not only mentioned the fate of him who, hanging between heaven and earth, had presented such a spectacle of horror to the whole band, but he acted anew the terrors of his situation, his resolution, and his death, on the branches of a sapling; and, finally, he rapidly recounted the manner in which each of their friends had fallen, never failing to touch upon their courage, and their most acknowledged virtues. When this recital of events was ended, his voice once more changed, and became plaintive and even musical, in its low guttural sounds. He now spoke of the wives and children of the slain; their destitution; their misery, both physical and moral; their distance; and, at last, of their unavenged wrongs. Then suddenly lifting his voice to a pitch of terrific energy, he concluded by demanding:

"Are the Hurons dogs to bear this? Who shall say to the wife of Menowgua that the fishes have his scalp and that his nation have not taken revenge! Who will dare meet the mother of Wassawattimie, that scornful woman, with his hands clean! What shall be said to the old men when they ask us for scalps, and we have not a hair from a white head to give them! The women will point their fingers at us. There is a dark spot on the names of the Hurons, and it must be hidden in blood!" His voice was no longer audible in the burst of rage which now broke into the air, as if the wood, instead of containing so small a band, was filled with the nation. During the foregoing address the progress of the speaker was too plainly read by those most interested in his success through the medium of the countenances of the men he addressed. They had answered his melancholy and mourning by sympathy and sorrow; his assertions, by gestures of confirmation; and his boasting, with the exultation of savages. When he spoke of courage, their looks were firm and responsive; when he alluded to their injuries, their eyes kindled with fury; when he mentioned the taunts of the women, they dropped their heads in shame; but when he pointed out their means of vengeance, he struck a chord which never failed to thrill in the breast of an Indian. With the first intimation that it was within their reach, the whole band sprang upon their feet as one man; giving utterance to their rage in the most frantic cries, they rushed upon their prisoners in a body with drawn knives and uplifted tomahawks. Heyward threw himself between the sisters and the foremost, whom he grappled with a desperate strength that for a moment checked his violence. This unexpected resistance gave Magua time to interpose, and with rapid enunciation and animated gesture, he drew the attention of the band again to himself. In that language he knew so well how to assume, he diverted his comrades from their instant purpose and invited them to prolong the misery of their victims. His proposal was received with acclamations and executed with the swiftness of thought.

Two powerful warriors cast themselves on Heyward, while another was occupied in securing the less active singing-master. Neither of the captives, however, submitted without a desperate, though fruitless, struggle. Even David hurled his assailant to the earth; nor was Heyward secured until the victory over his companion enabled the Indians to direct their united force to that object. He was then bound and fastened to the body of the sapling, on whose branches Magua had acted the pantomime of the falling Huron. When the young soldier regained his recollection, he had the painful certainty before his eyes that a common fate was intended for the whole party. On his right was Cora in a durance similar to his own, pale, and agitated, but with an eye whose steady look still read the proceedings of their enemies. On his left, the withes which bound her to a pine, performed that office for Alice which her trembling limbs refused and alone kept her fragile form from sinking. Her hands were clasped before her in prayer, but instead of looking upward toward that power which alone could rescue them, her unconscious looks wandered to the countenance of Duncan with infantile dependency. David had contended, and the novelty of the circumstance held him silent, in deliberation on the propriety of the unusual occurrence.

The vengeance of the Hurons had now taken a new direction, and they prepared to execute it with that barbarous ingenuity with which they were familiarized by the practice of centuries. Some sought knots, to raise the blazing pile; one was driving the splinters of pine, in order to pierce the flesh of their captives with the burning fragments; and others bent the tops of two saplings to the earth, in order to suspend Heyward by the arms between the recoiling branches. But the vengeance of Magua sought a deeper and more malignant enjoyment.

While the less refined monsters of the band prepared, before the eyes of those who were to suffer, these well-known and vulgar means of torture, he approached Cora, and pointed out, with the most malign expression of countenance, the speedy fate that awaited her:

"Ha!" he added, "what says the daughter of Munro? Her head is too good to find a pillow in the wigwam of Le Renard; will she like it better when it rolls about this hill a plaything for the wolves? Her bosom cannot nurse the children of a Huron; she will see it spit upon by Indians!"

"What means the monster!" demanded the astonished Heyward.

"Nothing!" was the firm reply. "He is a savage, a barbarous and ignorant savage, and knows not what he does. Let us find leisure, with our dying breath, to ask for him penitence and pardon."

"Pardon!" echoed the fierce Huron, mistaking in his anger, the meaning of her words; "the memory of an Indian is no longer than the arm of the pale faces; his mercy shorter than their justice! Say; shall I send the yellow hair to her father, and will you follow Magua to the great lakes, to carry his water, and feed him with corn?"

Cora beckoned him away with an emotion of disgust she could not control.

"Leave me," she said, with a solemnity that for a moment checked the barbarity of the Indian; "you mingle bitterness in my prayers; you stand between me and my God!"

The slight impression produced on the savage was, however, soon forgotten, and he continued pointing, with taunting irony, toward Alice.

"Look! the child weeps! She is too young to die! Send her to Munro, to comb his gray hairs, and keep life in the heart of the old man."

Cora could not resist the desire to look upon her youthful sister, in whose eyes she met an imploring glance, that betrayed the longings of nature.

"What says he, dearest Cora?" asked the trembling voice of Alice. "Did he speak of sending me to our father?"

For many moments the elder sister looked upon the younger, with a countenance that wavered with powerful and contending emotions. At length she spoke, though her tones had lost their rich and calm fullness, in an expression of tenderness that seemed maternal.

"Alice," she said, "the Huron offers us both life, nay, more than both; he offers to restore Duncan, our invaluable Duncan, as well as you, to our friends, to our father, to our heart-stricken, childless father, if I will bow down this rebellious, stubborn pride of mine, and consent"

Her voice became choked, and clasping her hands, she looked upward, as if seeking, in her agony, intelligence from a wisdom that was infinite.

"Say on," cried Alice; "to what, dearest Cora? Oh! that the proffer were made to me! to save you, to cheer our aged father, to restore Duncan, how cheerfully could I die!"

"Die!" repeated Cora, with a calmer and firmer voice, "that were easy! Perhaps the alternative may not be less so. He would have me," she continued, her accents sinking under a deep consciousness of the degradation of the proposal, "follow him to the wilderness; go to the habitations of the Hurons; to remain there; in short, to become his wife! Speak, then, Alice; child of my affections! sister of my love! And you, too, Major Heyward, aid my weak reason with your counsel. Is life to be purchased by such a sacrifice? Will you, Alice, receive it at my hands at such a price? And you, Duncan, guide me; control me between you; for I am wholly yours!"

"Would I!" echoed the indignant and astonished youth. "Cora! Cora! you jest with our misery! Name not the horrid alternative again; the thought itself is worse than a thousand deaths."

"That such would be your answer, I well knew!" exclaimed Cora, her cheeks flushing, and her dark eyes once more sparkling with the lingering emotions of a woman. "What says my Alice? for her will I submit without another murmur."

Although both Heyward and Cora listened with painful suspense and the deepest attention, no sounds were heard in reply. It appeared as if the delicate and sensitive form of Alice would shrink into itself, as she listened to this proposal. Her arms had fallen lengthwise before her, the fingers moving in slight convulsions; her head dropped upon her bosom, and her whole person seemed suspended against the tree, looking like some beautiful emblem of the wounded delicacy of her sex, devoid of animation and yet keenly conscious. In a few moments, however, her head began to move slowly, in a sign of deep, unconquerable disapprobation.

"No, no, no; better that we die as we have lived, together!"

"Then die!" shouted Magua, hurling his tomahawk with violence at the unresisting speaker

"Then die!" shouted Magua, hurling his tomahawk with violence at the unresisting speaker, and gnashing his teeth with a rage that could no longer be bridled at this sudden exhibition of firmness in the one he believed the weakest of the party. The axe cleaved the air in front of Heyward, and cutting some of the flowing ringlets of Alice, quivered in the tree above her head. The sight maddened Duncan to desperation. Collecting all his energies in one effort he snapped the twigs which bound him and rushed upon another savage, who was preparing, with loud yells and a more deliberate aim, to repeat the blow. They encountered, grappled, and fell to the earth together. The naked body of his antagonist afforded Heyward no means of holding his adversary, who glided from his grasp, and rose again with one knee on his chest, pressing him down with the weight of a giant. Duncan already saw the knife gleaming in the air, when a whistling sound swept past him, and was rather accompanied than followed by the sharp crack of a rifle. He felt his breast relieved from the load it had endured; he saw the savage expression of his adversary's countenance change to a look of vacant wildness when the Indian fell dead on the faded leaves by his side.

CHAPTER XII.

"Clo, I am gone, sire,
And anon, sire, I'll be with you again."
—Twelfth Night

The Hurons stood aghast at this sudden visitation of death on one of their bands. But as they regarded the fatal accuracy of an aim which had dared to immolate an enemy at so much hazard to a friend, the name of "La Longue Carabine" burst simultaneously from every lip and was succeeded by a wild and a sort of plaintive howl. The cry was answered by a loud shout from a little thicket, where the incautious party had piled their arms; and at the next moment, Hawkeye, too eager to load the rifle he had regained, was seen advancing upon them, brandishing the clubbed weapon, and cutting the air with wide and powerful sweeps. Bold and rapid as was the progress of the scout, it was exceeded by that of a light and vigorous form which, bounding past him, leaped, with incredible activity and daring, into the very center of the Hurons, where it stood, whirling a tomahawk, and flourishing a glittering knife, with fearful menaces, in front of Cora. Quicker than the thoughts could follow those unexpected and audacious movements, an image, armed in the emblematic panoply of death, glided before their eyes, and assumed a threatening attitude at the other's side. The savage tormentors recoiled before these warlike intruders, and uttered, as they appeared in such quick succession, the often repeated and peculiar exclamations of surprise, followed by the well-known and dreaded appellations of:

"Le Cerf Agile! Le Gros Serpent!"

But the wary and vigilant leader of the Hurons was not so easily disconcerted. Casting his keen eyes around the little plain, he comprehended the nature of the assault at a glance and encouraging his followers by his voice as well as by his example, he unsheathed his long and dangerous knife, and rushed with a loud whoop upon the expected Chingachgook. It was the signal for a general combat. Neither party had firearms, and the contest was to be decided in the deadliest manner, hand to hand, with weapons of offense, and none of defense.

Uncas answered the whoop, and leaping on an enemy, with a single, well-directed blow of his tomahawk, cleft him to the brain. Heyward tore the weapon of Magua from the sapling and rushed eagerly toward the fray. As the combatants were now equal in number, each singled an opponent from the adverse band. The rush and blows passed with the fury of a whirlwind, and the swiftness of lightning. Hawkeye soon got another enemy within reach of his arm, and with one sweep of his formidable weapon he beat down the slight and inartificial defenses of his antagonist, crushing him to the earth with the blow. Heyward ventured to hurl the tomahawk he had seized, too ardent to await the moment of closing. It struck the Indian he had selected on the forehead and checked for an instant his onward rush. Encouraged by this slight advantage, the impetuous young man continued his onset, and sprang upon his enemy with naked hands. A single instant was enough to assure him of the rashness of the measure, for he immediately found himself fully engaged, with all his activity and courage, in endeavoring to ward the desperate thrusts made with the knife of the Huron. Unable longer to foil an enemy so alert and vigilant, he threw his arms about him, and succeeded in pinning the limbs of the other to his side, with an iron grasp, but one that was far too exhausting to himself to continue long. In this extremity he heard a voice near him, shouting:

"Extarminate the varlets! no quarter to an accursed Mingo!"

At the next moment, the breech of Hawkeye's rifle fell on the naked head of his adversary, whose muscles appeared to wither under the shock, as he sank from the arms of Duncan, flexible and motionless.

When Uncas had brained his first antagonist, he turned, like a hungry lion, to seek another. The fifth and only Huron disengaged at the first onset had paused a moment, and then seeing that all around him were employed in the deadly strife, he had sought, with hellish vengeance, to complete the baffled work of revenge. Raising a shout of triumph, he sprang toward the defenseless Cora, sending his keen axe as the dreadful precursor of his approach. The tomahawk grazed her shoulder and cutting the withes which bound her to the tree, left the maiden at liberty to fly. She eluded the grasp of the savage, and reckless of her own safety, threw herself on the bosom of Alice, striving with convulsed and ill-directed fingers, to tear asunder the twigs which confined the person of her sister. Any other than a monster would have relented at such an act of generous devotion to the best and purest affection; but the breast of the Huron was a stranger to sympathy. Seizing Cora by the rich tresses which fell in confusion about her form, he tore her from her frantic hold, and bowed her down with brutal violence to her knees. The savage drew the flowing curls through his hand, and raising them on high with an outstretched arm, he passed the knife around the exquisitely molded head of his victim, with a taunting and exulting laugh. But he purchased this moment of fierce gratification with the loss of the fatal opportunity. It was just then the sight caught the eye of Uncas. Bounding from his footsteps he appeared for an instant darting through the air and descending in a ball he fell on the chest of his enemy, driving him many yards from the spot, headlong and prostrate. The violence of the exertion cast the young Mohican at his side. They arose together, fought, and bled, each in his turn. But the conflict was soon decided; the tomahawk of Heyward and the rifle of Hawkeye descended on the skull of the Huron, at the same moment that the knife of Uncas reached his heart.

The battle was now entirely terminated with the exception of the protracted struggle between "Le Renard Subtil" and "Le Gros Serpent." Well did these barbarous warriors prove that they deserved those significant names which had been bestowed for deeds in former wars. When they engaged, some little time was lost in eluding the quick and vigorous thrusts which had been aimed at their lives. Suddenly darting on each other, they closed, and came to the earth, twisted together like twining serpents, in pliant and subtle folds. At the moment when the victors found themselves unoccupied, the spot where these experienced and desperate combatants lay could only be distinguished by a cloud of dust and leaves, which moved from the center of the little plain toward its boundary, as if raised by the passage of a whirlwind. Urged by the different motives of filial affection, friendship and gratitude, Heyward and his companions rushed with one accord to the place, encircling the little canopy of dust which hung above the warriors. In vain did Uncas dart around the cloud, with a wish to strike his knife into the heart of his father's foe; the threatening rifle of Hawkeye was raised and suspended in vain, while Duncan endeavored to seize the limbs of the Huron with hands that appeared to have lost their power. Covered as they were with dust and blood, the swift evolutions of the combatants seemed to incorporate their bodies into one. The death-like looking figure of the Mohican, and the dark form of the Huron, gleamed before their eyes in such quick and confused succession, that the friends of the former knew not where to plant the succoring blow. It is true there were short and fleeting moments, when the fiery eyes of Magua were seen glittering, like the fabled organs of the basilisk through the dusty wreath by which he was enveloped, and he read by those short and deadly glances the fate of the combat in the presence of his enemies; ere, however, any hostile hand could descend on his devoted head, its place was filled by the scowling visage of Chingachgook. In this manner the scene of the combat was removed from the center of the little plain to its verge. The Mohican now found an opportunity to make a powerful thrust with his knife; Magua suddenly relinquished his grasp, and fell backward without motion, and seemingly without life. His adversary leaped on his feet, making the arches of the forest ring with the sounds of triumph.

"Well done for the Delawares! victory to the Mohicans!" cried Hawkeye, once more elevating the butt of the long and fatal rifle; "a finishing blow from a man without a cross will never tell against his honor, nor rob him of his right to the scalp."

But at the very moment when the dangerous weapon was in the act of descending, the subtle Huron rolled swiftly from beneath the danger, over the edge of the precipice, and falling on his feet, was seen leaping, with a single bound, into the center of a thicket of low bushes, which clung along its sides. The Delawares, who had believed their enemy dead, uttered their exclamation of surprise, and were following with speed and clamor, like hounds in open view of the deer, when a shrill and peculiar cry from the scout instantly changed their purpose, and recalled them to the summit of the hill.

"'Twas like himself!" cried the inveterate forester, whose prejudices contributed so largely to veil his natural sense of justice in all matters which concerned the Mingoes; "a lying and deceitful varlet as he is. An honest Delaware now, being fairly vanquished, would have lain still, and been knocked on the head, but these knavish Maquas cling to life like so many cats-o'-the-mountain. Let him go, let him go; 'tis but one man, and he without rifle or bow, many a long mile from his French comrades and like a rattler that lost his fangs, he can do no further mischief, until such time as he, and we too, may leave the prints of our moccasins over a long reach of sandy plain. See, Uncas," he added, in Delaware, "your father is flaying the scalps already. It may be well to go round and feel the vagabonds that are left, or we may have another of them loping through the woods and screeching like a jay that has been winged."

So, saying the honest but implacable scout made the circuit of the dead, into whose senseless bosoms he thrust his long knife, with as much coolness as though they had been so many brute carcasses. He had, however, been anticipated by the elder Mohican, who had already torn the emblems of victory from the unresisting heads of the slain.

But Uncas, denying his habits, we had almost said his nature, flew with instinctive delicacy, accompanied by Heyward, to the assistance of the females, and quickly releasing Alice, placed her in the arms of Cora. We shall not attempt to describe the gratitude to the Almighty Disposer of Events which glowed in the bosoms of the sisters, who were thus unexpectedly restored to life and to each other. Their thanksgivings were deep and silent; the offerings of their gentle spirits burning brightest and purest on the secret altars of their hearts; and their renovated and more earthly feelings exhibiting themselves in long and fervent though speechless caresses. As Alice rose from her knees, where she had sunk by the side of Cora, she threw herself on the bosom of the latter, and sobbed aloud the name of their aged father, while her soft, dove-like eyes, sparkled with the rays of hope.

"We are saved! we are saved!" she murmured; "to return to the arms of our dear, dear father, and his heart will not be broken with grief. And you, too, Cora, my sister, my more than sister, my mother; you, too, are spared. And Duncan," she added, looking round upon the youth with a smile of ineffable innocence, "even our own brave and noble Duncan has escaped without a hurt."

To these ardent and nearly innocent words Cora made no other answer than by straining the youthful speaker to her heart, as she bent over her in melting tenderness. The manhood of Heyward felt no shame in dropping tears over this spectacle of affectionate rapture; and Uncas stood, fresh and blood-stained from the combat, a calm, and, apparently, an unmoved looker-on, it is true, but with eyes that had already lost their fierceness, and were beaming with a sympathy that elevated him far above the intelligence, and advanced him probably centuries before, the practices of his nation.

During this display of emotions so natural in their situation, Hawkeye, whose vigilant distrust had satisfied itself that the Hurons, who disfigured the heavenly scene, no longer possessed the power to interrupt its harmony, approached David, and liberated him from the bonds he had, until that moment, endured with the most exemplary patience.

"There," exclaimed the scout, casting the last withe behind him, "you are once more master of your own limbs, though you seem not to use them with much greater judgment than that in which they were first fashioned. If advice from one who is not older than yourself, but who, having lived most of his time in the wilderness, may be said to have experience beyond his years, will give no offense, you are welcome to my thoughts; and these are, to part with the little tooting instrument in your jacket to the first fool you meet with, and buy some weapon with the money, if it be only the barrel of a horseman's pistol. By industry and care, you might thus come to some preferment; for by this time, I should think, your eyes would plainly tell you that a carrion crow is a better bird than a mocking-thresher. The one will, at least, remove foul sights from before the face of man, while the other is only good to brew disturbances in the woods, by cheating the ears of all that hear them."

"Arms and the clarion for the battle, but the song of thanksgiving to the victory!" answered the liberated David. "Friend," he added, thrusting forth his lean, delicate hand toward Hawkeye, in kindness, while his eyes twinkled and grew moist, "I thank thee that the hairs of my head still grow where they were first rooted by Providence; for, though those of other men may be glossier and curling, I have ever found mine own well suited to the brain they shelter. That I did not join myself to the battle, was less owing to disinclination, than to the bonds of the heathen. Valiant and skillful hast thou proved thyself in the conflict, and I hereby thank thee, before proceeding to discharge other and more important duties, because thou hast proved thyself well worthy of a Christian's praise."

"The thing is but a trifle, and what you may often see if you tarry long among us," returned the scout, a good deal softened toward the man of song, by this unequivocal expression of gratitude. "I have got back my old companion, 'killdeer'," he added, striking his hand on the breech of his rifle; "and that in itself is a victory. These Iroquois are cunning, but they outwitted themselves when they placed their firearms out of reach; and had Uncas or his father been gifted with only their common Indian patience, we should have come in upon the knaves with three bullets instead of one, and that would have made a finish of the whole pack; yon loping varlet, as well as his comrades. But 'twas all fore ordered, and for the best."

"Thou sayest well," returned David, "and hast caught the true spirit of Christianity. He that is to be saved will be saved, and he that is predestined to be damned will be damned. This is the doctrine of truth, and most consoling and refreshing it is to the true believer."

The scout, who by this time was seated, examining into the state of his rifle with a species of parental assiduity, now looked up at the other in a displeasure that he did not affect to conceal, roughly interrupting further speech.

"Doctrine or no doctrine," said the sturdy woodsman, "'tis the belief of knaves, and the curse of an honest man. I can credit that yonder Huron was to fall by my hand, for with my own eyes I have seen it; but nothing short of being a witness will cause me to think he has met with any reward, or that Chingachgook there will be condemned at the final day."

"You have no warranty for such an audacious doctrine, nor any covenant to support it," cried David who was deeply tinctured with the subtle distinctions which, in his time, and more especially in his province, had been drawn around the beautiful simplicity of revelation, by endeavoring to penetrate the awful mystery of the divine nature, supplying faith by self-sufficiency, and by consequence, involving those who reasoned from such human dogmas in absurdities and doubt; "your temple is reared on the sands, and the first tempest will wash away its foundation. I demand your authorities for such an uncharitable assertion (like other advocates of a system, David was not always accurate in his use of terms). Name chapter and verse; in which of the holy books do you find language to support you?"

"Book!" repeated Hawkeye, with singular and ill-concealed disdain; "do you take me for a whimpering boy at the apron strings of one of your old gals; and this good rifle on my knee for the feather of a goose's wing, my ox's horn for a bottle of ink, and my leather pouch for a cross-barred hand Kercher to carry my dinner? Book! what have such as I, who am a warrior of the wilderness, though a man without a cross, to do with books? I never read but in one, and the words that are written there are too simple and too plain to need much schooling; though I may boast that of forty long and hard-working years."

"What call you the volume?" said David, misconceiving the other's meaning.

"'Tis open before your eyes," returned the scout; "and he who owns it is not a niggard of its use. I have heard it said that there are men who read in books to convince themselves there is a God. I know not but man may so deform his works in the settlement, as to leave that which is so clear in the wilderness a matter of doubt among traders and priests. If any such there be, and he will follow me from sun to sun, through the windings of the forest, he shall see enough to teach him that he is a fool, and that the greatest of his folly lies in striving to rise to the level of One he can never equal, be it in goodness, or be it in power."

The instant David discovered that he battled with a disputant who imbibed his faith from the lights of nature, eschewing all subtleties of doctrine, he willingly abandoned a controversy from which he believed neither profit nor credit was to be derived. While the scout was speaking, he had also seated himself, and producing the ready little volume and the iron-rimmed spectacles, he prepared to discharge a duty, which nothing but the unexpected assault he had received in his orthodoxy could have so long suspended. He was, in truth, a minstrel of the western continent of a much later day, certainly, than those gifted bards, who formerly sang the profane renown of baron and prince, but after the spirit of his own age and country; and he was now prepared to exercise the cunning of his craft, in celebration of, or rather in thanksgiving for, the recent victory. He waited patiently for Hawkeye to cease, then lifting his eyes, together with his voice, he said, aloud:

"I invite you, friends, to join in praise for this signal deliverance from the hands of barbarians and infidels to the comfortable and solemn tones of the tune called 'Northampton'."

He next named the page and verse where the rhymes selected were to be found, and applied the pitchpipe to his lips, with the decent gravity that he had been wont to use in the temple. This time he was, however, without any accompaniment, for the sisters were just then pouring out those tender effusions of affection which have been already alluded to. Nothing deterred by the smallness of his audience, which, in truth, consisted only of the discontented scout, he raised his voice, commencing and ending the sacred song without accident or interruption of any kind.

Hawkeye listened while he coolly adjusted his flint and reloaded his rifle; but the sounds, wanting the extraneous assistance of scene and sympathy, failed to awaken his slumbering emotions. Never minstrel, or by whatever more suitable name David should be known, drew upon his talents in the presence of more insensible auditors; though considering the singleness and sincerity of his motive, it is probable that no bard of profane song ever uttered notes that ascended so near to that throne where all homage and praise is due. The scout shook his head, and muttering some unintelligible words, among which "throat" and "Iroquois" were alone audible, he walked away, to collect and to examine into the state of the captured arsenal of the Hurons. In this office he was now joined by Chingachgook, who found his own, as well as the rifle of his son, among the arms. Even Heyward and David were furnished with weapons; nor was ammunition wanting to render them all effectual.

When the foresters had made their selection, and distributed their prizes, the scout announced that the hour had arrived when it was necessary to move. By this time the song of Gamut had ceased, and the sisters had learned to still the exhibition of their emotions. Aided by Duncan and the younger Mohican, the two latter descended the precipitous sides of that hill which they had so lately ascended under so very different auspices, and whose summit had so nearly proved the scene of their massacre. At the foot they found the Narragansetts browsing the herbage of the bushes, and having mounted, they followed the movements of a guide, who, in the deadliest straits, had so often proved himself their friend. The journey was, however, short. Hawkeye, leaving the blind path that the Hurons had followed, turned short to his right, and entering the thicket, he crossed a babbling brook, and halted in a narrow dell, under the shade of a few water elms. Their distance from the base of the fatal hill was but a few rods, and the steeds had been serviceable only in crossing the shallow stream.

The scout and the Indians appeared to be familiar with the sequestered place where they now were; for, leaning their rifle against the trees, they commenced throwing aside the dried leaves, and opening the blue clay, out of which a clear and sparkling spring of bright, glancing water, quickly bubbled. The white man then looked about him, as though seeking for some object, which was not to be found as readily as he expected.

"Them careless imps, the Mohawks, with their Tuscarora and Onondaga brethren, have been here slaking their thirst," he muttered, "and the vagabonds have thrown away the gourd! This is the way with benefits when they are bestowed on such disremembering hounds! Here has the Lord laid his hand, in the midst of the howling wilderness, for their good, and raised a fountain of water from the bowels of the 'arth, that might laugh at the richest shop of apothecary's ware in all the colonies; and see! the knaves have trodden in the clay, and deformed the cleanliness of the place, as though they were brute beasts, instead of human men."

Uncas silently extended toward him the desired gourd, which the spleen of Hawkeye had hitherto prevented him from observing on a branch of an elm. Filling it with water, he retired a short distance, to a place where the ground was firmer and drier; here he coolly seated himself, and after taking a long, and, apparently, a grateful draught, he commenced a very strict examination of the fragments of food left by the Hurons, which had hung in a wallet on his arm.

"Thank you, lad!" he continued, returning the empty gourd to Uncas; "now we will see how these rampaging Hurons lived, when outlying in ambushments. Look at this! The varlets know the better pieces of the deer; and one would think they might carve and roast a saddle, equal to the best cook in the land! But everything is raw, for the Iroquois are thorough savages. Uncas, take my steel and kindle a fire; a mouthful of a tender broil will give nature' a helping hand, after so long a trail."

Heyward, perceiving that their guides now set about their repast in sober earnest, assisted the ladies to alight, and placed himself at their side, not unwilling to enjoy a few moments of grateful rest, after the bloody scene he had just gone through. While the culinary process was in hand, curiosity induced him to inquire into the circumstances which had led to their timely and unexpected rescue:

"How is it that we see you so soon, my generous friend," he asked, "and without aid from the garrison of Edward?"

"Had we gone to the bend in the river, we might have been in time to rake the leaves over your bodies, but too late to have saved your scalps," coolly answered the scout. "No, no; instead of throwing away strength and opportunity by crossing to the fort, we lay by, under the bank of the Hudson, waiting to watch the movements of the Hurons."

"You were, then, witnesses of all that passed?"

"Not of all; for Indian sight is too keen to be easily cheated, and we kept close. A difficult matter it was, too, to keep this Mohican boy snug in the ambushment. Ah! Uncas, Uncas, your behavior was more like that of a curious woman than of a warrior on his scent."

Uncas permitted his eyes to turn for an instant on the sturdy countenance of the speaker, but he neither spoke nor gave any indication of repentance. On the contrary, Heyward thought the manner of the young Mohican was disdainful, if not a little fierce, and that he suppressed passions that were ready to explode, as much in compliment to the listeners, as from the deference he usually paid to his white associate.

"You saw our capture?" Heyward next demanded.

"We heard it," was the significant answer. "An Indian yell is plain language to men who have passed their days in the woods. But when you landed, we were driven to crawl like serpents, beneath the leaves; and then we lost sight of you entirely, until we placed eyes on you again trussed to the trees, and ready bound for an Indian massacre."

"Our rescue was the deed of Providence. It was nearly a miracle that you did not mistake the path, for the Hurons divided, and each band had its horses."

"Ay! there we were thrown off the scent, and might, indeed, have lost the trail, had it not been for Uncas; we took the path, however, that led into the wilderness; for we judged, and judged rightly, that the savages would hold that course with their prisoners. But when we had followed it for many miles, without finding a single twig broken, as I had advised, my mind misgave me; especially as all the footsteps had the prints of moccasins."

"Our captors had the precaution to see us shod like themselves," said Duncan, raising a foot, and exhibiting the buckskin he wore.

"Aye, 'twas judgmatical and like themselves; though we were too expart to be thrown from a trail by so common an invention."

"To what, then, are we indebted for our safety?"

"To what, as a white man who has no taint of Indian blood, I should be ashamed to own; to the judgment of the young Mohican, in matters which I should know better than he, but which I can now hardly believe to be true, though my own eyes tell me it is so."

"'Tis extraordinary! will you not name the reason?"

"Uncas was bold enough to say, that the beasts ridden by the gentle ones," continued Hawkeye, glancing his eyes, not without curious interest, on the fillies of the ladies, "planted the legs of one side on the ground at the same time, which is contrary to the movements of all trotting four-footed animals of my knowledge, except the bear. And yet here are horses that always journey in this manner, as my own eyes have seen, and as their trail has shown for twenty long miles."

"'Tis the merit of the animal! They come from the shores of Narragansett Bay, in the small province of Providence Plantations, and are celebrated for their hardihood, and the ease of this peculiar movement; though other horses are not unfrequently trained to the same."

"It may be, it may be," said Hawkeye, who had listened with singular attention to this explanation; "though I am a man who has the full blood of the whites, my judgment in deer and beaver is greater than in beasts of burden. Major Effingham has many noble chargers, but I have never seen one travel after such a sidling gait."

"True; for he would value the animals for very different properties. Still is this a breed highly esteemed and, as you witness, much honored with the burdens it is often destined to bear."

The Mohicans had suspended their operations about the glimmering fire to listen; and, when Duncan had done, they looked at each other significantly, the father uttering the never-failing exclamation of surprise. The scout ruminated, like a man digesting his newly acquired knowledge, and once more stole a glance at the horses.

"I dare to say there are even stranger sights to be seen in the settlements!" he said, at length. "Nature' is sadly abused by man when he once gets the mastery. But go sidling or go straight, Uncas had seen the movement, and their trail led us on to the broken bush. The outer branch, near the prints of one of the horses, was bent upward, as a lady breaks a flower from its stem, but all the rest were ragged and broken down, as if the strong hand of a man had been tearing them! So, I concluded that the cunning varments had seen the twig bent, and had torn the rest, to make us believe a buck had been feeling the boughs with his antlers."

"I do believe your sagacity did not deceive you; for some such thing occurred!"

"That was easy to see," added the scout, in no degree conscious of having exhibited any extraordinary sagacity; "and a very different matter it was from a waddling horse! It then struck me the Mingoes would push for this spring, for the knaves well know the virtue of its waters!"

"Is it, then, so famous?" demanded Heyward, examining, with a more curious eye, the secluded dell, with its bubbling fountain, surrounded, as it was, by earth of a deep, dingy brown.

"Few red skins, who travel south and east of the great lakes but have heard of its qualities. Will you taste for yourself?"

Heyward took the gourd, and after swallowing a little of the water, threw it aside with grimaces of discontent. The scout laughed in his silent but heartfelt manner and shook his head with vast satisfaction.

"Ah! you want the flavor that one gets by habit; the time was when I liked it as little as yourself; but I have come to my taste, and I now crave it, as a deer does the licks[1]. Your high-spiced wines are not better liked than a red-skin relishes this water; especially when his nature' is ailing. But Uncas has made his fire, and it is time we think of eating, for our journey is long, and all before us."

Interrupting the dialogue by this abrupt transition, the scout had instant recourse to the fragments of food which had escaped the voracity of the Hurons. A very summary process completed the simple cookery, when he and the Mohicans commenced their humble meal, with the silence and characteristic diligence of men who ate in order to enable themselves to endure great and unremitting toil.

When this necessary, and, happily, grateful duty had been performed, each of the foresters stooped and took a long and parting draught at that solitary and silent spring[2], around which and its sister fountains, within fifty years, the wealth, beauty and talents of a hemisphere were to assemble in throngs, in pursuit of health and pleasure. Then Hawkeye announced his determination to proceed. The sisters resumed their saddles; Duncan and David grasped their rifles and followed on footsteps; the scout leading the advance, and the Mohicans bringing up the rear. The whole party moved swiftly

[1] Many of the animals of the American forests resort to those spots where salt springs are found. These are called "licks" or "salt licks," in the language of the country, from the circumstance that the quadruped is often obliged to lick the earth, in order to obtain the saline particles. These licks are great places of resort with the hunters, who waylay their game near the paths that lead to them.

[2] The scene of the foregoing incidents is on the spot where the village of Ballston now stands; one of the two principal watering places of America.

through the narrow path, toward the north, leaving the healing waters to mingle unheeded with the adjacent brooks and the bodies of the dead to fester on the neighboring mount, without the rites of sepulture; a fate but too common to the warriors of the woods to excite either commiseration or comment.

CHAPTER XIII.

"I'll seek a readier path."

—Parnell

The route taken by Hawkeye lay across those sandy plains, relived by occasional valleys and swells of land, which had been traversed by their party on the morning of the same day, with the baffled Magua for their guide. The sun had now fallen low toward the distant mountains; and as their journey lay through the interminable forest, the heat was no longer oppressive. Their progress, in consequence, was proportionate; and long before the twilight gathered about them, they had made good many toilsome miles on their return.

The hunter, like the savage whose place he filled, seemed to select among the blind signs of their wild route, with a species of instinct, seldom abating his speed, and never pausing to deliberate. A rapid and oblique glance at the moss on the trees, with an occasional upward gaze toward the setting sun, or a steady but passing look at the direction of the numerous water courses, through which he waded, were sufficient to determine his path and remove his greatest difficulties. In the meantime, the forest began to change its hues, losing that lively green which had embellished its arches, in the graver light which is the usual precursor of the close of day.

While the eyes of the sisters were endeavoring to catch glimpses through the trees, of the flood of golden glory which formed a glittering halo around the sun, tinging here and there with ruby streaks, or bordering with narrow edgings of shining yellow, a mass of clouds that lay piled at no great distance above the western hills, Hawkeye turned suddenly and pointing upward toward the gorgeous heavens, he spoke:

"Yonder is the signal given to man to seek his food and natural rest," he said; "better and wiser would it be, if he could understand the signs of nature, and take a lesson from the fowls of the air and the beasts of the field! Our night, however, will soon be over, for with the moon we must be up and moving again. I remember to have found the Maquas, hereaways, in the first war in which I ever drew blood from man; and we threw up a work of blocks, to keep the ravenous varmints from handling our scalps. If my marks do not fail me, we shall find the place a few rods further to our left."

Without waiting for an assent, or, indeed, for any reply, the sturdy hunter moved boldly into a dense thicket of young chestnuts, shoving aside the branches of the exuberant shoots which nearly covered the ground, like a man who expected, at each step, to discover some object he had formerly known. The recollection of the scout did not deceive him. After penetrating through the brush, matted as it was with briars, for a few hundred feet, he entered an open space, that surrounded a low, green hillock, which was crowned by the decayed blockhouse in question. This rude and neglected building was one of those deserted works, which, having been thrown up on an emergency, had been abandoned with the disappearance of danger, and was now quietly crumbling in the solitude of the forest, neglected, and nearly forgotten, like the circumstances which had caused it to be reared. Such memorials of the passage and struggles of man are yet frequent throughout the broad barrier of wilderness which once separated the hostile provinces and form a species of ruins that are intimately associated with the recollections of colonial history, and which are in appropriate keeping with the gloomy character of the surrounding scenery. The roof of bark had long since fallen, and mingled with the soil, but the huge logs of pine, which had been hastily thrown together, still preserved their relative positions, though one angle of the work had given way under the pressure and threatened a speedy downfall to the remainder of the rustic edifice. While Heyward and his companions hesitated to approach a building so decayed, Hawkeye and the Indians entered within the low walls, not only without fear, but with obvious interest. While the former surveyed the ruins, both internally and externally, with the curiosity of one whose recollections were reviving at each moment, Chingachgook related to his son, in the language of the Delawares, and with the pride of a conqueror, the brief history of the skirmish which had been fought, in his youth, in that secluded spot. A strain of melancholy, however, blended with his triumph, rendering his voice, as usual, soft, and musical.

In the meantime, the sisters gladly dismounted, and prepared to enjoy their halt in the coolness of the evening, and in a security which they believed nothing, but the beasts of the forest could invade.

"Would not our resting-place have been more retired, my worthy friend," demanded the more vigilant Duncan, perceiving that the scout had already finished his short survey, "had we chosen a spot less known, and one more rarely visited than this?"

"Few live who know the blockhouse was ever raised," was the slow and musing answer; "'tis not often that books are made, and narratives written of such a scrimmage as was here found between the Mohicans and the Mohawks, in a war of their own waging. I was then a younker and went out with the Delawares because I know had they were a scandalized and wronged race. Forty days and forty nights did the imps crave our blood around this pile of logs, which I designed and partly reared, being, as you'll remember, no Indian myself, but a man without a cross. The Delawares lent themselves to the work, and we made it good, ten to twenty, until our numbers were nearly equal, and then we sallied out upon the hounds, and not a man of them ever got back to tell the fate of his party. Yes, yes; I was then young, and new to the sight of blood; and not relishing the thought that creatures who had spirits like myself should lay on the naked ground, to be torn asunder by beasts, or to bleach in the rains, I buried the dead with my own hands, under that very little hillock where you have placed yourselves; and no bad seat does it make neither, though it be raised by the bones of mortal men."

Heyward and the sisters arose, on the instant, from the grassy sepulcher; nor could the two latter, notwithstanding the terrific scenes they had so recently passed through, entirely suppress an emotion of natural horror, when they found themselves in such familiar contact with the grave of the dead Mohawks. The gray light, the gloomy little area of dark grass, surrounded by its border of brush, beyond which the pines rose, in breathing silence, apparently into the very clouds, and the deathlike stillness of the vast forest, were all in unison to deepen such a sensation. "They are gone, and they are harmless," continued Hawkeye, waving his hand, with a melancholy smile at their manifest alarm; "they'll never shout the war-whoop nor strike a blow with the tomahawk again! And of all those who aided in placing them where they lie, Chingachgook and I only are living! The brothers and family of the Mohican formed our war party; and you see before you all that are now left of his race."

The eyes of the listeners involuntarily sought the forms of the Indians, with a compassionate interest in their desolate fortune. Their dark persons were still to be seen within the shadows of the blockhouse, the son listening to the relation of his father with that sort of intenseness which would be created by a narrative that redounded so much to the honor of those whose names he had long revered for their courage and savage virtues.

"I had thought the Delawares a pacific people," said Duncan, "and that they never waged war in person; trusting the defense of their hands to those very Mohawks that you slew!"

"'Tis true in part," returned the scout, "and yet, at the bottom, 'tis a wicked lie. Such a treaty was made in ages gone by, through the deviltries of the Dutchers, who wished to disarm the natives that had the best right to the country, where they had settled themselves. The Mohicans, though a part of the same nation, having to deal with the English, never entered into the silly bargain, but kept to their manhood; as in truth did the Delawares, when their eyes were open to their folly. You see before you a chief of the great Mohican Sagamores! Once his family could chase their deer over tracts of country wider than that which belongs to the Albany Patteroon, without crossing brook or hill that was not their own but what is left of their descendant? He may find his six feet of earth when God chooses, and keep it in peace, perhaps, if he has a friend who will take the pains to sink his head so low that the plowshares cannot reach it!"

"Enough!" said Heyward, apprehensive that the subject might lead to a discussion that would interrupt the harmony so necessary to the preservation of his fair companions; "we have journeyed far, and few among us are blessed with forms like that of yours, which seems to know neither fatigue nor weakness."

"The sinews and bones of a man carry me through it all," said the hunter, surveying his muscular limbs with a simplicity that betrayed the honest pleasure the compliment afforded him; "there are larger and heavier men to be found in the settlements, but you might travel many days in a city before you could meet one able to walk fifty miles without stopping to take breath, or who has kept the hounds within hearing during a chase of hours. However, as flesh and blood are not always the same, it is quite reasonable to suppose that the gentle ones are willing to rest, after all they have seen and done this day. Uncas, clear out the spring, while your father and I make a cover for their tender heads of these chestnut shoots, and a bed of grass and leaves."

The dialogue ceased, while the hunter and his companions busied themselves in preparations for the comfort and protection of those they guided. A spring, which many long years before had induced the natives to select the place for their temporary fortification, was soon cleared of leaves, and a fountain of crystal gushed from the bed, diffusing its waters over the verdant hillock. A corner of the building was then roofed in such a manner as to exclude the heavy dew of the climate, and piles of sweet shrubs and dried leaves were laid beneath it for the sisters to repose on.

While the diligent woodsmen were employed in this manner, Cora and Alice partook of that refreshment which duty required much more than inclination prompted them to accept. They then retired within the walls, and first offering up their thanksgivings for past mercies, and petitioning for a continuance of the Divine favor throughout the coming night, they laid their tender forms on the fragrant couch, and in spite of recollections and forebodings, soon sank into those slumbers which nature so imperiously demanded, and which were sweetened by hopes for the morrow. Duncan had prepared himself to pass the night in watchfulness near them, just without the ruin, but the scout, perceiving his intention, pointed toward Chingachgook, as he coolly disposed his own person on the grass, and said:

"The eyes of a white man are too heavy and too blind for such a watch as this! The Mohican will be our sentinel, therefore let us sleep."

"I proved myself a sluggard on my post during the past night," said Heyward, "and have less need of repose than you, who did more credit to the character of a soldier. Let all the party seek their rest, then, while I hold the guard."

"If we lay among the white tents of the Sixtieth, and in front of an enemy like the French, I could not ask for a better watchman," returned the scout; "but in the darkness and among the signs of the wilderness your judgment would be like the folly of a child, and your vigilance thrown away. Do then, like Uncas and myself, sleep, and sleep in safety."

Heyward perceived, in truth, that the younger Indian had thrown his form on the side of the hillock while they were talking, like one who sought to make the most of the time allotted to rest, and that his example had been followed by David, whose voice literally "clove to his jaws," with the fever of his wound, heightened, as it was, by their toilsome march. Unwilling to prolong a useless discussion, the young man affected to comply, by posting his back against the logs of the blockhouse, in a half recumbent posture, though resolutely determined, in his own mind, not to close an eye until he had delivered his precious charge into the arms of Munro himself. Hawkeye, believing he had prevailed, soon fell asleep, and a silence as deep as the solitude in which they had found it, pervaded the retired spot.

For many minutes Duncan succeeded in keeping his senses on the alert, and alive to every moaning sound that arose from the forest. His vision became more acute as the shades of evening settled on the place; and even after the stars were glimmering above his head, he was able to distinguish the recumbent forms of his companions, as they lay stretched on the grass, and to note the person of Chingachgook, who sat upright and motionless as one of the trees which formed the dark barrier on every side. He still heard the gentle breathings of the sisters, who lay within a few feet of him, and not a leaf was ruffled by the passing air of which his ear did not detect the whispering sound. At length, however, the mournful notes of a whip-poor-will became blended with the moaning's of an owl; his heavy eyes occasionally sought the bright rays of the stars, and he then fancied he saw them through the fallen lids. At instants of momentary wakefulness he mistook a bush for his associate sentinel; his head next sank upon his shoulder, which, in its turn, sought the support of the ground; and, finally, his whole person became relaxed and pliant, and the young man sank into a deep sleep, dreaming that he was a knight of ancient chivalry, holding his midnight vigils before the tent of a recaptured princess, whose favor he did not despair of gaining, by such a proof of devotion and watchfulness.

How long the tired Duncan lay in this insensible state he never knew himself, but his slumbering visions had been long lost in total forgetfulness, when he was awakened by a light tap on the shoulder. Aroused by this signal, slight as it was, he sprang upon his feet with a confused recollection of the self-imposed duty he had assumed with the commencement of the night.

"Who comes?" he demanded, feeling for his sword, at the place where it was usually suspended. "Speak! friend or enemy?"

"Friend," replied the low voice of Chingachgook; who, pointing upward at the luminary which was shedding its mild light through the opening in the trees, directly in their bivouac, immediately added, in his rude English: "Moon comes and white man's fort far...far off; time to move, when sleep shuts both eyes of the Frenchman!"

"You say true! Call up your friends and bridle the horses while I prepare my own companions for the march!"

"We are awake, Duncan," said the soft, silvery tones of Alice within the building, "and ready to travel very fast after so refreshing a sleep but you have watched through the tedious night in our behalf, after having endured so much fatigue the livelong day!"

"Say, rather, I would have watched, but my treacherous eyes betrayed me; twice have I proved myself unfit for the trust I bear."

"Nay, Duncan, deny it not," interrupted the smiling Alice, issuing from the shadows of the building into the light of the moon, in all the loveliness of her freshened beauty; "I know you to be a heedless one, when self is the object of your care, and but too vigilant in favor of others. Can we not tarry here a little longer while you find the rest you need? Cheerfully, most cheerfully, will Cora and I keep the vigils, while you and all these brave men endeavor to snatch a little sleep!"

"If shame could cure me of my drowsiness, I should never close an eye again," said the uneasy youth, gazing at the ingenuous countenance of Alice, where, however, in its sweet solicitude, he read nothing to confirm his half-awakened suspicion. "It is but too true, that after leading you into danger by my heedlessness, I have not even the merit of guarding your pillows as should become a soldier."

"No one but Duncan himself should accuse Duncan of such a weakness. Go, then, and sleep; believe me, neither of us, weak girls as we are, will betray our watch."

The young man was relieved from the awkwardness of making any further protestations of his own demerits, by an exclamation from Chingachgook, and the attitude of riveted attention assumed by his son.

"The Mohicans hear an enemy!" whispered Hawkeye, who, by this time, in common with the whole party, was awake and stirring. "They scent danger in the wind!"

"God forbid!" exclaimed Heyward. "Surely we have had enough of bloodshed!"

While he spoke, however, the young soldier seized his rifle, and advancing toward the front, prepared to atone for his venial remissness, by freely exposing his life in defense of those he attended.

"'Tis some creature of the forest prowling around us in quest of food," he said, in a whisper, as soon as the low, and apparently distant sounds, which had startled the Mohicans, reached his own ears.

"Hist!" returned the attentive scout; "'tis man; even I can now tell his tread, poor as my senses are when compared to an Indian's! That Scampering Huron has fallen in with one of Montcalm's outlying parties, and they have struck upon our trail. I shouldn't like, myself, to spill more human blood in this spot," he added, looking around with anxiety in his features, at the dim objects by which he was surrounded; "but what must be, must! Lead the horses into the blockhouse, Uncas; and, friends, do you follow to the same shelter. Poor and old as it is, it offers a cover, and has rung with the crack of a rifle afore to-night!"

He was instantly obeyed, the Mohicans leading the Narrangansetts within the ruin, whither the whole party repaired with the most guarded silence.

The sound of approaching footsteps were now too distinctly audible to leave any doubts as to the nature of the interruption. They were soon mingled with voices calling to each other in an Indian dialect, which the hunter, in a whisper, affirmed to Heyward was the language of the Hurons. When the party reached the point where the horses had entered the thicket which surrounded the blockhouse, they were evidently at fault, having lost those marks which, until that moment, had directed their pursuit.

It would seem by the voices that twenty men were soon collected at that one spot, mingling their different opinions and advice in noisy clamor.

"The knaves know our weakness," whispered Hawkeye, who stood by the side of Heyward, in deep shade, looking through an opening in the logs, "or they wouldn't indulge their idleness in such a squaw's march. Listen to the reptiles! each man among them seems to have two tongues, and but a single leg."

Duncan, brave as he was in the combat, could not, in such a moment of painful suspense, make any reply to the cool and characteristic remark of the scout. He only grasped his rifle more firmly, and fastened his eyes upon the narrow opening, through which he gazed upon the moonlight view with increasing anxiety. The deeper tones of one who spoke as having authority were next heard, amid a silence that denoted the respect with which his orders, or rather advice, was received. After which, by the rustling of leaves, and crackling of dried twigs, it was apparent the savages were separating in pursuit of the lost trail. Fortunately for the pursued, the light of the moon, while it shed a flood of mild luster upon the little area around the ruin, was not sufficiently strong to penetrate the deep arches of the forest, where the objects still lay in deceptive shadow. The search proved fruitless; for so short and sudden had been the passage from the faint path the travelers had journeyed into the thicket, that every trace of their footsteps was lost in the obscurity of the woods.

It was not long, however, before the restless savages were heard beating the brush, and gradually approaching the inner edge of that dense border of young chestnuts which encircled the little area.

"They are coming," muttered Heyward, endeavoring to thrust his rifle through the chink in the logs; "let us fire on their approach."

"Keep everything in the shade," returned the scout; "the snapping of a flint, or even the smell of a single karnel of the brimstone, would bring the hungry varlets upon us in a body. Should it please God that we must give battle for the scalps, trust to the experience of men who know the ways of the savages, and who are not often backward when the war-whoop is howled."

Duncan cast his eyes behind him and saw that the trembling sisters were cowering in the far corner of the building, while the Mohicans stood in the shadow, like two upright posts, ready, and apparently willing, to strike when the blow should be needed. Curbing his impatience, he again looked out upon the area, and awaited the result in silence. At that instant the thicket opened, and a tall and armed Huron advanced a few paces into the open space. As he gazed upon the silent blockhouse, the moon fell upon his swarthy countenance, and betrayed its surprise and curiosity. He made the exclamation which usually accompanies the former emotion in an Indian, and, calling in a low voice, soon drew a companion to his side.

These children of the woods stood together for several moments pointing at the crumbling edifice and conversing in the unintelligible language of their tribe. They then approached, though with slow and cautious steps, pausing every instant to look at the building, like startled deer whose curiosity struggled powerfully with their awakened apprehensions for the mastery. The foot of one of them suddenly rested on the mound, and he stopped to examine its nature. At this moment, Heyward observed that the scout loosened his knife in its sheath and lowered the muzzle of his rifle. Imitating these movements, the young man prepared himself for the struggle which now seemed inevitable.

The savages were so near, that the least motion in one of the horses, or even a breath louder than common, would have betrayed the fugitives. But in discovering the character of the mound, the attention of the Hurons appeared directed to a different object. They spoke together, and the sounds of their voices were low and solemn, as if influenced by a reverence that was deeply blended with awe. Then they drew warily back, keeping their eyes riveted on the ruin, as if they expected to see the apparitions of the dead issue from its silent walls, until, having reached the boundary of the area, they moved slowly into the thicket and disappeared.

Hawkeye dropped the breech of his rifle to the earth, and drawing a long, free breath, exclaimed, in an audible whisper:

"Ay! they respect the dead, and it has this time saved their own lives, and, it may be, the lives of better men too."

Heyward lent his attention for a single moment to his companion, but without replying, he again turned toward those who just then interested him more. He heard the two Hurons leave the bushes, and it was soon plain that all the pursuers were gathered about them, in deep attention to their report. After a few minutes of earnest and solemn dialogue, altogether different from the noisy clamor with which they had first collected about the spot, the sounds grew fainter and more distant, and finally were lost in the depths of the forest.

Hawkeye waited until a signal from the listening Chingachgook assured him that every sound from the retiring party was completely swallowed by the distance, when he motioned to Heyward to lead forth the horses, and to assist the sisters into their saddles. The instant this was done they issued through the broken gateway and stealing out by a direction opposite to the one by which they entered, they quitted the spot, the sisters casting furtive glances at the silent, grave, and crumbling ruin, as they left the soft light of the moon, to bury themselves in the gloom of the woods.

CHAPTER XIV.

"Guard...Qui est la?

Puc. —Paisans, pauvres gens de France."

—King Henry VI

The scout resumed his post in the advance

During the rapid movement from the blockhouse, and until the party was deeply buried in the forest, each individual was too much interested in the escape to hazard a word even in whispers. The scout resumed his post in advance, though his steps, after he had thrown a safe distance between himself and his enemies, were more deliberate than in their previous march, in consequence of his utter ignorance of the localities of the surrounding woods. More than once he halted to consult with his confederates, the Mohicans, pointing upward at the moon, and examining the barks of the trees with care. In these brief pauses, Heyward and the sisters listened, with senses rendered doubly acute by the danger, to detect any symptoms which might announce the proximity of their foes. At such moments, it seemed as if a vast range of country lay buried in eternal sleep; not the least sound arising from the forest, unless it was the distant and scarcely audible rippling of a watercourse. Birds, beasts, and man, appeared to slumber alike, if, indeed, any of the latter were to be found in that wide tract of wilderness. But the sounds of the rivulet, feeble and murmuring as they were, relieved the guides at once from no trifling embarrassment, and toward it they immediately held their way.

When the banks of the little stream were gained, Hawkeye made another halt; and taking the moccasins from his feet, he invited Heyward and Gamut to follow his example. He then entered the water, and for near an hour they traveled in the bed of the brook, leaving no trail. The moon had already sunk into an immense pile of black clouds, which lay impending above the western horizon, when they issued from the low and devious watercourse to rise again to the light and level of the sandy but wooded plain. Here the scout seemed to be once more at home, for he held on to this way with the certainty and diligence of a man who moved in the security of his own knowledge. The path soon became more uneven, and the travelers could plainly perceive that the mountains drew nigher to them on each hand, and that they were, in truth, about entering one of their gorges. Suddenly, Hawkeye made a pause, and, waiting until he was joined by the whole party, he spoke, though in tones so low and cautious, that they added to the solemnity of his words, in the quiet and darkness of the place.

"It is easy to know the pathways, and to find the licks and water-courses of the wilderness," he said; "but who that saw this spot could venture to say, that a mighty army was at rest among yonder silent trees and barren mountains?"

"We are, then, at no great distance from William Henry?" said Heyward, advancing nigher to the scout.

"It is yet a long and weary path, and when and where to strike it is now our greatest difficulty. See," he said, pointing through the trees toward a spot where a little basin of water reflected the stars from its placid bosom, "here is the 'bloody pond' and I am on ground that I have not only often traveled, but over which I have found the enemy, from the rising to the setting sun."

"Ha! that sheet of dull and dreary water, then, is the sepulcher of the brave men who fell in the contest. I have heard it named, but never have I stood on its banks before."

"Three battles did we make with the Dutch-Frenchman[1] in a day," continued Hawkeye, pursuing the train of his own thoughts, rather than replying to the remark of Duncan. "He met us hard by, in our outward march to ambush his advance, and scattered us, like driven deer, through the defile, to the shores of Horican. Then we rallied behind our fallen trees, and made head against him, under Sir William, who was made Sir William for that very deed and well did we pay him for the disgrace of the morning! Hundreds of Frenchmen saw the sun that day for the last time; and even their leader, Dieskau himself, fell into our hands, so cut and torn with the lead, that he has gone back to his own country, unfit for further acts in war."

"'Twas a noble repulse!" exclaimed Heyward, in the heat of his

[1] Baron Dieskau, a German, in the service of France. A few years previously to the period of the tale, this officer was defeated by Sir William Johnson, of Johnstown, New York, on the shores of Lake George.

youthful ardor; "the fame of it reached us early, in our southern army."

"Ay! but it did not end there. I was sent by Major Effingham, at Sir William's own bidding, to outflank the French, and carry the tidings of their disaster across the portage, to the fort on the Hudson. Just hereaway, where you see the trees rise into a mountain swell, I met a party coming down to our aid, and I led them where the enemy were taking their meal, little dreaming that they had not finished the bloody work of the day."

"And you surprised them?"

"If death can be a surprise to men who are thinking only of the cravings of their appetites. We gave them but little breathing time, for they had borne hard upon us in the fight of the morning, and there were few in our party who had not lost friend or relative by their hands."

"When all was over, the dead, and some say the dying, were cast into that little pond. These eyes have seen its waters colored with blood, as natural water never yet flowed from the bowels of the 'arth."

"It was a convenient, and, I trust, will prove a peaceful grave for a soldier. You have then seen much service on this frontier?"

"Ay!" said the scout, erecting his tall person with an air of military pride; "there are not many echoes among these hills that haven't rung with the crack of my rifle, nor is there the space of a square mile atwixt Horican and the river, that 'killdeer' hasn't dropped a living body on, be it an enemy or be it a brute beast. As for the grave there being as quiet as you mention, it is another matter. There are them in the camp who say and think, man, to lie still, should not be buried while the breath is in the body; and certain it is that in the hurry of that evening, the doctors had but little time to say who was living and who was dead. Hist! see you nothing walking on the shore of the pond?"

"'Tis not probable that any are as houseless as ourselves in this dreary forest."

"Such as he may care but little for house or shelter, and night dew can never wet a body that passes its days in the water," returned the scout, grasping the shoulder of Heyward with such convulsive strength as to make the young soldier painfully sensible how much superstitious terror had got the mastery of a man usually so dauntless.

"By heaven, there is a human form, and it approaches! Stand to your arms, my friends; for we know not whom we encounter."

"Qui vive?" demanded a stern, quick voice, which sounded like a challenge from another world, issuing out of that solitary and solemn place.

"What says it?" whispered the scout; "it speaks neither Indian nor English."

"Qui vive?" repeated the same voice, which was quickly followed by the rattling of arms, and a menacing attitude.

"France!" cried Heyward, advancing from the shadow of the trees to the shore of the pond, within a few yards of the sentinel.

"D'ou venez-vous...ou allez-vous, d'aussi bonne heure?" demanded the grenadier, in the language and with the accent of a man from old France.

"Je viens de la découverte, et je vais me coucher."

"Etes-vous officier du roi?"

"Sans doute, mon camarade; me prends-tu pour un provincial! Je suis capitaine de chasseurs (Heyward well knew that the other was of a regiment in the line); j'ai ici, avec moi, les filles du commandant de la fortification. Aha! tu en as entendu parler! je les ai fait prisonnières près de l'autre fort, et je les conduis au général."

"Ma foi! mesdames; j'en suis faché pour vous," exclaimed the young soldier, touching his cap with grace; "mais...fortune de guerre! vous trouverez notre général un brave homme, et bien poli avec les dames."

"C'est le caractere des gens de guerre," said Cora, with admirable self-possession. "Adieu, mon ami; je vous souhaiterais un devoir plus agréable a remplir."

The soldier made a low and humble acknowledgment for her civility; and Heyward adding a "Bonne nuit, mon camarade," they moved deliberately forward, leaving the sentinel pacing the banks of the silent pond, little suspecting an enemy of so much effrontery, and humming to himself those words which were recalled to his mind by the sight of women, and, perhaps, by recollections of his own distant and beautiful France:

"Vive le vin, vive l'amour," &c., &c.

"'Tis well you understood the knave!" whispered the scout, when they had gained a little distance from the place, and letting his rifle fall into the hollow of his arm again; "I soon saw that he was one of them uneasy Frenchers and well for him it was that his speech was friendly and his wishes kind or a place might have been found for his bones among those of his countrymen."

He was interrupted by a long and heavy groan which arose from the little basin, as though, in truth, the spirits of the departed lingered about their watery sepulcher.

"Surely it was of flesh," continued the scout; "no spirit could handle its arms so steadily."

"It was of flesh; but whether the poor fellow still belongs to this world may well be doubted," said Heyward, glancing his eyes around him, and missing Chingachgook from their little band. Another groan more faint than the former was succeeded by a heavy and sullen plunge into the water, and all was still again as if the borders of the dreary pool had never been awakened from the silence of creation. While they yet hesitated in uncertainty, the form of the Indian was seen gliding out of the thicket. As the chief rejoined them, with one hand he attached the reeking scalp of the unfortunate young Frenchman to his girdle, and with the other he replaced the knife and tomahawk that had drunk his blood. He then took his wonted station, with the air of a man who believed he had done a deed of merit.

The scout dropped one end of his rifle to the earth, and leaning his hands on the other, he stood musing in profound silence. Then, shaking his head in a mournful manner, he muttered:

"'Twould have been a cruel and an unhuman act for a white skin; but 'tis the gift and nature' of an Indian, and I suppose it should not be denied. I could wish, though, it had befallen an accursed Mingo, rather than that gay young boy from the old countries."

"Enough!" said Heyward, apprehensive the unconscious sisters might comprehend the nature of the detention and conquering his disgust by a train of reflections very much like that of the hunter; "'tis done; and though better it were left undone, cannot be amended. You see, we are, too obviously within the sentinels of the enemy; what course do you propose to follow?"

"Yes," said Hawkeye, rousing himself again; "'tis as you say, too late to harbor further thoughts about it. Ay, the French have gathered around the fort in good earnest, and we have a delicate needle to thread in passing them."

"And but little time to do it in," added Heyward, glancing his eyes upwards, toward the bank of vapor that concealed the setting moon.

"And little time to do it in!" repeated the scout. "The thing may be done in two fashions, by the help of Providence, without which it may not be done at all."

"Name them quickly for time presses."

"One would be to dismount the gentle ones, and let their beasts range the plain, by sending the Mohicans in front, we might then cut a lane through their sentries, and enter the fort over the dead bodies."

"It will not do...it will not do!" interrupted the generous Heyward; "a soldier might force his way in this manner, but never with such a convoy."

"'Twould be, indeed, a bloody path for such tender feet to wade in," returned the equally reluctant scout; "but I thought it befitting my manhood to name it. We must, then, turn in our trail and get without the line of their lookouts, when we will bend short to the west, and enter the mountains; where I can hide you, so that all the devil's hounds in Montcalm's pay would be thrown off the scent for months to come."

"Let it be done, and that instantly."

Further words were unnecessary; for Hawkeye, merely uttering the mandate to "follow," moved along the route by which they had just entered their present critical and even dangerous situation. Their progress, like their late dialogue, was guarded, and without noise; for none knew at what moment a passing patrol, or a crouching picket of the enemy, might rise upon their path. As they held their silent way along the margin of the pond, again Heyward and the scout stole furtive glances at its appalling dreariness. They looked in vain for the form they had so recently seen stalking along in silent shores, while a low and regular wash of the little waves, by announcing that the waters were not yet subsided, furnished a frightful memorial of the deed of blood they had just witnessed. Like all that passing and gloomy scene, the low basin, however, quickly melted in the darkness, and became blended with the mass of black objects in the rear of the travelers.

Hawkeye soon deviated from the line of their retreat, and striking off towards the mountains which form the western boundary of the narrow plain, he led his followers, with swift steps, deep within the shadows that were cast from their high and broken summits. The route was now painful; lying over ground ragged with rocks, and intersected with ravines, and their progress proportionately slow. Bleak and black hills lay on every side of them, compensating in some degree for the additional toil of the march by the sense of security they imparted. At length the party began slowly to rise a steep and rugged ascent, by a path that curiously wound among rocks and trees, avoiding the one and supported by the other, in a manner that showed it had been devised by men long practiced in the arts of the wilderness. As they gradually rose from the level of the valleys, the thick darkness which usually precedes the approach of day began to disperse, and objects were seen in the plain and palpable colors with which they had been gifted by nature. When they issued from the stunted woods which clung to the barren sides of the mountain, upon a flat and mossy rock that formed its summit, they met the morning, as it came blushing above the green pines of a hill that lay on the opposite side of the valley of the Horican.

The scout now told the sisters to dismount; and taking the bridles from the mouths, and the saddles off the backs of the jaded beasts, he turned them loose, to glean a scanty subsistence among the shrubs and meager herbage of that elevated region.

"Go," he said, "and seek your food where nature' gives it to you and beware that you become not food to ravenous wolves yourselves, among these hills."

"Have we no further needed of them?" demanded Heyward.

"See, and judge with your own eyes," said the scout, advancing toward the eastern brow of the mountain, whither he beckoned for the whole party to follow; "if it was as easy to look into the heart of man as it is to spy out the nakedness of Montcalm's camp from this spot, hypocrites would grow scarce, and the cunning of a Mingo might prove a losing game, compared to the honesty of a Delaware."

When the travelers reached the verge of the precipices they saw, at a glance, the truth of the scout's declaration, and the admirable foresight with which he had led them to their commanding station.

The mountain on which they stood, elevated perhaps a thousand feet in the air, was a high cone that rose a little in advance of that range which stretches for miles along the western shores of the lake, until meeting its sisters' miles beyond the water, it ran off toward the Canadas, in confused and broken masses of rock, thinly sprinkled with evergreens. Immediately at the feet of the party, the southern shore of the Horican swept in a broad semicircle from mountain to mountain, marking a wide strand, that soon rose into an uneven and somewhat elevated plain. To the north stretched the limpid, and, as it appeared from that dizzy height, the narrow sheet of the "holy lake," indented with numberless bays, embellished by fantastic headlands, and dotted with countless islands. At the distance of a few leagues, the bed of the water became lost among mountains or was wrapped in the masses of vapor that came slowly rolling along their bosom before a light morning air. But a narrow opening between the crests of the hills pointed out the passage by which they found their way still further north, to spread their pure and ample sheets again, before pouring out their tribute into the distant Champlain. To the south stretched the defile, or rather broken plain, so often mentioned. For several miles in this direction, the mountains appeared reluctant to yield their dominion, but within reach of the eye they diverged, and finally melted into the level and sandy lands, across which we have accompanied our adventurers in their double journey. Along both ranges of hills, which bounded the opposite sides of the lake and valley, clouds of light vapor were rising in spiral wreaths from the uninhabited woods, looking like the smoke of hidden cottages; or rolled lazily down the declivities, to mingle with the fogs of the lower land. A single, solitary, snow-white cloud floated above the valley, and marked the spot beneath which lay the silent pool of the "bloody pond."

Directly on the shore of the lake, and nearer to its western than to its eastern margin, lay the extensive earthen ramparts and low buildings of William Henry. Two of the sweeping bastions appeared to rest on the water which washed their bases, while a deep ditch and extensive morasses guarded its other sides and angles. The land had been cleared of wood for a reasonable distance around the work, but every other part of the scene lay in the green livery of nature, except where the limpid water mellowed the view, or the bold rocks thrust their black and naked heads above the undulating outline of the mountain ranges. In its front might be seen the scattered sentinels, who held a weary watch against their numerous foes; and within the walls themselves, the travelers looked down upon men still drowsy with a night of vigilance. Toward the southeast, but in immediate contact with the fort, was an entrenched camp, posted on a rocky eminence, that would have been far more eligible for the work itself, in which Hawkeye pointed out the presence of those auxiliary regiments that had so recently left the Hudson in their company. From the woods, a little further to the south, rose numerous dark and lurid smokes, that were easily to be distinguished from the purer exhalations of the springs, and which the scout also showed to Heyward, as evidence that the enemy lay in force in that direction.

But the spectacle which most concerned the young soldier was on the western bank of the lake, though quite near to its southern termination. On a strip of land, which appeared from his stand too narrow to contain such an army, but which, in truth, extended many hundreds of yards from the shores of the Horican to the base of the mountain, were to be seen the white tents and military engines of an encampment of ten thousand men. Batteries were already thrown up in their front, and even while the spectators above them were looking down, with such different emotions, on a scene which lay like a map beneath their feet, the roar of artillery rose from the valley, and passed off in thundering echoes along the eastern hills.

"Morning is just touching them below," said the deliberate and musing scout, "and the watchers have a mind to wake up the sleepers by the sound of cannon. We are a few hours too late! Montcalm has already filled the woods with his accursed Iroquois."

"The place is, indeed, invested," returned Duncan; "but is there no expedient by which we may enter? capture in the works would be far preferable to falling again into the hands of roving Indians."

"See!" exclaimed the scout, unconsciously directing the attention of Cora to the quarters of her own father, "how that shot has made the stones fly from the side of the commandant's house! Ay! these Frenchers will pull it to pieces faster than it was put together, solid, and thick though it be!"

"Heyward, I sicken at the sight of danger that I cannot share," said the undaunted but anxious daughter. "Let us go to Montcalm, and demand admission: he dare not deny a child the boon."

"You would scarce find the tent of the Frenchman with the hair on your head"; said the blunt scout. "If I had but one of the thousand boats which lie empty along that shore, it might be done! Ha! here will soon be an end of the firing, for yonder comes a fog that will turn day to night and make an Indian arrow more dangerous than a molded cannon. Now, if you are equal to the work, and will follow, I will make a push; for I long to get down into that camp, if it be only to scatter some Mingo dogs that I see lurking in the skirts of yonder thicket of birch."

"We are equal," said Cora, firmly; "on such an errand we will follow to any danger."

The scout turned to her with a smile of honest and cordial approbation, as he answered:

"I would I had a thousand men, of brawny limbs and quick eyes, that feared death as little as you! I'd send them jabbering Frenchers back into their den again, afore the week was ended, howling like so many fettered hounds or hungry wolves. But stir," he added, turning from her to the rest of the party, "the fog comes rolling down so fast, we shall have but just the time to meet it on the plain, and use it as a cover. Remember, if any accident should befall me, to keep the air blowing on your left cheeks or, rather, follow the Mohicans; they'd scent their way, be it in day or be it at night."

He then waved his hand for them to follow, and threw himself down the steep declivity, with free, but careful footsteps. Heyward assisted the sisters to descend, and in a few minutes, they were all far down a mountain whose sides they had climbed with so much toil and pain.

The direction taken by Hawkeye soon brought the travelers to the level of the plain, nearly opposite to a sally-port in the western curtain of the fort, which lay itself at the distance of about half a mile from the point where he halted to allow Duncan to come up with his charge. In their eagerness, and favored by the nature of the ground, they had anticipated the fog, which was rolling heavily down the lake, and it became necessary to pause, until the mists had wrapped the camp of the enemy in their fleecy mantle. The Mohicans profited by the delay, to steal out of the woods, and to make a survey of surrounding objects. They were followed at a little distance by the scout, with a view to profit early by their report and to obtain some faint knowledge for himself of the more immediate localities.

In a very few moments he returned, his face reddened with vexation, while he muttered his disappointment in words of no very gentle import.

"Here has the cunning Frenchman been posting a picket directly in our path," he said; "red-skins and whites; and we shall be as likely to fall into their midst as to pass them in the fog!"

"Cannot we make a circuit to avoid the danger," asked Heyward, "and come into our path again when it is passed?"

"Who that once bends from the line of his march in a fog can tell when or how to find it again! The mists of Horican are not like the curls from a peace-pipe, or the smoke which settles above a mosquito fire."

He was yet speaking, when a crashing sound was heard and a cannonball entered the thicket, striking the body of a sapling, and rebounding to the earth, its force being much expended by previous resistance. The Indians followed instantly like busy attendants on the terrible messenger, and Uncas commenced speaking earnestly and with much action, in the Delaware tongue.

"It may be so, lad," muttered the scout, when he had ended; "for desperate fevers are not to be treated like a toothache. Come, then, the fog is shutting in."

"Stop!" cried Heyward; "first explain your expectations."

"'Tis soon done, and a small hope it is but it is better than nothing. This shot that you see," added the scout, kicking the harmless iron with his foot, "has plowed the 'arth in its road from the fort, and we shall hunt for the furrow it has made, when all other signs may fail. No more words, but follow, or the fog may leave us in the middle of our path, a mark for both armies to shoot at."

Heyward perceiving that, in fact, a crisis had arrived, when acts were more required than words, placed himself between the sisters, and drew them swiftly forward, keeping the dim figure of their leader in his eye. It was soon apparent that Hawkeye had not magnified the power of the fog, for before they had proceeded twenty yards, it was difficult for the different individuals of the party to distinguish each other in the vapor.

They had made their little circuit to the left, and were already inclining again toward the right, having, as Heyward thought, got over nearly half the distance to the friendly works, when his ears were saluted with the fierce summons, apparently within twenty feet of them, of:

"Qui va là?"

"Push on!" whispered the scout, once more bending to the left.

"Push on!" repeated Heyward; when the summons was renewed by a dozen voices, each of which seemed charged with menace.

"C'est moi," cried Duncan, dragging rather than leading those he supported swiftly onward.

"Bête!..qui?...moi!"

"Ami de la France."

"Tu m'as plus l'air d'un *ennemi* de la France; arrete ou pardieu je te ferai ami du diable. Non! feu, camarades, feu!"

The order was instantly obeyed, and the fog was stirred by the explosion of fifty muskets. Happily, the aim was bad, and the bullets cut the air in a direction a little different from that taken by the fugitives; though still so nigh them, that to the unpractised ears of David and the two females, it appeared as if they whistled within a few inches of the organs. The outcry was renewed, and the order, not only to fire again, but to pursue, was too plainly audible. When Heyward briefly explained the meaning of the words they heard, Hawkeye halted and spoke with quick decision and great firmness.

"Let us deliver our fire," he said; "they will believe it a sortie, and give way, or they will wait for reinforcements."

The scheme was well conceived but failed in its effects. The instant the French heard the pieces, it seemed as if the plain was alive with men, muskets rattling along its whole extent, from the shores of the lake to the furthest boundary of the woods.

"We shall draw their entire army upon us, and bring on a general assault," said Duncan: "lead on, my friend, for your own life and ours."

The scout seemed willing to comply but, in the hurry of the moment, and in the change of position, he had lost the direction. In vain he turned either cheek toward the light air; they felt equally cool. In this dilemma, Uncas lit the furrow of the cannon ball, where it had cut the ground in three adjacent anthills.

"Give me the range!" said Hawkeye, bending to catch a glimpse of the direction, and then instantly moving onward.

Cries, oaths, voices calling to each other, and the reports of muskets, were now quick and incessant, and, apparently, on every side of them. Suddenly a strong glare of light flashed across the scene, the fog rolled upward in thick wreaths, and several cannons belched across the plain, and the roar was thrown heavily back from the bellowing echoes of the mountain.

"'Tis from the fort!" exclaimed Hawkeye, turning short on his tracks; "and we, like stricken fools, were rushing to the woods, under the very knives of the Maquas."

The instant their mistake was rectified, the whole party retraced the error with the utmost diligence. Duncan willingly relinquished the support of Cora to the arm of Uncas and Cora as readily accepted the welcome assistance. Men, hot and angry in pursuit, were evidently on their footsteps, and each instant threatened their capture, if not their destruction.

"Point de quartier aux coquins!" cried an eager pursuer, who seemed to direct the operations of the enemy.

"Stand firm, and be ready, my gallant Sixtieths!" suddenly exclaimed a voice above them; "wait to see the enemy, fire low and sweep the glacis."

"Father! father!" exclaimed a piercing cry from out the mist: "it is I! Alice! thy own Elsie! Spare, oh! save your daughters!"

"Hold!" shouted the former speaker, in the awful tones of parental agony, the sound reaching even to the woods, and rolling back in solemn echo. "'Tis she! God has restored me to my children! Throw open the sally-port; to the field, Sixtieths, to the field; pull not a trigger, lest ye kill my lambs! Drive off these dogs of France with your steel."

Duncan heard the grating of the rusty hinges, and darting to the spot, directed by the sound, he met a long line of dark red warriors, passing swiftly toward the glacis. He knew them for his own battalion of the Royal Americans, and flying to their head, soon swept every trace of his pursuers from before the works.

For an instant, Cora and Alice had stood trembling and bewildered by this unexpected desertion; but before either had leisure for speech, or even thought, an officer of gigantic frame, whose locks were bleached with years and service, but whose air of military grandeur had been rather softened than destroyed by time, rushed out of the body of mist, and folded them to his bosom, while large scalding tears rolled down his pale and wrinkled cheeks, and he exclaimed, in the peculiar accent of Scotland:

"For this I thank thee, Lord! Let danger come as it will, thy servant is now prepared!"

CHAPTER XV.

"Then go we in, to know his embassy;
Which I could, with ready guess, declare,
Before the Frenchmen speak a word of it."
—King Henry V

A few succeeding days were passed amid the privations, the uproar, and the dangers of the siege, which was vigorously pressed by a power, against whose approaches Munro possessed no competent means of resistance. It appeared as if Webb, with his army, which lay slumbering on the banks of the Hudson, had utterly forgotten the strait to which his countrymen were reduced. Montcalm had filled the woods of the portage with his savages, every yell and whoop from whom rang through the British encampment, chilling the hearts of men who were already but too much disposed to magnify the danger.

Not so, however, with the besieged. Animated by the words, and stimulated by the examples of their leaders, they had found their courage, and maintained their ancient reputation, with a zeal that did justice to the stern character of their commander. As if satisfied with the toil of marching through the wilderness to encounter his enemy, the French general, though of approved skill, had neglected to seize the adjacent mountains; whence the besieged might have been exterminated with impunity and which, in the more modern warfare of the country, would not have been neglected for a single hour. This sort of contempt for eminences, or rather dread of the labor of ascending them, might have been termed the besetting weakness of the warfare of the period. It originated in the simplicity of the Indian contests, in which, from the nature of the combats, and the density of the forests, fortresses were rare, and artillery next to useless. The carelessness engendered by these usages descended even to the war of the Revolution and lost the States the important fortress of Ticonderoga opening a way for the army of Burgoyne into what was then the bosom of the country. We look back at this ignorance, or infatuation, whichever it may be called, with wonder, knowing that the neglect of an eminence, whose difficulties, like those of Mount Defiance, have been so greatly exaggerated, would, at the present time, prove fatal to the reputation of the engineer who had planned the works at their base, or to that of the general whose lot it was to defend them.

The tourist, the valetudinarian, or the amateur of the beauties of nature, who, in the train of his four-in-hand, now rolls through the scenes we have attempted to describe, in quest of information, health, or pleasure, or floats steadily toward his object on those artificial waters which have sprung up under the administration of a statesman[1] who has dared to stake his political character on the hazardous issue, is not to suppose that his ancestors traversed those hills, or struggled with the same currents with equal facility. The transportation of a single heavy gun was often considered equal to a victory gained; if happily, the difficulties of the passage had not so far separated it from its necessary concomitant, the ammunition, as to render it no more than a useless tube of unwieldy iron.

The evils of this state of things pressed heavily on the fortunes of the resolute Scotsman who now defended William Henry. Though his adversary neglected the hills, he had planted his batteries with judgment on the plain and caused them to be served with vigor

[1] Evidently the late De Witt Clinton, who died governor of New York in 1828.

and skill. Against this assault, the besieged could only oppose the imperfect and hasty preparations of a fortress in the wilderness.

It was in the afternoon of the fifth day of the siege, and the fourth of his own service in it, that Major Heyward profited by a parley that had just been beaten, by repairing to the ramparts of one of the water bastions, to breathe the cool air from the lake, and to take a survey of the progress of the siege. He was alone, if the solitary sentinel who paced the mound be excepted; for the artillerists had hastened also to profit by the temporary suspension of their arduous duties. The evening was delightfully calm, and the light air from the limpid water fresh and soothing. It seemed as if, with the termination of the roar of artillery and the plunging of shot, nature had also seized the moment to assume her mildest and most captivating form. The sun poured down his parting glory on the scene, without the oppression of those fierce rays that belong to the climate and the season. The mountains looked green, and fresh, and lovely, tempered with the milder light, or softened in shadow, as thin vapors floated between them and the sun. The numerous islands rested on the bosom of the Horican, some low and sunken, as if embedded in the waters, and others appearing to hover about the element, in little hillocks of green velvet; among which the fishermen of the beleaguering army peacefully rowed their skiffs or floated at rest on the glassy mirror in quiet pursuit of their employment.

The scene was at once animated and still. All that pertained to nature was sweet, or simply grand; while those parts which depended on the temper and movements of man were lively and playful.

Two little spotless flags were abroad, the one on a salient angle of the fort, and the other on the advanced battery of the besiegers; emblems of the truth which existed, not only to the acts, but it would seem, also, to the enmity of the combatants.

Behind these again swung, heavily opening, and closing in silken folds, the rival standards of England and France.

A hundred gay and thoughtless young Frenchmen were drawing a net to the pebbly beach, within dangerous proximity to the sullen but silent cannon of the fort, while the eastern mountain was sending back the loud shouts and gay merriment that attended their sport. Some were rushing eagerly to enjoy the aquatic games of the lake, and others were already toiling their way up the neighboring hills, with the restless curiosity of their nation. To all these sports and pursuits, those of the enemy who watched the besieged, and the besieged themselves, were, however, merely the idle though sympathizing spectators. Here and there a picket had, indeed, raised a song, or mingled in a dance, which had drawn the dusky savages around them, from their lairs in the forest. In short, everything wore rather the appearance of a day of pleasure, than of an hour stolen from the dangers and toil of a bloody and vindictive warfare.

Duncan had stood in a musing attitude, contemplating this scene a few minutes, when his eyes were directed to the glacis in front of the sally-port already mentioned, by the sounds of approaching footsteps. He walked to an angle of the bastion, and beheld the scout advancing, under the custody of a French officer, to the body of the fort. The countenance of Hawkeye was haggard and careworn, and his air dejected, as though he felt the deepest degradation at having fallen into the power of his enemies. He was without his favorite weapon, and his arms were even bound behind him with thongs, made of the skin of a deer. The arrival of flags to cover the messengers of summons, had occurred so often of late, that when Heyward first threw his careless glance on this group, he expected to see another of the officers of the enemy, charged with a similar office but the instant he recognized the tall person and still sturdy though downcast features of his friend, the woodsman, he started with surprise, and turned to descend from the bastion into the bosom of the work.

The sounds of other voices, however, caught his attention, and for a moment caused him to forget his purpose. At the inner angle of the mound, he met the sisters, walking along the parapet, in search, like himself, of air and relief from confinement. They had not met from that painful moment when he deserted them on the plain, only to assure their safety. He had parted from them worn with care and jaded with fatigue; he now saw them refreshed and blooming, though timid, and anxious. Under such an inducement it will cause no surprise that the young man lost sight for a time, of other objects in order to address them. He was, however, anticipated by the voice of the ingenuous and youthful Alice.

"Ah! thou tyrant! thou recreant knight! he who abandons his damsels in the very lists," she cried; "here have we been days, nay, ages, expecting you at our feet, imploring mercy and forgetfulness of your craven backsliding, or I should rather say, back running for verily you fled in the manner that no stricken deer, as our worthy friend the scout would say, could equal!"

"You know that Alice means our thanks and our blessings," added the graver and more thoughtful Cora. "In truth, we have a little wonder why you should so rigidly absent yourself from a place where the gratitude of the daughters might receive the support of a parent's thanks."

"Your father himself could tell you, that, though absent from your presence, I have not been altogether forgetful of your safety," returned the young man; "the mastery of yonder village of huts," pointing to the neighboring entrenched camp, "has been keenly disputed; and he who holds it is sure to be possessed of this fort, and that which it contains. My days and nights have all been passed there since we separated, because I thought that duty called me thither. But" he added, with an air of chagrin, which he endeavored, though unsuccessfully, to conceal, "had I been aware that what I then believed a soldier's conduct could be so construed, shame would have been added to the list of reasons."

"Heyward! Duncan!" exclaimed Alice, bending forward to read his half-averted countenance, until a lock of her golden hair rested on her flushed cheek, and nearly concealed the tear that had started to her eye; "did I think this idle tongue of mine had pained you, I would silence it forever. Cora can say, if Cora would, how justly we have prized your services, and how deep I had almost said, how fervent is our gratitude."

"And will Cora attest the truth of this?" cried Duncan, suffering the cloud to be chased from his countenance by a smile of open pleasure. "What says our graver sister? Will she find an excuse for the neglect of the knight in the duty of a soldier?"

Cora made no immediate answer, but turned her face toward the water, as if looking on the sheet of the Horican. When she did bend her dark eyes on the young man, they were yet filled with an expression of anguish that at once drove every thought but that of kind solicitude from his mind.

"You are not well, dearest Miss Munro!" he exclaimed; "we have trifled while you are in suffering!"

"'Tis nothing," she answered, refusing his support with feminine reserve. "That I cannot see the sunny side of the picture of life, like this artless but ardent enthusiast," she added, laying her hand lightly, but affectionately, on the arm of her sister, "is the penalty of experience, and, perhaps, the misfortune of my nature. See," she continued, as if determined to shake off infirmity, in a sense of duty; "look around you, Major Heyward, and tell me what a prospect is this for the daughter of a soldier whose greatest happiness is his honor and his military renown."

"Neither ought nor shall be tarnished by circumstances over which he has had no control," Duncan warmly replied. "But your words recall me to my own duty. I go now to your gallant father, to hear his determination in matters of the last moment to the defense. God bless you in every fortune, noble Cora I may and must call you." She frankly gave him her hand, though her lip quivered, and her cheeks gradually became of Ashly paleness. "In every fortune, I know you will be an ornament and honor to your sex. Alice, adieu" his voice changed from admiration to tenderness "adieu, Alice; we shall soon meet again; as conquerors, I trust, and amid rejoicings!"

Without waiting for an answer from either, the young man threw himself down the grassy steps of the bastion, and moving rapidly across the parade, he was quickly in the presence of their father. Munro was pacing his narrow apartment with a disturbed air and gigantic strides as Duncan entered.

"You have anticipated my wishes, Major Heyward," he said; "I was about to request this favor."

"I am sorry to see, sir, that the messenger I so warmly recommended has returned in custody of the French! I hope there is no reason to distrust his fidelity?"

"The fidelity of 'The Long Rifle' is well known to me," returned Munro, "and is above suspicion; though his usual good fortune seems, at last, to have failed. Montcalm has got him, and with the accursed politeness of his nation, he has sent him in with a doleful tale, of 'knowing how I valued the fellow, he could not think of retaining him.' A Jesuitical way that, Major Duncan Heyward, of telling a man of his misfortunes!"

"But the general and his succor?"

"Did ye look to the south as ye entered and could ye not see them?" said the old soldier, laughing bitterly. "Hoot! hoot! you're an impatient boy, sir, and cannot give the gentlemen leisure for their march!"

"They are coming, then? The scout has said as much?"

"When? and by what path? for the dunce has omitted to tell me this. There is a letter, it would seem, too; and that is the only agreeable part of the matter. For the customary attentions of your Marquis of Montcalm, I warrant me, Duncan, that he of Lothian would buy a dozen such marquisates but if the news of the letter were bad, the gentility of this French monsieur would certainly compel him to let us know it."

"He keeps the letter, then, while he releases the messenger?"

"Ay, that does he, and all for the sake of what you call your 'bonhomie.' I would venture, if the truth was known, the fellow's grandfather taught the noble science of dancing."

"But what says the scout? he has eyes and ears, and a tongue. What verbal report does he make?"

"Oh! sir, he is not wanting in natural organs, and he is free to tell all that he has seen and heard. The whole amount is this; there is a fort of his majesties on the banks of the Hudson, called Edward, in honor of his gracious highness of York, you'll know; and it is well filled with armed men, as such a work should be."

"But was there no movement, no signs of any intention to advance to our relief?"

"There were the morning and evening parades and when one of the provincial loons you'll know, Duncan, you're half a Scotsman yourself, when one of them dropped his powder over his porretch, if it touched the coals, it just burned!" Then, suddenly changing his bitter, ironical manner, to one graver and more thoughtful, he continued: "and yet there might, and must be, something in that letter which it would be well to know!"

"Our decision should be speedy," said Duncan, gladly availing himself of this change of humor, to press the more important objects of their interview; "I cannot conceal from you, sir, that the camp will not be much longer tenable, and I am sorry to add, that things appear no better in the fort; more than half the guns are busted."

"And how should it be otherwise? Some were fished from the bottom of the lake; some have been rusting in woods since the discovery of the country and some were never guns at all, mere privateersmen's playthings! Do you think, sir, you can have Woolwich Warren in the midst of a wilderness, three thousand miles from Great Britain?"

"The walls are crumbling about our ears, and provisions begin to fail us," continued Heyward, without regarding the new burst of indignation; "even the men show signs of discontent and alarm."

"Major Heyward," said Munro, turning to his youthful associate with the dignity of his years and superior rank; "I should have served his majesty for half a century, and earned these gray hairs in vain, were I ignorant of all you say, and of the pressing nature of our circumstances; still, there is everything due to the honor of the king's arms, and something to ourselves. While there is hope of succor, this fortress will I defend, though it be to be done with pebbles gathered on the lake shore. It is a sight of the letter, therefore, that we want, that we may know the intentions of the man the earl of Loudon has left among us as his substitute."

"And can I be of service in the matter?"

"Sir, you can; the marquis of Montcalm has, in addition to his other civilities, invited me to a personal interview between the works and his own camp; in order, as he says, to impart some additional information. Now, I think it would not be wise to show any undue solicitude to meet him, and I would employ you, an officer of rank, as my substitute; for it would but ill comport with the honor of Scotland to let it be said one of her gentlemen was outdone in civility by a native of any other country on earth."

Without assuming the supererogatory task of entering into a discussion of the comparative merits of national courtesy, Duncan cheerfully assented to supply the place of the veteran in the approaching interview. A long and confidential communication now succeeded, during which the young man received some additional insight into his duty, from the experience and native acuteness of his commander, and then the former took his leave.

As Duncan could only act as the representative of the commandant of the fort, the ceremonies which should have accompanied a meeting between the heads of the adverse forces were, of course, dispensed with. The truce still existed, and with a roll and beat of the drum, and covered by a little white flag, Duncan left the sally-port, within ten minutes after his instructions were ended. He was received by the French officer in advance with the usual formalities, and immediately accompanied to a distant marquee of the renowned soldier who led the forces of France.

The general of the enemy received the youthful messenger, surrounded by his principal officers, and by a swarthy band of the native chiefs, who had followed him to the field, with the warriors of their several tribes. Heyward paused short, when, in glancing his eyes rapidly over the dark group of the latter, he beheld the malignant countenance of Magua, regarding him with the calm but sullen attention which marked the expression of that subtle savage. A slight exclamation of surprise even burst from the lips of the young man, but instantly, recollecting his errand, and the presence in which he stood, he suppressed every appearance of emotion, and turned to the hostile leader, who had already advanced a step to receive him.

The marquis of Montcalm was, at the period of which we write, in the flower of his age, and, it may be added, in the zenith of his fortunes. But even in that enviable situation, he was affable, and distinguished as much for his attention to the forms of courtesy, as for that chivalrous courage which, only two short years afterward, induced him to throw away his life on the plains of Abraham. Duncan, in turning his eyes from the malign expression of Magua, suffered them to rest with pleasure on the smiling and polished features, and the noble military air, of the French general.

"Monsieur," said the latter, "j'ai beaucoup de plaisir à—bah! où est cet interpréte?"

"Je crois, monsieur, qu'il ne sear pas nécessaire," Heyward modestly replied; "je parle un peu Français."

"Ah! j'en suis bien aise," said Montcalm, taking Duncan familiarly by the arm, and leading him deep into the marquee, a little out of earshot; "je déteste ces fripons-là; on ne sait jamais sur quel piè on est avec eux. Eh, bien! monsieur," he continued still speaking in French; "though I should have been proud of receiving your commandant, I am very happy that he has seen proper to employ an officer so distinguished, and who, I am sure, is so amiable, as yourself."

Duncan bowed low, pleased with the compliment, in spite of a most heroic determination to suffer no artifice to allure him into forgetfulness of the interest of his prince; and Montcalm, after a pause of a moment, as if to collect his thoughts, proceeded:

"Your commandant is a brave man, and well qualified to repel my assault. Mais, monsieur, is it not time to begin to take more counsel of humanity, and less of your courage? The one as strongly characterizes the hero as the other."

"We consider the qualities as inseparable," returned Duncan, smiling; "but while we find in the vigor of your excellency every motive to stimulate the one, we can, as yet see no particular call for the exercise of the other."

Montcalm, in his turn, slightly bowed, but it was with the air of a man too practiced remembering the language of flattery. After musing a moment, he added:

"It is possible my glasses have deceived me, and that your works resist our cannon better than I had supposed. You know our force?"

"Our accounts vary," said Duncan, carelessly; "the highest, however, has not exceeded twenty thousand men."

The Frenchman bit his lip, and fastened his eyes keenly on the other as if to read his thoughts; then, with a readiness peculiar to himself, he continued, as if assenting to the truth of an enumeration which quite doubled his army:

"It is a poor compliment to the vigilance of us soldiers, monsieur, that, do what we will, we never can conceal our numbers. If it were to be done at all, one would believe it might succeed in these woods. Though you think it too soon to listen to the calls of humanity," he added, smiling archly, "I may be permitted to believe that gallantry is not forgotten by one so young as yourself. The daughters of the commandant, I learn, have passed into the fort since it was invested?"

"It is true, monsieur but, so far from weakening our efforts, they set us an example of courage in their own fortitude. We're nothing but resolution necessary to repel so accomplished a soldier as M. de Montcalm, I would gladly trust the defense of William Henry to the elder of those ladies."

"We have a wise ordinance in our Salique laws, which says, 'The crown of France shall never degrade the lance to the distaff'," said Montcalm, dryly, and with a little hauteur; but instantly adding, with his former frank and easy air: "as all the nobler qualities are hereditary, I can easily credit you; though, as I said before, courage has its limits, and humanity must not be forgotten. I trust, monsieur, you come authorized to treat for the surrender of the place?"

"Has your excellency found our defense so feeble as to believe the measure necessary?"

"I should be sorry to have the defense protracted in such a manner as to irritate my red friends there," continued Montcalm, glancing his eyes at the group of grave and attentive Indians, without attending to the other's questions; "I find it difficult, even now, to limit them to the usages of war."

Heyward was silent for a painful recollection of the dangers he had so recently escaped came over his mind and recalled the images of those defenseless beings who had shared in all his sufferings.

"Ces messieurs-là," said Montcalm, following up the advantage which he conceived he had gained, "are most formidable when baffled; and it is unnecessary to tell you with what difficulty they are restrained in their anger. Eh bien, monsieur! shall we speak of the terms?"

"I fear your excellency has been deceived as to the strength of William Henry, and the resources of its garrison!"

"I have not sat down before Quebec, but an earthen work, that is defended by twenty-three hundred gallant men," was the laconic reply.

"Our mounds are earthen, certainly nor are they seated on the rocks of Cape Diamond; but they stand on that shore which proved so destructive to Dieskau and his army. There is also a powerful force within a few hours' march of us, which we account upon as a part of our means."

"Some six or eight thousand men," returned Montcalm, with much apparent indifference, "whom their leader wisely judges to be safer in their works than in the field."

It was now Heyward's turn to bite his lip with vexation as the other so coolly alluded to a force which the young man knew to be overrated. Both mused a little while in silence, when Montcalm renewed the conversation, in a way that showed he believed the visit of his guest was solely to propose terms of capitulation. On the other hand, Heyward began to throw sundry inducements in the way of the French general, to betray the discoveries he had made through the intercepted letter. The artifice of neither, however, succeeded; and after a protracted and fruitless interview, Duncan took his leave, favorably impressed with an opinion of the courtesy and talents of the enemy's captain, but as ignorant of what he came to learn as when he arrived. Montcalm followed him as far as the entrance of the marquee, renewing his invitations to the commandant of the fort to give him an immediate meeting in the open ground between the two armies.

There they separated, and Duncan returned to the advanced post of the French, accompanied as before; whence he instantly proceeded to the fort, and to the quarters of his own commander

CHAPTER XVI.

"EDG.—Before you fight the battle ope this letter."

—Lear

Major Heyward found Munro attended only by his daughters. Alice sat upon his knee, parting the gray hairs on the forehead of the old man with her delicate fingers; and whenever he affected to frown on her trifling, appeasing his assumed anger by pressing her ruby lips fondly on his wrinkled brow. Cora was seated nigh them, a calm and amused looker-on; regarding the wayward movements of her more youthful sister with that species of maternal fondness which characterized her love for Alice. Not only the dangers through which they had passed, but those which still impended above them, appeared to be momentarily forgotten, in the soothing indulgence of such a family meeting. It seemed as if they had profited by the short truce, to devote an instant to the purest and best affection; the daughters forgetting their fears, and the veteran his cares, in the security of the moment. Of this scene, Duncan, who, in his eagerness to report his arrival, had entered unannounced, stood many moments an unobserved and a delighted spectator. But the quick and dancing eyes of Alice soon caught a glimpse of his figure reflected from a glass and she sprang blushing from her father's knee, exclaiming aloud:

"Major Heyward!"

"What of the lad?" demanded her father; "I have sent him to crack a little with the Frenchman. Ha, sir, you are young, and you're nimble! Away with you, ye baggage; as if there were not troubles enough for a soldier, without having his camp filled with such prattling hussies as yourself!"

Alice laughingly followed her sister, who instantly led the way from an apartment where she perceived their presence was no longer desirable. Munro, instead of demanding the result of the young man's mission, paced the room for a few moments, with his hands behind his back, and his head inclined toward the floor, like a man lost in thought. At length he raised his eyes, glistening with a father's fondness, and exclaimed:

"They are a pair of excellent girls, Heyward, and such as anyone may boast of."

"You are not now to learn my opinion of your daughters, Colonel Munro."

"True, lad, true," interrupted the impatient old man; "you were about opening your mind more fully on that matter the day you got in, but I did not think it becoming in an old soldier to be talking of nuptial blessings and wedding jokes when the enemies of his king were likely to be unbidden guests at the feast. But I was wrong, Duncan, boy, I was wrong there; and I am now ready to hear what you have to say."

"Notwithstanding the pleasure your assurance gives me, dear sir, I have just now, a message from Montcalm..."

"Let the Frenchman and all his host go to the devil, sir!" exclaimed the hasty veteran. "He is not yet master of William Henry, nor shall he ever be, provided Webb proves himself the man he should. No, sir, thank Heaven we are not yet in such a strait that it can be said Munro is too much pressed to discharge the little domestic duties of his own family. Your mother was the only child of my bosom friend, Duncan; and I'll just give you a hearing, though all the knights of

St. Louis were in a body at the sally-port, with the French saint at their head, crying to speak a word under favor. A pretty degree of knighthood, sir, is that which can be bought with sugar hogsheads! and then your two penny marquisates. The thistle is the order for dignity and antiquity; the veritable 'nemo me impune lacessit' of chivalry. Ye had ancestors in that degree, Duncan, and they were an ornament to the nobles of Scotland."

Heyward, who perceived that his superior took a malicious pleasure in exhibiting his contempt for the message of the French general, was fain to humor a spleen that he knew would be short-lived; he therefore, replied with as much indifference as he could assume on such a subject:

"My request, as you know, sir, went so far as to presume to the honor of being your son."

"Ay, boy, you found words to make yourself very plainly comprehended. But, let me ask ye, sir, have you been as intelligible to the girl?"

"On my honor, no," exclaimed Duncan, warmly; "there would have been an abuse of a confided trust, had I taken advantage of my situation for such a purpose."

"Your notions are those of a gentleman, Major Heyward, and well enough in their place. But Cora Munro is a maiden too discreet, and of a mind too elevated and improved, to need the guardianship even of a father."

"Cora!"

"Ay—Cora! we are talking of your pretensions to Miss Munro, are we not, sir?"

"I—I—I was not conscious of having mentioned her name," said Duncan, stammering.

"And to marry whom, then, did you wish my consent, Major Heyward?" demanded the old soldier, erecting himself in the dignity of offended feeling.

"You have another, and not less lovely child."

"Alice!" exclaimed the father, in an astonishment equal to that with which Duncan had just repeated the name of her sister.

"Such was the direction of my wishes, sir."

The young man awaited in silence the result of the extraordinary effect produced by a communication, which, as it now appeared, was so unexpected. For several minutes Munro paced the chamber with long and rapid strides, his rigid features working convulsively, and every faculty seemingly absorbed in the musings of his own mind. At length, he paused directly in front of Heyward and riveting his eyes upon those of the other, he said, with a lip that quivered violently:

"Duncan Heyward, I have loved you for the sake of him whose blood is in your veins; I have loved you for your own good qualities; and I have loved you, because I thought you would contribute to the happiness of my child. But all this love would turn to hatred, were I assured that what I so much apprehend is true."

"God forbid that any act or thought of mine should lead to such a change!" exclaimed the young man, whose eye never quailed under the penetrating look it encountered. Without adverting to the impossibility of the other's comprehending those feelings which were hid in his own bosom, Munro suffered himself to be appeased by the unaltered countenance he met, and with a voice sensibly softened, he continued:

"You would be my son, Duncan, and you're ignorant of the history of the man you wish to call your father. Sit ye down, young man, and I will open to you the wounds of a seared heart, in as few words as may be suitable."

By this time, the message of Montcalm was as much forgotten by him who bore it as by the man for whose ears it was intended. Each drew a chair, and while the veteran communed a few moments with his own thoughts, apparently in sadness, the youth suppressed his impatience in a look and attitude of respectful attention. At length, the former spoke:

"You'll know, already, Major Heyward, that my family was both ancient and honorable," commenced the Scotsman; "though it might not altogether be endowed with that amount of wealth that should correspond with its degree. I was, maybe, such a one as yourself when I plighted my faith to Alice Graham, the only child of a neighboring laird of some estate. But the connection was disagreeable to her father, on more accounts than my poverty. I did, therefore, what an honest man should restored the maiden her troth and departed the country in the service of my king. I had seen many regions and had shed much blood in different lands before duty called me to the islands of the West Indies. There it was my lot to form a connection with one who in time became my wife, and the mother of Cora. She was the daughter of a gentleman of those isles, by a lady whose misfortune it was, if you will," said the old man, proudly, "to be descended, remotely, from that unfortunate class who are so basely enslaved to administer to the wants of a luxurious people. Ay, sir, that is a curse, entailed on Scotland by her unnatural union with a foreign and trading people. But could I find a man among them who would dare to reflect on my child, he should feel the weight of a father's anger! Ha! Major Heyward, you are yourself born at the south, where these unfortunate beings are considered of a race inferior to your own."

"'Tis most unfortunately true, sir," said Duncan, unable any longer to prevent his eyes from sinking to the floor in embarrassment.

"And you cast it on my child as a reproach! You scorn to mingle the blood of the Heywards with one so degraded lovely and virtuous though she be?" fiercely demanded the jealous parent.

"Heaven protect me from a prejudice so unworthy of my reason!" returned Duncan, at the same time conscious of such a feeling, and that as deeply rooted as if it had been ingrafted in his nature. "The sweetness, the beauty, the witchery of your younger daughter, Colonel Munro, might explain my motives without imputing to me this injustice."

"Ye are right, sir," returned the old man, again changing his tones to those of gentleness, or rather softness; "the girl is the image of what her mother was at her years, and before she had become acquainted with grief. When death deprived me of my wife I returned to Scotland, enriched by the marriage; and, would you think it, Duncan! the suffering angel had remained in the heartless state of celibacy twenty long years, and that for the sake of a man who could forget her! She did more, sir; she overlooked my want of faith, and, all difficulties being now removed, she took me for her husband."

"And became the mother of Alice?" exclaimed Duncan, with an eagerness that might have proved dangerous at a moment when the thoughts of Munro were less occupied that at present.

"She did, indeed," said the old man, "and dearly did she pay for the blessing she bestowed. But she is a saint in heaven, sir; and it ill becomes one whose footrests on the grave to mourn a lot so blessed. I had her but a single year, though; a short term of happiness for one who had seen her youth fade in hopeless pining."

There was something so commanding in the distress of the old man, that Heyward did not dare to venture a syllable of consolation. Munro sat utterly unconscious of the other's presence, his features exposed and working with the anguish of his regrets, while heavy tears fell from his eyes, and rolled unheeded from his cheeks to the floor. At length he moved, and as if suddenly recovering his recollection; when he arose, and taking a single turn across the room, he approached his companion with an air of military grandeur, and demanded:

"Have you not, Major Heyward, some communication that I should hear from the marquis de Montcalm?"

Duncan started in his turn, and immediately commenced in an embarrassed voice, the half-forgotten message. It is unnecessary to dwell upon the evasive though polite manner with which the French general had eluded every attempt of Heyward to worm from him the purport of the communication he had proposed making, or on the decided, though still polished message, by which he now gave his enemy to understand, that, unless he chose to receive it in person, he should not receive it at all. As Munro listened to the detail of Duncan, the excited feelings of the father gradually gave way before the obligations of his station, and when the other was done, he saw before him nothing but the veteran, swelling with the wounded feelings of a soldier.

"You have said enough, Major Heyward," exclaimed the angry old man; "enough to make a volume of commentary on French civility. Here has this gentleman invited me to a conference, and when I send him a capable substitute, for ye're all that, Duncan, though your years are but few, he answers me with a riddle."

"He may have thought less favorably of the substitute, my dear sir; and you will remember that the invitation, which he now repeats, was to the commandant of the works, and not to his second."

"Well, sir, is not a substitute clothed with all the power and dignity of him who grants the commission? He wishes to confer with Munro! Faith, sir, I have much inclination to indulge the man, if it should only be to let him behold the firm countenance we maintain in spite of his numbers and his summons. There might be not bad policy in such a stroke, young man."

Duncan, who believed it of the last importance that they should speedily come to the contents of the letter borne by the scout, gladly encouraged this idea.

"Without doubt, he could gather no confidence by witnessing our indifference," he said.

"You never said truer word. I could wish, sir, that he would visit the works in open day, and in the form of a storming party; that is the least failing method of proving the countenance of an enemy and would be far preferable to the battering system he has chosen. The beauty and manliness of warfare has been much deformed, Major Heyward, by the arts of your Monsieur Vauban. Our ancestors were far above such scientific cowardice!"

"It may be very true, sir; but we are now obliged to repel art by art. What is your pleasure in the matter of the interview?"

"I will meet the Frenchman, and that without fear or delay; promptly, sir, as becomes a servant of my royal master. Go, Major Heyward, and give them a flourish of the music; and send out a messenger to let them know who is coming. We will follow with a small guard, for such respect is due to one who holds the honor of his king in keeping; and hark'ee, Duncan," he added, in a half whisper, though they were alone, "it may be prudent to have some aid at hand, in case there should be treachery at the bottom of it all."

The young man availed himself of this order to quit the apartment; and, as the day was fast coming to a close, he hastened without delay, to make the necessary arrangements. A very few minutes only were necessary to parade a few files, and to dispatch an orderly with a flag to announce the approach of the commandant of the fort. When Duncan had done both these, he led the guard to the sally-port, near which he found his superior ready, waiting his appearance. As soon as the usual ceremonials of a military departure were observed, the veteran and his more youthful companion left the fortress, attended by the escort.

They had proceeded only a hundred yards from the works, when the little array which attended the French general to the conference was seen issuing from the hollow way which formed the bed of a brook that ran between the batteries of the besiegers and the fort.

From the moment that Munro left his own works to appear in front of his enemy's, his air had been grand, and his step and countenance highly military. The instant he caught a glimpse of the white plume that waved in the hat of Montcalm, his eye lighted, and age no longer appeared to possess any influence over his vast and still muscular person.

"Speak to the boys to be watchful, sir," he said, in an undertone, to Duncan; "and to look well to their flints and steel, for one is never safe with a servant of these Louis's; at the same time, we shall show them the front of men in deep security. Ye'll understand me, Major Heyward!"

He was interrupted by the clamor of a drum from the approaching Frenchmen, which was immediately answered, when each party pushed an orderly in advance, bearing a white flag, and the wary Scotsman halted with his guard close at his back. As soon as this slight salutation had passed, Montcalm moved toward them with a quick but graceful step, baring his head to the veteran, and dropping his spotless plume nearly to the earth in courtesy. If the air of Munro was more commanding and manly, it wanted both the ease and insinuating polish of that of the Frenchman. Neither spoke for a few moments, each regarding the other with curious and interested eyes. Then, as became his superior rank and the nature of the interview, Montcalm broke the silence. After uttering the usual words of greeting, he turned to Duncan, and continued, with a smile of recognition, speaking always in French:

"I am rejoiced, monsieur, that you have given us the pleasure of your company on this occasion. There will be no necessity to employ an ordinary interpreter; for, in your hands, I feel the same security as if I spoke your language myself."

Duncan acknowledged the compliment, when Montcalm, turning to his guard, which in imitation of that of their enemies, pressed close upon him, continued:

"En arriere, mes enfants, il fait chaud...retirez-vous un peu."

Before Major Heyward would imitate this proof of confidence, he glanced his eyes around the plain, and beheld with uneasiness the numerous dusky groups of savages, who looked out from the margin of the surrounding woods, curious spectators of the interview.

"Monsieur de Montcalm will readily acknowledge the difference in our situation," he said, with some embarrassment, pointing at the same time toward those dangerous foes, who were to be seen in almost every direction. "Were we to dismiss our guard, we should stand here at the mercy of our enemies."

"Monsieur, you have the plighted faith of 'un gentilhomme Français', for your safety," returned Montcalm, laying his hand impressively on his heart; "it should suffice."

"It shall. Fall back," Duncan added to the officer who led the escort; "fall back, sir, beyond hearing, and wait for orders."

Munro witnessed this movement with manifest uneasiness; nor did he fail to demand an instant explanation.

"Is it not our interest, sir, to betray no distrust?" retorted Duncan. "Monsieur de Montcalm pledges his word for our safety, and I have ordered the men to withdraw a little, in order to prove how much we depend on his assurance."

"It may be all right, sir, but I have no overweening reliance on the faith of these marquesses, or marquis, as they call themselves. Their patents of nobility are too common to be certain that they bear the seal of true honor."

"You forget, dear sir, that we confer with an officer, distinguished alike in Europe and America for his deeds. From a soldier of his reputation, we can have nothing to apprehend."

The old man made a gesture of resignation, though his rigid features still betrayed his obstinate adherence to a distrust, which he derived from a sort of hereditary contempt of his enemy, rather than from any present signs which might warrant so uncharitable a feeling. Montcalm waited patiently until this little dialogue in demi-voice was ended, when he drew nigher, and opened the subject of their conference.

"I have solicited this interview from your superior, monsieur," he said, "because I believe he will allow himself to be persuaded that he has already done everything which is necessary for the honor of his prince and will now listen to the admonitions of humanity. I will forever bear testimony that his resistance has been gallant and was continued as long as there was hope."

When this opening was translated to Munro, he answered with dignity, but with sufficient courtesy:

"However, I may prize such testimony from Monsieur Montcalm, it will be more valuable when it shall be better merited."

The French general smiled, as Duncan gave him the purport of this reply, and observed:

"What is now so freely accorded to approved courage, may be refused to useless obstinacy. Monsieur would wish to see my camp, and witness for himself our numbers, and the impossibility of his resisting them with success?"

"I know that the king of France is well served," returned the unmoved Scotsman, as soon as Duncan ended his translation; "but my own royal master has as many and as faithful troops."

"Though not at hand, fortunately for us," said Montcalm, without waiting, in his ardor, for the interpreter. "There is a destiny in war, to which a brave man knows how to submit with the same courage that he faces his foes."

"Had I been conscious that Monsieur Montcalm was master of the English, I should have spared myself the trouble of so awkward a translation," said the vexed Duncan, dryly, remembering instantly his recent by-play with Munro.

"Your pardon, monsieur," rejoined the Frenchman, suffering a slight color to appear on his dark cheek. "There is a vast difference between understanding and speaking a foreign tongue; you will, therefore, please to assist me still." Then, after a short pause, he added; "These hills afford us every opportunity of reconnoitering your works, messieurs and I am possibly as well acquainted with their weak condition as you can be yourselves."

"Ask the French general if his glasses can reach to the Hudson," said Munro, proudly; "and if he knows when and where to expect the army of Webb."

"Let General Webb be his own interpreter," returned the politic Montcalm, suddenly extending an open letter toward Munro as he spoke; "you will there learn, monsieur, that his movements are not likely to prove embarrassing to my army."

The veteran seized the offered paper, without waiting for Duncan to translate the speech, and with an eagerness that betrayed how important he deemed its contents. As his eye passed hastily over the words, his countenance changed from its look of military pride to one of deep chagrin; his lip began to quiver and suffering the paper to fall from his hand, his head dropped upon his chest, like that of a man whose hopes were withered at a single blow. Duncan caught the letter from the ground, and without apology for the liberty he took, he read at a glance its cruel purport. Their common superior, so far from encouraging them to resist, advised a speedy surrender, urging in the plainest language, as a reason, the utter impossibility of his sending a single man to their rescue.

"Here is no deception!" exclaimed Duncan, examining the billet both inside and out; "this is the signature of Webb, and must be the captured letter."

"The man has betrayed me!" Munro at length bitterly exclaimed; "he has brought dishonor to the door of one where disgrace was never before known to dwell and shame has, he heaped heavily on my gray hairs."

"Say not so," cried Duncan; "we are yet masters of the fort, and of our honor. Let us, then, sell our lives at such a rate as shall make our enemies believe the purchase too dear."

"Boy, I thank thee," exclaimed the old man, rousing himself from his stupor; "you have, for once, reminded Munro of his duty. We will go back and dig our graves behind those ramparts."

"Messieurs," said Montcalm, advancing toward them a step, in generous interest, "you little know Louis de St. Veran if you believe him capable of profiting by this letter to humble brave men, or to build up a dishonest reputation for himself. Listen to my terms before you leave me."

"What says the Frenchman?" demanded the veteran, sternly; "does he make a merit of having captured a scout, with a note from headquarters? Sir, he had better raise this siege, to go and sit down before Edward if he wishes to frighten his enemy with words."

Duncan explained the other's meaning.

"Monsieur de Montcalm, we will hear you," the veteran added, more calmly, as Duncan ended.

"To retain the fort is now impossible," said his liberal enemy; "it is necessary to the interests of my master that it should be destroyed but as for yourselves and your brave comrades, there is no privilege dear to a soldier that shall be denied."

"Our colors?" demanded Heyward.

"Carry them to England and show them to your king."

"Our arms?"

"Keep them; none can use them better."

"Our march; the surrender of the place?"

"Shall all be done in a way most honorable to yourselves."

Duncan now turned to explain these proposals to his commander, who heard him with amazement, and a sensibility that was deeply touched by so unusual and unexpected generosity.

"Go you, Duncan," he said; "go with this marquess, as, indeed, marquess he should be, go to his marquee and arrange it all. I have lived to see two things in my old age that never did I expect to behold. An Englishman afraid to support a friend, and a Frenchman too honest to profit by his advantage."

So, saying, the veteran again dropped his head to his chest, and returned slowly toward the fort, exhibiting, by the dejection of his air, to the anxious garrison, a harbinger of evil tidings.

From the shock of this unexpected blow the haughty feelings of Munro never recovered but from that moment there commenced a change in his determined character, which accompanied him to a speedy grave. Duncan remained to settle the terms of the capitulation. He was seen to re-enter the works during the first watches of the night, and immediately after a private conference with the commandant, to leave them again. It was then openly announced that hostilities must cease, Munro having signed a treaty by which the place was to be yielded to the enemy, with the morning; the garrison to retain their arms, the colors, and their baggage, and, consequently, according to military opinion, their honor.

CHAPTER XVII.

"Weave we the woof.
The thread is spun.
The web is wove.
The work is done."—Gray

The hostile armies, which lay in the wilds of the Horican, passed the night of the ninth of August 1757, much in the manner they would, had they encountered on the fairest field of Europe. While the conquered were still, sullen, and dejected, the victors triumphed. But there are limits alike to grief and joy; and long before the watches of the morning came the stillness of those boundless woods was only broken by a gay call from some exulting young Frenchman of the advanced pickets, or a menacing challenge from the fort, which sternly forbade the approach of any hostile footsteps before the stipulated moment. Even these occasional threatening sounds ceased to be heard in that dull hour which precedes the day, at which period a listener might have sought in vain any evidence of the presence of those armed powers that then slumbered on the shores of the "holy lake."

It was during these moments of deep silence that the canvas which concealed the entrance to a spacious marquee in the French encampment was shoved aside, and a man issued from beneath the drapery into the open air. He was enveloped in a cloak that might have been intended as a protection from the chilling damps of the woods, but which served equally well as a mantle to conceal his person. He was permitted to pass the grenadier, who watched over the slumbers of the French commander, without interruption, the man making the usual salute which betokens military deference, as the other passed swiftly through the little city of tents, in the direction of William Henry. Whenever this unknown individual encountered one of the numberless sentinels who crossed his path, his answer was prompt, and, as it appeared, satisfactory; for he was uniformly allowed to proceed without further interrogation.

With the exception of such repeated but brief interruptions, he had moved silently from the center of the camp to its most advanced outposts, when he drew nigh the soldier who held his watch nearest to the works of the enemy. As he approached, he was received with the usual challenge:

"Qui vive?"

"France," was the reply.

"Le mot d'ordre?"

"La victorie," said the other, drawing so nigh as to be heard in a loud whisper.

"C'est bien," returned the sentinel, throwing his musket from the charge to his shoulder; "vous promenez bien matin, monsieur!"

"Il est necessaire d'être vigilant, mon enfant," the other observed, dropping a fold of his cloak, and looking the soldier close in the face as he passed him, still continuing his way toward the British fortification. The man started; his arms rattled heavily as he threw them forward in the lowest and most respectful salute; and when he had again recovered his piece, he turned to walk his post, muttering between his teeth:

"Il faut être vigilant, en vérité! je crois que nous avons là, un caporal qui ne dort jamais!"

The officer proceeded, without affecting to hear the words which escaped the sentinel in his surprise; nor did he again pause until he had reached the low strand, and in a somewhat dangerous vicinity to the western water bastion of the fort. The light of an obscure moon was just sufficient to render objects, though dim, perceptible in their outlines. He, therefore, took the precaution to place himself against the trunk of a tree, where he leaned for many minutes, and seemed to contemplate the dark and silent mounds of the English works in profound attention. His gaze at the ramparts was not that of a curious or idle spectator; but his looks wandered from point to point, denoting his knowledge of military usages, and betraying that his search was not unaccompanied by distrust. At length he appeared satisfied; and having cast his eyes impatiently upward toward the summit of the eastern mountain, as if anticipating the approach of the morning, he was in the act of turning on his footsteps, when a light sound on the nearest angle of the bastion caught his ear and induced him to remain.

Just then a figure was seen to approach the edge of the rampart, where it stood, apparently contemplating in its turn the distant tents of the French encampment. Its head was then turned toward the east, as though equally anxious for the appearance of light, when the form leaned against the mound, and seemed to gaze upon the glassy expanse of the waters, which, like a submarine firmament, glittered with its thousand mimic stars. The melancholy air, the hour, together with the vast frame of the man who thus leaned, musing, against the English ramparts, left no doubt as to his person in the mind of the observant spectator. Delicacy, no less than prudence, now urged him to retire; and he had moved cautiously round the body of the tree for that purpose, when another sound drew his attention, and once more arrested his footsteps. It was a low and almost inaudible movement of the water and was succeeded by a grating of pebbles one against the other. In a moment he saw a dark form rise, as it were, out of the lake, and steal without further noise to the land, within a few feet of the place where he himself stood. A rifle next slowly rose between his eyes and the watery mirror; but before it could be discharged his own hand was on the lock.

"Hugh!" exclaimed the savage, whose treacherous aim was so singularly and so unexpectedly interrupted.

Without making any reply, the French officer laid his hand on the shoulder of the Indian and led him in profound silence to a distance from the spot, where their subsequent dialogue might have proved dangerous, and where it seemed that one of them, at least, sought a victim. Then throwing open his cloak, so as to expose his uniform and the cross of St. Louis, which was suspended at his breast, Montcalm sternly demanded:

"What means this? Does not my son know that the hatchet is buried between the English and his Canadian Father?"

"What can the Hurons do?" returned the savage, speaking also, though imperfectly, in the French language.

"Not a warrior has a scalp, and the pale faces make friends!"

"Ha, Le Renard Subtil! Methinks this is an excess of zeal for a friend who was so late an enemy! How many suns have set since Le Renard struck the war-post of the English?"

"Where is that sun?" demanded the sullen savage. "Behind the hill; and it is dark and cold. But when he comes again, it will be bright and warm. Le Subtil is the sun of his tribe. There have been clouds, and many mountains between him and his nation but now he shines, and it is a clear sky!"

"That Le Renard has power with his people, I well know," said Montcalm; "for yesterday he hunted for their scalps, and to-day they hear him at the council-fire."

"Magua is a great chief."

"Let him prove it, by teaching his nation how to conduct themselves toward our new friends."

"Why did the chief of the Canadas bring his young men into the woods and fire his cannon at the earthen house?" demanded the subtle Indian.

"To subdue it. My master owns the land, and your father was ordered to drive off these English squatters. They have consented to go, and now he calls them enemies no longer."

"'Tis well. Magua took the hatchet to color it with blood. It is now bright; when it is red, it shall be buried."

"But Magua is pledged not to sully the lilies of France. The enemies of the great king across the salt lake are his enemies; his friends, the friends of the Hurons."

"Friends!" repeated the Indian in scorn. "Let his father give Magua a hand."

Montcalm, who felt that his influence over the warlike tribes he had gathered was to be maintained by concession rather than by power, complied reluctantly with the other's request. The savage placed the fingers of the French commander on a deep scar in his bosom, and then exultingly demanded:

"Does my father know that?"

"What warrior does not? 'Tis where a leaden bullet has cut."

"And this?" continued the Indian, who had turned his naked back to the other, his body being without its usual calico mantle.

"This! my son has been sadly injured here; who has done this?"

"Magua slept hard in the English wigwams, and the sticks have left their mark," returned the savage, with a hollow laugh, which did not conceal the fierce temper that nearly choked him. Then, recollecting himself, with sudden and native dignity, he added: "Go; teach your young men it is peace. Le Renard Subtil knows how to speak to a Huron warrior."

Without deigning to bestow further words, or to wait for any answer, the savage cast his rifle into the hollow of his arm, and moved silently through the encampment toward the woods where his own tribe was known to lie. Every few yards as he proceeded, he was challenged by the sentinels; but he stalked sullenly onward, utterly disregarding the summons of the soldiers, who only spared his life because they knew the air and tread no less than the obstinate daring of an Indian.

Montcalm lingered long and melancholy on the strand where he had been left by his companion, brooding deeply on the temper which his ungovernable ally had just discovered. Already had his fair fame been tarnished by one horrid scene, and in circumstances fearfully resembling those under which he now found himself. As he mused, he became keenly sensible of the deep responsibility they assume who disregard the means to attain the end, and of all the danger of setting in motion an engine which it exceeds human power to control. Then shaking off a train of reflections that he accounted a weakness in such a moment of triumph, he retraced his steps toward his tent, giving the order as he passed to make the signal that should arouse the army from its slumbers.

The first tap of the French drums was echoed from the bosom of the fort, and presently the valley was filled with the strains of martial music, rising long, thrilling, and lively above the rattling accompaniment. The horns of the victors sounded merry and cheerful flourishes, until the last laggard of the camp was at his post; but the instant the British fifes had blown their shrill signal, they became mute. In the meantime, the day had dawned, and when the line of the French army was ready to receive its general, the rays of a brilliant sun were glancing along the glittering array.

Then that success, which was already so well known, was officially announced; the favored band who were selected to guard the gates of the fort were detailed and defiled before their chief; the signal of their approach was given, and all the usual preparations for a change of masters were ordered and executed directly under the guns of the contested works.

A very different scene presented itself within the lines of the Anglo-American army. As soon as the warning signal was given, it exhibited all the signs of a hurried and forced departure. The sullen soldiers shouldered their empty tubes and fell into their places, like men whose blood had been heated by the past contest, and who only desired the opportunity to revenge an indignity which was still wounding to their pride, concealed as it was under the observances of military etiquette.

Women and children ran from place to place, some bearing the scanty remnants of their baggage, and others searching in the ranks for those countenances they looked up to for protection.

Munro appeared among his silent troops firm but dejected. It was evident that the unexpected blow had struck deep into his heart, though he struggled to sustain his misfortune with the port of a man.

Duncan was touched at the quiet and impressive exhibition of his grief. He had discharged his own duty, and he now pressed to the side of the old man, to know in what particular he might serve him.

"My daughters," was the brief but expressive reply.

"Good heavens! are not arrangements already made for their convenience?"

"Today I am only a soldier, Major Heyward," said the veteran. "All that you see here, claim alike to be my children."

Duncan had heard enough. Without losing one of those moments which had now become so precious, he flew toward the quarters of Munro, in quest of the sisters. He found them on the threshold of the low edifice, already prepared to depart, and surrounded by a clamorous and weeping assemblage of their own sex, that had gathered about the place, with a sort of instinctive consciousness that it was the point most likely to be protected. Though the cheeks of Cora were pale and her countenance anxious, she had lost none of her firmness; but the eyes of Alice were inflamed and betrayed how long and bitterly she had wept. They both, however, received the young man with undisguised pleasure; the former, for a novelty, being the first to speak.

"The fort is lost," she said, with a melancholy smile; "though our good name, I trust, remains."

"'Tis brighter than ever. But dearest Miss Munro, it is time to think less of others, and to make some provision for yourself. Military usage pride that pride on which you so much value yourself, demands that your father and I should for a little while continue with the troops. Then where to seek a proper protector for you against the confusion and chances of such a scene?"

"None is necessary," returned Cora; "who will dare to injure or insult the daughter of such a father, at a time like this?"

"I would not leave you alone," continued the youth, looking about him in a hurried manner, "for the command of the best regiment in the pay of the king. Remember, our Alice is not gifted with all your firmness, and God only knows the terror she might endure."

"You may be right," Cora replied, smiling again, but far more sadly than before. "Listen! chance has already sent us a friend when he is most needed."

Duncan did listen, and on the instant comprehended her meaning. The low and serious sounds of the sacred music, so well-known to the eastern provinces, caught his ear, and instantly drew him to an apartment in an adjacent building, which had already been deserted by its customary tenants. There he found David, pouring out his pious feelings through the only medium in which he ever indulged. Duncan waited, until, by the cessation of the movement of the hand, he believed the strain was ended, when, by touching his shoulder, he drew the attention of the other to himself, and in a few words explained his wishes.

"Even so," replied the single-minded disciple of the King of Israel, when the young man had ended; "I have found much that is comely and melodious in the maidens, and it is fitting that we who have consorted in so much peril, should abide together in peace. I will attend them, when I have completed my morning praise, to which nothing is now wanting but the doxology. Wilt thou bear a part, friend? The meter is common, and the tune 'South well'."

Then, extending the little volume, and giving the pitch of the air anew with considerate attention, David recommenced and finished his strains, with a fixedness of manner that it was not easy to interrupt. Heyward was fain to wait until the verse was ended; when, seeing David relieving himself from the spectacles and replacing the book, he continued.

"It will be your duty to see that none dare to approach the ladies with any rude intention, or to offer insult or taunt at the misfortune of their brave father. In this task you will be seconded by the domestics of their household."

"Even so."

"It is possible that the Indians and stragglers of the enemy may intrude, in which case you will remind them of the terms of the capitulation and threaten to report their conduct to Montcalm. A word will suffice."

"If not, I have that here which shall," returned David, exhibiting his book, with an air in which meekness and confidence were singularly blended. Here are words which, uttered, or rather thundered, with proper emphasis, and in measured time, shall quiet the unruliest temper:

"'Why rage the heathen furiously'?"

"Enough," said Heyward, interrupting the burst of his musical invocation; "we understand each other; it is time that we should now assume our respective duties."

Gamut cheerfully assented, and together they sought the females. Cora received her new and somewhat extraordinary protector courteously, at least; and even the pallid features of Alice lighted again with some of their native archness as she thanked Heyward for his care. Duncan took occasion to assure them he had done the best that circumstances permitted, and, as he believed, quite enough for the security of their feelings; of danger there was none. He then spoke gladly of his intention to rejoin them the moment he had led the advance a few miles toward the Hudson, and immediately took his leave.

By this time the signal for departure had been given, and the head of the English column was in motion. The sisters started at the sound, and glancing their eyes around, they saw the white uniforms of the French grenadiers, who had already taken possession of the gates of the fort. At that moment an enormous cloud seemed to pass suddenly above their heads, and, looking upward, they discovered that they stood beneath the wide folds of the standard of France.

"Let us go," said Cora; "this is no longer a fit place for the children of an English officer."

Alice clung to the arm of her sister, and together they left the parade, accompanied by the moving throng that surrounded them.

As they passed the gates, the French officers, who had learned their rank, bowed often and low, forbearing, however, to intrude those attentions which they saw, with peculiar tact, might not be agreeable. As every vehicle and each beast of burden was occupied by the sick and wounded, Cora had decided to endure the fatigues of a foot march, rather than interfere with their comforts. Indeed, many a maimed and feeble soldier was compelled to drag his exhausted limbs in the rear of the columns, for the want of the necessary means of conveyance in that wilderness. The whole, however, was in motion; the weak and wounded, groaning and in suffering; their comrades silent and sullen; and the women and children in terror, they knew not of what.

As the confused and timid throng left the protecting mounds of the fort, and issued on the open plain, the whole scene was at once presented to their eyes. At a little distance on the right, and somewhat in the rear, the French army stood to their arms, Montcalm having collected his parties, so soon as his guards had possession of the works. They were attentive but silent observers of the proceedings of the vanquished, failing in none of the stipulated military honors, and offering no taunt or insult, in their success, to their less fortunate foes. Living masses of the English, to the amount, in the whole, of near three thousand, were moving slowly across the plain, toward the common center, and gradually approached each other, as they converged to the point of their march, a vista cut through the lofty trees, where the road to the Hudson entered the forest. Along the sweeping borders of the woods hung a dark cloud of savages, eyeing the passage of their enemies and hovering at a distance, like vultures who were only kept from swooping on their prey by the presence and restraint of a superior army. A few had straggled among the conquered columns, where they stalked in sullen discontent; attentive, though, as yet passive observers of the moving multitude.

The advance, with Heyward at its head, had already reached the defile, and was slowly disappearing, when the attention of Cora was drawn to a collection of stragglers by the sounds of contention. A truant provincial was paying the forfeit of his disobedience, by being plundered of those very effects which had caused him to desert his place in the ranks. The man was of powerful frame, and too avaricious to part with his goods without a struggle. Individuals from either party interfered; the one side to prevent and the other to aid in the robbery. Voices grew loud and angry, and a hundred savages appeared, as it were, by magic, where a dozen only had been seen a minute before. It was then that Cora saw the form of Magua gliding among his countrymen and speaking with his fatal and artful eloquence. The mass of women and children stopped and hovered together like alarmed and fluttering birds. But the cupidity of the Indian was soon gratified, and the different bodies again moved slowly onward.

The savages now fell back, and seemed content to let their enemies advance without further molestation. But, as the female crowd approached them, the gaudy colors of a shawl attracted the eyes of a wild and untutored Huron. He advanced to seize it without the least hesitation. The woman, more in terror than through love of the ornament, wrapped her child in the coveted article, and folded both more closely to her bosom. Cora was in the act of speaking, with an intent to advise the woman to abandon the trifle, when the savage relinquished his hold of the shawl, and tore the screaming infant from her arms. Abandoning everything to the greedy grasp of those around her, the mother darted, with distraction in her mien, to reclaim her child. The Indian smiled grimly, and extended one hand, in sign of a willingness to exchange, while, with the other, he flourished the babe over his head, holding it by the feet as if to enhance the value of the ransom.

"Here...here...there...all...any...everything!" exclaimed the breathless woman, tearing the lighter articles of dress from her person with ill-directed and trembling fingers; "take all, but give me my babe!"

The savage spurned the worthless rags and perceiving that the shawl had already become a prize to another, his bantering but sullen smile changing to a gleam of ferocity, he dashed the head of the infant against a rock, and cast its quivering remains to her very feet. For an instant the mother stood, like a statue of despair, looking wildly down at the unseemly object, which had so lately nestled in her bosom and smiled in her face; and then she raised her eyes and countenance toward heaven, as if calling on God to curse the perpetrator of the foul deed. She was spared the sin of such a prayer for, maddened at his disappointment, and excited at the sight of blood, the Huron mercifully drove his tomahawk into her own brain. The mother sank under the blow, and fell, grasping at her child, in death, with the same engrossing love that had caused her to cherish it when living.

At that dangerous moment, Magua placed his hands to his mouth, and raised the fatal and appalling whoop. The scattered Indians started at the well-known cry, as coursers bound at the signal to quit the goal; and directly there arose such a yell along the plain, and through the arches of the wood, as seldom burst from human lips before. They who heard it listened with a curdling horror at the heart, little inferior to that dread which may be expected to attend the blasts of the final summons.

More than two thousand raving savages broke from the forest at the signal and threw themselves across the fatal plain with instinctive alacrity. We shall not dwell on the revolting horrors that succeeded. Death was everywhere, and in his most terrific and disgusting aspects. Resistance only served to inflame the murderers, who inflicted their furious blows long after their victims were beyond the power of their resentment. The flow of blood might be likened to the outbreaking of a torrent; and as the natives became heated and maddened by the sight, many among them even kneeled to the earth, and drank freely, exultingly, hellishly, of the crimson tide.

The trained bodies of the troops threw themselves quickly into solid masses, endeavoring to awe their assailants by the imposing appearance of a military front. The experiment in some measure succeeded, though far too many suffered their unloaded muskets to be torn from their hands, in the vein hope of appeasing the savages.

In such a scene none had leisure to note the fleeting moments. It might have been ten minutes (it seemed an age) that the sisters had stood riveted to one spot, horror-stricken and nearly helpless. When the first blow was struck, their screaming companions had pressed upon them in a body, rendering flight impossible; and now that fear or death had scattered most, if not all, from around them, they saw no avenue open, but such as conducted to the tomahawks of their foes. On every side arose shrieks, groans, exhortations, and curses. At this moment, Alice caught a glimpse of the vast form of her father, moving rapidly across the plain, in the direction of the French army. He was, in truth, proceeding to Montcalm, fearless of every danger, to claim the tardy escort for which he had before conditioned. Fifty glittering axes and barbed spears were offered unheeded at his life, but the savages respected his rank and calmness, even in their fury. The dangerous weapons were brushed aside by the still nervous arm of the veteran, or fell of themselves, after menacing an act that it would seem no one had courage to perform. Fortunately, the vindictive Magua was searching for his victim in the very band the veteran had just quitted.

"Father...father...we are here!" shrieked Alice, as he passed, at no great distance, without appearing to heed them. "Come to us, father, or we die!"

The cry was repeated, and in terms and tones that might have melted a heart of stone, but it was unanswered. Once, indeed, the old man appeared to catch the sound, for he paused and listened, but Alice had dropped senseless on the earth, and Cora had sunk at her side, hovering in untiring tenderness over her lifeless form. Munro shook his head in disappointment, and proceeded, bent on the high duty of his station.

"Lady," said Gamut, who, helpless and useless as he was, had not yet dreamed of deserting his trust, "it is the jubilee of the devils, and this is not a meet place for Christians to tarry in. Let us up and fly."

"Go," said Cora, still gazing at her unconscious sister; "save thyself. To me thou canst not be of further use."

David comprehended the unyielding character of her resolution, by the simple but expressive gesture that accompanied her words. He gazed for a moment at the dusky forms that were acting their hellish rites on every side of him, and his tall person grew more erect while his chest heaved, and every feature swelled, and seemed to speak with the power of the feelings by which he was governed.

"If the Jewish boy might tame the great spirit of Saul by the sound of his harp, and the words of sacred song, it may not be amiss," he said, "to try the potency of music here."

Then raising his voice to its highest tone, he poured out a strain so powerful as to be heard even amid the din of that bloody field. More than one savage rushed toward them, thinking to rifle the unprotected sisters of their attire, and bear away their scalps but when they found this strange and unmoved figure riveted to his post, they paused to listen. Astonishment soon changed to admiration, and they passed on to other and less courageous victims, openly expressing their satisfaction at the firmness with which the white warrior sang his death song. Encouraged and deluded by his success, David exerted all his powers to extend what he believed so holy an influence. The unwonted sounds caught the ears of a distant savage, who flew raging from group to group, like one who, scorning to touch the vulgar herd, hunted for some victim more worthy of his renown. It was Magua, who uttered a yell of pleasure when he beheld his ancient prisoners again at his mercy.

"Come," he said, laying his soiled hands on the dress of Cora, "the wigwam of the Huron is still open. Is it not better than this place?"

"Away!" cried Cora, veiling her eyes from his revolting aspect.

The Indian laughed tauntingly, as he held up his reeking hand, and answered: "It is red, but it comes from white veins!"

"Monster! there is blood, oceans of blood, upon thy soul; thy spirit has moved this scene."

"Magua is a great chief!" returned the exulting savage, "will the dark-hair go to his tribe?"

"Never! strike if thou wilt and complete thy revenge." He hesitated a moment, and then catching the light and senseless form of Alice in his arms, the subtle Indian moved swiftly across the plain toward the woods.

"Hold!" shrieked Cora, following wildly on his footsteps; "release the child! wretch! what isn't you do?"

But Magua was deaf to her voice; or, rather, he knew his power, and was determined to maintain it.

"Stay...lady...stay," called Gamut, after the unconscious Cora. "The holy charm is beginning to be felt, and soon shalt thou see this horrid tumult stilled."

Perceiving that, in his turn, he was unheeded, the faithful David followed the distracted sister, raising his voice again in sacred song, and sweeping the air to the measure, with his long arm, in diligent accompaniment. In this manner they traversed the plain, through the flying, the wounded, and the dead. The fierce Huron was, at any time, sufficient for himself and the victim that he bore; though Cora would have fallen more than once under the blows of her savage enemies, but for the extraordinary being who stalked in her rear, and who now appeared to the astonished natives gifted with the protecting spirit of madness.

Magua, who knew how to avoid the more pressing dangers, and also to elude pursuit, entered the woods through a low ravine, where he quickly found the Narragansetts, which the travelers had abandoned so shortly before, awaiting his appearance, in custody of a savage as fierce and malign in his expression as himself. Laying Alice on one of the horses, he made a sign to Cora to mount the other.

Notwithstanding the horror excited by the presence of her captor, there was a present relief in escaping from the bloody scene enacting on the plain, to which Cora could not be altogether insensible. She took her seat, and held forth her arms for her sister, with an air of entreaty and love that even the Huron could not deny. Placing Alice, then, on the same animal with Cora, he seized the bridle, and commenced his route by plunging deeper into the forest. David, perceiving that he was left alone, utterly disregarded as a subject too worthless even to destroy, threw his long limb across the saddle of the beast they had deserted, and made such progress in the pursuit as the difficulties of the path permitted.

They soon began to ascend; but as the motion had a tendency to revive the dormant faculties of her sister, the attention of Cora was too much divided between the tenderest solicitude in her behalf, and in listening to the cries which were still too audible on the plain, to note the direction in which they journeyed. When, however, they gained the flattened surface of the mountain-top, and approached the eastern precipice, she recognized the spot to which she had once before been led under the more friendly auspices of the scout. Here Magua suffered them to dismount; and notwithstanding their own captivity, the curiosity which seems inseparable from horror, induced them to gaze at the sickening sight below.

The cruel work was still unchecked. On every side the captured were flying before their relentless persecutors, while the armed columns of the Christian king stood fast in an apathy which has never been explained, and which has left an immovable blot on the otherwise fair escutcheon of their leader. Nor was the sword of death stayed until cupidity got the mastery of revenge. Then, indeed, the shrieks of the wounded, and the yells of their murderers grew less frequent, until, finally, the cries of horror were lost to their ear, or were drowned in the loud, long, and piercing whoops of the triumphant savage

CHAPTER XVIII.

"Why, anything;
An honorable murderer, if you will;
For naught I did in hate, but all in honor."
—Othello

The bloody and inhuman scene rather incidentally mentioned than described in the preceding chapter, is conspicuous in the pages of colonial history by the merited title of "The Massacre of William Henry." It so far deepened the stain which a previous and very similar event had left upon the reputation of the French commander that it was not entirely erased by his early and glorious death. It is now becoming obscured by time; and thousands, who know that Montcalm died like a hero on the plains of Abraham, have yet to learn how much he was deficient in that moral courage without which no man can be truly great. Pages might yet be written to prove, from this illustrious example, the defects of human excellence; to show how easy it is for generous sentiments, high courtesy, and chivalrous courage to lose their influence beneath the chilling blight of selfishness, and to exhibit to the world a man who was great in all the minor attributes of character, but who was found wanting when it became necessary to prove how much principle is superior to policy. But the task would exceed our prerogatives; and, as history, like love, is so apt to surround her heroes with an atmosphere of imaginary brightness, it is probable that Louis de Saint Veran will be viewed by posterity only as the gallant defender of his country, while his cruel apathy on the shores of the Oswego and of the Horican will be forgotten. Deeply regretting this weakness on the part of a sister muse, we shall at once retire from her sacred precincts, within the proper limits of our own humble vocation.

The third day from the capture of the fort was drawing to a close, but the business of the narrative must still detain the reader on the shores of the "holy lake." When last seen, the environs of the works were filled with violence and uproar. They were now possessed by stillness and death. The blood-stained conquerors had departed; and their camp, which had so lately rung with the merry rejoicings of a victorious army, lay a silent and deserted city of huts. The fortress was a smoldering ruin; charred rafters, fragments of exploded artillery, and rent mason-work covering its earthen mounds in confused disorder.

A frightful change had also occurred in the season. The sun had hidden its warmth behind an impenetrable mass of vapor, and hundreds of human forms, which had blackened beneath the fierce heats of August, were stiffening in their deformity before the blasts of a premature November. The curling and spotless mists, which had been seen sailing above the hills toward the north, were now returning in an interminable dusky sheet, that was urged along by the fury of a tempest. The crowded mirror of the Horican was gone; and, in its place, the green and angry waters lashed the shores, as if indignantly casting back its impurities to the polluted strand. Still the clear fountain retained a portion of its charmed influence, but it reflected only the somber gloom that fell from the impending heavens. That humid and congenial atmosphere which commonly adorned the view, veiling its harshness, and softening its asperities, had disappeared, the northern air poured across the waste of water so harsh and unmingled, that nothing was left to be conjectured by the eye, or fashioned by the fancy.

The fiercer element had cropped the verdure of the plain, which looked as though it were scathed by the consuming lightning. But, here and there, a dark green tuft rose in the midst of the desolation; the earliest fruits of a soil that had been fattened with human blood. The whole landscape, which, seen by a favoring light, and in a genial temperature, had been found so lovely, appeared now like some pictured allegory of life, in which objects were arrayed in their harshest but truest colors, and without the relief of any shadowing.

The solitary and arid blades of grass arose from the passing gusts fearfully perceptible; the bold and rocky mountains were too distinct in their barrenness, and the eye even sought relief, in vain, by attempting to pierce the illimitable void of heaven, which was shut to its gaze by the dusky sheet of ragged and driving vapor.

The wind blew unequally; sometimes sweeping heavily along the ground, seeming to whisper its moaning's in the cold ears of the dead, then rising in a shrill and mournful whistling, it entered the forest with a rush that filled the air with the leaves and branches it scattered in its path. Amid the unnatural shower, a few hungry ravens struggled with the gale; but no sooner was the green ocean of woods which stretched beneath them, passed, than they gladly stopped at random, to their hideous banquet.

In short, it was a scene of wildness and desolation, and it appeared as if all who had profanely entered it had been stricken, at a blow, by the relentless arm of death. But the prohibition had ceased and for the first time since the perpetrators of those foul deeds which had assisted to disfigure the scene were gone, living human beings had now presumed to approach the place.

About an hour before the setting of the sun, on the day already mentioned, the forms of five men might have been seen issuing from the narrow vista of trees, where the path to the Hudson entered the forest, and advancing in the direction of the ruined works. At first their progress was slow and guarded, as though they entered with reluctance amid the horrors of the post or dreaded the renewal of its frightful incidents. A light figure preceded the rest of the party, with the caution and activity of a native; ascending every hillock to reconnoiter, and indicating by gestures, to his companions, the route he deemed it most prudent to pursue. Nor were those in the rear wanting in every caution and foresight known to forest warfare. One among them, he also was an Indian, moved a little on one flank, and watched the margin of the woods, with eyes long accustomed to read the smallest sign of danger. The remaining three were white, though clad investments adapted, both in quality and color, to their present hazardous pursuit—that of hanging on the skirts of a retiring army in the wilderness.

The effects produced by the appalling sights that constantly arose in their path to the lake shore, were as different as the characters of the respective individuals who composed the party. The youth in front threw serious but furtive glances at the mangled victims, as he stepped lightly across the plain, afraid to exhibit his feelings, and yet too inexperienced to quell entirely their sudden and powerful influence. His red associate, however, was superior to such a weakness. He passed the groups of dead with a steadiness of purpose, and an eye so calm, that nothing but long and inveterate practice could enable him to maintain. The sensations produced in the minds of even the white men were different, though uniformly sorrowful. One, whose gray locks and furrowed lineaments, blending with a martial air and tread, betrayed, in spite of the disguise of a woodsman's dress, a man long experienced in scenes of war, was not ashamed to groan aloud, whenever a spectacle of more than usual horror came under his view. The young man at his elbow shuddered but seemed to suppress his feelings in tenderness to his companion. Of them all, the straggler who brought up the rear appeared alone to betray his real thoughts, without fear of observation or dread of consequences. He gazed at the most appalling sight with eyes and muscles that knew not how to waver, but with execrations so bitter and deep as to denote how much he denounced the crime of his enemies.

The reader will perceive at once, in these respective characters, the Mohicans, and their white friend, the scout, together with Munro and Heyward. It was, in truth, the father in quest of his children, attended by the youth who felt so deep a stake in their happiness, and those brave and trusty foresters, who had already proved their skill and fidelity through the trying scenes related.

When Uncas, who moved in front, had reached the center of the plain, he raised a cry that drew his companions in a body to the spot. The young warrior had halted over a group of females who lay in a cluster, a confused mass of dead. Notwithstanding the revolting horror of the exhibition, Munro and Heyward flew toward the festering heap, endeavoring, with a love that no unseemliness could extinguish, to discover whether any vestiges of those they sought were to be seen among the tattered and many-colored garments. The father and the lover found instant relief in the search; though each was condemned again to experience the misery of an uncertainty that was hardly less insupportable than the most revolting truth. They were standing, silent and thoughtful, around the melancholy pile when the scout approached. Eyeing the sad spectacle with an angry countenance, the sturdy woodsman, for the first time since his entering the plain, spoke intelligibly and aloud:

"I have been on many a shocking field and have followed a trail of blood for weary miles," he said, "but never have I found the hand of the devil so plain as it is here to be seen! Revenge is an Indian feeling, and all who know me know that there is no cross in my veins; but this much will I say here, in the face of heaven, and with the power of the Lord so manifest in this howling wilderness that should these Frenches ever trust themselves again within the range of a ragged bullet, there is one rifle which shall play its part so long as flint will fire or powder burn! I leave the tomahawk and knife to such as have a natural gift to use them. What say you, Chingachgook," he added, in Delaware; "shall the Hurons boast of this to their women when the deep snows come?"

A gleam of resentment flashed across the dark lineaments of the Mohican chief; he loosened his knife in his sheath and then turning calmly from the sight, his countenance settled into a repose as deep as if he knew the instigation of passion.

"Montcalm! Montcalm!" continued the deeply resentful and less self-restrained scout; "they say a time must come when all the deeds done in the flesh will be seen at a single look; and that by eyes cleared from mortal infirmities. Woe betide the wretch who is born to behold this plain, with the judgment hanging about his soul! Ha—as I am a man of white blood, yonder lies a red-skin, without the hair of his head where nature rooted it! Look to him, Delaware; it may be one of your missing people; and he should have burial like a stout warrior. I see it in your eye, Sagamore; a Huron pays for this, afore the fall winds have blown away the scent of the blood!"

Chingachgook approached the mutilated form, and, turning it over, he found the distinguishing marks of one of those six allied tribes, or nations, as they were called, who, while they fought in the English ranks, were so deadly hostile to his own people. Spurning the loathsome object with his foot, he turned from it with the same indifference he would have quitted a brute carcass. The scout comprehended the action, and very deliberately pursued his own way, continuing, however, his denunciations against the French commander in the same resentful strain.

"Nothing but vast wisdom and unlimited power should dare to sweep off men in multitudes," he added; "for it is only the one that can know the necessity of the judgment; and what is there, short of the other, that can replace the creatures of the Lord? I hold it a sin to kill the second buck afore the first is eaten, unless a march in front, or an ambushment, be contemplated. It is a different matter with a few warriors in open and rugged fight, for 'tis their gift to die with the rifle or the tomahawk in hand; according as their natures may happen to be, white or red. Uncas, come this way, lad, and let the ravens settle upon the Mingo. I know, from often seeing it, that they have a craving for the flesh of an Oneida, and it is as well to let the bird follow the gift of its natural appetite."

"Hugh!" exclaimed the young Mohican, rising on the extremities of his feet, and gazing intently in his front, frightening the ravens to some other prey by the sound and the action.

"What is it, boy?" whispered the scout, lowering his tall form into a crouching attitude, like a panther about to take his leap; "God send it be a tardy Frencher, skulking for plunder. I do believe 'killdeer' would take an uncommon range today!"

Uncas, without making any reply, bounded away from the spot, and in the next instant he was seen tearing from a bush, and waving in triumph, a fragment of the green riding-veil of Cora. The movement, the exhibition, and the cry which again burst from the lips of the young Mohican, instantly drew the whole party about him.

"My child!" said Munro, speaking quickly and wildly; "give me my child!"

"Uncas will try," was the short and touching answer.

The simple but meaning assurance was lost on the father, who seized the piece of gauze, and crushed it in his hand, while his eyes roamed fearfully among the bushes, as if he equally dreaded and hoped for the secrets they might reveal.

"Here are no dead," said Heyward; "the storm seems not to have passed this way."

"That's manifest; and clearer than the heavens above our heads," returned the undisturbed scout; "but either she, or they that have robbed her, have passed the bush; for I remember the rag she wore to hide a face that all did love to look upon. Uncas, you are right; the dark hair has been here, and she has fled like a frightened fawn, to the wood; none who could fly would remain to be murdered. Let us search for the marks she left; for, to Indian eyes, I sometimes think a hummingbird leaves his trail in the air."

The young Mohican darted away at the suggestion, and the scout had hardly done speaking, before the former raised a cry of success from the margin of the forest. On reaching the spot, the anxious party perceived another portion of the veil fluttering on the lower branch of a beech.

"Softly, softly," said the scout, extending his long rifle in front of the eager Heyward; "we now know our work, but the beauty of the trail must not be deformed. A step too soon may give us hours of trouble. We have them, though; that much is beyond denial."

"Bless ye, bless ye, worthy man!" exclaimed Munro; "whither then, have they fled, and where are my babes?"

"The path they have taken depends on many chances. If they have gone alone, they are quite as likely to move in a circle as straight, and they may be within a dozen miles of us; but if the Hurons, or any of the French Indians, have laid hands on them, 'tis probably they are now near the borders of the Canadas. But what matters that?" continued the deliberate scout, observing the powerful anxiety and disappointment the listeners exhibited; "here are the Mohicans and I on one end of the trail and rely on it, we find the other, though they should be a hundred leagues asunder! Gently, gently, Uncas, you are as impatient as a man in the settlements; you forget that light feet leave but faint marks!"

"Hugh!" exclaimed Chingachgook, who had been occupied in examining an opening that had been evidently made through the low underbrush which skirted the forest; and who now stood erect, as he pointed downward, in the attitude and with the air of a man who beheld a disgusting serpent.

"Here is the palpable impression of the footstep of a man," cried Heyward, bending over the indicated spot; "he has trod in the margin of this pool, and the mark cannot be mistaken. They are captives."

"Better so than left to starve in the wilderness," returned the scout "and they will leave a wider trail. I would wager fifty beaver skins against as many flints, that the Mohicans and I enter their wigwams within the month! Stoop to it, Uncas, and try what you can make of the moccasin; for moccasin it plainly is, and no shoe."

The young Mohican bent over the track, and removing the scattered leaves from around the place, he examined it with much of that sort of scrutiny that a money dealer, in these days of pecuniary doubts, would bestow on a suspected due bill. At length he arose from his knees, satisfied with the result of the examination.

"Well, boy," demanded the attentive scout; "what does it say? Can you make anything of the tell-tale?"

"Well, boy," demanded the attentive scout; "what does it say? Can you make anything of the tell-tale?"

"Le Renard Subtil!"

"Ha! that rampaging devil again! there will never be an end of his loping till 'killdeer' has said a friendly word to him."

Heyward reluctantly admitted the truth of this intelligence, and now expressed rather his hopes than his doubts by saying:

"One moccasin is so much like another; it is probable there is some mistake."

"One moccasin like another! you may as well say that one foot is like another; though we all know that some are long, and others short; some broad and others narrow; some with high, and some with low insteps; some intoed, and some out. One moccasin is no more like another than one book is like another: though they who can read in one are seldom able to tell the marks of the other. Which is all ordered for the best, giving to every man his natural advantages. Let me get down to it, Uncas; neither book nor moccasin is the worse for having two opinions, instead of one." The scout stooped to the task, and instantly added:

"You are right, boy; here is the patch we saw so often in the other chase. And the fellow will drink when he can get an opportunity; your drinking Indian always learns to walk with a wider toe than the natural savage, it being the gift of a drunkard to straddle, whether of white or red skin. 'Tis just the length and breadth, too! look at it, Sagamore; you measured the prints more than once, when we hunted the varmints from Glenn's to the health springs."

Chingachgook complied; and after finishing his short examination, he arose, and with a quiet demeanor, he merely pronounced the word:

"Magua!"

"Ay, 'tis a settled thing; here, then, have passed the dark-hair and Magua."

"And not Alice?" demanded Heyward.

"Of her we have not yet seen the signs," returned the scout, looking closely around at the trees, the bushes, and the ground. "What have we there? Uncas, bring hither the thing you see dangling from yonder thornbush."

When the Indian had complied, the scout received the prize, and holding it on high, he laughed in his silent but heartfelt manner.

"'Tis the tooting we'pon of the singer! now we shall have a trail a priest might travel," he said. "Uncas, look for the marks of a shoe that is long enough to uphold six feet two of tottering human flesh. I begin to have some hopes of the fellow, since he has given up squalling to follow some better trade."

"At least he has been faithful to his trust," said Heyward. "And Cora and Alice are not without a friend."

"Yes," said Hawkeye, dropping his rifle, and leaning on it with an air of visible contempt, "he will do their singing. Can he slay a buck for their dinner; journey by the moss on the beaches or cut the throat of a Huron? If not, the first catbird[1] he meets is the cleverer of the two. Well, boy, any signs of such a foundation?"

"Here is something like the footstep of one who has worn a shoe; can it be that of our friend?"

"Touch the leaves lightly or you'll disconcert the formation. That! that is the print of a foot, but 'tis the dark hair's and small it is, too, for one of such a noble height and grand appearance. The singer

[1] The powers of the American mockingbird are generally known. But the true mockingbird is not found so far north as the state of New York, where it has, however, two substitutes of inferior excellence, the catbird, so often named by the scout, and the bird vulgarly called ground- thresher. Either of these last two birds is superior to the nightingale or the lark, though, in general, the American birds are less musical than those of Europe.

would cover it with his heel."

"Where! let me look on the footsteps of my child," said Munro, shoving the bushes aside, and bending fondly over the nearly obliterated impression. Though the tread which had left the mark had been light and rapid, it was still plainly visible. The aged soldier examined it with eyes that grew dim as he gazed; nor did he rise from this stooping posture until Heyward saw that he had watered the trace of his daughter's passage with a scalding tear. Willing to divert a distress which threatened each moment to break through the restraint of appearances, by giving the veteran something to do, the young man said to the scout:

"As we now possess these infallible signs, let us commence our march. A moment, at such a time, will appear an age to the captives."

"It is not the swiftest leaping deer that gives the longest chase," returned Hawkeye, without moving his eyes from the different marks that had come under his view; "we know that the rampaging Huron has passed, and the dark-hair, and the singer, but where is she of the yellow locks and blue eyes? Though little and far from being as bold as her sister, she is fair to the view, and pleasant in discourse. Has she no friend, that none care for her?"

"God forbid she should ever want hundreds! Are we not now in her pursuit? For one, I will never cease the search till she be found."

"In that case we may have to journey by different paths; for here she has not passed, light and little as her footsteps would be."

Heyward drew back all his ardor to proceed seeming to vanish on the instant. Without attending to this sudden change in the other's humor, the scout after musing a moment continued:

"There is no woman in this wilderness could leave such a print as that, but the dark-hair or her sister. We know that the first has been here, but where are the signs of the other? Let us push deeper on the trail, and if nothing offers, we must go back to the plain and strike another scent. Move on, Uncas, and keep your eyes on the dried leaves. I will watch the bushes, while your father shall run with a low nose to the ground. Move on, friends; the sun is getting behind the hills."

"Is there nothing that I can do?" demanded the anxious Heyward.

"You?" repeated the scout, who, with his red friends, was already advancing in the order he had prescribed; "yes, you can keep in our rear and be careful not to cross the trail."

Before they had proceeded many rods, the Indians stopped, and appeared to gaze at some signs on the earth with more than their usual keenness. Both father and son spoke quick and loud now looking at the object of their mutual admiration, and now regarding each other with the most unequivocal pleasure.

"They have found the little foot!" exclaimed the scout, moving forward, without attending further to his own portion of the duty. "What have we here? An ambushment has been planted in the spot! No, by the truest rifle on the frontiers, here have been them one-sided horses again! Now the whole secret is out, and all is plain as the north star at midnight. Yes, here they have mounted. There the beasts have been bound to a sapling, in waiting; and yonder runs the broad path away to the north, in full sweep for the Canadas."

"But still there are no signs of Alice, of the younger Miss Munro," said Duncan.

"Unless the shining bauble Uncas has just lifted from the ground should prove one. Pass it this way, lad, that we may look at it."

Heyward instantly knew it for a trinket that Alice was fond of wearing, and which he recollected, with the tenacious memory of a lover, to have seen, on the fatal morning of the massacre, dangling from the fair neck of his mistress. He seized the highly prized jewel; and as he proclaimed the fact, it vanished from the eyes of the wondering scout, who in vain looked for it on the ground, long after it was warmly pressed against the beating heart of Duncan.

"Pshaw!" said the disappointed Hawkeye, ceasing to rake the leaves with the breech of his rifle; "'tis a certain sign of age, when the sight begins to weaken. Such a glittering gewgaw, and not to be seen! Well, well, I can squint along a clouded barrel yet, and that is enough to settle all disputes between me and the Mingoes. I should like to find the thing, too, if it were only to carry it to the right owner, and that would be bringing the two ends of what I call a long trail together, for by this time the broad St. Lawrence, or perhaps, the Great Lakes themselves, are between us."

"So much the more reason why we should not delay our march," returned Heyward; "let us proceed."

"Young blood and hot blood, they say, are much the same thing. We are not about to start on a squirrel hunt, or to drive a deer into the Horican, but to outlie for days and nights, and to stretch across a wilderness where the feet of men seldom go and where no bookish knowledge would carry you through harmless. An Indian never starts on such an expedition without smoking over his council-fire and, though a man of white blood, I honor their customs in this particular, seeing that they are deliberate and wise. We will, therefore, go back and light our fire tonight in the ruins of the old fort and in the morning, we shall be fresh, and ready to undertake our work like men and not like babbling women or eager boys."

Heyward saw, by the manner of the scout, that altercation would be useless. Munro had again sunk into that sort of apathy which had beset him since his late overwhelming misfortunes, and from which he was apparently to be roused only by some new and powerful excitement. Making a merit of necessity, the young man took the veteran by the arm, and followed in the footsteps of the Indians and the scout, who had already begun to retrace the path which conducted them to the plain.

CHAPTER XIX.

"Salar.—Why, I am sure, if he forfeit, thou wilt not take his flesh; what's that good for?
Shy.—To bait fish withal; if it will feed nothing else, it will feed my revenge."
—Merchant of Venice

The shades of evening had come to increase the dreariness of the place when the party entered the ruins of William Henry. The scout and his companions immediately made their preparations to pass the night there; but with an earnestness and sobriety of demeanor that betrayed how much the unusual horrors they had just witnessed worked on even their practiced feelings. A few fragments of rafters were reared against a blackened wall and when Uncas had covered them slightly with brush, the temporary accommodations were deemed sufficient. The young Indian pointed toward his rude hut when his labor was ended and Heyward, who understood the meaning of the silent gestures, gently urged Munro to enter. Leaving the bereaved old man alone with his sorrows, Duncan immediately returned into the open air, too much excited himself to seek the repose he had recommended to his veteran friend.

While Hawkeye and the Indians lighted their fire and took their evening's repast, a frugal meal of dried bear's meat, the young man paid a visit to that curtain of the dilapidated fort which looked out on the sheet of the Horican. The wind had fallen, and the waves were already rolling on the sandy beach beneath him, in a more regular and tempered succession. The clouds, as if tired of their furious chase, were breaking asunder; the heavier volumes, gathering in black masses about the horizon, while the lighter scud still hurried above the water, or eddied among the tops of the mountains, like broken flights of birds, hovering around their roosts. Here and there, a red and fiery star struggled through the drifting vapor, furnishing a lurid gleam of brightness to the dull aspect of the heavens. Within the bosom of the encircling hills, an impenetrable darkness had already settled; and the plain lay like a vast and deserted charnel-house, without omen or whisper to disturb the slumbers of its numerous and hapless tenants.

Of this scene, so chillingly in accordance with the past, Duncan stood for many minutes a rapt observer. His eyes wandered from the bosom of the mound, where the foresters were seated around their glimmering fire, to the fainter light which still lingered in the skies, and then rested long and anxiously on the embodied gloom, which lay like a dreary void on that side of him where the dead reposed. He soon fancied those inexplicable sounds arose from the place, though so indistinct and stolen, as to render not only their nature but even their existence uncertain. Ashamed of his apprehensions, the young man turned toward the water, and strove to divert his attention to the mimic stars that dimly glimmered on its moving surface. Still, his too-conscious ears performed their ungrateful duty, as if to warn him of some lurking danger. At length, a swift trampling seemed, quite audibly, to rush athwart the darkness. Unable any longer to quiet his uneasiness, Duncan spoke in a low voice to the scout, requesting him to ascend the mound to the place where he stood. Hawkeye threw his rifle across an arm and complied, but with an air so unmoved and calm, as to prove how much he counted on the security of their position.

"Listen!" said Duncan, when the other placed himself deliberately at his elbow; "there are suppressed noises on the plain which may show Montcalm has not yet entirely deserted his conquest."

"Then ears are better than eyes," said the undisturbed scout, who, having just deposited a portion of a bear between his grinders, spoke thick and slow, like one whose mouth was doubly occupied. "I myself saw him caged in Ty, with all his host; for your Frenchers, when they have done a clever thing, like to get back, and have a dance, or a merry-making, with the women over their success."

"I know not. An Indian seldom sleeps in war, and plunder may keep a Huron here after his tribe has departed. It would be well to extinguish the fire and have a watch listen! you hear the noise I mean!"

"An Indian more rarely lurks about the graves. Though ready to slay, and not over regardful of the means, he is commonly content with the scalp, unless when blood is hot, and temper up; but after spirit is once fairly gone, he forgets his enmity, and is willing to let the dead find their natural rest. Speaking of spirits, major, are you of opinion that the heaven of a red-skin and of us whites will be of one and the same?"

"No doubt...no doubt. I thought I heard it again! or was it the rustling of the leaves in the top of the beech?"

"For my own part," continued Hawkeye, turning his face for a moment in the direction indicated by Heyward, but with a vacant and careless manner, "I believe that paradise is ordained for happiness and that men will be indulged in it according to their dispositions and gifts. I, therefore, judge that a red-skin is not far from the truth when he believes he is to find them glorious hunting grounds of which his traditions tell; nor, for that matter, do I think it would be any disparagement to a man without a cross to pass his time—"

"You hear it again?" interrupted Duncan.

"Ay, ay; when food is scarce, and when food is plenty, a wolf grows bold," said the unmoved scout. "There would be picking, too, among the skins of the devils, if there was light and time for the sport. But, concerning the life that is to come, major; I have heard preachers say, in the settlements, that heaven was a place of rest. Now, men's minds differ as to their ideas of enjoyment. For myself, and I say it with reverence to the ordering of Providence, it would be no great indulgence to be kept shut up in those mansions of which they preach, having a natural longing for motion and the chase."

Duncan, who was now made to understand the nature of the noise he had heard, answered, with more attention to the subject which the humor of the scout had chosen for discussion, by saying:

"It is difficult to account for the feelings that may attend the last great change."

"It would be a change, indeed, for a man who has passed his days in the open air," returned the single-minded scout; "and who has so often broken his fast on the head waters of the Hudson, to sleep within sound of the roaring Mohawk. But it is a comfort to know we serve a merciful Master, though we do it each after his fashion and with great tracts of wilderness atween us...what goes there?"

"Is it not the rushing of the wolves you have mentioned?"

Hawkeye slowly shook his head and beckoned for Duncan to follow him to a spot to which the glare from the fire did not extend. When he had taken this precaution, the scout placed himself in an attitude of intense attention and listened long and keenly for a repetition of the low sound that had so unexpectedly startled him. His vigilance, however, seemed exercised in vain; for after a fruitless pause, he whispered to Duncan:

"We must give a call to Uncas. The boy has Indian senses, and he may hear what is hid from us; for, being a white-skin, I will not deny my nature."

The young Mohican, who was conversing in a low voice with his father, started as he heard the moaning of an owl, and, springing on his feet, he looked toward the black mounds, as if seeking the place whence the sounds proceeded. The scout repeated the call, and in a few moments, Duncan saw the figure of Uncas stealing cautiously along the rampart, to the spot where they stood.

Hawkeye explained his wishes in a very few words, which were spoken in the Delaware tongue. So soon as Uncas was in possession of the reason why he was summoned, he threw himself flat on the turf; where, to the eyes of Duncan, he appeared to lie quiet and motionless. Surprised at the immovable attitude of the young warrior, and curious to observe the manner in which he employed his faculties to obtain the desired information, Heyward advanced a few steps, and bent over the dark object on which he had kept his eye riveted. Then it was he discovered that the form of Uncas vanished, and that he beheld only the dark outline of an inequality in the embankment.

"What has become of the Mohican?" he demanded of the scout, stepping back in amazement; "it was here that I saw him fall, and could have sworn that here he yet remained."

"Hist! speak lower; for we know not what ears are open, and the Mingoes are a quick-witted breed. As for Uncas, he is out on the plain, and the Maquas, if any such are about us, will find their equal."

"You think that Montcalm has not called off all his Indians? Let us give the alarm to our companions, that we may stand to our arms. Here are five of us, who are not unused to meet an enemy."

"Not a word to either, as you value your life. Look at the Sagamore, how like a grand Indian chief he sits by the fire. If there are any skulkers out in the darkness, they will never discover, by his countenance, that we suspect danger at hand."

"But they may discover him, and it will prove his death. His person can be too plainly seen by the light of that fire, and he will become the first and most certain victim."

"It is undeniable that now you speak the truth," returned the scout, betraying more anxiety than was usual; "yet what can be done? A single suspicious look might bring on an attack before we are ready to receive it. He knows, by the call I gave to Uncas, that we have struck a scent; I will tell him that we are on the trail of the Mingoes; his Indian nature will teach him how to act."

The scout applied his fingers to his mouth, and raised a low hissing sound, that caused Duncan at first to start aside, believing that he heard a serpent. The head of Chingachgook was resting on a hand, as he sat musing by himself but the moment, he had heard the warning of the animal whose name he bore, he arose to an upright position, and his dark eyes glanced swiftly and keenly on every side of him. With his sudden and, perhaps, involuntary movement, every appearance of surprise or alarm ended. His rifle lay untouched, and apparently unnoticed, within reach of his hand. The tomahawk that he had loosened in his belt for the sake of ease, was even suffered to fall from its usual situation to the ground, and his form seemed to sink, like that of a man whose nerves and sinews were suffered to relax for the purpose of rest. Cunningly resuming his former position, though with a change of hands, as if the movement had been made merely to relieve the limb, the native awaited the result with a calmness and fortitude that none, but an Indian warrior would have known how to exercise.

But Heyward saw that while to a less instructed eye the Mohican chief appeared to slumber, his nostrils were expanded, his head was turned a little to one side, as if to assist the organs of hearing, and that his quick and rapid glances ran incessantly over every object within the power of his vision.

"See the noble fellow!" whispered Hawkeye, pressing the arm of Heyward; "he knows that a look or a motion might disconcert our schemes, and put us at the mercy of them imps—"

He was interrupted by the flash and report of a rifle. The air was filled with sparks of fire, around that spot where the eyes of Heyward were still fastened, with admiration and wonder. A second look told him that Chingachgook had disappeared in the confusion. In the meantime, the scout had thrown forward his rifle, like one prepared for service and waited impatiently the moment when an enemy might rise to view. But with the solitary and fruitless attempt made on the life of Chingachgook, the attack appeared to have terminated. Once or twice the listeners thought they could distinguish the distant rustling of bushes, as bodies of some unknown description rushed through them; nor was it long before Hawkeye pointed out the "scampering of the wolves," as they fled precipitately before the passage of some intruder on their proper domains. After an impatient and breathless pause, a plunge was heard in the water, and it was immediately followed by the report of another rifle.

"There goes Uncas!" said the scout; "the boy bears a smart piece! I know its crack, as well as a father knows the language of his child, for I carried the gun myself until a better offered."

"What can this mean?" demanded Duncan, "we are watched, and, as it would seem, marked for destruction."

"Yonder scattered brand can witness that no good was intended, and this Indian will testify that no harm has been done," returned the scout, dropping his rifle across his arm again, and following Chingachgook, who just then reappeared within the circle of light, into the bosom of the work. "How is it, Sagamore? Are the Mingoes upon us in earnest, or is it only one of those reptiles who hang upon the skirts of a war-party, to scalp the dead, go in, and make their boast among the squaws of the valiant deeds done on the pale faces?"

Chingachgook very quietly resumed his seat; nor did he make any reply, until after he had examined the firebrand which had been struck by the bullet that had nearly proved fatal to himself. After which he was content to reply, holding a single finger up to view, with the English monosyllable:

"One."

"I thought as much," returned Hawkeye, seating himself; "and as he had got the cover of the lake afore Uncas pulled upon him, it is more than probable the knave will sing his lies about some great ambushment, in which he was outlying on the trail of two Mohicans and a white hunter for the officers can be considered as little better than idlers in such a scrimmage. Well, let him...let him. There are always some honest men in every nation, though heaven knows, too, that they are scarce among the Maquas, to look down an upstart when he brags again the face of reason. The varlet sent his lead within whistle of your ears, Sagamore."

Chingachgook turned a calm and incurious eye toward the place where the ball had struck, and then resumed his former attitude, with a composure that could not be disturbed by so trifling an incident. Just then Uncas glided into the circle, and seated himself at the fire, with the same appearance of indifference as was maintained by his father.

Of these several moments Heyward was a deeply interested and wondering observer. It appeared to him as though the foresters had some secret means of intelligence, which had escaped the vigilance of his own faculties. In place of that eager and garrulous narration with which a white youth would have endeavored to communicate, and perhaps exaggerate, that which had passed out in the darkness of the plain, the young warrior was seemingly content to let his deeds speak for themselves. It was, in fact, neither the moment nor the occasion for an Indian to boast of his exploits; and it is probably that, had Heyward neglected to inquire, not another syllable would, just then, have been uttered on the subject.

"What has become of our enemy, Uncas?" demanded Duncan; "we

heard your rifle and hoped you had not fired in vain."

The young chief removed a fold of his hunting skirt, and quietly exposed the fatal tuft of hair, which he bore as the symbol of victory. Chingachgook laid his hand on the scalp and considered it for a moment with deep attention. Then dropping it, with disgust depicted in his strong features, he ejaculated:

"Oneida!"

"Oneida!" repeated the scout, who was fast losing his interest in the scene, in an apathy nearly assimilated to that of his red associates, but who now advanced in uncommon earnestness to regard the bloody badge. "By the Lord, if the Oneidas are outlying upon the trail, we shall by flanked by devils on every side of us! Now, to white eyes there is no difference between this bit of skin and that of any other Indian, and yet the Sagamore declares it came from the poll of a Mingo; nay, he even names the tribe of the poor devil, with as much ease as if the scalp was the leaf of a book, and each hair a letter. What right have Christian whites to boast of their learning, when a savage can read a language that would prove too much for the wisest of them all! What say you, lad, of what people was the knave?"

Uncas raised his eyes to the face of the scout, and answered, in his soft voice:

"Oneida."

"Oneida, again! when one Indian makes a declaration it is commonly true but when he is supported by his people, set it down as gospel!"

"The poor fellow has mistaken us for French," said Heyward; "or he would not have attempted the life of a friend."

"He mistake a Mohican in his paint for a Huron! You would be as likely to mistake the white-coated grenadiers of Montcalm for the scarlet jackets of the Royal Americans," returned the scout. "No, no, the serpent knew his errand; nor was there any great mistake in the matter, for there is but little love atween a Delaware and a Mingo, let their tribes go out to fight for whom they may, in a white quarrel. For that matter, though the Oneidas do serve his sacred majesty, who is my sovereign lord and master, I should not have deliberated long about letting off 'killdeer' at the imp myself, had luck thrown him in my way."

"That would have been an abuse of our treaties, and unworthy of your character."

"When a man consort much with a people," continued Hawkeye, "if they were honest and he no knave, love will grow up atwixt them. It is true that white cunning has managed to throw the tribes into great confusion, as respects friends and enemies; so that the Hurons and the Oneidas, who speak the same tongue, or what may be called the same, take each other's scalps, and the Delawares are divided among themselves; a few hanging about their great council-fire on their own river, and fighting on the same side with the Mingoes while the greater part are in the Canadas, out of natural enmity to the Maquas thus throwing everything into disorder, and destroying all the harmony of warfare. Yet a red nature is not likely to alter with every shift of policy; so that the love atwixt a Mohican and a Mingo is much like the regard between a white man and a serpent."

"I regret to hear it; for I had believed those natives who dwelt within our boundaries had found us too just and liberal, not to identify themselves fully with our quarrels."

"Why, I believe it is nature to give a preference to one's own quarrels before those of strangers. Now, for myself, I do love justice; and, therefore, I will not say I hate a Mingo, for that may be unsuitable to my color and my religion, though I will just repeat, it may have been owing to the night that 'killdeer' had no hand in the death of this skulking Oneida."

Then, as if satisfied with the force of his own reasons, whatever might be their effect on the opinions of the other disputant, the honest but implacable woodsman turned from the fire, content to let the controversy slumber. Heyward withdrew to the rampart, too uneasy and too little accustomed to the warfare of the woods to remain at ease under the possibility of such insidious attacks. Not so, however, with the scout and the Mohicans. Those acute and long-practiced senses, whose powers so often exceed the limits of all ordinary credulity, after having detected the danger, had enabled them to ascertain its magnitude and duration. Not one of the three appeared in the least to doubt their perfect security, as was indicated by the preparations that were soon made to sit in council over their future proceedings.

The confusion of nations, and even of tribes, to which Hawkeye alluded, existed at that period in the fullest force. The great tie of language, and, of course, of a common origin, was severed in many places and it was one of its consequences, that the Delaware and the Mingo (as the people of the Six Nations were called) were found fighting in the same ranks, while the latter sought the scalp of the Huron, though believed to be the root of his own stock. The Delawares were even divided among themselves. Though love for the soil which had belonged to his ancestors kept the Sagamore of the Mohicans with a small band of followers who were serving at Edward, under the banners of the English king, by far the largest portion of his nation were known to be in the field as allies of Montcalm. The reader probably knows, if enough has not already been gleaned from this narrative, that the Delaware, or Lenape, claimed to be the progenitors of that numerous people, who once were masters of most of the eastern and northern states of America, of whom the community of the Mohicans was an ancient and highly honored member.

It was, of course, with a perfect understanding of the minute and intricate interests which had armed friend against friend, and brought natural enemies to combat by each other's side, that the scout and his companions now disposed themselves to deliberate on the measures that were to govern their future movements, amid so many jarring and savage races of men. Duncan knew enough of Indian customs to understand the reason that the fire was replenished, and why the warriors, not excepting Hawkeye, took their seats within the curl of its smoke with so much gravity and decorum. Placing himself at an angle of the works, where he might be a spectator of the scene without, he awaited the result with as much patience as he could summon.

After a short and impressive pause, Chingachgook lighted a pipe whose bowl was curiously carved in one of the soft stones of the country, and whose stem was a tube of wood, and commenced smoking. When he had inhaled enough of the fragrance of the soothing weed, he passed the instrument into the hands of the scout. In this manner the pipe had made its rounds three several times, amid the most profound silence, before either of the party opened his lips. Then the Sagamore, as the oldest and highest in rank, in a few calm and dignified words, proposed the subject for deliberation. He was answered by the scout; and Chingachgook rejoined, when the other objected to his opinions. But the youthful Uncas continued a silent and respectful listener, until Hawkeye, in complaisance, demanded his opinion. Heyward gathered from the manners of the different speakers, that the father and son espoused one side of a disputed question, while the white man maintained the other. The contest gradually grew warmer, until it was quite evident the feelings of the speakers began to be somewhat enlisted in the debate.

Notwithstanding the increasing warmth of the amicable contest, the most decorous Christian assembly, not even excepting those in which its reverend ministers are collected, might have learned a wholesome lesson of moderation from the forbearance and courtesy of the disputants. The words of Uncas were received with the same deep attention as those which fell from the mature wisdom of his father and so far from manifesting any impatience, neither spoke in reply, until a few moments of silent meditation were, seemingly, bestowed in deliberating on what had already been said.

The language of the Mohicans was accompanied by gestures so direct and natural that Heyward had but little difficulty in following the thread of their argument. On the other hand, the scout was obscure; because from the lingering pride of color, he rather affected the cold and artificial manner which characterizes all classes of Anglo-Americans when unexcited. By the frequency with which the Indians described the marks of a forest trial, it was evident they urged a pursuit by land, while the repeated sweep of Hawkeye's arm toward the Horican denoted that he was for a passage across its waters.

The latter was to every appearance fast losing ground, and the point was about to be decided against him, when he arose to his feet, and shaking off his apathy, he suddenly assumed the manner of an Indian, and adopted all the arts of native eloquence. Elevating an arm, he pointed out the track of the sun, repeating the gesture for every day that was necessary to accomplish their objects. Then he delineated a long and painful path, amid rocks and watercourses. The age and weakness of the slumbering and unconscious Munro were indicated by signs too palpable to be mistaken. Duncan perceived that even his own powers were spoken lightly of, as the scout extended his palm, and mentioned him by the appellation of the "Open Hand", a name his liberality had purchased of all the friendly tribes. Then came a representation of the light and graceful movements of a canoe, set in forcible contrast to the tottering steps of one enfeebled and tired. He concluded by pointing to the scalp of the Oneida, and apparently urging the necessity of their departing speedily, and in a manner that should leave no trail.

The Mohicans listened gravely, and with countenances that reflected the sentiments of the speaker.

The Mohicans listened gravely, and with countenances that reflected the sentiments of the speaker. Conviction gradually wrought its influence, and toward the close of Hawkeye's speech, his sentences were accompanied by the customary exclamation of commendation. In short, Uncas and his father became converts to his way of thinking, abandoning their own previously expressed opinions with a liberality and candor that, had they been the representatives of some great and civilized people, would have infallibly worked their political ruin, by destroying forever their reputation for consistency.

The instant the matter in discussion was decided, the debate, and everything connected with it, except the result appeared to be forgotten. Hawkeye, without looking round to read his triumph in applauding eyes, very composedly stretched his tall frame before the dying embers and closed his own organs in sleep.

Left now in a measure to themselves, the Mohicans, whose time had been so much devoted to the interests of others, seized the moment to devote some attention to themselves. Casting off at once the grave and austere demeanor of an Indian chief, Chingachgook commenced speaking to his son in the soft and playful tones of affection. Uncas gladly met the familiar air of his father and before the hard breathing of the scout announced that he slept, a complete change was affected in the manner of his two associates.

It is impossible to describe the music of their language, while thus engaged in laughter and endearments, in such a way as to render it intelligible to those whose ears have never listened to its melody. The compass of their voices, particularly that of the youth, was wonderful extending from the deepest bass to tones that were even feminine in softness. The eyes of the father followed the plastic and ingenious movements of the son with open delight, and he never failed to smile in reply to the other's contagious but low laughter. While under the influence of these gentle and natural feelings, no trace of ferocity was to be seen in the softened features of the Sagamore. His figured panoply of death looked more like a disguise assumed in mockery than a fierce annunciation of a desire to carry destruction in his footsteps.

After an hour had passed in the indulgence of their better feelings, Chingachgook abruptly announced his desire to sleep, by wrapping his head in his blanket and stretching his form on the naked earth. The merriment of Uncas instantly ceased; and carefully raking the coals in such a manner that they should impart their warmth to his father's feet, the youth sought his own pillow among the ruins of the place.

Imbibing renewed confidence from the security of these experienced foresters, Heyward soon imitated their example; and long before the night had turned, they who lay in the bosom of the ruined work, seemed to slumber as heavily as the unconscious multitude whose bones were already beginning to bleach on the surrounding plain.

CHAPTER XX

"Land of Albania! let me bend mine eyes
On thee; thou rugged nurse of savage men!"
—Childe Harold

The heavens were still studded with stars when Hawkeye came to arouse the sleepers. Casting aside their cloaks Munro and Heyward were on their feet while the woodsman was still making his low calls, at the entrance of the rude shelter where they had passed the night. When they issued from beneath its concealment, they found the scout awaiting their appearance nigh by, and the only salutation between them was the significant gesture for silence, made by their sagacious leader.

"Think over your prayers," he whispered, as they approached him; "for He to whom you make them, knows all tongues; that of the heart, as well as those of the mouth. But speak not a syllable; it is rare for a white voice to pitch itself properly in the woods, as we have seen by the example of that miserable devil, the singer. Come," he continued, turning toward a curtain of the works; "let us get into the ditch on this side, and be regardful to step on the stones and fragments of wood as you go."

His companions complied, though to two of them the reasons of this extraordinary precaution were yet a mystery. When they were in the low cavity that surrounded the earthen fort on three sides, they found that passage nearly choked by the ruins. With care and patience, however, they succeeded in clambering after the scout, until they reached the sandy shore of the Horican.

"That's a trail that nothing but a nose can follow," said the satisfied scout, looking back along their difficult way; "grass is a treacherous carpet for a flying party to tread on, but wood and stone take no print from a moccasin. Had you worn your armed boots, there might, indeed, have been something to fear but with the deerskin suitably prepared, a man may trust himself, generally, on rocks with safety. Shove in the canoe nigher to the land, Uncas; this sand will take a stamp as easily as the butter of the Jarmans on the Mohawk. Softly, lad, softly; it must not touch the beach, or the knaves will know by what road we have left the place."

The young man observed the precaution; and the scout, laying a board from the ruins to the canoe, made a sign for the two officers to enter. When this was done, everything was studiously restored to its former disorder and then Hawkeye succeeded in reaching his little birchen vessel, without leaving behind him any of those marks which he appeared so much to dread. Heyward was silent until the Indians had cautiously paddled the canoe some distance from the fort, and within the broad and dark shadows that fell from the eastern mountain on the glassy surface of the lake; then he demanded:

"What need have we for this stolen and hurried departure?"

"If the blood of an Oneida could stain such a sheet of pure water as this we float on," returned the scout, "your two eyes would answer your own question. Have you forgotten the skulking reptile Uncas slew?"

"By no means. But he was said to be alone, and dead men give no cause for fear."

"Ay, he was alone in his deviltry! but an Indian whose tribe counts so many warriors, need seldom fear his blood will run without the death shriek coming speedily from some of his enemies."

"But our presence the authority of Colonel Munro would prove sufficient protection against the anger of our allies, especially in a case where the wretch so well merited his fate. I trust in Heaven you have not deviated a single foot from the direct line of our course with so slight a reason!"

"Do you think the bullet of that varlet's rifle would have turned aside, though his sacred majesty the king had stood in its path?" returned the stubborn scout. "Why did not the grand Frencher, he who is captain-general of the Canadas, bury the tomahawks of the Hurons, if a word from a white can work so strongly on the nature of an Indian?"

The reply of Heyward was interrupted by a groan from Munro but after he had paused a moment in deference to the sorrow of his aged friend, he resumed the subject.

"The marquis of Montcalm can only settle that error with his God," said the young man solemnly.

"Ay, ay, now there is reason in your words, for they are bottomed on religion and honesty. There is a vast difference between throwing a regiment of white coats atwixt the tribes and the prisoners, and coaxing an angry savage to forget he carries a knife and rifle, with words that must begin with calling him your son. No, no," continued the scout, looking back at the dim shore of William Henry, which was now fast receding, and laughing in his own silent but heartfelt manner; "I have put a trail of water atween us; and unless the imps can make friends with the fishes, and hear who has paddled across their basin this fine morning, we shall throw the length of the Horican behind us before they have made up their minds which path to take."

"With foes in front, and foes in our rear, our journey is like to be one of danger."

"Danger!" repeated Hawkeye, calmly; "no, not absolutely of danger; for, with vigilant ears and quick eyes, we can manage to keep a few hours ahead of the knaves; or, if we must try the rifle, there are three of us who understand its gifts as well as any you can name on the borders. No, not of danger; but that we shall have what you may call a brisk push of it, is probable; and it may happen, a brush, a scrimmage, or some such diversion, but always where covers are good, and ammunition abundant."

It is possible that Heyward's estimate of danger differed in some degree from that of the scout, for, instead of replying, he now sat in silence, while the canoe glided over several miles of water. Just as the day dawned, they entered the narrows of the lake[1], and stole swiftly and cautiously among their numberless little islands. It was by this road that Montcalm had retired with his army, and the adventurers knew not but he had left some of his Indians in ambush, to protect the rear of his forces and collect the stragglers. They, therefore, approached the passage with the customary silence of their guarded habits.

Chingachgook laid aside his paddle; while Uncas and the scout urged the light vessel through crooked and intricate channels, where every foot that they advanced exposed them to the danger of some sudden rising on their progress. The eyes of the Sagamore moved warily from islet to islet and copse to copse, as the canoe proceeded and, when a clearer sheet of water permitted, his keen vision was bent along the bald rocks and impending forests that frowned upon the narrow strait.

Heyward, who was a doubly interested spectator, as well from the beauties of the place as from the apprehension natural to his

---

[1] The beauties of Lake George are well known to every American tourist. In the height of the mountains which surround it, and in artificial accessories, it is inferior to the finest of the Swiss and Italian lakes, while in outline and purity of water it is fully their equal; and in the number and disposition of its isles and islets much superior to them all together. There are said to be some hundreds of islands in a sheet of water less than thirty miles long. The narrows, which connect what may be called, in truth, two lakes, are crowded with islands to such a degree as to leave passages between them frequently of only a few feet in width. The lake itself varies in breadth from one to three miles.

situation, was just believing that he had permitted the latter to be excited without sufficient reason, when the paddle ceased moving, in obedience to a signal from Chingachgook.

"Hugh!" exclaimed Uncas, nearly at the moment that the light tap his father had made on the side of the canoe notified them of the vicinity of danger.

"What now?" asked the scout; "the lake is as smooth as if the winds had never blown, and I can see along its sheet for miles; there is not so much as the black head of a loon dotting the water."

The Indian gravely raised his paddle, and pointed in the direction in which his own steady look was riveted. Duncan's eyes followed the motion. A few rods in their front lay another of the wooded islets, but it appeared as calm and peaceful as if its solitude had never been disturbed by the foot of man.

"I see nothing," he said, "but land and water; and a lovely scene it is."

"Hist!" interrupted the scout. "Ay, Sagamore, there is always a reason for what you do. 'Tis but a shade, and yet it is not natural. You see the mist, major, that is rising above the island; you can't call it a fog, for it is more like a streak of thin cloud"

"It is vapor from the water."

"That a child could tell. But what is the edging of blacker smoke that hangs along its lower side, and which you may trace down into the thicket of hazel? 'Tis from a fire; but one that, in my judgment, has been suffered to burn low."

"Let us, then, push for the place, and relieve our doubts," said the impatient Duncan; "the party must be small that can lie on such a bit of land."

"If you judge of Indian cunning by the rules you find in books, or by white sagacity, they will lead you astray, if not to your death," returned Hawkeye, examining the signs of the place with that acuteness which distinguished him. "If I may be permitted to speak in this matter, it will be to say, that we have but two things to choose between: the one is, to return, and give up all thoughts of following the Hurons..."

"Never!" exclaimed Heyward, in a voice far too loud for their circumstances.

"Well, well," continued Hawkeye, making a hasty sign to repress his impatience; "I am much of your mind myself; though I thought it becoming my experience to tell the whole. We must, then, make a push, and if the Indians or Frenchers are in the narrows, run the gauntlet through these toppling mountains. Is there reason in my words, Sagamore?"

The Indian made no other answer than by dropping his paddle into the water and urging forward the canoe. As he held the office of directing its course, his resolution was sufficiently indicated by the movement. The whole party now plied their paddles vigorously, and in a very few moments they had reached a point whence they might command an entire view of the northern shore of the island, the side that had hitherto been concealed.

"There they are, by all the truth of signs," whispered the scout, "two canoes and a smoke. The knaves haven't yet got their eyes out of the mist, or we should hear the accursed whoop. Together, friends! we are leaving them, and are already nearly out of whistle of a bullet."

The well-known crack of a rifle, whose ball came skipping along the placid surface of the strait, and a shrill yell from the island, interrupted his speech, and announced that their passage was discovered. In another instant several savages were seen rushing into canoes, which were soon dancing over the water in pursuit. These fearful precursors of a coming struggle produced no change in the countenances and movements of his three guides, so far as Duncan could discover, except that the strokes of their paddles were longer and more in unison and caused the little bark to spring forward like a creature possessing life and volition.

"Hold them there, Sagamore," said Hawkeye, looking coolly backward over this left shoulder, while he still plied his paddle; "keep them just there. Them Hurons have never a piece in their nation that will execute at this distance; but 'killdeer' has a barrel on which a man may calculate."

The scout having ascertained that the Mohicans were sufficient of themselves to maintain the requisite distance, deliberately laid aside his paddle, and raised the fatal rifle. Three several times he brought the piece to his shoulder, and when his companions were expecting its report, he as often lowered it to request the Indians would permit their enemies to approach a little nigher. At length his accurate and fastidious eye seemed satisfied, and, throwing out his left arm on the barrel, he was slowly elevating the muzzle, when an exclamation from Uncas, who sat in the bow, once more caused him to suspend the shot.

"What, now, lad?" demanded Hawkeye; "you save a Huron from the death-shriek by that word; have you reason for what you do?"

Uncas pointed toward a rocky shore a little in their front, whence another war canoe was darting directly across their course. It was too obvious now that their situation was imminently perilous to need the aid of language to confirm it. The scout laid aside his rifle, and resumed the paddle, while Chingachgook inclined the bows of the canoe a little toward the western shore, in order to increase the distance between them and this new enemy. In the meantime, they were reminded of the presence of those who pressed upon their rear, by wild and exulting shouts. The stirring scene awakened even Munro from his apathy.

"Let us make for the rocks on the main," he said, with the mien of a tired soldier, "and give battle to the savages. God forbid that I, or those attached to me and mine, should ever trust again to the faith of any servant of the Louis's!"

"He who wishes to prosper in Indian warfare," returned the scout, "must not be too proud to learn from the wit of a native. Lay her more along the land, Sagamore; we are doubling on the varlets, and perhaps they may try to strike our trail on the long calculation."

Hawkeye was not mistaken; for when the Hurons found their course was likely to throw them behind their chase, they rendered it less direct, until, by gradually bearing more and more obliquely, the two canoes were, ere long, gliding on parallel lines, within two hundred yards of each other. It now became entirely a trial of speed. So rapid was the progress of the light vessels, that the lake curled in their front, in miniature waves, and their motion became undulating by its own velocity. It was, perhaps, owing to this circumstance, in addition to the necessity of keeping every hand employed at the paddles, that the Hurons had not immediate recourse to their firearms. The exertions of the fugitives were too severe to continue long, and the pursuers had the advantage of numbers. Duncan observed with uneasiness, that the scout began to look anxiously about him, as if searching for some further means of assisting their flight.

"Edge her a little more from the sun, Sagamore," said the stubborn woodsman; "I see the knaves are sparing a man to the rifle. A single broken bone might lose us our scalps. Edge more from the sun and we will put the island between us."

The expedient was not without its use. A long, low island lay at a little distance before them, and, as they closed with it, the chasing canoe was compelled to take a side opposite to that on which the pursued passed. The scout and his companions did not neglect this advantage, but the instant they were hid from observation by the bushes, they redoubled efforts that before had seemed prodigious. The two canoes came round the last low point, like two coursers at the top of their speed, the fugitives taking the lead. This change had brought them nigher to each other, however, while it altered their relative positions.

"You showed knowledge in the shaping of a birchen bark, Uncas, when you chose this from among the Huron canoes," said the scout, smiling, apparently more in satisfaction at their superiority in the race than from that prospect of final escape which now began to open a little upon them. "The imps have put all their strength again at the paddles, and we are to struggle for our scalps with bits of flattened wood, instead of clouded barrels and true eyes. A long stroke, and together, friends."

"They are preparing for a shot," said Heyward; "and as we are in a line with them, it can scarcely fail."

"Get you, then, into the bottom of the canoe," returned the scout; "you and the colonel; it will be so much taken from the size of the mark."

Heyward smiled, as he answered:

"It would be but an ill example for the highest in rank to dodge, while the warriors were under fire."

"Lord! Lord! That is now a white man's courage!" exclaimed the scout; "and like to many of his notions, not to be maintained by reason. Do you think the Sagamore, or Uncas, or even I, who am a man without a cross, would deliberate about finding a cover in the scrimmage, when an open body would do no good? For what have the Frenchers reared up their Quebec, if fighting is always to be done in the clearings?"

"All that you say is very true, my friend," replied Heyward; "still, our customs must prevent us from doing as you wish."

A volley from the Hurons interrupted the discourse, and as the bullets whistled about them, Duncan saw the head of Uncas turned, looking back at himself and Munro. Notwithstanding the nearness of the enemy, and his own great personal danger, the countenance of the young warrior expressed no other emotion, as the former was compelled to think, than amazement at finding men willing to encounter so useless an exposure. Chingachgook was probably better acquainted with the notions of white men, for he did not even cast a glance aside from the riveted look his eye maintained on the object by which he governed their course. A ball soon struck the light and polished paddle from the hands of the chief, and drove it through the air, far in the advance. A shout arose from the Hurons, who seized the opportunity to fire another volley. Uncas described an arc in the water with his own blade, and as the canoe passed swiftly on, Chingachgook recovered his paddle, and flourishing it on high, he gave the war-whoop of the Mohicans, and then lent his strength and skill again to the important task.

The clamorous sounds of "Le Gros Serpent!" "La Longue Carabine!" "Le Cerf Agile!" burst at once from the canoes behind and seemed to give new zeal to the pursuers. The scout seized "killdeer" in his left hand, and elevating it about his head, he shook it in triumph at his enemies. The savages answered the insult with a yell, and immediately another volley succeeded. The bullets pattered along the lake, and one even pierced the bark of their little vessel. No perceptible emotion could be discovered in the Mohicans during this critical moment, their rigid features expressing neither hope nor alarm; but the scout again turned his head, and, laughing in his own silent manner, he said to Heyward:

"The knaves love to hear the sounds of their pieces; but the eye is not to be found among the Mingoes that can calculate a true range in a dancing canoe! You see the dumb devils have taken off a man to charge, and by the smallest measurement that can be allowed, we move three feet to their two!"

Duncan, who was not altogether as easy under this nice estimate of distances as his companions, was glad to find, however, that owing to their superior dexterity, and the diversion among their enemies, they were very sensibly obtaining the advantage. The Hurons soon fired again, and a bullet struck the blade of Hawkeye's paddle without injury.

"That will do," said the scout, examining the slight indentation with a curious eye; "it would not have cut the skin of an infant, much less of men, who, like us, have been blown upon by the heavens in their anger. Now, major, if you will try to use this piece of flattened wood, I'll let 'killdeer' take a part in the conversation."

Heyward seized the paddle, and applied himself to the work with an eagerness that supplied the place of skill, while Hawkeye was engaged in inspecting the priming of his rifle. The latter then took a swift aim and fired. The Huron in the bows of the leading canoe had risen with a similar object, and he now fell backward, suffering his gun to escape from his hands into the water. In an instant, however, he recovered his feet, though his gestures were wild and bewildered. At the same moment his companions suspended their efforts, and the chasing canoes clustered together, and became stationary. Chingachgook and Uncas profited by the interval to regain their wind, though Duncan continued to work with the most persevering industry. The father and son now cast calm but inquiring glances at each other, to learn if either had sustained any injury by the fire; for both well knew that no cry or exclamation would, in such a moment of necessity have been permitted to betray the accident. A few large drops of blood were trickling down the shoulder of the Sagamore, who, when he perceived that the eyes of Uncas dwelt too long on the sight, raised some water in the hollow of his hand, and washing off the stain, was content to manifest, in this simple manner, the slightness of the injury.

"Softly, softly, major," said the scout, who by this time had reloaded his rifle; "we are a little too far already for a rifle to put forth its beauties, and you see yonder imps are holding a council. Let them come up within striking distance, my eye may well be trusted in such a matter, and I will trail the varlets the length of the Horican, guaranteeing that not a shot of theirs shall, at the worst, more than break the skin, while 'killdeer' shall touch the life twice in three times."

"We forget our errand," returned the diligent Duncan. "For God's sake let us profit by this advantage and increase our distance from the enemy."

"Give me my children," said Munro, hoarsely; "trifle no longer with a father's agony, but restore me my babes."

Long and habitual deference to the mandates of his superiors had taught the scout the virtue of obedience. Throwing a last and lingering glance at the distant canoes, he laid aside his rifle, and, relieving the wearied Duncan, resumed the paddle, which he wielded with sinews that never tired. His efforts were seconded by those of the Mohicans and a very few minutes served to place such a sheet of water between them and their enemies, that Heyward once more breathed freely.

The lake now began to expand, and their route lay along a wide reach, that was lined, as before, by high and ragged mountains. But the islands were few, and easily avoided. The strokes of the paddles grew more measured and regular, while they who plied them continued their labor, after the close and deadly chase from which they had just relieved themselves, with as much coolness as though their speed had been tried in sport, rather than under such pressing, nay, almost desperate, circumstances.

Instead of following the western shore, whither their errand led them, the wary Mohican inclined his course more toward those hills behind which Montcalm was known to have led his army into the formidable fortress of Ticonderoga. As the Hurons, to every appearance, had abandoned the pursuit, there was no apparent reason for this excess of caution. It was, however, maintained for hours, until they had reached a bay, nigh the northern termination of the lake. Here the canoe was driven upon the beach, and the whole party landed. Hawkeye and Heyward ascended an adjacent bluff, where the former, after considering the expanse of water beneath him, pointed out to the latter a small black object, hovering under a headland, at the distance of several miles.

"Do you see it?" demanded the scout. "Now, what would your account that spot, were you left alone to white experience to find your way through this wilderness?"

"But for its distance and its magnitude, I should suppose it a bird. Can it be a living object?"

"'Tis a canoe of good birchen bark and paddled by fierce and crafty

Mingoes. Though Providence has lent to those who inhabit the woods eyes that would be needless to men in the settlements, where there are inventions to assist the sight, yet no human organs can see all the dangers which at this moment circumvent us. These varlets pretend to be bent chiefly on their sun-down meal, but the moment it is dark they will be on our trail, as true as hounds on the scent. We must throw them off, or our pursuit of Le Renard Subtil may be given up. These lakes are useful at times, especially when the game take the water," continued the scout, gazing about him with a countenance of concern; "but they give no cover, except it be to the fishes. God knows what the country would be if the settlements should ever spread far from the two rivers. Both hunting and war would lose their beauty."

"Let us not delay a moment, without some good and obvious cause."

"I little like that smoke, which you may see worming up along the rock above the canoe," interrupted the abstracted scout. "My life on it, other eyes than ours see it, and know its meaning. Well, words will not mend the matter, and it is time that we were doing."

Hawkeye moved away from the lookout, and descended, musing profoundly, to the shore. He communicated the result of his observations to his companions, in Delaware, and a short and earnest consultation succeeded. When it terminated, the three instantly set about executing their new resolutions.

The canoe was lifted from the water, and borne on the shoulders of the party, they proceeded into the wood, making as broad and obvious a trail as possible. They soon reached the watercourse, which they crossed and, continuing onward, until they came to an extensive and naked rock. At this point, where their footsteps might be expected to be no longer visible, they retraced their route to the brook, walking backward, with the utmost care. They now followed the bed of the little stream to the lake, into which they immediately launched their canoe again. A low point concealed them from the headland, and the margin of the lake was fringed for some distance with dense and overhanging bushes. Under the cover of these natural advantages, they toiled their way, with patient industry, until the scout pronounced that he believed it would be safe once more to land.

The halt continued until evening rendered objects indistinct and uncertain to the eye. Then they resumed their route, and, favored by the darkness, pushed silently and vigorously toward the western shore. Although the rugged outline of mountain, to which they were steering, presented no distinctive marks to the eyes of Duncan, the Mohican entered the little haven he had selected with the confidence and accuracy of an experienced pilot.

The boat was again lifted and borne into the woods, where it was carefully concealed under a pile of brush. The adventurers assumed their arms and packs, and the scout announced to Munro and Heyward that he and the Indians were at last in readiness to proceed.

CHAPTER XXI.

"If you find a man there, he shall die a flea's death."
—Merry Wives of Windsor.

The party had landed on the border of a region that is, even to this day, less known to the inhabitants of the States than the deserts of Arabia, or the steppes of Tartary. It was the sterile and rugged district which separates the tributaries of Champlain from those of the Hudson, the Mohawk, and the St. Lawrence. Since the period of our tale the active spirit of the country has surrounded it with a belt of rich and thriving settlements, though none but the hunter or the savage is ever known even now to penetrate its wild recesses.

As Hawkeye and the Mohicans had, however, often traversed the mountains and valleys of this vast wilderness, they did not hesitate to plunge into its depth, with the freedom of men accustomed to its privations and difficulties. For many hours the travelers toiled on their laborious way, guided by a star, or following the direction of some watercourse, until the scout called a halt, and holding a short consultation with the Indians, they lighted their fire and made the usual preparations to pass the remainder of the night where they then were.

Imitating the example, and emulating the confidence of their more experienced associates, Munro and Duncan slept without fear, if not without uneasiness. The dews were suffered to exhale, and the sun had dispersed the mists, and was shedding a strong and clear light in the forest, when the travelers resumed their journey.

After proceeding a few miles, the progress of Hawkeye, who led the advance, became more deliberate and watchful. He often stopped to examine the trees; nor did he cross a rivulet without attentively considering the quantity, the velocity, and the color of its waters. Distrusting his own judgment, his appeals to the opinion of Chingachgook were frequent and earnest. During one of these conferences Heyward observed that Uncas stood a patient and silent, though, as he imagined, an interested listener. He was strongly tempted to address the young chief and demand his opinion of their progress; but the calm and dignified demeanor of the native induced him to believe, that, like himself, the other was wholly dependent on the sagacity and intelligence of the seniors of the party. At last, the scout spoke in English, and at once explained the embarrassment of their situation.

"When I found that the home path of the Hurons run north," he said, "it did not need the judgment of many long years to tell that they would follow the valleys and keep atween the waters of the Hudson and the Horican, until they might strike the springs of the Canada streams, which would lead them into the heart of the country of the Frenchers. Yet here are we, within a short range of the Scaroons, and not a sign of a trail have we crossed! Human nature' is weak and it is possible we may not have taken the proper scent."

"Heaven protect us from such an error!" exclaimed Duncan. "Let us retrace our steps, and examine as we go, with keener eyes. Has Uncas no counsel to offer in such a strait?"

The young Mohican cast a glance at his father but maintaining his quiet and reserved mien, he continued silent. Chingachgook had caught the look, and motioning with his hand, he bade him speak. The moment this permission was accorded, the countenance of Uncas changed from its grave composure to a gleam of intelligence and joy. Bounding forward like a deer, he sprang up the side of a little acclivity, a few rods in advance, and stood, exultingly, over a spot of fresh earth, that looked as though it had been recently upturned by the passage of some heavy animal. The eyes of the whole party followed the unexpected movement and read their success in the air of triumph that the youth assumed.

"'Tis the trail!" exclaimed the scout, advancing to the spot; "the lad is quick of sight and keen of wit for his years."

"'Tis extraordinary that he should have withheld his knowledge so long," muttered Duncan, at his elbow.

"It would have been more wonderful had he spoken without a bidding. No, no; your young white, who gathers his learning from books and can measure what he knows by the page, may conceit that his knowledge, like his legs, outruns that of his fathers', but, where experience is the master, the scholar is made to know the value of years, and respects them accordingly."

"See!" said Uncas, pointing north and south, at the evident marks of the broad trail on either side of him, "the dark-hair has gone toward the forest."

"Hound never ran on a more beautiful scent," responded the scout, dashing forward, at once, on the indicated route; "we are favored, greatly favored, and can follow with high noses. Ay, here are both your waddling beasts: this Huron travels like a white general. The fellow is stricken with a judgment and is mad! Look sharp for wheels, Sagamore," he continued, looking back, and laughing in his newly awakened satisfaction; "we shall soon have the fool journeying in a coach, and that with three of the best pair of eyes on the borders in his rear."

The spirits of the scout, and the astonishing success of the chase, in which a circuitous distance of more than forty miles had been passed, did not fail to impart a portion of hope to the whole party.

Their advance was rapid and made with as much confidence as a traveler would proceed along a wide highway. If a rock, or a rivulet, or a bit of earth harder than common, severed the links of the clew they followed, the true eye of the scout recovered them at a distance, and seldom rendered the delay of a single moment necessary. Their progress was much facilitated by the certainty that Magua had found it necessary to journey through the valleys; a circumstance which rendered the general direction of the route sure. Nor had the Huron entirely neglected the arts uniformly practiced by the natives when retiring in front of an enemy. False trails and sudden turnings were frequent, wherever a brook or the formation of the ground rendered them feasible; but his pursuers were rarely deceived, and never failed to detect their error before they had lost either time or distance on the deceptive track.

By the middle of the afternoon, they had passed the Scaroons, and were following the route of the declining sun. After descending an eminence to a low bottom, through which a swift stream glided, they suddenly came to a place where the party of Le Renard had made a halt. Extinguished brands were lying around a spring, the offal's of a deer were scattered about the place, and the trees bore evident marks of having been browsed by the horses. At a little distance, Heyward discovered, and contemplated with tender emotion, the small bower under which he was fain to believe that Cora and Alice had reposed. But while the earth was trodden, and the footsteps of both men and beasts were so plainly visible around the place, the trail appeared to have suddenly ended.

It was easy to follow the tracks of the Narragansetts, but they seemed only to have wandered without guides, or any other object than the pursuit of food. At length Uncas, who, with his father, had endeavored to trace the route of the horses, came upon a sign of their presence that was quite recent. Before following the clew, he communicated his success to his companions; and while the latter were consulting on the circumstance, the youth reappeared, leading the two fillies, with their saddles broken, and the housings soiled, as though they had been permitted to run at will for several days.

"What should this prove?" said Duncan, turning pale, and glancing his eyes around him, as if he feared the brush and leaves were about to give up some horrid secret.

"That our march is come to a quick end, and that we are in an enemy's country," returned the scout. "Had the knave been pressed, and the gentle ones wanted horses to keep up with the party, he might have taken their scalps; but without an enemy at his heels, and with such rugged beasts as these, he would not hurt a hair of their heads. I know your thoughts, and shame be it to our color that you have reason for them; but he who thinks that even a Mingo would ill-treat a woman, unless it be to tomahawk her, knows nothing of Indian nature, or the laws of the woods. No, no; I have heard that the French Indians had come into these hills to hunt the moose, and we are getting within scent of their camp. Why should they not? The morning and evening guns of Ty may be heard any day among these mountains; for the Frenchers are running a new line atween the provinces of the king and the Canadas. It is true that the horses are here, but the Hurons are gone; let us, then, hunt for the path by which they parted."

Hawkeye and the Mohicans now applied themselves to their task in good earnest. A circle of a few hundred feet in circumference was drawn, and each of the party took a segment for his portion. The examination, however, resulted in no discovery. The impressions of footsteps were numerous, but they all appeared like those of men who had wandered about the spot, without any design to quit it. Again, the scout and his companions made the circuit of the halting place, each slowly following the other, until they assembled in the center once more, no wiser than when they started.

"Such cunning is not without its deviltry," exclaimed Hawkeye, when he met the disappointed looks of his assistants.

"We must get down to it, Sagamore, beginning at the spring, and going over the ground by inches. The Huron shall never brag in his tribe that he has a foot which leaves no print."

Setting the example himself, the scout engaged in the scrutiny with renewed zeal. Not a leaf was left unturned. The sticks were removed, and the stones lifted for Indian cunning was known frequently to adopt these objects as covers, laboring with the utmost patience and industry, to conceal each footstep as they proceeded. Still no discovery was made. At length Uncas, whose activity had enabled him to achieve his portion of the task the soonest, raked the earth across the turbid little rill which ran from the spring, and diverted its course into another channel. So soon as its narrow bed below the dam was dry, he stooped over it with keen and curious eyes. A cry of exultation immediately announced the success of the young warrior. The whole party crowded to the spot where Uncas pointed out the impression of a moccasin in the moist alluvion.

"This lad will be an honor to his people," said Hawkeye, regarding the trail with as much admiration as a naturalist would expend on the tusk of a mammoth or the rib of a mastodon; "ay, and a thorn in the sides of the Hurons. Yet that is not the footstep of an Indian! the weight is too much on the heel, and the toes are squared, as though one of the French dancers had been in, pigeon-winging his tribe! Run back, Uncas, and bring me the size of the singer's foot. You will find a beautiful print of it just opposite yon rock, again the hillside."

While the youth was engaged in this commission, the scout and Chingachgook were attentively considering the impressions. The measurements agreed, and the former unhesitatingly pronounced that the footstep was that of David, who had once more been made to exchange his shoes for moccasins.

"I can now read the whole of it, as plainly as if I had seen the arts of Le Subtil," he added; "the singer being a man whose gifts lay chiefly in his throat and feet, was made to go first, and the others have trod in his steps, imitating their formation."

"But" cried Duncan, "I see no signs of..."

"The gentle ones," interrupted the scout; "the varlet has found a way to carry them, until he supposed he had thrown any followers off the scent. My life on it, we see their pretty little feet again before many rods go by."

The whole party now proceeded, following the course of the rill, keeping anxious eyes on the regular impressions. The water soon flowed into its bed again, but watching the ground on either side, the foresters pursued their way content with knowing that the trail lay beneath. More than half a mile was passed before the rill rippled close around the base of an extensive and dry rock. Here they paused to make sure that the Hurons had not quitted the water.

It was fortunate they did so. For the quick and active Uncas soon found the impression of a foot on a bunch of moss, where it would seem an Indian had inadvertently trodden. Pursuing the direction given by this discovery, he entered the neighboring thicket, and struck the trail, as fresh and obvious as it had been before they reached the spring. Another shout announced the good fortune of the youth to his companions and at once terminated the search.

"Ay, it has been planned with Indian judgment," said the scout, when the party was assembled around the place, "and would have blinded white eyes."

"Shall we proceed?" demanded Heyward.

"Softly, softly, we know our path; but it is good to examine the formation of things. This is my schooling, major; and if one neglects the book, there is little chance of learning from the open land of Providence. All is plain but one thing, which is the manner that the knave contrived to get the gentle ones along the blind trail. Even a Huron would be too proud to let their tender feet touch the water."

"Will this assist in explaining the difficulty?" said Heyward, pointing toward the fragments of a sort of handbarrow, that had been rudely constructed of boughs, and bound together with withes, and which now seemed carelessly cast aside as useless.

"'Tis explained!" cried the delighted Hawkeye. "If them varlets have passed a minute, they have spent hours in striving to fabricate a lying end to their trail! Well, I've known them to waste a day in the same manner to as little purpose. Here we have three pair of moccasins, and two of little feet. It is amazing that any mortal beings can journey on limbs so small! Pass me the thong of buckskin, Uncas, and let me take the length of this foot. By the Lord, it is no longer than a child's and yet the maidens are tall and comely. That Providence is partial in its gifts, for its own wise reasons, the best and most contented of us must allow."

"The tender limbs of my daughters are unequal to these hardships," said Munro, looking at the light footsteps of his children, with a parent's love; "we shall find their fainting forms in this desert."

"Of that there is little cause of fear," returned the scout, slowly shaking his head; "this is a firm and straight, though a light step, and not over long. See, the heel has hardly touched the ground and there the dark-hair has made a little jump, from root to root. No, no; my knowledge for it, neither of them was nigh fainting, hereaway. Now, the singer was beginning to be footsore and leg-weary, as is plain by his trail. There, you see, he slipped; here he has traveled wide and tottered; and there again it looks as though he journeyed on snowshoes. Ay, ay, a man who uses his throat altogether, can hardly give his legs a proper training."

From such undeniable testimony did the practiced woodsman arrive at the truth, with nearly as much certainty and precision as if he had been a witness of all those events which his ingenuity so easily elucidated. Cheered by these assurances, and satisfied by a reasoning that was so obvious, while it was so simple, the party resumed its course, after making a short halt, to take a hurried repast.

When the meal was ended, the scout cast a glance upward at the setting sun and pushed forward with a rapidity which compelled Heyward and the still vigorous Munro to exert all their muscles to equal. Their route now lay along the bottom which has already been mentioned. As the Hurons had made no further efforts to conceal their footsteps, the progress of the pursuers was no longer delayed by uncertainty. Before an hour had elapsed, however, the speed of Hawkeye sensibly abated, and his head, instead of maintaining its former direct and forward look, began to turn suspiciously from side to side, as if he were conscious of approaching danger. He soon stopped again and waited for the whole party to come up.

"I sent the Hurons," he said, speaking to the Mohicans; "yonder is open sky, through the treetops and we are getting too nigh their encampment. Sagamore, you will take the hillside, to the right; Uncas will bend along the brook to the left, while I will try the trail. If anything should happen, the call will be three croaks of a crow. I saw one of the birds fanning himself in the air, just beyond the dead oak, another sign that we are approaching an encampment."

The Indians departed their several ways without reply, while Hawkeye cautiously proceeded with the two gentlemen. Heyward soon pressed to the side of their guide, eager to catch an early glimpse of those enemies he had pursued with so much toil and anxiety. His companion told him to steal to the edge of the wood, which, as usual, was fringed with a thicket, and wait his coming, for he wished to examine certain suspicious signs a little on one side. Duncan obeyed, and soon found himself in a situation to command a view which he found as extraordinary as it was novel.

The trees of many acres had been felled, and the glow of a mild summer's evening had fallen on the clearing, in beautiful contrast to the gray light of the forest. A short distance from the place where Duncan stood, the stream had seemingly expanded into a little lake, covering most of the low land, from mountain to mountain. The water fell out of this wide basin, in a cataract so regular and gentle, that it appeared rather to be the work of human hands than fashioned by nature. A hundred earthen dwellings stood on the margin of the lake, and even in its waters, as though the latter had overflowed its usual banks. Their rounded roofs, admirably molded for defense against the weather, denoted more of industry and foresight than the natives were wont to bestow on their regular habitations, much less on those they occupied for the temporary purposes of hunting and war. In short, the whole village or town, whichever it might be termed, possessed more of method and neatness of execution, than the white men had been accustomed to believing belonged, ordinarily, to the Indian habits. It appeared, however, to be deserted. At least, so thought Duncan for many minutes; but, at length, he fancied he discovered several human forms advancing toward him on all fours, and apparently dragging in the train some heavy, and as he was quick to apprehend, some formidable engine. Just then a few dark-looking heads gleamed out of the dwellings, and the place seemed suddenly alive with beings, which, however, glided from cover to cover so swiftly, as to allow no opportunity of examining their humors or pursuits. Alarmed at these suspicious and inexplicable movements, he was about to attempt the signal of the crows, when the rustling of leaves at hand drew his eyes in another direction.

The young man started and recoiled a few paces instinctively, when he found himself within a hundred yards of a stranger Indian. Recovering his recollection on the instant, instead of sounding an alarm, which might prove fatal to himself, he remained stationary, an attentive observer of the other's motions.

An instant of calm observation served to assure Duncan that he was undiscovered. The native, like himself, seemed occupied in considering the low dwellings of the village, and the stolen movements of its inhabitants. It was impossible to discover the expression of his features through the grotesque mask of paint under which they were concealed, though Duncan fancied it was rather melancholy than savage. His head was shaved, as usual, with the exception of the crown, from whose tuft three or four faded feathers from a hawk's wing were loosely dangling. A ragged calico mantle half encircled his body, while his nether garment was composed of an ordinary shirt, the sleeves of which were made to perform the office that is usually executed by a much more commodious arrangement. His legs were, however, covered with a pair of good deer-skin moccasins. Altogether, the appearance of the individual was forlorn and miserable.

Duncan was still curiously observing the person of his neighbor when the scout stole silently and cautiously to his side.

"You see we have reached their settlement or encampment," whispered the young man; "and here is one of the savages himself, in a very embarrassing position for our further movements."

Hawkeye started, and dropped his rifle, when, directed by the finger of his companion, the stranger came under his view. Then lowering the dangerous muzzle, he stretched forward his long neck, as if to assist a scrutiny that was already intensely keen.

"The imp is not a Huron," he said, "nor of any of the Canada tribes; and yet you see, by his clothes, the knave has been plundering a white. Ay, Montcalm has raked the woods for his inroad, and a whooping, murdering set of varlets has he gathered together. Can you see where he has put his rifle or his bow?"

"He appears to have no arms; nor does he seem to be viciously inclined. Unless he communicate the alarm to his fellows, who, as you see, are dodging about the water, we have but little to fear from him."

The scout turned to Heyward and regarded him a moment with unconcealed amazement. Then opening wide his mouth, he indulged in unrestrained and heartfelt laughter, though in that silent and peculiar manner which danger had so long taught him to practice.

Repeating the words, "Fellows who are dodging about the water!" he added, "so much for schooling and passing a boyhood in the settlements! The knave has long legs, though, and shall not be trusted. Do you keep him under your rifle while I creep in behind, through the bush, and take him alive. Fire on no account."

Heyward had already permitted his companion to bury part of his person in the thicket, when, stretching forth his arm, he arrested him, in order to ask:

"If I see you in danger, may I not risk a shot?"

Hawkeye regarded him a moment, like one who knew not how to take the question; then, nodding his head, he answered, still laughing, though inaudibly:

"Fire a whole platoon, major."

In the next moment he was concealed by the leaves. Duncan waited several minutes in feverish impatience before he caught another glimpse of the scout. Then he reappeared, creeping along the earth, from which his dress was hardly distinguishable, directly in the rear of his intended captive. Having reached within a few yards of the latter, he arose to his feet, silently and slowly. At that instant, several loud blows were struck on the water and Duncan turned his eyes just in time to perceive that a hundred dark forms were plunging, in a body, into the troubled little sheet. Grasping his rifle his looks were again bent on the Indian near him. Instead of taking the alarm, the unconscious savage stretched forward his neck, as if he also watched the movements about the gloomy lake, with a sort of silly curiosity. In the meantime, the uplifted hand of Hawkeye was above him. But, without any apparent reason, it was withdrawn, and its owner indulged in another long, though still silent, fit of merriment. When the peculiar and hearty laughter of Hawkeye was ended, instead of grasping his victim by the throat, he tapped him lightly on the shoulder, and exclaimed aloud:

"How now, friend! have you a mind to teach the beavers to sing?"

"Even so," was the ready answer. "It would seem that the Being that gave them power to improve His gifts so well, would not deny them voices to proclaim His praise."

CHAPTER XXII.

"Bot.—Abibl we all met?

Qui.—Pat—pat and here's a marvelous convenient place for our rehearsal."

—Midsummer Night's Dream

The reader may better imagine, than we describe the surprise of Heyward. His lurking Indians were suddenly converted into four-footed beasts; his lake into a beaver pond; his cataract into a dam, constructed by those industrious and ingenious quadrupeds; and a suspected enemy into his tried friend, David Gamut, the master of psalmody. The presence of the latter created so many unexpected hopes relative to the sisters that, without a moment's hesitation, the young man broke out of his ambush, and sprang forward to join the two principal actors in the scene.

The merriment of Hawkeye was not easily appeased. Without ceremony, and with a rough hand, he twirled the supple Gamut around on his heel, and more than once affirmed that the Hurons had done themselves great credit in the fashion of his costume. Then, seizing the hand of the other, he squeezed it with a grip that brought tears into the eyes of the placid David and wished him joy of his new condition.

"You were about opening your throat-practicing's among the

beavers, were ye?" he said. "The cunning devils know half the trade already, for they beat the time with their tails, as you heard just now and in good time it was, too, or 'killdeer' might have sounded the first note among them. I have known greater fools, who could read and write, than an experienced old beaver; but as for squalling, the animals are born dumb! What think you of such a song as this?"

David shut his sensitive ears, and even Heyward apprised as he was of the nature of the cry, looked upward in quest of the bird, as the cawing of a crow rang in the air about them.

"See!" continued the laughing scout, as he pointed toward the remainder of the party, who, in obedience to the signal, were already approaching; "this is music which has its natural virtues; it brings two good rifles to my elbow, to say nothing of the knives and tomahawks. But we see that you are safe; now tell us what has become of the maidens."

"They are captives to the heathen," said David; "and, though greatly troubled in spirit, enjoying comfort and safety in the body."

"Both!" demanded the breathless Heyward.

"Even so. Though our wayfaring has been sore and our sustenance scanty, we have had little other cause for complaint, except the violence done our feelings, by being thus led in captivity into a far land."

"Bless ye for these very words!" exclaimed the trembling Munro; "I shall then receive my babes, spotless and angel-like, as I lost them!"

"I know not that their delivery is at hand," returned the doubting David; "the leader of these savages is possessed of an evil spirit that no power short of Omnipotence can tame. I have tried him sleeping and waking, but neither sounds nor language seem to touch his soul."

"Where is the knave?" bluntly interrupted the scout.

"He hunts the moose today, with his young men and tomorrow, as I hear, they pass further into the forests, and nigher to the borders of Canada. The elder maiden is conveyed to a neighboring people, whose lodges are situated beyond yonder black pinnacle of rock; while the younger is detained among the women of the Hurons, whose dwellings are but two short miles hence, on a tableland, where the fire had done the office of the axe and prepared the place for their reception."

"Alice, my gentle Alice!" murmured Heyward; "she has lost the consolation of her sister's presence!"

"Even so. But so far as praise and thanksgiving in psalmody can temper the spirit in affliction, she has not suffered."

"Has she then a heart for music?"

"Of the graver and more solemn character; though it must be acknowledged that, in spite of all my endeavors, the maiden weeps oftener than she smiles. At such moments I forbear to press the holy songs; but there are many sweet and comfortable periods of satisfactory communication, when the ears of the savages are astounded with the uplifting's of our voices."

"And why are you permitted to go at large, unwatched?"

David composed his features into what he intended should express an air of modest humility, before he meekly replied:

"Little be the praise to such a worm as I. But, though the power of psalmody was suspended in the terrible business of that field of blood through which we have passed, it has recovered its influence even over the souls of the heathen, and I am suffered to go and come at will."

The scout laughed, and, tapping his own forehead significantly, he perhaps explained the singular indulgence more satisfactorily when he said:

"The Indians never harm a non-composer. But why, when the path lay open before your eyes, did you not strike back on your own trail (it is not so blind as that which a squirrel would make) and bring in the tidings to Edward?"

The scout, remembering only his own sturdy and iron nature, had probably exacted a task that David, under no circumstances, could have performed. But, without entirely losing the meekness of his air, the latter was content to answer:

"Though my soul would rejoice to visit the habitations of Christendom once more, my feet would rather follow the tender spirits entrusted to my keeping, even into the idolatrous province of the Jesuits, than take one step backward, while they pined in captivity and sorrow."

Though the figurative language of David was not very intelligible, the sincere and steady expression of his eye, and the glow of his honest countenance, were not easily mistaken. Uncas pressed closer to his side, and regarded the speaker with a look of commendation, while his father expressed his satisfaction by the ordinary pithy exclamation of approbation. The scout shook his head as he rejoined:

"The Lord never intended that the man should place all his endeavors in his throat, to the neglect of other and better gifts! But he has fallen into the hands of some silly woman, when he should have been gathering his education under a blue sky, among the beauties of the forest. Here, friend; I did intend to kindle a fire with this tooting-whistle of thine; but, as you value the thing, take it, and blow your best on it."

Gamut received his pitchpipe with as strong an expression of pleasure as he believed compatible with the grave functions he exercised. After essaying its virtues repeatedly, in contrast with his own voice, and, satisfying himself that none of its melody was lost, he made a very serious demonstration toward achieving a few stanzas of one of the longest effusions in the little volume so often mentioned.

Heyward, however, hastily interrupted his pious purpose by continuing questions concerning the past and present condition of his fellow captives, and in a manner more methodical than had been permitted by his feelings in the opening of their interview. David, though he regarded his treasure with longing eyes, was constrained to answer, especially as the venerable father took a part in the interrogatories, with an interest too imposing to be denied. Nor did the scout fail to throw in a pertinent inquiry, whenever a fitting occasion presented. In this manner, though with frequent interruptions which were filled with certain threatening sounds from the recovered instrument, the pursuers were put in possession of such leading circumstances as were likely to prove useful in accomplishing their great and engrossing object, the recovery of the sisters. The narrative of David was simple, and the facts but few.

Magua had waited on the mountain until a safe moment to retire presented itself, when he had descended, and taken the route along the western side of the Horican in direction of the Canadas. As the subtle Huron was familiar with the paths, and well knew there was no immediate danger of pursuit, their progress had been moderate, and far from fatiguing. It appeared from the unembellished statement of David, that his own presence had been rather endured than desired; though even Magua had not been entirely exempt from that veneration with which the Indians regard those whom the Great Spirit had visited in their intellects. At night, the utmost care had been taken of the captives, both to prevent injury from the damps of the woods and to guard against an escape. At the spring, the horses were turned loose, as has been seen; and, notwithstanding the remoteness and length of their trail, the artifices already named were resorted to, in order to cut off every clue to their place of retreat. On their arrival at the encampment of his people, Magua, in obedience to a policy seldom departed from, separated his prisoners. Cora had been sent to a tribe that temporarily occupied an adjacent valley, though David was far too ignorant of the customs and history of the natives, to be able to declare anything satisfactory concerning their name or character. He only knew that they had not engaged in the late expedition against William Henry; that, like the Hurons themselves they were allies of Montcalm; and that they maintained an amicable, though a watchful intercourse with the warlike and savage people whom chance had, for a time, brought in such close and disagreeable contact with themselves.

The Mohicans and the scout listened to his interrupted and imperfect narrative, with an interest that obviously increased as he proceeded; and it was while attempting to explain the pursuits of the community in which Cora was detained, that the latter abruptly demanded:

"Did you see the fashion of their knives? were they of English or French formation?"

"My thoughts were bent on no such vanities, but rather mingled in consolation with those of the maidens."

"The time may come when you will not consider the knife of a savage such a despicable vanity," returned the scout, with a strong expression of contempt for the other's dullness. "Had they held their corn feast, or can you say anything of the totems of the tribe?"

"Of corn, we had many and plentiful feasts; for the grain, being in the milk is both sweet to the mouth and comfortable to the stomach. Of totem, I know not the meaning; but if it appertained in any wise to the art of Indian music, it need not be inquired after at their hands. They never join their voices in praise, and it would seem that they are among the profanest of the idolatrous."

"There in you believe the nature' of an Indian. Even the Mingo adores but the true and loving God. 'Tis wicked fabrication of the whites, and I say it to the shame of my color that would make the warrior bow down before images of his own creation. It is true, they endeavor to make truces to the wicked one, as who would not with an enemy he cannot conquer! but they look up for favor and assistance to the Great and Good Spirit only."

"It may be so," said David; "but I have seen strange and fantastic images drawn in their paint, of which their admiration and care savored of spiritual pride; especially one, and that, too, a foul and loathsome object."

"Was it a sarpent?" quickly demanded the scout.

"Much the same. It was in the likeness of an abject and creeping tortoise."

"Hugh!" exclaimed both the attentive Mohicans in a breath; while the scout shook his head with the air of one who had made an important but by no means a pleasing discovery. Then the father spoke, in the language of the Delawares, and with a calmness and dignity that instantly arrested the attention even of those to whom his words were unintelligible. His gestures were impressive, and at times energetic. Once he lifted his arm on high; and, as it descended, the action threw aside the folds of his light mantle, a finger resting on his breast, as if he would enforce his meaning by the attitude. Duncan's eyes followed the movement, and he perceived that the animal just mentioned was beautifully, though faintly, worked in blue tint, on the swarthy breast of the chief. All that he had ever heard of the violent separation of the vast tribes of the Delawares rushed across his mind, and he awaited the proper moment to speak, with a suspense that was rendered nearly intolerable by his interest in the stake. His wish, however, was anticipated by the scout who turned from his red friend, saying:

"We have found that which may be good or evil to us, as heaven disposes. The Sagamore is of the high blood of the Delawares and is the great chief of their Tortoises! That some of these stocks are among the people of whom the singer tells us, is plain by his words and had he but spent half the breath in prudent questions that he has blown away in making a trumpet of his throat, we might have known how many warriors they numbered. It is, altogether, a dangerous path we move in; for a friend whose face is turned from you often bears a bloodier mind than the enemy who seeks your scalp."

"Explain," said Duncan.

"'Tis a long and melancholy tradition, and one I little like to think of; for it is not to be denied that the evil has been mainly done by men with white skins. But it has ended in turning the tomahawk of brother against brother and brought the Mingo and the Delaware to travel in the same path."

"You, then, suspect it is a portion of that people among whom Cora resides?"

The scout nodded his head in assent, though he seemed anxious to waive the further discussion of a subject that appeared painful. The impatient Duncan now made several hasty and desperate propositions to attempt the release of the sisters. Munro seemed to shake off his apathy, and listened to the wild schemes of the young man with a deference that his gray hairs and reverend years should have denied. But the scout, after suffering the ardor of the lover to expend itself a little, found means to convince him of the folly of precipitation, in a manner that would require their coolest judgment and utmost fortitude.

"It would be well," he added, "to let this man go in again, as usual, and for him to tarry in the lodges, giving notice to the gentle ones of our approach, until we call him out, by signal, to consult. You know the cry of a crow, friend, from the whistle of the whip-poor-will?"

"'Tis a pleasing bird," returned David, "and has a soft and melancholy note! though the time is rather quick and ill-measured."

"He speaks of the wish-ton-wish," said the scout; "well, since you like his whistle, it shall be your signal. Remember, then, when you hear the whip-poor-will's call three times repeated, you are to come into the bushes where the bird might be supposed..."

"Stop," interrupted Heyward; "I will accompany him."

"You!" exclaimed the astonished Hawkeye; "are you tired of seeing the sun rise and set?"

"David is a living proof that the Hurons can be merciful."

"Ay, but David can use his throat, as no man in his senses would pervert the gift."

"I too can play the madman, the fool, the hero; in short, any or everything to rescue her I love. Name your objections no longer: I am resolved."

Hawkeye regarded the young man a moment in speechless amazement. But Duncan, who, in deference to the other's skill and services, had hitherto submitted somewhat implicitly to his dictation, now assumed the superior, with a manner that was not easily resisted. He waved his hand, in sign of his dislike to all remonstrance, and then, in more tempered language, he continued:

"You have the means of disguise; change me; paint me, too, if you will; in short, alter me to anything...a fool."

"It is not for one like me to say that he who is already formed by so powerful a hand as Providence, stands in need of a change," muttered the discontented scout. "When you send your parties abroad in war, you find it prudent, at least, to arrange the marks and places of encampment, in order that they who fight on your side may know when and where to expect a friend."

"Listen," interrupted Duncan; "you have heard from this faithful follower of the captives, that the Indians are of two tribes, if not of different nations. With one, whom you think to be a branch of the Delawares, is she you call the 'dark-hair'; the other, and younger, of the ladies, is undeniably with our declared enemies, the Hurons. It becomes my youth and rank to attempt the latter adventure. While you, therefore, are negotiating with your friends for the release of one of the sisters, I will effect that of the other, or die."

The awakened spirit of the young soldier gleamed in his eyes, and his form became imposing under its influence. Hawkeye, though too much accustomed to Indian artifices not to foresee the danger of the experiment, knew not well how to combat this sudden resolution.

Perhaps there was something in the proposal that suited his own hardy nature and that secret love of desperate adventure, which had increased with his experience, until hazard and danger had become, in some measure, necessary to the enjoyment of his existence. Instead of continuing to oppose the scheme of Duncan, his humor suddenly altered, and he lent himself to its execution.

"Come," he said, with a good-humored smile; "the buck that will take to the water must be headed, and not followed. Chingachgook has as many different paints as the engineer officer's wife, who takes down nature on scraps of paper, making the mountains look like cocks of rusty hay, and placing the blue sky in reach of your hand. The Sagamore can use them, too. Seat yourself on the log and my life on it, he can soon make a natural fool of you, and that well to your liking."

Duncan complied; and the Mohican, who had been an attentive listener to the discourse, readily undertook the office. Long practiced in all the subtle arts of his race, he drew, with great dexterity and quickness, the fantastic shadow that the natives were accustomed to considering as the evidence of a friendly and jocular disposition. Every line that could possibly be interpreted into a secret inclination for war, was carefully avoided; while, on the other hand, he studied those conceits that might be construed into amity.

In short, he entirely sacrificed every appearance of the warrior to the masquerade of a buffoon. Such exhibitions were not uncommon among the Indians, and as Duncan was already sufficiently disguised in his dress, there certainly did exist some reason for believing that, with his knowledge of French, he might pass for a juggler from Ticonderoga, straggling among the allied and friendly tribes.

When he was thought to be sufficiently painted, the scout gave him much friendly advice; concerted signals, and appointed the place where they should meet, in the event of mutual success. The parting between Munro and his young friend was more melancholy; still, the former submitted to the separation with an indifference that his warm and honest nature would never have permitted in a more healthful state of mind. The scout led Heyward aside and acquainted him with his intention to leave the veteran in some safe encampment, in charge of Chingachgook, while he and Uncas pursued their inquires among the people, they had reason to believe were Delawares. Then, renewing his cautions and advice, he concluded by saying, with a solemnity and warmth of feeling, with which Duncan was deeply touched:

"And now, God bless you! You have shown a spirit that I like; for it is the gift of youth, more especially one of warm blood and a stout heart. But believe the warning of a man who has reason to know all he says to be true. You will have occasion for your best manhood, and for a sharper wit than what is to be gathered in books, afore you outdo the cunning or get the better of the courage of a Mingo. God bless you! if the Hurons master your scalp, rely on the promise of one who has two stout warriors to back him. They shall pay for their victory, with a life for every hair it holds. I say, young gentleman, may Providence bless your undertaking, which is altogether for good and remember that to outwit the knaves it is lawful to practice things that may not be naturally the gift of a white skin."

Duncan shook his worthy and reluctant associate warmly by the hand, once more recommended his aged friend to his care, and returning his good wishes, he motioned to David to proceed. Hawkeye gazed after the high-spirited and adventurous young man for several moments, in open admiration; then, shaking his head doubtingly, he turned, and led his own division of the party into the concealment of the forest.

The route taken by Duncan and David lay directly across the clearing of the beavers, and along the margin of their pond.

When the former found himself alone with one so simple, and so little qualified to render any assistance in desperate emergencies, he first began to be sensible of the difficulties of the task he had undertaken. The fading light increased the gloominess of the bleak and savage wilderness that stretched so far on every side of him, and there was even a fearful character in the stillness of those little huts, that he knew were so abundantly peopled. It struck him, as he gazed at the admirable structures and the wonderful precautions of their sagacious inmates, that even the brutes of these vast wilds were possessed of an instinct nearly commensurate with his own reason; and he could not reflect, without anxiety, on the unequal contest that he had so rashly courted. Then came the glowing image of Alice; her distress; her actual danger; and all the peril of his situation was forgotten. Cheering David, he moved on with the light and vigorous step of youth and enterprise.

After making nearly a semicircle around the pond, they diverged from the watercourse and began to ascend to the level of a slight elevation in that bottom land, over which they journeyed. Within half an hour they gained the margin of another opening that bore all the signs of having been also made by the beavers, and which those sagacious animals had probably been induced, by some accident, to abandon, for the more eligible position they now occupied. A very natural sensation caused Duncan to hesitate a moment, unwilling to leave the cover of their bushy path, as a man pauses to collect his energies before he essays any hazardous experiment, in which he is secretly conscious they will all be needed. He profited by the halt, to gather such information as might be obtained from his short and hasty glances.

On the opposite side of the clearing, and near the point where the brook tumbled over some rocks, from a still higher level, some fifty or sixty lodges, rudely fabricated of logs brush, and earth intermingled, were to be discovered. They were arranged without any order and seemed to be constructed with very little attention to neatness or beauty. Indeed, so very inferior were they in the two latter particulars to the village Duncan had just seen, that he began to expect a second surprise, no less astonishing that the former. This expectation was in no degree diminished, when, by the doubtful twilight, he beheld twenty or thirty forms rising alternately from the cover of the tall, coarse grass, in front of the lodges, and then sinking again from the sight, as it were to burrow in the earth. By the sudden and hasty glimpses that he caught of these figures, they seemed more like dark, glancing specters, or some other unearthly beings, than creatures fashioned with the ordinary and vulgar materials of flesh and blood. A gaunt, naked form was seen, for a single instant, tossing its arms wildly in the air, and then the spot it had filled was vacant; the figure appearing suddenly in some other and distant place, or being succeeded by another, possessing the same mysterious character. David, observing that his companion lingered, pursued the direction of his gaze, and in some measure recalled the recollection of Heyward, by speaking.

"There is much fruitful soil uncultivated here," he said; "and, I may add, without the sinful leaven of self-commendation, that, since my short sojourn in these heathenish abodes, much good seed has been scattered by the wayside."

"The tribes are fonder of the chase than of the arts of men of labor," returned the unconscious Duncan, still gazing at the objects of his wonder.

"It is rather joy than labor to the spirit, to lift up the voice in praise but sadly do these boys abuse their gifts. Rarely have I found any of their age, on whom nature has so freely bestowed the elements of psalmody; and surely, surely, there are none who neglect them more. Three nights have I now tarried here, and three several times have I assembled the urchins to join in sacred song; and as often have they responded to my efforts with whooping's and howling's that have chilled my soul!"

"Of whom speak you?"

"Of those children of the devil, who waste the precious moments in yonder idle antics. Ah! the wholesome restraint of discipline is but little known among this self-abandoned people. In a country of birches, a rod is never seen, and it ought not to appear a marvel in my eyes, that the choicest blessings of Providence are wasted in such cries as these."

David closed his ears against the juvenile pack, whose yell just then rang shrilly through the forest; and Duncan, suffering his lip to curl, as in mockery of his own superstition, said firmly:

"We will proceed."

Without removing the safeguards form his ears, the master of song complied, and together they pursued their way toward what David was sometimes wont to call the "tents of the Philistines."

CHAPTER XXIII.

"But though the beast of game
The privilege of chase may claim;
Though space and law the stag we lend
Ere hound we slip, or bow we bend;
Whoever recked, where, how, or when
The prowling fox was trapped or slain?"
—Lady of the Lake.

It is unusual to find an encampment of the natives, like those of the more instructed whites, guarded by the presence of armed men. Well informed of the approach of every danger, while it is yet at a distance, the Indian generally rests secure under his knowledge of the signs of the forest, and the long and difficult paths that separate him from those he has most reason to dread. But the enemy who, by any lucky concurrence of accidents, has found means to elude the vigilance of the scouts, will seldom meet with sentinels nearer home to sound the alarm. In addition to this general usage, the tribes friendly to the French knew too well the weight of the blow that had just been struck, to apprehend any immediate danger from the hostile nations that were tributary to the crown of Britain.

When Duncan and David, therefore, found themselves in the center of the children, who played the antics already mentioned, it was without the least previous intimation of their approach. But so soon as they were observed the whole of the juvenile pack raised, by common consent, a shrill and warning whoop; and then sank, as it were, by magic, from before the sight of their visitors. The naked, tawny bodies of the crouching urchins blended so nicely at that hour, with the withered herbage, that at first it seemed as if the earth had, in truth, swallowed up their forms; though when surprise permitted Duncan to bend his look more curiously about the spot, he found it everywhere met by dark, quick, and rolling eyeballs.

Gathering no encouragement from this startling presage of the nature of the scrutiny he was likely to undergo from the more mature judgments of the men, there was an instant when the young soldier would have retreated. It was, however, too late to appear to hesitate. The cry of the children had drawn a dozen warriors to the door of the nearest lodge, where they stood clustered in a dark and savage group, gravely awaiting the nearer approach of those who had unexpectedly come among them.

David, in some measure familiarized to the scene, led the way with a steadiness that no slight obstacle was likely to disconcert, into this very building. It was the principal edifice of the village, though roughly constructed of the bark and branches of trees; being the lodge in which the tribe held its councils and public meetings during their temporary residence on the borders of the English province. Duncan found it difficult to assume the necessary appearance of unconcern, as he brushed the dark and powerful frames of the savages who thronged its threshold but conscious that his existence depended on his presence of mind, he trusted to the discretion of his companion, whose footsteps he closely followed, endeavoring, as he proceeded, to rally his thoughts for the occasion. His blood curdled when he found himself in absolute contact with such fierce and implacable enemies; but he so far mastered his feelings as to pursue his way into the center of the lodge, with an exterior that did not betray the weakness. Imitating the example of the deliberate

Gamut, he drew a bundle of fragrant brush from beneath a pile that filled the corner of the hut and seated himself in silence.

So soon as their visitor had passed, the observant warriors fell back from the entrance, and arranging themselves about him, they seemed patiently to await the moment when it might comport with the dignity of the stranger to speak. By far the greater number stood leaning, in lazy, lounging attitudes, against the upright posts that supported the crazy building, while three or four of the oldest and most distinguished of the chiefs placed themselves on the earth a little more in advance.

A flaring torch was burning in the place and set its red glare from face to face and figure to figure, as it waved in the currents of air. Duncan profited by its light to read the probable character of his reception, in the countenances of his hosts. But his ingenuity availed him little, against the cold artifices of the people he had encountered. The chiefs in front scarce cast a glance at his person, keeping their eyes on the ground, with an air that might have been intended for respect, but which it was quite easy to construe into distrust. The men in the shadow were less reserved. Duncan soon detected their searching, but stolen, looks which, in truth, scanned his person and attire inch by inch leaving no emotion of the countenance, no gesture, no line of the paint, nor even the fashion of a garment, unheeded, and without comment.

At length one whose hair was beginning to be sprinkled with gray, but whose sinewy limbs and firm tread announced that he was still equal to the duties of manhood, advanced out of the gloom of a corner, whither he had probably posted himself to make his observations unseen, and spoke. He used the language of the Wyandots, or Hurons; his words were, consequently, unintelligible to Heyward, though they seemed, by the gestures that accompanied them, to be uttered more in courtesy than anger. The latter shook his head and made a gesture indicative of his inability to reply.

"Do none of my brothers speak the French or the English?" he said, in the former language, looking about him from countenance to countenance, in hopes of finding a nod of assent.

Though more than one had turned, as if to catch the meaning of his words, they remained unanswered.

"I should be grieved to think," continued Duncan, speaking slowly, and using the simplest French of which he was the master, "to believe that none of this wise and brave nation understand the language that the 'Grand Monarque' uses when he talks to his children. His heart would be heavy did he believe his red warriors paid him so little respect!"

A long and grave pause succeeded, during which no movement of a limb, nor any expression of an eye, betrayed the expression produced by his remark. Duncan, who knew that silence was a virtue among his hosts, gladly had recourse to the custom, in order to arrange his ideas. At length the same warrior who had before addressed him replied, by dryly demanding, in the language of the Canadas:

"When our Great Father speaks to his people, is it with the tongue of a Huron?"

"He knows no difference in his children, whether the color of the skin be red, or black, or white," returned Duncan, evasively; "though chiefly is he satisfied with the brave Hurons."

"In what manner will he speak," demanded the wary chief, "when the runners count to him the scalps which five nights ago grew on the heads of the Yengeese?"

"They were his enemies," said Duncan, shuddering involuntarily; "and doubtless, he will say, it is good; my Hurons are very gallant."

"Our Canada father does not think it. Instead of looking forward to rewarding his Indians, his eyes are turned backward. He sees the dead Yengeese, but no Huron. What can this mean?"

"A great chief, like him, has more thoughts than tongues. He looks to see that no enemies are on his trail."

"The canoe of a dead warrior will not float on the Horican," returned the savage, gloomily. "His ears are open to the Delawares, who are not our friends, and they fill them with lies."

"It cannot be. See; he has bid me, who am a man that knows the art of healing, to go to his children, the red Hurons of the great lakes, and ask if any are sick!"

Another silence succeeded this annunciation of the character Duncan had assumed. Every eye was simultaneously bent on his person, as if to inquire into the truth or falsehood of the declaration, with an intelligence and keenness that caused the subject of their scrutiny to tremble for the result. He was, however, relieved again by the former speaker.

"Do the cunning men of the Canadas paint their skins?" the Huron coldly continued; "we have heard them boast that their faces were pale."

"When an Indian chief comes among his white fathers," returned Duncan, with great steadiness, "he lays aside his buffalo robe, to carry the shirt that is offered him. My brothers have given me paint and I wear it."

A low murmur of applause announced that the compliment of the tribe was favorably received. The elderly chief made a gesture of commendation, which was answered by most of his companions, who each threw forth a hand and uttered a brief exclamation of pleasure. Duncan began to breathe more freely, believing that the weight of his examination was past; and, as he had already prepared a simple and probable tale to support his pretended occupation, his hopes of ultimate success grew brighter.

After a silence of a few moments, as if adjusting his thoughts, in order to make a suitable answer to the declaration their guests had just given, another warrior arose, and placed himself in an attitude to speak. While his lips were yet in the act of parting, a low but fearful sound arose from the forest, and was immediately succeeded by a high, shrill yell, that was drawn out, until it equaled the longest and most plaintive howl of the wolf. The sudden and terrible interruption caused Duncan to start from his seat, unconscious of everything but the effect produced by so frightful a cry. At the same moment, the warriors glided in a body from the lodge, and the outer air was filled with loud shouts, that nearly drowned those awful sounds, which were still ringing beneath the arches of the woods. Unable to command himself any longer, the youth broke from the place, and presently stood in the center of a disorderly throng, that included nearly everything having life, within the limits of the encampment. Men, women, and children; the aged, the inform, the active and the strong, were alike abroad, some exclaiming aloud, others clapping their hands with a joy that seemed frantic, and all expressing their savage pleasure in some unexpected event. Though astounded, at first, by the uproar, Heyward was soon enabled to find its solution by the scene that followed.

There yet lingered sufficient light in the heavens to exhibit those bright openings among the tree-tops, where different paths left the clearing to enter the depths of the wilderness. Beneath one of them, a line of warriors issued from the woods, and advanced slowly toward the dwellings. One in front bore a short pole, on which, as it afterwards appeared, were suspended several human scalps. The startling sounds that Duncan had heard were what the whites have not inappropriately called the "death-hallo"; and each repetition of the cry was intended to announce to the tribe the fate of an enemy. Thus far the knowledge of Heyward assisted him in the explanation; and as he now knew that the interruption was caused by the unlooked-for return of a successful war-party, every disagreeable sensation was quieted in inward congratulation, for the opportune relief and insignificance it conferred on himself.

When at the distance of a few hundred feet from the lodges the newly arrived warriors halted. Their plaintive and terrific cry, which was intended to represent equally the wailings of the dead and the triumph to the victors, had entirely ceased. One of their number now called aloud, in words that were far from appalling, though not more intelligible to those for whose ears they were intended, than their expressive yells. It would be difficult to convey a suitable idea of the savage ecstasy with which the news thus imparted was received. The whole encampment, in a moment, became a scene of the most violent bustle and commotion. The warriors drew their knives, and flourishing them, they arranged themselves in two lines, forming a lane that extended from the war-party to the lodges. The squaws seized clubs, axes, or whatever weapon of offense first offered itself to their hands, and rushed eagerly to act their part in the cruel game that was at hand. Even the children would not be excluded; but boys, little able to wield the instruments, tore the tomahawks from the belts of their fathers, and stole into the ranks, apt imitators of the savage traits exhibited by their parents.

Large piles of brush lay scattered about the clearing, and a wary and aged squaw was occupied in firing as many as might serve to light the coming exhibition. As the flame arose, its power exceeded that of the parting day and assisted to render objects at the same time more distinct and more hideous. The whole scene formed a striking picture, whose frame was composed of the dark and tall border of pines. The warriors just arrived were the most distant figures. A little in advance stood two men, who were apparently selected from the rest, as the principal actors in what was to follow. The light was not strong enough to render their features distinct, though it was quite evident that they were governed by very different emotions. While one stood erect and firm, prepared to meet his fate like a hero, the other bowed his head, as if palsied by terror or stricken with shame. The high-spirited Duncan felt a powerful impulse of admiration and pity toward the former, though no opportunity could offer to exhibit his generous emotions. He watched his slightest movement, however, with eager eyes and as he traced the fine outline of his admirably proportioned and active frame, he endeavored to persuade himself, that, if the powers of man, seconded by such noble resolution, could bear one harmless through so severe a trial, the youthful captive before him might hope for success in the hazardous race he was about to run. Insensibly the young man drew nigher to the swarthy lines of the Hurons, and scarcely breathed, so intense became his interest in the spectacle. Just then the signal yell was given, and the momentary quiet which had preceded it was broken by a burst of cries, that far exceeded any before heard. The more abject of the two victims continued motionless but the other bounded from the place at the cry, with the activity and swiftness of a deer. Instead of rushing through the hostile lines, as had been expected, he just entered the dangerous defile, and before time was given for a single blow, turned short, and leaping the heads of a row of children, he gained at once the exterior and safer side of the formidable array. The artifice was answered by a hundred voices raised in imprecations; and the whole of the excited multitude broke from their order and spread themselves about the place in wild confusion.

A dozen blazing piles now shed their lurid brightness on the place, which resembled some unhallowed and supernatural arena, in which malicious demons had assembled to act their bloody and lawless rites. The forms in the background looked like unearthly beings, gliding before the eye, and cleaving the air with frantic and unmeaning gestures; while the savage passions of such as passed the flames were rendered fearfully distinct by the gleams that shot athwart their inflamed visages.

It will easily be understood that, amid such a concourse of vindictive enemies, no breathing time was allowed the fugitive. There was a single moment when it seemed as if he would have reached the forest, but the whole body of his captors threw themselves before him and drove him back into the center of his relentless persecutors. Turning like a headed deer, he shot, with the swiftness of an arrow, through a pillar of forked flame, and passing the whole multitude harmless, he appeared on the opposite side of the clearing. Here, too, he was met and turned by a few of the older and more subtle of the Hurons. Once more he tried the throng, as if seeking safety in its blindness, and then several moments succeeded, during which Duncan believed the active and courageous young stranger was lost.

Nothing could be distinguished but a dark mass of human forms tossed and involved in inexplicable confusion. Arms, gleaming knives and formidable clubs, appeared above them, but the blows were evidently given at random. The awful effect was heightened by the piercing shrieks of the women and the fierce yells of the warriors.

Now and then, Duncan caught a glimpse of a light form cleaving the air in some desperate bound, and he rather hoped than believed that the captive yet retained the command of his astonishing powers of activity. Suddenly the multitude rolled backward and approached the spot where he himself stood. The heavy body in the rear pressed upon the women and children in front and bore them to the earth. The stranger reappeared in the confusion. Human power could not, however, much longer endure so severe a trial. Of this the captive seemed conscious. Profiting by the momentary opening, he darted from among the warriors, and made a desperate, and what seemed to Duncan a final effort to gain the wood. As if aware that no danger was to be apprehended from the young soldier, the fugitive nearly brushed his person in his flight. A tall and powerful Huron, who had husbanded his forces, pressed close upon his heels, and with an uplifted arm menaced a fatal blow. Duncan thrust forth a foot, and the shock precipitated the eager savage headlong, many feet in advance of his intended victim. Thought itself is not quicker than was the motion with which the latter profited by the advantage; he turned, gleamed like a meteor again before the eyes of Duncan, and, at the next moment, when the latter recovered his recollection, and gazed around in quest of the captive, he saw him quietly leaning against a small painted post, which stood before the door of the principal lodge.

Apprehensive that the part he had taken in the escape might prove fatal to himself, Duncan left the place without delay. He followed the crowd, which drew nigh the lodges, gloomy and sullen, like any other multitude that had been disappointed in an execution. Curiosity, or perhaps a better feeling, induced him to approach the stranger. He found him, standing with one arm cast about the protecting post, and breathing thick and hard, after his exertions, but disdaining to permit a single sign of suffering to escape. His person was now protected by immemorial and sacred usage, until the tribe in council had deliberated and determined on his fate. It was not difficult, however, to foretell the result, if any presage could be drawn from the feelings of those who crowded the place.

There was no term of abuse known to the Huron vocabulary that the disappointed women did not lavishly expend on the successful stranger. They flouted at his efforts, and told him, with bitter scoffs, that his feet were better than his hands; and that he merited wings, while he knew not the use of an arrow or a knife. To all this the captive made no reply; but was content to preserve an attitude in which dignity was singularly blended with disdain. Exasperated as much by his composure as by his good fortune, their words became unintelligible, and were succeeded by shrill, piercing yells. Just then the crafty squaw, who had taken the necessary precaution to fire the piles, made her way through the throng, and cleared a place for herself in front of the captive. The squalid and withered person of this hag might well have obtained for her the character of possessing more than human cunning. Throwing back her light vestment, she stretched forth her long, skinny arm, in derision, and using the language of the Lenape, as more intelligible to the subject of her gibes, she commenced aloud:

"Look you, Delaware," she said, snapping her fingers in his face; "your nation is a race of women, and the hoe is better fitted to your hands than the gun. Your squaws are the mothers of deer; but if a bear, or a wildcat, or a serpent were born among you, ye would flee. The Huron girls shall make you petticoats, and we will find you a husband."

A burst of savage laughter succeeded this attack, during which the soft and musical merriment of the younger females strangely chimed with the cracked voice of their older and more malignant companion. But the stranger was superior to all their efforts. His head was immovable; nor did he betray the slightest consciousness that any were present, except when his haughty eye rolled toward the dusky forms of the warriors, who stalked in the background silent and sullen observers of the scene.

Infuriated at the self-command of the captive, the woman placed her arms akimbo; and, throwing herself into a posture of defiance, she broke out anew, in a torrent of words that no art of ours could commit successfully to paper. Her breath was, however, expended in vain; for, although distinguished in her nation as a proficient in the art of abuse, she was permitted to work herself into such a fury as actually to foam at the mouth, without causing a muscle to vibrate in the motionless figure of the stranger. The effect of his indifference began to extend itself to the other spectators; and a youngster, who was just quitting the condition of a boy to enter the state of manhood, attempted to assist the termagant, by flourishing his tomahawk before their victim, and adding his empty boasts to the taunts of the women. Then, indeed, the captive turned his face toward the light, and looked down on the stripling with an expression that was superior to contempt. At the next moment he resumed his quiet and reclining attitude against the post. But the change of posture had permitted Duncan to exchange glances with the firm and piercing eyes of Uncas.

Breathless with amazement, and heavily oppressed with the

critical situation of his friend, Heyward recoiled before the look, trembling lest its meaning might, in some unknown manner, hasten the prisoner's fate. There was not, however, any instant cause for such an apprehension. Just then a warrior forced his way into the exasperated crowd. Motioning the women and children aside with a stern gesture, he took Uncas by the arm, and led him toward the door of the council-lodge. Thither all the chiefs, and most of the distinguished warriors, followed; among whom the anxious Heyward found means to enter without attracting any dangerous attention to himself.

A few minutes were consumed in disposing of those present in a manner suitable to their rank and influence in the tribe. An order very similar to that adopted in the preceding interview was observed; the aged and superior chiefs occupying the area of the spacious apartment, within the powerful light of a glaring torch, while their juniors and inferiors were arranged in the background, presenting a dark outline of swarthy and marked visages. In the very center of the lodge, immediately under an opening that admitted the twinkling light of one or two stars, stood Uncas, calm, elevated, and collected. His high and haughty carriage was not lost on his captors, who often bent their looks on his person, with eyes which, while they lost none of their inflexibility of purpose, plainly betrayed their admiration of the stranger's daring.

The case was different with the individual whom Duncan had observed to stand forth with his friend, previously to the desperate trial of speed; and who, instead of joining in the chase, had remained, throughout its turbulent uproar, like a cringing statue, expressive of shame and disgrace. Though not a hand had been extended to greet him, nor yet an eye had condescended to watch his movements, he had also entered the lodge, as though impelled by a fate to whose decrees he submitted, seemingly, without a struggle. Heyward profited by the first opportunity to gaze in his face, secretly apprehensive he might find the features of another acquaintance; but they proved to be those of a stranger and what was still more inexplicable, of one who bore all the distinctive marks of a Huron warrior. Instead of mingling with his tribe, however, he sat apart, a solitary being in a multitude, his form shrinking into a crouching and abject attitude, as if anxious to fill as little space as possible. When each individual had taken his proper station, and silence reigned in the place, the gray-haired chief already introduced to the reader, spoke aloud, in the language of the Lenni Lenape.

"Delaware," he said, "though one of a nation of women, you have proved yourself a man. I would give you food; but he who eats with a Huron should become his friend. Rest in peace till the morning sun when our last words shall be spoken."

"Seven nights, and as many summer days, have I fasted on the trail of the Hurons," Uncas coldly replied; "the children of the Lenape know how to travel the path of the just without lingering to eat."

"Two of my young men are in pursuit of your companion," resumed the other, without appearing to regard the boast of his captive; "when they get back, then will our wise man say to you 'live' or 'die'."

"Has a Huron no ears?" scornfully exclaimed Uncas; "twice, since he has been your prisoner, has the Delaware heard a gun that he knows. Your young men will never come back!"

A short and sullen pause succeeded this bold assertion. Duncan, who understood the Mohican to allude to the fatal rifle of the scout, bent forward in earnest observation of the effect it might produce on the conquerors; but the chief was content with simply retorting:

"If the Lenape are so skillful, why is one of their bravest warriors here?"

"He followed in the steps of a flying coward and fell into a snare. The cunning beaver may be caught."

As Uncas thus replied, he pointed with his finger toward the solitary Huron, but without deigning to bestow any other notice on so unworthy an object. The words of the answer and the air of the speaker produced a strong sensation among his auditors. Every eye rolled sullenly toward the individual indicated by the simple gesture, and a low, threatening murmur passed through the crowd. The ominous sounds reached the outer door, and the women and children pressing into the throng, no gap had been left, between shoulder and shoulder, that was not now filled with the dark lineaments of some eager and curious human countenance.

In the meantime, the more aged chiefs, in the center, communed with each other in short and broken sentences. Not a word was uttered that did not convey the meaning of the speaker, in the simplest and most energetic form. Again, a long and deeply solemn pause took place. It was known, by all present, to be the brave precursor of a weighty and important judgment. They who composed the outer circle of faces were on tiptoe to gaze; and even the culprit for an instant forgot his shame in a deeper emotion, and exposed his abject features, in order to cast an anxious and troubled glance at the dark assemblage of chiefs. The silence was finally broken by the aged warrior so often named. He arose from the earth, and moving past the immovable form of Uncas, placed himself in a dignified attitude before the offender. At that moment, the withered squaw already mentioned moved into the circle, in a slow, sidling sort of a dance, holding the torch, and muttering the indistinct words of what might have been a species of incantation. Though her presence was altogether an intrusion, it was unheeded.

Approaching Uncas, she held the blazing brand in such a manner as to cast its red glare on his person, and to expose the slightest emotion of his countenance. The Mohican maintained his firm and haughty attitude; and his eyes, so far from deigning to meet her inquisitive look, dwelt steadily on the distance, as though it penetrated the obstacles which impeded the view and looked into futurity. Satisfied with her examination, she left him, with a slight expression of pleasure and proceeded to practice the same trying experiment on her delinquent countryman.

The young Huron was in his war paint, and very little of a finely molded form was concealed by his attire. The light rendered every limb and joint discernible, and Duncan turned away in horror when he saw they were writhing in irrepressible agony. The woman was commencing a low and plaintive howl at the sad and shameful spectacle, when the chief put forth his hand and gently pushed her aside.

"Reed-that-bends," he said, addressing the young culprit by name, and in his proper language, "though the Great Spirit has made you pleasant to the eyes, it would have been better that you had not been born. Your tongue is loud in the village, but in battle it is still. None of my young men strike the tomahawk deeper into the war-post none of them so lightly on the Yengeese. The enemy know the shape of your back, but they have never seen the color of your eyes. Three times have they called on you to come, and as often did you forget to answer. Your name will never be mentioned again in your tribe, it is already forgotten."

As the chief slowly uttered these words, pausing impressively between each sentence, the culprit raised his face, in deference to the other's rank and years. Shame, horror, and pride struggled in its lineaments. His eye, which was contracted with inward anguish, gleamed on the persons of those whose breath was his fame; and the latter emotion for an instant predominated. He arose to his feet, and baring his bosom, looked steadily on the keen, glittering knife, that was already upheld by his inexorable judge. As the weapon passed slowly into his heart he even smiled, as if in joy at having found death less dreadful than he had anticipated and fell heavily on his face, at the feet of the rigid and unyielding form of Uncas.

The squaw gave a loud and plaintive yell, dashed the torch to the earth, and buried everything in darkness. The whole shuddering group of spectators glided from the lodge like troubled sprites; and Duncan thought that he and the yet throbbing body of the victim of an Indian judgment had now become its only tenants.

CHAPTER XXIV.

"Thus spoke the sage: the kings without delay
Dissolve the council, and their chief obey."
—Pope's Iliad

IA single moment served to convince the youth that he was mistaken. A hand was laid, with a powerful pressure, on his arm, and the low voice of Uncas muttered in his ear:

"The Hurons are dogs. The sight of a coward's blood can never make a warrior tremble. The 'Gray Head' and the Sagamore are safe, and the rifle of Hawkeye is not asleep. Go, Uncas and the 'Open Hand' are now strangers. It is enough."

Heyward would gladly have heard more, but a gentle push from his friend urged him toward the door and admonished him of the danger that might attend the discovery of their intercourse. Slowly and reluctantly yielding to the necessity, he quitted the place, and mingled with the throng that hovered nigh. The dying fires in the clearing cast a dim and uncertain light on the dusky figures that were silently stalking to and from and occasionally a brighter gleam than common glanced into the lodge and exhibited the figure of Uncas still maintaining its upright attitude near the dead body of the Huron.

A knot of warriors soon entered the place again, and reissuing, they bore the senseless remains into the adjacent woods. After this termination of the scene, Duncan wandered among the lodges, unquestioned and unnoticed, endeavoring to find some trace of her in whose behalf he incurred the risk he ran. In the present temper of the tribe, it would have been easy to have fled and rejoined his companions, had such a wish crossed his mind. But, in addition to the never-ceasing anxiety on account of Alice, a fresher though feebler interest in the fate of Uncas assisted to chain him to the spot. He continued, therefore, to stray from hut to hut, looking into each only to encounter additional disappointment, until he had made the entire circuit of the village. Abandoning a species of inquiry that proved so fruitless, he retraced his steps to the council-lodge, resolved to seek and question David, in order to put an end to his doubts.

On reaching the building, which had proved alike the seat of judgment and the place of execution, the young man found that the excitement had already subsided. The warriors had reassembled, and were now calmly smoking, while they conversed gravely on the chief incidents of their recent expedition to the head of the Horican. Though the return of Duncan was likely to remind them of his character, and the suspicious circumstances of his visit, it produced no visible sensation. So far, the terrible scene that had just occurred proved favorable to his views, and he required no other prompter than his own feelings to convince him of the expediency of profiting by so unexpected an advantage.

Without seeming to hesitate, he walked into the lodge, and took his seat with a gravity that accorded admirably with the deportment of his hosts. A hasty but searching glance sufficed to tell him that, though Uncas still remained where he had left him, David had not reappeared. No other restraint was imposed on the former than the watchful looks of a young Huron, who had placed himself at hand; though an armed warrior leaned against the post that formed one side of the narrow doorway. In every other respect, the captive seemed at liberty; still he was excluded from all participation in the discourse and possessed much more of the air of some finely molded statue than a man having life and volition.

Heyward had too recently witnessed a frightful instance of the prompt punishments of the people into whose hands he had fallen to hazard an exposure by any officious boldness. He would greatly have preferred silence and meditation to speech when a discovery of his real condition might prove so instantly fatal. Unfortunately for this prudent resolution, his entertainers appeared otherwise disposed. He had not long occupied the seat wisely taken a little in the shade, when another of the elder warriors, who spoke the French language, addressed him:

"My Canada father does not forget his children," said the chief; "I thank him. An evil spirit lives in the wife of one of my young men. Can the cunning stranger frighten him away?"

Heyward possessed some knowledge of the mummery practiced among the Indians, in the cases of such supposed visitations. He saw, at a glance, that the circumstance might possibly be improved to further his own ends. It would, therefore, have been difficult, just then to have uttered a proposal that would have given him more satisfaction. Aware of the necessity of preserving the dignity of his imaginary character, however, he repressed his feelings, and answered with suitable mystery:

"Spirits differ; some yield to the power of wisdom, while others are too strong."

"My brother is a great medicine," said the cunning savage; "he will try?"

A gesture of assent was the answer. The Huron was content with the assurance, and, resuming his pipe, he awaited the proper moment to move. The impatient Heyward, inwardly execrating the cold customs of the savages, which required such sacrifices to appearance, was fair to assume an air of indifference, equal to that maintained by the chief, who was, in truth, a near relative of the afflicted woman.

The minutes lingered, and the delay had seemed an hour to the adventurer in empiricism, when the Huron laid aside his pipe and drew his robe across his breast, as if about to lead the way to the lodge of the invalid. Just then, a warrior of powerful frame, darkened the door, and stalking silently among the attentive group, he seated himself on one end of the low pile of brush which sustained Duncan. The latter cast an impatient look at his neighbor and felt his flesh creep with uncontrollable horror when he found himself in actual contact with Magua.

The sudden return of this artful and dreaded chief caused a delay in the departure of the Huron. Several pipes, that had been extinguished, were lighted again; while the newcomer, without speaking a word, drew his tomahawk from his girdle, and filling the bowl on its head began to inhale the vapors of the weed through the hollow handle, with as much indifference as if he had not been absent two weary days on a long and toilsome hunt. Ten minutes, which appeared so many ages to Duncan, might have passed in this manner; and the warriors were fairly enveloped in a cloud of white smoke before any of them spoke.

"Welcome!" one at length uttered; "has my friend found the moose?"

"The young men stagger under their burdens," returned Magua. "Let 'Reed-that-bends' go on the hunting path; he will meet them."

A deep and awful silence succeeded the utterance of the forbidden name. Each pipe dropped from the lips of its owner as though all had inhaled an impurity at the same instant. The smoke wreathed above their heads in little eddies, and curling in a spiral form it ascended swiftly through the opening in the roof of the lodge, leaving the place beneath clear of its fumes, and each dark visage distinctly visible. The looks of most of the warriors were riveted on the earth; though a few of the younger and less gifted of the party suffered their wild and glaring eyeballs to roll in the direction of a white-headed savage, who sat between two of the most venerated chiefs of the tribe. There was nothing in the air or attire of this Indian that would seem to entitle him to such a distinction. The former was rather depressed, than remarkable for the bearing of the natives; and the latter was such as was commonly worn by the ordinary men of the nation. Like most around him for more than a minute his look, too, was on the ground but trusting his eyes at length to steal a glance aside, he perceived that he was becoming an object of general attention. Then he arose and lifted his voice in the general silence.

"It was a lie," he said; "I had no son. He who was called by that name is forgotten; his blood was pale, and it came not from the veins of a Huron; the wicked Chippewas cheated my squaw. The Great Spirit has said that the family of Wiss-entush should end; he is happy who knows that the evil of his race dies with himself. I have done."

The speaker, who was the father of the recreant young Indian, looked round and about him, as if seeking commendation of his stoicism in the eyes of the auditors. But the stern customs of his people had made too severe an exaction of the feeble old man. The expression of his eye contradicted his figurative and boastful language, while every muscle in his wrinkled visage was working with anguish. Standing a single minute to enjoy his bitter triumph, he turned away, as if sickening at the gaze of men and veiling his face in his blanket, he walked from the lodge with the noiseless step of an Indian seeking, in the privacy of his own abode, the sympathy of one like himself, aged, forlorn and childless.

The Indians, who believe in the hereditary transmission of virtues and defects in character, suffered him to depart in silence. Then, with an elevation of breeding that many in a more cultivated state of society might profitably emulate, one of the chiefs drew the attention of the young men from the weakness they had just witnessed, by saying, in a cheerful voice, addressing himself in courtesy to Magua, as the newest comer:

"The Delawares have been like bears after the honey pots, prowling around my village. But who has ever found a Huron asleep?"

The darkness of the impending cloud which precedes a burst of thunder was not blacker than the brow of Magua as he exclaimed:

"The Delawares of the Lakes!"

"Not so. They who wear the petticoats of squaws, on their own river. One of them has been passing the tribe."

"Did my young men take his scalp?"

"His legs were good, though his arm is better for the hoe than the tomahawk," returned the other, pointing to the immovable form of Uncas.

Instead of manifesting any womanish curiosity to feast his eyes with the sight of a captive from a people he was known to have so much reason to hate, Magua continued to smoke, with the meditative air that he usually maintained, when there was no immediate call on his cunning or his eloquence. Although secretly amazed at the facts communicated by the speech of the aged father, he permitted himself to ask no questions, reserving his inquiries for a more suitable moment. It was only after a sufficient interval that he shook the ashes from his pipe, replaced the tomahawk, tightened his girdle, and arose, casting for the first time a glance in the direction of the prisoner, who stood a little behind him. The wary, though seemingly abstracted Uncas caught a glimpse of the movement, and turning suddenly to the light, their looks met. Near a minute these two bold and untamed spirits stood regarding one another steadily in the eye, neither quailing in the least before the fierce gaze he encountered. The form of Uncas dilated, and his nostrils opened like those of a tiger at bay but so rigid and unyielding was his posture, that he might easily have been converted by the imagination into an exquisite and faultless representation of the warlike deity of his tribe. The lineaments of the quivering features of Magua proved more ductile; his countenance gradually lost its character of defiance in an expression of ferocious joy and heaving a breath from the very bottom of his chest, he pronounced aloud the formidable name of:

"Le Cerf Agile!"

Each warrior sprang upon his feet at the utterance of the well-known appellation, and there was a short period during which the stoical constancy of the natives was completely conquered by surprise. The hated and yet respected name was repeated as by one voice, carrying the sound even beyond the limits of the lodge. The women and children, who lingered around the entrance, took up the words in an echo, which was succeeded by another shrill and plaintive howl. The latter was not yet ended, when the sensation among the men had entirely abated. Each one in presence seated himself, as though ashamed of his precipitation; but it was many minutes before their meaning eyes ceased to roll toward their captive, in curious examination of a warrior who had so often proved his prowess on the best and proudest of their nation. Uncas enjoyed his victory but was content with merely exhibiting his triumph by a quiet smile, an emblem of scorn which belongs to all time and every nation.

Magua caught the expression, and raising his arm, he shook it at the captive, the light silver ornaments attached to his bracelet rattling with the trembling agitation of the limb, as, in a tone of vengeance, he exclaimed, in English:

"Mohican, you die!"

"The healing waters will never bring the dead Hurons to life," returned Uncas, in the music of the Delawares; "the tumbling river washes their bones; their men are squaws: their women owls. Go! call together the Huron dogs, that they may look upon a warrior, My nostrils are offended; they sent the blood of a coward."

The latter allusion struck deep, and the injury rankled. Many of the Hurons understood the strange tongue in which the captive spoke, among which number was Magua. This cunning savage beheld and instantly profited by his advantage. Dropping the light robe of skin from his shoulder, he stretched forth his arm, and commenced a burst of his dangerous and artful eloquence. However much his influence among his people had been impaired by his occasional and besetting weakness, as well as by his desertion of the tribe, his courage and his fame as an orator were undeniable. He never spoke without auditors, and rarely without making converts to his opinions. On the present occasion, his native powers were stimulated by the thirst of revenge.

He again recounted the events of the attack on the island at Glenn's, the death of his associates and the escape of their most formidable enemies. Then he described the nature and position of the mount whither he had led such captives as had fallen into their hands. Of his own bloody intentions toward the maidens, and of his baffled malice he made no mention, but passed rapidly on to the surprise of the party by "La Longue Carabine," and its fatal termination. Here he paused, and looked about him, in affected veneration for the departed, but, in truth, to note the effect of his opening narrative. As usual, every eye was riveted on his face. Each dusky figure seemed a breathing statue, so motionless was the posture, so intense the attention of the individual.

Then Magua dropped his voice which had hitherto been clear, strong, and elevated, and touched upon the merits of the dead. No quality that was likely to command the sympathy of an Indian escaped his notice. One had never been known to follow the chase in vain; another had been indefatigable on the trail of their enemies. This was brave, that generous. In short, he so managed his allusions, that in a nation which was composed of so few families, he contrived to strike every chord that might find, in its turn, some breast in which to vibrate.

"Are the bones of my young men," he concluded, "in the burial-place of the Hurons? You know they are not. Their spirits are gone toward the setting sun, and are already crossing the great waters, to the happy hunting-grounds. But they departed without food, without guns or knives, without moccasins, naked and poor as they were born. Shall this be? Are their souls to enter the land of the just like hungry Iroquois or unmanly Delawares, or shall they meet their friends with arms in their hands and robes on their backs? What will our fathers think the tribes of the Wyandots have become? They will look on their children with a dark eye, and say, 'Go! a Chippewa has come hither with the name of a Huron.' Brothers, we must not forget the dead; a red skin never ceases to remember. We will load the back of this Mohican until he staggers under our bounty and dispatch him after my young men. They call to us for aid, though our ears are not open; they say, 'Forget us not.' When they see the spirit of this Mohican toiling after them with his burden, they will know we are of that mind. Then will they go on happy; and our children will say, 'So did our fathers to their friends, so must we do to them.' What is a Yengee? we have slain many, but the earth is still pale. A stain on the name of Huron can only be hid by blood that comes from the veins of an Indian. Let this Delaware die."

The effect of such a harangue, delivered in the nervous language and with the emphatic manner of a Huron orator, could scarcely be mistaken. Magua had so artfully blended the natural sympathies with the religious superstition of his auditors, that their minds, already prepared by custom to sacrifice a victim to the manes of their countrymen, lost every vestige of humanity in a wish for revenge. One warrior in particular, a man of wild and ferocious mien, had been conspicuous for the attention he had given to the words of the speaker. His countenance had changed with each passing emotion, until it settled into a look of deadly malice. As Magua ended he arose and, uttering the yell of a demon, his polished little axe was seen glancing in the torchlight as he whirled it above his head. The motion and the cry were too sudden for words to interrupt his bloody intention. It appeared as if a bright gleam shot from his hand, which was crossed at the same moment by a dark and powerful line. The former was the tomahawk in its passage; the latter the arm that Magua darted forward to divert its aim. The quick and ready motion of the chief was not entirely too late. The keen weapon cut the war plume from the scalping tuft of Uncas, and passed through the frail wall of the lodge as though it were hurled from some formidable engine.

Duncan had seen the threatening action, and sprang upon his feet, with a heart which, while it leaped into his throat, swelled with the most generous resolution in behalf of his friend. A glance told him that the blow had failed, and terror changed to admiration. Uncas stood still, looking his enemy in the eye with features that seemed superior to emotion. Marble could not be colder, calmer, or steadier than the countenance he put upon this sudden and vindictive attack. Then, as if pitying a want of skill which had proved so fortunate to himself, he smiled and muttered a few words of contempt in his own tongue.

"No!" said Magua, after satisfying himself of the safety of the captive; "the sun must shine on his shame; the squaws must see his flesh tremble, or our revenge will be like the play of boys. Go! take him where there is silence; let us see if a Delaware can sleep at night, and in the morning die."

The young men whose duty it was to guard the prisoner instantly passed their ligaments of bark across his arms, and led him from the lodge, amid a profound and ominous silence. It was only as the figure of Uncas stood in the opening of the door that his firm step hesitated. There he turned and in the sweeping and haughty glance that he threw around the circle of his enemies, Duncan caught a look which he was glad to construe into an expression that he was not entirely deserted by hope.

Magua was content with his success or too much occupied with his secret purposes to push his inquiries any further. Shaking his mantle and folding it on his bosom, he also quitted the place, without pursuing a subject which might have proved so fatal to the individual at his elbow. Notwithstanding his rising resentment, his natural firmness, and his anxiety on behalf of Uncas, Heyward felt sensibly relieved by the absence of so dangerous and so subtle a foe. The excitement produced by the speech gradually subsided. The warriors resumed their seats and clouds of smoke once more filled the lodge. For near half an hour, not a syllable was uttered, or scarcely a look cast aside; a grave and meditative silence being the ordinary succession to every scene of violence and commotion among these beings, who were alike so impetuous and yet so self-restrained.

When the chief, who had solicited the aid of Duncan, finished his pipe, he made a final and successful movement toward departing. A motion of a finger was the intimation he gave the supposed physician to follow and passing through the clouds of smoke, Duncad was glad, on more accounts than one, to be able at last to breathe the pure air of a cool and refreshing summer evening.

Instead of pursuing his way among those lodges where Heyward had already made his unsuccessful search, his companion turned aside, and proceeded directly toward the base of an adjacent mountain, which overhung the temporary village. A thicket of brush skirted its foot, and it became necessary to proceed through a crooked and narrow path. The boys had resumed their sports in the clearing and were enacting a mimic chase to the post among themselves. In order to render their games as like the reality as possible, one of the boldest of their number had conveyed a few brands into some piles of treetops that had hitherto escaped the burning. The blaze of one of these fires lighted the way of the chief and Duncan and gave a character of additional wildness to the rude scenery. At a little distance from a bald rock, and directly in its front, they entered a grassy opening, which they prepared to cross. Just then fresh fuel was added to the fire, and a powerful light penetrated even to that distant spot. It fell upon the white surface of the mountain and was reflected downward upon a dark and mysterious looking being that arose, unexpectedly, in their path. The Indian paused, as if doubtful whether to proceed, and permitted his companion to approach his side. A large black ball, which at first seemed stationary, now began to move in a manner that to the latter was inexplicable. Again, the fire brightened, and its glare fell more distinctly on the object. Then even Duncan knew it, by its restless and sidling attitudes, which kept the upper part of its form in constant motion, while the animal itself appeared seated, to be a bear. Though it growled loudly and fiercely, and there were instants when its glistening eyeballs might be seen, it gave no other indications of hostility. The Huron, at least, seemed assured that the intentions of this singular intruder were peaceable, for after giving it an attentive examination, he quietly pursued his course.

Duncan, who knew that the animal was often domesticated among the Indians, followed the example of his companion, believing that some favorite of the tribe had found its way into the thicket, in search of food. They passed it unmolested. Though obliged to come nearly in contact with the monster, the Huron, who had at first so warily determined the character of his strange visitor, was now content with proceeding without wasting a moment in further examination; but Heyward was unable to prevent his eyes from looking backward, in salutary watchfulness against attacks in the rear. His uneasiness was in no degree diminished when he perceived the beast rolling along their path and following their footsteps. He would have spoken, but the Indian at that moment shoved aside a door of bark and entered a cavern in the bosom of the mountain.

Profiting by so easy a method of retreat, Duncan stepped after him, and was gladly closing the slight cover to the opening, when he felt it drawn from his hand by the beast, whose shaggy form immediately darkened the passage. They were now in a straight and long gallery, in a chasm of the rocks, where retreat without encountering the animal was impossible. Making the best of the circumstances, the young man pressed forward, keeping as close as possible to his conductor. The bear growled frequently at his heels, and once or twice its enormous paws were laid on his person, as if disposed to prevent his further passage into the den.

How long the nerves of Heyward would have sustained him in this extraordinary situation, it might be difficult to decide, for, happily, he soon found relief. A glimmer of light had constantly been in their front, and they now arrived at the place whence it proceeded.

A large cavity in the rock had been rudely fitted to answer the purposes of many apartments. The subdivisions were simple but ingenious, being composed of stone, sticks, and bark, intermingled. Openings above admitted the light by day, and at night fires and torches supplied the place of the sun. Hither the Hurons had brought most of their valuables, especially those which more particularly pertained to the nation; and hither, as it now appeared, the sick woman, who was believed to be the victim of supernatural power, had been transported also, under an impression that her tormentor would find more difficulty in making his assaults through walls of stone than through the leafy coverings of the lodges. The apartment into which Duncan and his guide first entered, had been exclusively devoted to her accommodation. The latter approached her bedside, which was surrounded by females, in the center of whom Heyward was surprised to find his missing friend David.

A single look was sufficient to apprise the pretended leech that the invalid was far beyond his powers of healing. She lay in a sort of paralysis, indifferent to the objects which crowded before her sight, and happily unconscious of suffering. Heyward was far from regretting that his mummeries were to be performed on one who was much too ill to take an interest in their failure or success. The slight qualm of conscience which had been excited by the intended deception was instantly appeased and he began to collect his thoughts, in order to enact his part with suitable spirit, when he found he was about to be anticipated in his skill by an attempt to prove the power of music.

Gamut, who had stood prepared to pour forth his spirit in song when the visitors entered, after delaying a moment, drew a strain from his pipe and commenced a hymn that might have worked a miracle, had faith in its efficacy been of much avail. He was allowed to proceed to the close, the Indians respecting his imaginary infirmity, and Duncan too glad of the delay to hazard the slightest interruption. As the dying cadence of his strains was falling on the ears of the latter, he started aside at hearing them repeated behind him, in a voice half human and half sepulchral. Looking around, he beheld the shaggy monster seated on end in a shadow of the cavern, where, while his restless body swung in the uneasy manner of the animal, it repeated, in a sort of low growl, sounds, if not words, which bore some slight resemblance to the melody of the singer.

The effect of so strange an echo on David may better be imagined than described. His eyes opened as if he doubted their truth; and his voice became instantly mute in excess of wonder. A deep-laid scheme, of communicating some important intelligence to Heyward, was driven from his recollection by an emotion which very nearly resembled fear, but which he was fain to believe was admiration. Under its influence, he exclaimed aloud: "She expects you, and is at hand"; and precipitately left the cavern.

CHAPTER XXV.

"Snug.—Have you the lion's part written? Pray you, if it be, give it to me, for I am slow of study.

Quince.—You may do it extempore, for it is nothing but roaring."

—Midsummer Night's Dream.

There was a strange blending of the ridiculous with that which was solemn in this scene. The beast still continued its rolling, and apparently untiring movements, though its ludicrous attempt to imitate the melody of David ceased the instant the latter abandoned the field. The words of Gamut were, as has been seen, in his native tongue; and to Duncan they seem pregnant with some hidden meaning, though nothing present assisted him in discovering the object of their allusion. A speedy end was, however, put to every conjecture on the subject, by the manner of the chief, who advanced to the bedside of the invalid, and beckoned away the whole group of female attendants that had clustered there to witness the skill of the stranger. He was implicitly, though reluctantly, obeyed; and when the low echo which rang along the hollow, natural gallery, from the distant closing door, had ceased, pointing toward his insensible daughter, he said:

"Now let my brother show his power."

Thus, unequivocally called on to exercise the functions of his assumed character, Heyward was apprehensive that the smallest delay might prove dangerous. Endeavoring, then, to collect his ideas, he prepared to perform that species of incantation, and those uncouth rites, under which the Indian conjurers are accustomed to concealing their ignorance and impotency. It is more than probable that, in the disordered state of his thoughts, he would soon have fallen into some suspicious, if not fatal, error had not his incipient attempts been interrupted by a fierce growl from the quadruped. Three several times did he renew his efforts to proceed, and as often was he met by the same unaccountable opposition, each interruption seeming more savage and threatening than the preceding.

"The cunning ones are jealous," said the Huron; "I go. Brother, the woman is the wife of one of my bravest young men; deal justly by her. Peace!" he added, beckoning to the discontented beast to be quiet; "I go."

The chief was as good as his word, and Duncan now found himself alone in that wild and desolate abode with the helpless invalid and the fierce and dangerous brute. The latter listened to the movements of the Indian with that air of sagacity that a bear is known to possess, until another echo announced that he had also left the cavern, when it turned and came waddling up to Duncan before whom it seated itself in its natural attitude, erect like a man. The youth looked anxiously about him for some weapon, with which he might make a resistance against the attack he now seriously expected.

It seemed, however, as if the humor of the animal had suddenly changed. Instead of continuing its discontented growls, or manifesting any further signs of anger, the whole of its shaggy body shook violently, as if agitated by some strange internal convulsion. The huge and unwieldy talons pawed stupidly about the grinning muzzle, and while Heyward kept his eyes riveted on its movements with jealous watchfulness, the grim head fell on one side and in its place appeared the honest sturdy countenance of the scout, who was indulging from the bottom of his soul in his own peculiar expression of merriment.

"Hist!" said the wary woodsman, interrupting Heyward's exclamation of surprise; "the varlets are about the place, and any sounds that are not natural to witchcraft would bring them back upon us in a body."

"Tell me the meaning of this masquerade; and why you have attempted so desperate an adventure?"

"Ah, reason and calculation are often outdone by accident," returned the scout. "But, as a story should always commence at the beginning, I will tell you the whole in order. After we parted I placed the commandant and the Sagamore in an old beaver lodge, where they are safer from the Hurons than they would be in the garrison of Edward; for your high north-west Indians, not having as yet got the traders among them, continued to venerate the beaver. After which Uncas and I pushed for the other encampment as was agreed. Have you seen the lad?"

"To my great grief! He is captive and condemned to die at the rising of the sun."

"I had misgivings that such would be his fate," resumed the scout, in a less confident and joyous tone. But soon regaining his naturally firm voice, he continued: "His bad fortune is the true reason of my being here, for it would never do to abandon such a boy to the Hurons. A rare time the knaves would have of it, could they tie 'The Bounding Elk' and 'The Long Carabine', as they call me, to the same stake! Though why they have given me such a name I never knew, there being as little likeness between the gifts of 'killdeer' and the performance of one of your real Canada carabynes, as there is between the nature of a pipestone and a flint."

"Keep to your tale," said the impatient Heyward; "we know not at what moment the Hurons may return."

"No fear of them. A conjurer must have his time, like a straggling priest in the settlements. We are as safe from interruption as a missionary would be at the beginning of a two hours' discourse. Well, Uncas and I fell in with a return party of the varlets; the lad was much too forward for a scout; nay, for that matter, being of hot blood, he was not so much to blame; and, after all, one of the Hurons proved a coward, and in fleeing led him into an ambushment."

"And dearly has he paid for the weakness."

The scout significantly passed his hand across his own throat, and nodded, as if he said, "I comprehend your meaning." After which he continued, in a more audible though scarcely more intelligible language:

"After the loss of the boy I turned upon the Hurons, as you may judge. There have been scrimmages atween one or two of their outliers and myself, but that is neither here nor there. So, after I had shot the imps, I got in pretty nigh to the lodges without further commotion. Then what should luck do in my favor but lead me to the very spot where one of the most famous conjurers of the tribe was dressing himself, as I well knew, for some great battle with Satan though why should I call that luck, which it now seems was an especial ordering of Providence. So, a judgmatical rap over the head stiffened the lying impostor for a time and leaving him a bit of walnut for his supper, to prevent an uproar, and stringing him up atween two saplings, I made free with his finery, and took the part of the bear on myself, in order that the operations might proceed."

"And admirably did you enact the character; the animal itself might have been shamed by the representation."

"Lord, major," returned the flattered woodsman, "I should be but a poor scholar for one who has studied so long in the wilderness, did I not know how to set forth the movements or nature of such a beast. Had it been now a catamount, or even a full-size panther, I would have embellished a performance for you worth regarding. But it is no such marvelous feat to exhibit the feats of so dull a beast; though, for that matter, too, a bear may be overacted. Yes, yes; it is not every imitator that knows nature may be outdone easier than she is equaled. But all our work is yet before us. Where is the gentle one?"

"Heaven knows. I have examined every lodge in the village, without discovering the slightest trace of her presence in the tribe."

"You heard what the singer said, as he left us: 'She is at hand, and expects you'?"

"I have been compelled to believe he alluded to this unhappy woman."

"The simpleton was frightened and blundered through his message; but he had a deeper meaning. Here are walls enough to separate the whole settlement. A bear ought to climb; therefore, will I take a look above them. There may be honeypots hid in these rocks and I am a beast, you know, that has a hankering for the sweets."

The scout looked behind him, laughing at his own conceit, while he clambered up the partition, imitating, as he went, the clumsy motions of the beast he represented; but the instant the summit was gained he made a gesture for silence, and slid down with the utmost precipitation.

"She is here," he whispered, "and by that door you will find her. I would have spoken a word of comfort to the afflicted soul; but the sight of such a monster might upset her reason. Though for that matter, major, you are none of the most inviting yourself in your paint."

Duncan, who had already swung eagerly forward, drew instantly back on hearing these discouraging words.

"Am I, then, so very revolting?" he demanded, with an air of chagrin.

"You might not startle a wolf or turn the Royal Americans from a discharge; but I have seen the time when you had a better favored look; your streaked countenances are not ill-judged of by the squaws, but young women of white blood give the preference to their own color. See," he added, pointing to a place where the water trickled from a rock, forming a little crystal spring, before it found an issue through the adjacent crevices; "you may easily get rid of the Sagamore's daub, and when you come back, I will try my hand at a new embellishment. It's as common for a conjurer to alter his paint as for a buck in the settlements to change his finery."

The deliberate woodsman had little occasion to hunt for arguments to enforce his advice. He was yet speaking when Duncan availed himself of the water. In a moment every frightful or offensive mark was obliterated, and the youth appeared again in the lineaments with which he had been gifted by nature. Thus, prepared for an interview with his mistress, he took a hasty leave of his companion, and disappeared through the indicated passage. The scout witnessed his departure with complacency, nodding his head after him, and muttering his good wishes; after which he very coolly set about an examination of the state of the larder, among the Hurons, the cavern, among other purposes, being used as a receptacle for the fruits of their hunts.

Duncan had no other guide than a distant glimmering light, which served, however, the office of a polar star to the lover. By its aid he was enabled to enter the haven of his hopes, which was merely another apartment of the cavern, that had been solely appropriated to the safekeeping of so important a prisoner as a daughter of the commandant of William Henry. It was profusely strewed with the plunder of that unlucky fortress. In the midst of this confusion, he found her he sought, pale, anxious and terrified, but lovely. David had prepared her for such a visit.

"Duncan!" she exclaimed, in a voice that seemed to tremble at the sounds created by itself.

"Alice!" he answered, leaping carelessly among trunks, boxes, arms, and furniture, until he stood at her side.

"I knew that you would never desert me," she said, looking up with a momentary glow on her otherwise dejected countenance. "But you are alone! Grateful as it is to be thus remembered, I could wish to think you are not entirely alone."

Duncan, observing that she trembled in a manner which betrayed her inability to stand, gently induced her to be seated, while he recounted those leading incidents which it has been our task to accord. Alice listened with breathless interest; and though the young man touched lightly on the sorrows of the stricken father; taking care, however, not to wound the self-love of his auditor, the tears ran as freely down the cheeks of the daughter as though she had never wept before. The soothing tenderness of Duncan, however, soon quieted the first burst of her emotions and she then heard him to the close with undivided attention, if not with composure.

"And now, Alice," he added, "you will see how much is still expected of you. By the assistance of our experienced and invaluable friend, the scout, we may find our way from this savage people, but you will have to exert your utmost fortitude. Remember that you fly to the arms of your venerable parent and how much his happiness, as well as your own, depends on those exertions."

"Can I do otherwise for a father who has done so much for me?"

"And for me, too," continued the youth, gently pressing the hand he held in both his own.

The look of innocence and surprise which he received in return convinced Duncan of the necessity of being more explicit.

"This is neither the place nor the occasion to detain you with selfish wishes," he added; "but what heart loaded like mine would not wish to cast its burden? They say misery is the closest of all ties; our common suffering in your behalf left but little to be explained between your father and myself."

"And dearest Cora, Duncan; surely Cora was not forgotten?"

"Not forgotten! no; regretted, as woman was seldom mourned before. Your venerable father knew no difference between his children but I—Alice, you will not be offended when I say, that to me her worth was in a degree obscured—"

"Then you knew not the merit of my sister," said Alice, withdrawing her hand; "of you she ever speaks as of one who is her dearest friend."

"I would gladly believe her such," returned Duncan, hastily; "I could wish her to be even more; but with you, Alice, I have the permission of your father to aspire to a still nearer and dearer tie."

Alice trembled violently, and there was an instant during which she bent her face aside, yielding to the emotions common to her sex; but they quickly passed away, leaving her mistress of her deportment, if not of her affections.

"Heyward," she said, looking him full in the face with a touching expression of innocence and dependency, "give me the sacred presence and the holy sanction of that parent before you urge me further."

"Though more I should not, less I could not say," the youth was about to answer, when he was interrupted by a light tap on his shoulder. Starting to his feet, he turned, and, confronting the intruder, his looks fell on the dark form and malignant visage of Magua. The deep guttural laugh of the savage sounded, at such a moment, to Duncan, like the hellish taunt of a demon. Had he pursued the sudden and fierce impulse of the instant, he would have cast himself on the Huron, and committed their fortunes to the issue of a deadly struggle. But, without arms of any description, ignorant of what succor his subtle enemy could command, and charged with the safety of one who was just then dearer than ever to his heart, he no sooner entertained than he abandoned the desperate intention.

"What is your purpose?" said Alice, meekly folding her arms on her bosom, and struggling to conceal an agony of apprehension in behalf of Heyward, in the usual cold and distant manner with which she received the visits of her captor.

The exulting Indian had resumed his austere countenance, though he drew warily back before the menacing glance of the young man's fiery eye. He regarded both his captives for a moment with a steady look, and then, stepping aside, he dropped a log of wood across a door different from that by which Duncan had entered. The latter now comprehended the manner of his surprise and believing himself irretrievably lost, he drew Alice to his bosom, and stood prepared to meet a fate which he hardly regretted, since it was to be suffered in such company. But Magua meditated no immediate violence. His first measures were very evidently taken to secure his new captive; nor did he even bestow a second glance at the motionless forms in the center of the cavern, until he had completely cut off every hope of retreat through the private outlet, he had himself used. He was watched in all his movements by Heyward, who, however, remained firm, still folding the fragile form of Alice to his heart, at once too proud and too hopeless to ask favor of an enemy so often foiled. When Magua had affected his object he approached his prisoners, and said in English:

"The pale faces trap the cunning beavers; but the red-skins know how to take the Yengeese."

"Huron, do your worst!" exclaimed the excited Heyward, forgetful that a double stake was involved in his life; "you and your vengeance are alike despised."

"Will the white man speak these words at the stake?" asked Magua; manifesting, at the same time, how little faith he had in the other's resolution by the sneer that accompanied his words.

"Here; singly to your face, or in the presence of your nation."

"Le Renard Subtil is a great chief!" returned the Indian; "he will go and bring his young men, to see how bravely a pale face can laugh at tortures."

He turned away while speaking and was about to leave the place through the avenue by which Duncan had approached, when a growl caught his ear, and caused him to hesitate. The figure of the bear appeared in the door, where it sat, rolling from side to side in its customary restlessness. Magua, like the father of the sick woman, eyed it keenly for a moment, as if to ascertain its character. He was far above the more vulgar superstitions of his tribe and so soon as he recognized the well-known attire of the conjurer, he prepared to pass it in cool contempt. But a louder and more threatening growl caused him again to pause. Then he seemed as if suddenly resolved to trifle no longer and moved resolutely forward.

The mimic animal, which had advanced a little, retired slowly in his front, until it arrived again at the pass, when, rearing on his hinder legs, it beat the air with its paws, in the manner practiced by its brutal prototype.

"Fool!" exclaimed the chief, in Huron, "go play with the children and squaws; leave men to their wisdom."

He once more endeavored to pass the supposed empiric, scorning even the parade of threatening to use the knife, or tomahawk, that was pendent from his belt. Suddenly the beast extended its arms, or rather legs, and enclosed him in a grasp that might have vied with the far-famed power of the "bear's hug" itself. Heyward had watched the whole procedure, on the part of Hawkeye, with breathless interest. At first, he relinquished his hold of Alice; then he caught up a thong of buckskin, which had been used around some bundle and when he beheld his enemy with his two arms pinned to his side by the iron muscles of the scout, he rushed upon him, and effectually secured them there. Arms, legs, and feet were encircled in twenty folds of the thong, in less time than we have taken to record the circumstance. When the formidable Huron was completely pinioned, the scout released his hold, and Duncan laid his enemy on his back, utterly helpless.

Throughout the whole of this sudden and extraordinary operation, Magua, though he had struggled violently, until assured he was in the hands of one whose nerves were far better strung than his own, had not uttered the slightest exclamation. But when Hawkeye, by way of making a summary explanation of his conduct, removed the shaggy jaws of the beast, and exposed his own rugged and earnest countenance to the gaze of the Huron, the philosophy of the latter was so far mastered as to permit him to utter the never failing:

"Hugh!"

"Ay, you've found your tongue," said his undisturbed conqueror; "now, in order that you shall not use it to our ruin, I must make free to stop your mouth."

As there was no time to be lost, the scout immediately set about effecting so necessary a precaution; and when he had gagged the Indian, his enemy might safely have been considered as "hors de combat."

"By what place did the imp enter?" asked the industrious scout when his work was ended. "Not a soul has passed my way since you left me."

Duncan pointed out the door by which Magua had come, and which now presented too many obstacles to a quick retreat.

"Bring on the gentle one, then," continued his friend; "we must make a push for the woods by the other outlet."

"'Tis impossible!" said Duncan; "fear has overcome her, and she is helpless. Alice! my sweet, my own Alice, arouse yourself; now is the moment to fly. 'Tis in vain! she hears but is unable to follow. Go, noble and worthy friend; save yourself, and leave me to my fate."

"Every trail has its end, and every calamity brings its lesson!" returned the scout. "There, wrap her in them Indian cloths. Conceal all of her little form. Nay, that foot has no fellow in the wilderness; it will betray her. All, every part. Now take her in your arms and follow. Leave the rest to me."

Duncan, as may be gathered from the words of his companion, was eagerly obeying; and, as the other finished speaking, he took the light person of Alice in his arms and followed in the footsteps of the scout. They found the sick woman as they had left her, still alone, and passed swiftly on, by the natural gallery, to the place of entrance. As they approached the little door of bark, a murmur of voices without announced that the friends and relatives of the invalid were gathered about the place, patiently awaiting a summons to re-enter.

"If I open my lips to speak," Hawkeye whispered, "my English, which is the genuine tongue of a white-skin, will tell the varlets that an enemy is among them. You must give them your jargon, major and say that we have shut the evil spirit in the cave and are taking the woman to the woods in order to find strengthening roots. Practice all your cunning, for it is a lawful undertaking."

The door opened a little, as if one without was listening to the proceedings within, and compelled the scout to cease his directions. A fierce growl repelled the eavesdropper, and then the scout boldly threw open the covering of bark and left the place, enacting the character of a bear as he proceeded. Duncan kept close at his heels, and soon found himself in the center of a cluster of twenty anxious relatives and friends.

The crowd fell back a little, and permitted the father, and one who appeared to be the husband of the woman, to approach.

"Has my brother driven away the evil spirit?" demanded the former. "What has he in his arms?"

"Thy child," returned Duncan, gravely; "the disease has gone out of her; it is shut up in the rocks. I take the woman to a distance, where I will strengthen her against any further attacks. She will be in the wigwam of the young man when the sun comes again."

When the father had translated the meaning of the stranger's words into the Huron language, a suppressed murmur announced the satisfaction with which this intelligence was received. The chief himself waved his hand for Duncan to proceed, saying aloud, in a firm voice, and with a lofty manner:

"Go; I am a man, and I will enter the rock and fight the wicked one."

Heyward had gladly obeyed, and was already past the little group, when these startling words arrested him.

"Is my brother mad?" he exclaimed; "is he cruel? He will meet the disease, and it will enter him or he will drive out the disease, and it will chase his daughter into the woods. No; let my children wait without, and if the spirit appears beat him down with clubs. He is cunning, and will bury himself in the mountain, when he sees how many are ready to fight him."

This singular warning had the desired effect. Instead of entering the cavern, the father and husband drew their tomahawks, and posted themselves in readiness to deal their vengeance on the imaginary tormentor of their sick relative, while the women and children broke branches from the bushes, or seized fragments of the rock, with a similar intention. At this favorable moment the counterfeit conjurers disappeared.

Hawkeye, at the same time that he had presumed so far on the nature of the Indian superstitions, was not ignorant that they were rather tolerated than relied on by the wisest of the chiefs. He well knew the value of time in the present emergency. Whatever might be the extent of the self-delusion of his enemies, and however it had tended to assist his schemes, the slightest cause of suspicion, acting on the subtle nature of an Indian, would be likely to prove fatal. Taking the path, therefore, that was most likely to avoid observation, he rather skirted than entered the village. The warriors were still to be seen in the distance, by the fading light of the fires, stalking from lodge to lodge. But the children had abandoned their sports for their beds of skins, and the quiet of night was already beginning to prevail over the turbulence and excitement of so busy and important an evening.

Alice revived under the renovating influence of the open air, and, as her physical rather than her mental powers had been the subject of weakness, she stood in no need of any explanation of that which had occurred.

"Now let me make an effort to walk," she said, when they had entered the forest, blushing, though unseen, that she had not been sooner able to quit the arms of Duncan; "I am indeed restored."

"Nay, Alice, you are yet too weak."

The maiden struggled gently to release herself, and Heyward was compelled to part with his precious burden. The representative of the bear had certainly been an entire stranger to the delicious emotions of the lover while his arms encircled his mistress; and he was, perhaps, a stranger also to the nature of that feeling of ingenuous shame that oppressed the trembling Alice. But when he found himself at a suitable distance from the lodges he made a halt, and spoke on a subject of which he was thoroughly the master.

"This path will lead you to the brook," he said; "follow its northern bank until you come to a fall; mount the hill on your right, and you will see the fires of the other people. There you must go and demand protection; if they are true Delawares you will be safe. A distant flight with that gentle one, just now, is impossible. The Hurons would follow up our trail and master our scalps before we had got a dozen miles. Go, and Providence be with you."

"And you!" demanded Heyward, in surprise; "surely we part not here?"

"The Hurons hold the pride of the Delawares; the last of the high blood of the Mohicans is in their power," returned the scout; "I go to see what can be done in his favor. Had they mastered your scalp, major, a knave should have fallen for every hair it held, as I promised; but if the young Sagamore is to be led to the stake, the Indians shall see also how a man without a cross can die."

Not in the least offended with the decided preference that the sturdy woodsman gave to one who might, in some degree, be called the child of his adoption, Duncan still continued to urge such reasons against so desperate an effort as presented themselves. He was aided by Alice, who mingled her entreaties with those of Heyward that he would abandon a resolution that promised so much danger, with so little hope of success. Their eloquence and ingenuity were expended in vain. The scout heard them attentively, but impatiently, and finally closed the discussion, by answering, in a tone that instantly silenced

Alice, while it told Heyward how fruitless any further remonstrances would be.

"I have heard," he said, "that there is a feeling in youth which binds man to woman closer than the father is tied to the son. It may be so. I have seldom been where women of my color dwell, but such may be the gifts of nature in the settlements. You have risked life, and all that is dear to you, to bring off this gentle one, and I suppose that some such disposition is at the bottom of it all. As for me, I taught the lad the real character of a rifle; and well has he paid me for it. I have fou't at his side in many a bloody scrimmage; and so long as I could hear the crack of his piece in one ear, and that of the Sagamore in the other, I knew no enemy was on my back. Winters and summer, nights, and days, have we roved the wilderness in company, eating of the same dish, one sleeping while the other watched and afore it shall be said that Uncas was taken to the torment, and I at hand. There is but a single Ruler of us all, whatever may the color of the skin and Him I call to witness, that before the Mohican boy shall perish for the want of a friend, good faith shall depart the 'arth, and 'killdeer' become as harmless as the tooting weapon of the singer!"

Duncan released his hold on the arm of the scout, who turned, and steadily retraced his steps toward the lodges. After pausing a moment to gaze at his retiring form, the successful and yet sorrowful Heyward and Alice took their way together toward the distant village of the Delawares.

CHAPTER XXVI.

"Bot.—Let me play the lion too."
—Midsummer Night's Dream

Notwithstanding the high resolution of Hawkeye, he fully comprehended all the difficulties and danger he was about to incur. In his return to the camp, his acute and practiced intellects were intently engaged in devising means to counteract a watchfulness and suspicion on the part of his enemies, that he knew were, in no degree, inferior to his own. Nothing but the color of his skin had saved the lives of Magua and the conjurer, who would have been the first victims sacrificed to his own security, had not the scout believed such an act, however congenial it might be to the nature of an Indian, utterly unworthy of one who boasted a descent from men that knew no cross of blood. Accordingly, he trusted to the withes and ligaments with which he had bound his captives and pursued his way directly toward the center of the lodges. As he approached the buildings, his steps become more deliberate, and his vigilant eye suffered no sign, whether friendly or hostile, to escape him. A neglected hut was a little in advance of the others and appeared as if it had been deserted when half completed most probably on account of failing in some of the more important requisites, such as wood or water. A faint light glimmered through its cracks, however, and announced that, notwithstanding its imperfect structure, it was not without a tenant. Thither, then, the scout proceeded, like a prudent general, who was about to feel the advanced positions of his enemy, before he hazarded the main attack.

Throwing himself into a suitable posture for the beast he represented, Hawkeye crawled to a little opening, where he might command a view of the interior. It proved to be the abiding place of David Gamut. Hither the faithful singing-master had now brought himself, together with all his sorrows, his apprehensions, and his meek dependence on the protection of Providence. At the precise moment when his ungainly person came under the observation of the scout, in the manner just mentioned, the woodsman himself, though in his assumed character, was the subject of the solitary being's propounded reflections.

However implicit the faith of David was in the performance of ancient miracles; he eschewed the belief of any direct supernatural agency in the management of modern morality. In other words, while he had implicit faith in the ability of Balaam's ass to speak, he was somewhat skeptical on the subject of a bear's singing; and yet he had been assured of the latter, on the testimony of his own exquisite organs. There was something in his air and manner that betrayed to the scout the utter confusion of the state of his mind. He was seated on a pile of brush, a few twigs from which occasionally fed his low fire, with his head leaning on his arm, in a posture of melancholy musing. The costume of the votary of music had undergone no other alteration from that so lately described, except that he had covered his bald head with the triangular beaver, which had not proved sufficiently alluring to excite the cupidity of any of his captors.

The ingenious Hawkeye, who recalled the hasty manner in which the other had abandoned his post at the bedside of the sick woman, was not without his suspicions concerning the subject of so much solemn deliberation. First making the circuit of the hut, and ascertaining that it stood quite alone, and that the character of its inmate was likely to protect it from visitors, he ventured through its low door, into the very presence of Gamut. The position of the latter brought the fire between them; and when Hawkeye had seated himself on end, near a minute elapsed, during which the two remained regarding each other without speaking. The suddenness and the nature of the surprise had nearly proved too much for we will not say the philosophy but for the pitch and resolution of David. He fumbled for his pitchpipe and arose with a confused intention of attempting a musical exorcism.

"Dark and mysterious monster!" he exclaimed, while with trembling hands he disposed of his auxiliary eyes, and sought his never-failing resource in trouble, the gifted version of the psalms; "I know not your nature nor intents but if aught you meditate against the person and rights of one of the humblest servants of the temple, listen to the inspired language of the youth of Israel, and repent."

The bear shook his shaggy sides, and then a well-known voice replied:

"Put up the tooting weapon and teach your throat modesty. Five words of plain and comprehendible English are worth just now an hour of squalling."

"What art thou?" demanded David, utterly disqualified to pursue his original intention, and nearly gasping for breath.

"A man like yourself; and one whose blood is as little tainted by the cross of a bear, or an Indian, as your own. Have you so soon forgotten from whom you received the foolish instrument you hold in your hand?"

"Can these things be?" returned David, breathing more freely, as the truth began to dawn upon him. "I have found many marvels during my sojourn with the heathen but surely nothing to excel this."

"Come, come," returned Hawkeye, uncasing his honest countenance, the better to assure the wavering confidence of his companion; "you may see a skin, which, if it be not as white as one of the gentle ones, has no tinge of red to it that the winds of the heaven and the sun have not bestowed. Now let us to business."

"First tell me of the maiden, and of the youth who so bravely sought her," interrupted David.

"Ay, they are happily freed from the tomahawks of these varlets. But can you put me on the scent of Uncas?"

"The young man is in bondage, and much I fear his death is decreed. I greatly mourn that one so well disposed should die in his ignorance, and I have sought a goodly hymn—"

"Can you lead me to him?"

"The task will not be difficult," returned David, hesitating; "though I greatly fear your presence would rather increase than mitigate his unhappy fortunes."

"No more words, but lead on," returned Hawkeye, concealing his face again and setting the example in his own person, by instantly quitting the lodge.

As they proceeded, the scout ascertained that his companion found access to Uncas, under privilege of his imaginary infirmity, aided by the favor he had acquired with one of the guards, who, in consequence of speaking a little English, had been selected by David as the subject of a religious conversion. How far the Huron comprehended the intentions of his new friend may well be doubted; but as exclusive attention is as flattering to a savage as to a more civilized individual, it had produced the effect we have mentioned. It is unnecessary to repeat the shrewd manner with which the scout extracted these particulars from the simple David; neither shall we dwell in this place on the nature of the instruction he delivered, when completely master of all the necessary facts as a whole will be sufficiently explained to the reader in the course of the narrative.

The lodge in which Uncas was confined was in the very center of the village, and in a situation, perhaps, more difficult than any other to approach, or leave, without observation. But it was not the policy of Hawkeye to affect the least concealment. Presuming on his disguise and his ability to sustain the character he had assumed; he took the most plain and direct route to the place. The hour, however, afforded him some little of that protection which he appeared so much to despise. The boys were already buried in sleep, and all the women, and most of the warriors, had retired to their lodges for the night. Four or five of the latter only lingered about the door of the prison of Uncas, wary but close observers of the manner of their captive.

At the sight of Gamut, accompanied by one in the well-known masquerade of their most distinguished conjurer, they readily made way for them both. Still, they betrayed no intention to depart. On the other hand, they were evidently disposed to remain bound to the place by an additional interest in the mysterious mummeries that they of course expected from such a visit.

From the total inability of the scout to address the Hurons in their own language, he was compelled to trust the conversation entirely to David. Notwithstanding the simplicity of the latter, he did ample justice to the instructions he had received, more than fulfilling the strongest hopes of his teacher.

"The Delawares are women!" he exclaimed, addressing himself to the savage who had a slight understanding of the language in which he spoke; "the Yengeese, my foolish countrymen, have told them to take up the tomahawk, and strike their fathers in the Canadas, and they have forgotten their sex. Does my brother wish to hear 'Le Cerf Agile' ask for his petticoats, and see him weep before the Hurons, at the stake?"

The exclamation "Hugh!" delivered in a strong tone of assent, announced the gratification the savage would receive in witnessing such an exhibition of weakness in an enemy so long hated and so much feared.

"Then let him step aside and the cunning man will blow upon the dog. Tell it to my brothers."

The Huron explained the meaning of David to his fellows, who, in their turn, listened to the project with that sort of satisfaction that their untamed spirits might be expected to find in such a refinement in cruelty. They drew back a little from the entrance and motioned to the supposed conjurer to enter. But the bear, instead of obeying, maintained the seat it had taken and growled:

"The cunning man is afraid that his breath will blow upon his brothers, and take away their courage too," continued David, improving the hint he received; "they must stand further off."

The Hurons, who would have deemed such a misfortune the heaviest calamity that could befall them, fell back in a body, taking a position where they were out of earshot, though at the same time they could command a view of the entrance to the lodge. Then, as if satisfied of their safety, the scout left his position, and slowly entered the place. It was silent and gloomy, being tenanted solely by the captive, and lighted by the dying embers of a fire, which had been used for the purposed of cookery.

Uncas occupied a distant corner, in a reclining attitude, being rigidly bound, both hands and feet, by strong and painful withes. When the frightful object first presented itself to the young Mohican, he did not deign to bestow a single glance on the animal. The scout, who had left David at the door, to ascertain they were not observed, thought it prudent to preserve his disguise until assured of their privacy. Instead of speaking, therefore, he exerted himself to enact one of the antics of the animal he represented. The young Mohican, who at first believed his enemies had sent in a real beast to torment him, and try his nerves, detected in those performances that to Heyward had appeared so accurate, certain blemishes, that at once betrayed the counterfeit. Had Hawkeye been aware of the low estimation in which the skillful Uncas held his representations, he would probably have prolonged the entertainment a little in pique. But the scornful expression of the young man's eye admitted of so many constructions, that the worthy scout was spared the mortification of such a discovery. As soon, therefore, as David gave the preconcerted signal, a low hissing sound was heard in the lodge in place of the fierce growling's of the bear.

His keen eye rested on the shaggy monster.

Uncas had cast his body back against the wall of the hut and closed his eyes, as if willing to exclude so contemptible and disagreeable an object from his sight. But the moment the noise of the serpent was heard, he arose, and cast his looks on each side of him, bending his head low, and turning it inquiringly in every direction, until his keen eye rested on the shaggy monster, where it remained riveted, as though fixed by the power of a charm. Again, the same sounds were repeated, evidently proceeding from the mouth of the beast. Once more the eyes of the youth roamed over the interior of the lodge, and returning to the former resting place, he uttered, in a deep, suppressed voice:

"Hawkeye!"

"Cut his bands," said Hawkeye to David, who just then approached them.

The singer did as he was ordered, and Uncas found his limbs released. At the same moment the dried skin of the animal rattled, and presently the scout arose to his feet, in proper person. The Mohican appeared to comprehend the nature of the attempt his friend had made, intuitively, neither tongue nor feature betraying another symptom of surprise. When Hawkeye had cast his shaggy vestment, which was done by simply loosing certain thongs of skin, he drew a long, glittering knife, and put it in the hands of Uncas.

"The red Hurons are without," he said; "let us be ready." At the same time, he laid his finger significantly on another similar weapon, both being the fruits of his prowess among their enemies during the evening.

"We will go," said Uncas.

"Whither?"

"To the Tortoises; they are the children of my grandfathers."

"Ay, lad," said the scout in English, a language he was apt to use when a little abstracted in mind; "the same blood runs in your veins, I believe; but time and distance has a little changed its color. What shall we do with the Mingoes at the door? They count six, and this singer is as good as nothing."

"The Hurons are boasters," said Uncas, scornfully; "their 'totem' is a moose, and they run like snails. The Delawares are children of the tortoise, and they outstrip the deer."

"Ay, lad, there is truth in what you say; and I doubt not, on a rush, you would pass the whole nation; and, in a straight race of two miles, would be in, and get your breath again, afore a knave of them all was within hearing of the other village. But the gift of a white man lies more in his arms than in his legs. As for myself, I can brain a Huron as well as a better man; but when it comes to a race the knaves would prove too much for me."

Uncas, who had already approached the door, in readiness to lead the way, now recoiled, and placed himself, once more, in the bottom of the lodge. But Hawkeye, who was too much occupied with his own thoughts to note the movement, continued speaking more to himself than to his companion.

"After all," he said, "it is unreasonable to keep one man in bondage to the gifts of another. So, Uncas, you had better take the lead, while I will put on the skin again, and trust to cunning for want of speed."

The young Mohican made no reply, but quietly folded his arms, and leaned his body against one of the upright posts that supported the wall of the hut.

"Well," said the scout looking up at him, "why do you tarry? There will be time enough for me, as the knaves will give chase to you at first."

"Uncas will stay," was the calm reply.

"For what?"

"To fight with his father's brother and die with the friend of the Delawares."

"Ay, lad," returned Hawkeye, squeezing the hand of Uncas between his own iron fingers; "'It would have been more like a Mingo than a Mohican had you left me. But I thought I would make the offer, seeing that youth commonly loves life. Well, what can't be done by main courage, in war, must be done by circumvention. Put on the skin; I doubt not you can play the bear nearly as well as myself."

Whatever might have been the private opinion of Uncas of their respective abilities in this particular, his grave countenance manifested no opinion of his superiority. He silently and expeditiously encased himself in the covering of the beast, and then awaited such other movements as his more aged companion saw fit to dictate.

"Now, friend," said Hawkeye, addressing David, "an exchange of garments will be a great convenience to you, inasmuch as you are but little accustomed to the makeshifts of the wilderness. Here, take my hunting shirt and cap, and give me your blanket and hat. You must trust me with the book and spectacles, as well as the tooter, too; if we ever meet again, in better times, you shall have all back again, with many thanks into the bargain."

David parted with the several articles named with a readiness that would have done great credit to his liberality, had he not certainly profited, in many particulars, by the exchange. Hawkeye was not long in assuming his borrowed garments; and when his restless eyes were hidden behind the glasses and his head was surmounted by the triangular beaver, as their statures were not dissimilar, he might readily have passed for the singer, by starlight. As soon as these dispositions were made, the scout turned to David, and gave him his parting instructions.

"Are you much given to cowardice?" he bluntly asked, by way of obtaining a suitable understanding of the whole case before he ventured a prescription.

"My pursuits are peaceful, and my temper, I humbly trust, is greatly given to mercy and love," returned David, a little nettled at so direct an attack on his manhood; "but there are none who can say that I have ever forgotten my faith in the Lord, even in the greatest straits."

"Your chiefest danger will be at the moment when the savages find out that they have been deceived. If you are not then knocked on the head, you're being a non-composer will protect you and you'll then have a good reason to expect to die in your bed. If you stay, it must be to sit down here in the shadow, and take the part of Uncas, until such times as the cunning of the Indians discover the cheat, when, as I have already said, your times of trial will come. So, choose for yourself to make a rush or tarry here."

"Even so," said David, firmly; "I will abide in the place of the Delaware. Bravely and generously has he battled in my behalf, and this, and more, will I dare in his service."

"You have spoken as a man, and like one who, under wiser schooling, would have been brought to better things. Hold your head down and draw in your legs; their formation might tell the truth too early. Keep silent as long as may be and it would be wise, when you do speak, to break out suddenly in one of your shouting's, which will serve to remind the Indians that you are not altogether as responsible as men should be. If, however, they take your scalp, as I trust and believe they will not, depend on it, Uncas and I will not forget the deed but revenge it as becomes true warriors and trusty friends."

"Hold!" said David, perceiving that with this assurance they were about to leave him; "I am an unworthy and humble follower of one who taught not the damnable principle of revenge. Should I fall, therefore, seek no victims to my manes, but rather forgive my destroyers and if you remember them at all, let it be in prayers for the enlightening of their minds, and for their eternal welfare."

The scout hesitated and appeared to muse.

"There is a principle in that," he said, "different from the law of the woods; and yet it is fair and noble to reflect upon." Then heaving a heavy sigh, probably among the last he ever drew in pining for a condition he had so long abandoned, he added: "it is what I would wish to practice myself, as one without a cross of blood, though it is not always easy to deal with an Indian as you would with a fellow Christian. God bless you, friend; I do believe your scent is not greatly wrong, when the matter is duly considered, and keeping eternity before the eyes, though much depends on the natural gifts, and the force of temptation."

So, saying, the scout returned and shook David cordially by the hand; after which act of friendship, he immediately left the lodge, attended by the new representative of the beast.

The instant Hawkeye found himself under the observation of the Hurons, he drew up his tall form in the rigid manner of David, threw out his arm in the act of keeping time, and commenced what he intended for an imitation of his psalmody. Happily, for the success of this delicate adventure, he had to deal with ears, but little practiced in the concord of sweet sounds, or the miserable effort would infallibly have been detected. It was necessary to pass within a dangerous proximity of the dark group of the savages, and the voice of the scout grew louder as they drew nigher. When at the nearest point the Huron who spoke, the English thrust out an arm and stopped the supposed singing-master.

"The Delaware dog!" he said, leaning forward, and peering through the dim light to catch the expression of the other's features; "is he afraid? Will the Hurons hear his groans?"

A growl, so exceedingly fierce and natural, proceeded from the beast, that the young Indian released his hold and started aside, as if to assure himself that it was not a veritable bear, and no counterfeit, that was rolling before him. Hawkeye, who feared his voice would betray him to his subtle enemies, gladly profited by the interruption, to break out anew in such a burst of musical expression as would, probably, in a more refined state of society have been termed "a grand crash." Among his actual auditors, however, it merely gave him an additional claim to that respect which they never withhold from such as are believed to be the subjects of mental alienation. The little knot of Indians drew back in a body, and suffered, as they thought, the conjurer and his inspired assistant to proceed.

It required no common exercise of fortitude in Uncas and the scout to continue the dignified and deliberate pace they had assumed in passing the lodge; especially as they immediately perceived that curiosity had so far mastered fear, as to induce the watchers to approach the hut, in order to witness the effect of the incantations. The least injudicious or impatient movement on the part of David might betray them and time was absolutely necessary to ensure the safety of the scout. The loud noise the latter conceived it politic to continue, drew many curious gazers to the doors of the different huts as thy passed; and once or twice a dark-looking warrior stepped across their path, led to the act by superstition and watchfulness. They were not, however, interrupted, the darkness of the hour, and the boldness of the attempt, proving their principal friends.

The adventurers had got clear of the village and were now swiftly approaching the shelter of the woods, when a loud and long cry arose from the lodge where Uncas had been confined. The Mohican started on his feet, and shook his shaggy covering, as though the animal he counterfeited was about to make some desperate effort.

"Hold!" said the scout, grasping his friend by the shoulder, "let them yell again! 'Twas nothing but wonderment."

He had no occasion to delay, for at the next instant a burst of cries filled the outer air and ran along the whole extent of the village. Uncas cast his skin and stepped forth in his own beautiful proportions. Hawkeye tapped him lightly on the shoulder and glided ahead.

"Now let the devils strike our scent!" said the scout, tearing two rifles, with all their attendant accouterments, from beneath a bush, and flourishing "killdeer" as he handed Uncas his weapon; "two, at least, will find it to their deaths."

Then, throwing their pieces to a low trail, like sportsmen in readiness for their game, they dashed forward, and were soon buried in the somber darkness of the forest.

CHAPTER XXVII.

"Ant. I shall remember: When C'sar says
Do this, it is performed."
—Julius Caesar

The impatience of the savages who lingered about the prison of Uncas, as has been seen, had overcome their dread of the conjurer's breath. They stole cautiously and with beating hearts, to a crevice, through which the faint light of the fire was glimmering. For several minutes they mistook the form of David for that of the prisoner but the very accident which Hawkeye had foreseen occurred. Tired of keeping the extremities of his long person so near together, the singer gradually suffered the lower limbs to extend themselves, until one of his misshapen feet actually came in contact with and shoved aside the embers of the fire. At first the Hurons believed the Delaware had been thus deformed by witchcraft. But when David, unconscious of being observed, turned his head, and exposed his simple, mild countenance, in place of the haughty lineaments of their prisoner, it would have exceeded the credulity of even a native to have doubted any longer. They rushed together into the lodge, and, laying their hands, with but little ceremony, on their captive, immediately detected the imposition. Then arose the cry first heard by the fugitives. It was succeeded by the most frantic and angry demonstrations of vengeance. David, however, firm in his determination to cover the retreat of his friends, was compelled to believe that his own final hour had come. Deprived of his book and his pipe, he was fain to trust to a memory that rarely failed him on such subjects and breaking forth in a loud and impassioned strain, he endeavored to smooth his passage into the other world by singing the opening verse of a funeral anthem. The Indians were seasonably reminded of his infirmity, and, rushing into the open air, they aroused the village in the manner described.

A native warrior fights as he sleeps, without the protection of anything defensive. The sounds of the alarm were, therefore, hardly uttered before two hundred men were afoot, and ready for the battle or the chase, as either might be required. The escape was soon known; and the whole tribe crowded, in a body, around the council-lodge, impatiently awaiting the instruction of their chiefs. In such a sudden demand on their wisdom, the presence of the cunning Magua could scarcely fail of being needed. His name was mentioned, and all looked round in wonder that he did not appear. Messengers were then dispatched to his lodge requiring his presence.

In the meantime, some of the swiftest and most discreet of the young men were ordered to make the circuit of the clearing, under cover of the woods, in order to ascertain that their suspected neighbors, the Delawares, designed no mischief. Women and children ran to and from and in short, the whole encampment exhibited another scene of wild and savage confusion. Gradually, however, these symptoms of disorder diminished; and in a few minutes the oldest and most distinguished chiefs were assembled in the lodge, in grave consultation.

The clamor of many voices soon announced that a party approached, who might be expected to communicate some intelligence that would explain the mystery of the novel surprise. The crowd without gave way and several warriors entered the place, bringing with them the hapless conjurer, who had been left so long by the scout in duress.

Notwithstanding this man was held in very unequal estimation among the Hurons, some believing implicitly in his power and others deeming him an impostor, he was now listened to by all with the deepest attention. When his brief story was ended, the father of the sick woman stepped forth and in a few pithy expressions, related, in his turn, what he knew. These two narratives gave a proper direction to the subsequent inquiries, which were now made with the characteristic cunning of savages.

Instead of rushing in a confused and disorderly throng to the cavern, ten of the wisest and firmest among the chiefs were selected to prosecute the investigation. As no time was to be lost, the instant the choice was made the individuals appointed rose in a body and left the place without speaking. On reaching the entrance, the younger men in advance made way for their seniors and the whole proceeded along the low, dark gallery, with the firmness of warriors ready to devote themselves to the public good, though, at the same time, secretly doubting the nature of the power with which they were about to contend.

The outer apartment of the cavern was silent and gloomy. The woman lay in her usual place and posture, though there were those present who affirmed they had seen her borne to the woods by the supposed "medicine of the white men." Such a direct and palpable contradiction of the tale related by the father caused all eyes to be turned on him. Chafed by the silent imputation, and inwardly troubled by so unaccountable a circumstance, the chief advanced to the side of the bed, and, stooping, cast an incredulous look at the features, as if distrusting their reality. His daughter was dead.

The unerring feeling of nature for a moment prevailed and the old warrior hid his eyes in sorrow. Then, recovering his self-possession, he faced his companions, and, pointing toward the corpse, he said, in the language of his people:

"The wife of my young man has left us! The Great Spirit is angry with his children."

The mournful intelligence was received in solemn silence. After a short pause, one of the elder Indians was about to speak, when a dark-looking object was seen rolling out of an adjoining apartment, into the very center of the room where they stood. Ignorant of the nature of the beings they had to deal with, the whole party drew back a little, and, rising on end, exhibited the distorted but still fierce and sullen features of Magua. The discovery was succeeded by a general exclamation of amazement.

As soon, however, as the true situation of the chief was understood, several knives appeared, and his limbs and tongue were quickly released. The Huron arose and shook himself like a lion quitting his lair. Not a word escaped him, though his hand played convulsively with the handle of his knife, while his lowering eyes scanned the whole party, as if they sought an object suited to the first burst of his vengeance.

It was happy for Uncas and the scout, and even David, that they were all beyond the reach of his arm at such a moment; for, assuredly, no refinement in cruelty would then have deferred their deaths, in opposition to the promptings of the fierce temper that nearly choked him. Meeting everywhere faces that he knew as friends, the savage grated his teeth together like rasps of iron and swallowed his passion for want of a victim on whom to vent it. This exhibition of anger was noted by all present; and from an apprehension of exasperating a temper that was already chafed nearly to madness, several minutes were suffered to pass before another word was uttered. When, however, suitable time had elapsed, the oldest of the party spoke.

"My friend has found an enemy," he said. "Is he nigh that the Hurons might take revenge?"

"Let the Delaware die!" exclaimed Magua, in a voice of thunder.

Another longer and expressive silence was observed, and was broken, as before, with due precaution, by the same individual.

"The Mohican is swift of foot, and leaps far," he said; "but my young men are on his trail."

"Is he gone?" demanded Magua, in tones so deep and guttural, that they seemed to proceed from his inmost chest.

"An evil spirit has been among us, and the Delaware has blinded our eyes."

"An evil spirit!" repeated the other, mockingly; "'tis the spirit that has taken the lives of so many Hurons; the spirit that slew my young men at 'the tumbling river'; that took their scalps at the 'healing spring' and who has, now, bound the arms of Le Renard Subtil!"

"Of whom does my friend speak?"

"Of the dog who carries the heart and cunning of a Huron under a pale skin...La Longue Carabine."

The pronunciation of so terrible a name produced the usual effect among his auditors. But when time was given for reflection, and the warriors remembered that their formidable and daring enemy had even been in the bosom of their encampment, working injury, fearful rage took the place of wonder, and all those fierce passions with which the bosom of Magua had just been struggling were suddenly transferred to his companions. Some among them gnashed their teeth in anger, others vented their feelings in yells, and some again beat the air as frantically as if the object of their resentment were suffering under their blows. But this sudden outbreaking of temper as quickly subsided in the still and sullen restraint they most affected in their moments of inaction.

Magua, who had in his turn found leisure for reflection, now changed his manner, and assumed the air of one who knew how to think and act with a dignity worthy of so grave a subject.

"Let us go to my people," he said; "they wait for us."

His companions consented in silence, and the whole of the savage party left the cavern and returned to the council-lodge. When they were seated, all eyes turned on Magua, who understood, from such an indication, that, by common consent, they had devolved the duty of relating what had passed on him. He arose and told his tale without duplicity or reservation. The whole deception practiced by both Duncan and Hawkeye was, of course, laid naked, and no room was found, even for the most superstitious of the tribe, any longer to affix a doubt on the character of the occurrences. It was but too apparent that they had been insultingly, shamefully, disgracefully deceived. When he had ended and resumed his seat, the collected tribe for his auditors, in substance, included all the fighting men of the party sat regarding each other like men astonished equally at the audacity and the success of their enemies. The next consideration, however, was the means and opportunities for revenge.

Additional pursuers were sent on the trail of the fugitives; and then the chiefs applied themselves, in earnest, to the business of consultation. Many different expedients were proposed by the elder warriors, in succession, to all of which Magua was a silent and respectful listener. That subtle savage had recovered his artifice and self-command, and now proceeded toward his object with his customary caution and skill. It was only when each one disposed to speak had uttered his sentiments, that he prepared to advance his own opinions. They were given with additional weight from the circumstance that some of the runners had already returned and reported that their enemies had been traced so far as to leave no doubt of their having sought safety in the neighboring camp of their suspected allies, the Delawares. With the advantage of possessing this important intelligence, the chief warily laid his plans before his fellows, and, as might have been anticipated from his eloquence and cunning, they were adopted without a dissenting voice. They were, briefly, as follows, both in opinions and in motives.

It has been already stated that, in obedience to a policy rarely departed from, the sisters were separated so soon as they reached the Huron village. Magua had early discovered that in retaining the person of Alice, he possessed the most effectual check on Cora. When they parted, therefore, he kept the former within reach of his hand, consigning the one he most valued to the keeping of their allies. The arrangement was understood to be merely temporary and was made as much with a view to flatter his neighbors as in obedience to the invariable rule of Indian policy.

While goaded incessantly by these revengeful impulses that in a savage seldom slumber, the chief was still attentive to his more permanent personal interests. The follies and disloyalty committed in his youth were to be expiated by a long and painful penance, ere he could be restored to the full enjoyment of the confidence of his ancient people; and without confidence there could be no authority in an Indian tribe. In this delicate and arduous situation, the crafty native had neglected no means of increasing his influence; and one of the happiest of his expedients had been the success with which he had cultivated the favor of their powerful and dangerous neighbors. The result of his experiment had answered all the expectations of his policy; for the Hurons were in no degree exempt from that governing principle of nature, which induces man to value his gifts precisely in the degree that they are appreciated by others.

But, while he was making this ostensible sacrifice to general considerations, Magua never lost sight of his individual motives. The latter had been frustrated by the unlooked-for events which had placed all his prisoners beyond his control; and he now found himself reduced to the necessity of suing for favors to those whom it had so lately been his policy to oblige.

Several of the chiefs had proposed deep and treacherous schemes to surprise the Delawares and, by gaining possession of their camp, to recover their prisoners by the same blow; for all agreed that their honor, their interests, and the peace and happiness of their dead countrymen, imperiously required them speedily to immolate some victims to their revenge. But plans so dangerous to attempt, and of such doubtful issue, Magua found little difficulty in defeating. He exposed their risk and fallacy with his usual skill; and it was only after he had removed every impediment, in the shape of opposing advice, that he ventured to propose his own projects.

He commenced by flattering the self-love of his auditors, a never-failing method of commanding attention. When he had enumerated the many different occasions on which the Hurons had exhibited their courage and prowess, in the punishment of insults, he digressed in a high encomium on the virtue of wisdom. He painted the quality as forming the great point of difference between the beaver and other brutes; between the brutes and men; and, finally, between the Hurons, in particular, and the rest of the human race. After he had sufficiently extolled the property of discretion, he undertook to exhibit in what manner its use was applicable to the present situation of their tribe. On the one hand, he said, was their great pale father, the governor of the Canadas, who had looked upon his children with a hard eye since their tomahawks had been so red; on the other, a people as numerous as themselves, who spoke a different language, possessed different interests and loved them not, and who would be glad of any pretense to bring them in disgrace with the great white chief. Then he spoke of their necessities; of the gifts they had a right to expect for their past services of their distance from their proper hunting-grounds and native villages; and of the necessity of consulting prudence more, and inclination less, in so critical circumstances. When he perceived that, while the old men applauded his moderation, many of the fiercest and most distinguished of the warriors listened to these politic plans with lowering looks, he cunningly led them back to the subject which they most loved. He spoke openly of the fruits of their wisdom, which he boldly pronounced would be a complete and final triumph over their enemies. He even darkly hinted that their success might be extended, with proper caution, in such a manner as to include the destruction of all whom they had reason to hate. In short, he so blended the warlike with the artful, the obvious with the obscure, as to flatter the propensities of both parties and to leave to each subject of hope, while neither could say it clearly comprehended his intentions.

The orator, or the politician, who can produce such a state of things, is commonly popular with his contemporaries, however he may be treated by posterity. All perceived that more was meant than was uttered and each one believed that the hidden meaning was precisely such as his own faculties enabled him to understand, or his own wishes led him to anticipate.

In this happy state of things, it is not surprising that the management of Magua prevailed. The tribe consented to act with deliberation, and with one voice they committed the direction of the whole affair to the government of the chief who had suggested such wise and intelligible expedients.

Magua had now attained one great object of all his cunning and enterprise. The ground he had lost in the favor of his people was completely regained, and he found himself even placed at the head of affairs. He was, in truth, their ruler; and, so long as he could maintain his popularity, no monarch could be more despotic, especially while the tribe continued in a hostile country. Throwing off, therefore, the appearance of consultation, he assumed the grave air of authority necessary to support the dignity of his office.

Runners were dispatched for intelligence in different directions; spies were ordered to approach and feel the encampment of the Delawares; the warriors were dismissed to their lodges, with an intimation that their services would soon be needed; and the women and children were ordered to retire, with a warning that it was their province to be silent. When these several arrangements were made, Magua passed through the village, stopping here and there to pay a visit where he thought his presence might be flattering to the individual. He confirmed his friends in their confidence, fixed the wavering, and gratified all. Then he sought his own lodge. The wife the Huron chief had abandoned, when he was chased from among his people, was dead. Children he had none; and he now occupied a hut, without companion of any sort. It was, in fact, the dilapidated and solitary structure in which David had been discovered, and whom he had tolerated in his presence, on those few occasions when they met, with the contemptuous indifference of a haughty superiority.

Hither, then, Magua retired when his labors of policy were ended. While others slept, however, he neither knew nor sought repose. Had there been one sufficiently curious to have watched the movements of the newly elected chief, he would have seen him seated in a corner of his lodge, musing on the subject of his future plans, from the hour of his retirement to the time he had appointed for the warriors to assemble again. Occasionally the air breathed through the crevices of the hut, and the low flame that fluttered about the embers of the fire threw their wavering light on the person of the sullen recluse. At such moments it would not have been difficult to have fancied the dusky savage the Prince of Darkness brooding on his own fancied wrongs and plotting evil.

Long before the day dawned, however, warrior after warrior entered the solitary hut of Magua, until they had collected to the number of twenty. Each bore his rifle, and all the other accouterments of war, though the paint was uniformly peaceful. The entrance of these fierce-looking beings was unnoticed: some seating themselves in the shadows of the place and others standing like motionless statues, until the whole of the designated band was collected.

Then Magua arose and gave the signal to proceed, marching himself in advance. They followed their leader singly and in that well-known order which has obtained the distinguishing appellation of "Indian file." Unlike other men engaged in the spirit-stirring business of war, they stole from their camp unostentatiously and unobserved resembling a band of gliding specters, more than warriors seeking the bubble reputation by deeds of desperate daring.

Instead of taking the path which led directly toward the camp of the Delawares, Magua led his party for some distance down the windings of the stream and along the little artificial lake of the beavers. The day began to dawn as they entered the clearing which had been formed by those sagacious and industrious animals. Though Magua, who had resumed his ancient garb, bore the outline of a fox on the dressed skin which formed his robe, there was one chief of his party who carried the beaver as his peculiar symbol, or "totem." There would have been a species of profanity in the omission, had this man passed so powerful a community of his fancied kindred, without bestowing some evidence of his regard. Accordingly, he paused, and spoke in words as kind and friendly as if he were addressing more intelligent beings. He called the animals his cousins and reminded them that his protecting influence was the reason they remained unharmed, while many avaricious traders were prompting the Indians to take their lives. He promised a continuance of his favors and admonished them to be grateful. After which, he spoke of the expedition in which he was himself engaged, and intimated, though with sufficient delicacy and circumlocution, the expediency of bestowing on their relative a portion of that wisdom for which they were so renowned.[1]

During the utterance of this extraordinary address, the companions of the speaker were as grave and as attentive to his language as though they were all equally impressed with its propriety. Once or twice black objects were seen rising to the surface of the water, and the Huron expressed pleasure, conceiving that his words were not bestowed in vain. Just as he ended his address, the head of a large beaver was thrust from the door of a lodge, whose earthen walls had been much injured, and which the party had believed, from its situation, to be uninhabited. Such an extraordinary sign of confidence was received by the orator as a highly favorable omen and though the animal retreated a little precipitately, he was lavish of his thanks and commendations.

[1] These harangues of the beasts were frequent among the Indians. They often address their victims in this way, reproaching them for cowardice or commending their resolution, as they may happen to exhibit fortitude or the reverse, in suffering.

When Magua thought sufficient time had been lost in gratifying the family affection of the warrior, he again made the signal to proceed. As the Indians moved away in a body, and with a step that would have been inaudible to the ears of any common man, the same venerable-looking beaver once more ventured his head from its cover. Had any of the Hurons turned to look behind them, they would have seen the animal watching their movements with an interest and sagacity that might easily have been mistaken for reason. Indeed, so very distinct, and intelligible were the devices of the quadruped, that even the most experienced observer would have been at a loss to account for its actions, until the moment when the party entered the forest, when the whole would have been explained, by seeing the entire animal issue from the lodge, uncasing, by the act, the grave features of Chingachgook from his mask of fur.

CHAPTER XXVIII.

"Brief, I pray for you; for you see, 'tis a busy time with me."
—Much Ado About Nothing.

The tribe, or rather half tribe, of Delawares, which has been so often mentioned, and whose present place of encampment was so nigh the temporary village of the Hurons, could assemble about an equal number of warriors with the latter people. Like their neighbors, they had followed Montcalm into the territories of the English crown and were making heavy and serious inroads on the hunting-grounds of the Mohawks; though they had seen fit, with the mysterious reserve so common among the natives, to withhold their assistance at the moment when it was most required. The French had accounted for this unexpected defection on the part of their ally in various ways. It was the prevalent opinion, however, that they had been influenced by veneration for the ancient treaty, that had once made them dependent on the Six Nations for military protection, and now rendered them reluctant to encounter their former masters. As for the tribe itself, it had been content to announce to Montcalm, through his emissaries, with Indian brevity, that their hatchets were dull, and time was necessary to sharpen them. The politic captain of the Canadas had deemed it wiser to submit to entertain a passive friend, than by any acts of ill-judged severity to convert him into an open enemy.

On that morning when Magua led his silent party from the settlement of the beavers into the forests, in the manner described, the sun rose upon the Delaware encampment as if it had suddenly burst upon a busy people, actively employed in all the customary avocations of high noon. The women ran from lodge to lodge, some engaged in preparing their morning's meal, a few earnestly bent on seeking the comforts necessary to their habits, but more pausing to exchange hasty and whispered sentences with their friends. The warriors were lounging in groups, musing more than they conversed and when a few words were uttered, speaking like men who deeply weighed their opinions. The instruments of the chase were to be seen in abundance among the lodges; but none departed. Here and there a warrior was examining his arms, with an attention that is rarely bestowed on the implements, when no other enemy than the beast of the forest is expected to be encountered. And occasionally, the eyes of a whole group were turned simultaneously toward a large and silent lodge in the center of the village, as if it contained the subject of their common thoughts.

During the existence of this scene, a man suddenly appeared at the furthest extremity of a platform of rock which formed the level of the village. He was without arms, and his paint tended rather to soften than increase the natural sternness of his austere countenance. When in full view of the Delawares he stopped, and made a gesture of amity, by throwing his arm upward toward heaven, and then letting it fall impressively on his breast. The inhabitants of the village answered his salute by a low murmur of welcome and encouraged him to advance by similar indications of friendship. Fortified by these assurances, the dark figure left the brow of the natural rocky terrace, where it had stood a moment, drawn in a strong outline against the blushing morning sky, and moved with dignity into the very center of the huts. As he approached, nothing was audible but the rattling of the light silver ornaments that loaded his arms and neck, and the tinkling of the little bells that fringed his deerskin moccasins. He made, as he advanced, many courteous signs of greeting to the men he passed, neglecting to notice the women, however, like one who deemed their favor, in the present enterprise, of no importance. When he had reached the group in which it was evident, by the haughtiness of their common mien, that the principal chiefs were collected, the stranger paused and then the Delawares saw that the active and erect form that stood before them was that of the well-known Huron chief, Le Renard Subtil.

His reception was grave, silent, and wary. The warriors in front stepped aside, opening the way to their most approved orator by the action; one who spoke all those languages that were cultivated among the northern aborigines.

"The wise Huron is welcome," said the Delaware, in the language of the Maquas; "he is come to eat his 'succotash',[1] with his brothers of the lakes."

"He is come," repeated Magua, bending his head with the dignity of an eastern prince.

The chief extended his arm and taking the other by the wrist, they once more exchanged friendly salutations. Then the Delaware invited his guest to enter his own lodge and share his morning meal. The invitation was accepted; and the two warriors, attended by three or four of the old men, walked calmly away, leaving the rest of the tribe devoured by a desire to understand the reasons of so unusual a visit, and yet not betraying the least impatience by sign or word.

During the short and frugal repast that followed, the conversation was extremely circumspect, and related entirely to the events of the hunt, in which Magua had so lately been engaged. It would have been impossible for the most finished breeding to wear more of the appearance of considering the visit as a thing of course, than did his hosts, notwithstanding every individual present was perfectly aware

[1] A dish composed of cracked corn and beans. It is much used also by the whites. By corn is meant maise.

that it must be connected with some secret object and that probably of importance to themselves. When the appetites of the whole were appeased, the squaws removed the trenchers and gourds, and the two parties began to prepare themselves for a subtle trial of their wits.

"Is the face of my great Canada father turned again toward his Huron children?" demanded the orator of the Delawares.

"When was it ever otherwise?" returned Magua. "He calls my people 'most beloved'."

The Delaware gravely bowed his acquiescence to what he knew to be false, and continued:

"The tomahawks of your young men have been very red."

"It is so; but they are now bright and dull; for the Yengeese are dead, and the Delawares are our neighbors."

The other acknowledged the pacific compliment by a gesture of the hand and remained silent. Then Magua, as if recalled to such a recollection, by the allusion to the massacre, demanded:

"Does my prisoner give trouble to my brothers?"

"She is welcome."

"The path between the Hurons and the Delawares is short, and it is open; let her be sent to my squaws, if she gives trouble to my brother."

"She is welcome," returned the chief of the latter nation, still more emphatically.

The baffled Magua continued silent several minutes, apparently indifferent, however, to the repulse he had received in this his opening effort to regain possession of Cora.

"Do my young men leave the Delawares room on the mountains for their hunts?" he at length continued.

"The Lenape are rulers of their own hills," returned the other a little haughtily.

"It is well. Justice is the master of a red skin. Why should they brighten their tomahawks and sharpen their knives against each other? Are not the pale faces thicker than the swallows in the season of flowers?"

"Good!" exclaimed two or three of his auditors at the same time.

Magua waited a little, to permit his words to soften the feelings of the Delawares, before he added:

"Have there not been strange moccasins in the woods? Have not my brothers scented the feet of white men?"

"Let my Canada father come," returned the other, evasively; "his children are ready to see him."

"When the great chief comes, it is to smoke with the Indians in their wigwams. The Hurons say, too, he is welcome. But the Yengeese have long arms, and legs that never tire! My young men dreamed they had seen the trail of the Yengeese nigh the village of the Delawares!"

"They will not find the Lenape asleep."

"It is well. The warrior whose eye is open can see his enemy," said Magua, once more shifting his ground, when he found himself unable to penetrate the caution of his companion. "I have brought gifts to my brother. His nation would not go on the warpath, because they did not think it well, but their friends have remembered where they lived."

When he had thus announced his liberal intention, the crafty chief arose and gravely spread his presents before the dazzled eyes of his hosts. They consisted principally of trinkets of little value, plundered from the slaughtered females of William Henry. In the division of the baubles the cunning Huron discovered no less art than in their selection. While he bestowed those of greater value on the two most distinguished warriors, one of whom was his host, he seasoned his offerings to their inferiors with such well-timed and apposite compliments, as left them no ground of complaint. In short, the whole ceremony contained such a happy blending of the profitable with the flattering, that it was not difficult for the donor immediately to read the effect of a generosity so aptly mingled with praise, in the eyes of those he addressed.

This well-judged and politic stroke on the part of Magua was not without instantaneous results. The Delawares lost their gravity in a much more cordial expression; and the host, in particular, after contemplating his own liberal share of the spoil for some moments with peculiar gratification, repeated with strong emphasis, the words:

"My brother is a wise chief. He is welcome."

"The Hurons love their friends the Delawares," returned Magua. "Why should they not? they are colored by the same sun, and their just men will hunt in the same grounds after death. The red skins should be friends and look with open eyes on the white men. Has not my brother scented spies in the woods?"

The Delaware, whose name in English signified "Hard Heart," an appellation that the French had translated into "le Coeur-dur," forgot that obduracy of purpose, which had probably obtained him so significant a title. His countenance grew very sensibly less stern, and he now deigned to answer more directly.

"There have been strange moccasins about my camp. They have been tracked into my lodges."

"Did my brother beat out the dogs?" asked Magua, without adverting in any manner to the former equivocation of the chief.

"It would not do. The stranger is always welcome to the children of the Lenape."

"The stranger, but not the spy."

"Would the Yengeese send their women as spies? Did not the Huron chief say he took women in the battle?"

"He told no lie. The Yengeese have sent out their scouts. They have been in my wigwams, but they found there no one to say welcome. Then they fled to the Delawares for, say they, the Delawares are our friends; their minds are turned from their Canada father!"

This insinuation was a home thrust, and one that in a more advanced state of society would have entitled Magua to the reputation of a skillful diplomatist. The recent defection of the tribe had, as they well knew themselves, subjected the Delawares to much reproach among their French allies; and they were now made to feel that their future actions were to be regarded with jealousy and distrust. There was no deep insight into causes and effects necessary to foresee that such a situation of things was likely to prove highly prejudicial to their future movements. Their distant villages, their hunting-grounds and hundreds of their women and children, together with a material part of their physical force, were actually within the limits of the French territory. Accordingly, this alarming annunciation was received, as Magua intended, with manifest disapprobation, if not with alarm.

"Let my father look in my face," said Le Coeur-dur; "he will see no change. It is true, my young men did not go out on the warpath; they had dreams for not doing so. But they love and venerate the great white chief."

"Will he think so when he hears that his greatest enemy is fed in the camp of his children? When is he told a bloody Yengee smokes at your fire? That the pale face who has slain so many of his friends goes in and out among the Delawares? Go! my great Canada father is not a fool!"

"Where is the Yengee that the Delawares fear?" returned the other; "who has slain my young men? Who is the mortal enemy of my Great Father?"

"La Longue Carabine!"

The Delaware warriors started at the well-known name, betraying by their amazement, that they now learned, for the first time, one so famous among the Indian allies of France was within their power.

"What does my brother mean?" demanded Le Coeur-dur, in a tone that, by its wonder, far exceeded the usual apathy of his race.

"A Huron never lies!" returned Magua, coldly, leaning his head against the side of the lodge, and drawing his slight robe across his tawny breast. "Let the Delawares count their prisoners; they will find one whose skin is neither red nor pale."

A long and musing pause succeeded. The chief consulted apart with his companions, and messengers dispatched to collect certain others of the most distinguished men of the tribe.

As warrior after warrior dropped in, they were each made acquainted, in turn, with the important intelligence that Magua had just communicated. The air of surprise, and the usual low, deep, guttural exclamation, were common to them all. The news spread from mouth to mouth, until the whole encampment became powerfully agitated. The women suspended their labors, to catch such syllables as unguardedly fell from the lips of the consulting warriors. The boys deserted their sports, and walking fearlessly among their fathers, looked up in curious admiration, as they heard the brief exclamations of wonder they so freely expressed the temerity of their hated foe. In short, every occupation was abandoned for the time, and all other pursuits seemed discarded in order that the tribe might freely indulge, after their own peculiar manner, in an open expression of feeling.

When the excitement had a little abated, the old men disposed themselves seriously to consider that which it became the honor and safety of their tribe to perform, under circumstances of so much delicacy and embarrassment. During all these movements, and in the midst of the general commotion, Magua had not only maintained his seat, but the very attitude he had originally taken, against the side of the lodge, where he continued as immovable and apparently, as unconcerned, as if he had no interest in the result. Not a single indication of the future intentions of his hosts, however, escaped his vigilant eyes. With his consummate knowledge of the nature of the people with whom he had to deal, he anticipated every measure on which they decided; and it might almost be said, that, in many instances, he knew their intentions, even before they became known to themselves.

The council of the Delawares was short. When it was ended, a general bustle announced that it was to be immediately succeeded by a solemn and formal assemblage of the nation. As such meetings were rare, and only called on occasions of the last importance, the subtle Huron, who still sat apart, a wily and dark observer of the proceedings, now knew that all his projects must be brought to their final issue. He, therefore, left the lodge and walked silently forth to the place, in front of the encampment, whither the warriors were already beginning to collect.

It might have been half an hour before each individual, including even the women and children, was in his place. The delay had been created by the grave preparations that were deemed necessary to so solemn and unusual a conference. But when the sun was seen climbing above the tops of that mountain, against whose bosom the Delawares had constructed their encampment, most were seated; and as his bright rays darted from behind the outline of trees that fringed the eminence, they fell upon as grave, as attentive, and as deeply interested a multitude, as was probably ever before lighted by his morning beams. Its number somewhat exceeded a thousand souls.

In a collection of so serious savages, there is never to be found any impatient aspirant after premature distinction, standing ready to move his auditors to some hasty, and, perhaps, injudicious discussion, in order that his own reputation may be the gainer. An act of so much precipitancy and presumption would seal the downfall of precocious intellect forever. It rested solely with the oldest and most experienced of the men to lay the subject of the conference before the people. Until such a one chose to make some movement, no deeds in arms, no natural gifts, nor any renown as an orator, would have justified the slightest interruption. On the present occasion, the aged warrior whose privilege it was to speak, was silent, seemingly oppressed with the magnitude of his subject. The delay had already continued long beyond the usual deliberative pause that always preceded a conference; but no sign of impatience or surprise escaped even the youngest boy. Occasionally an eye was raised from the earth, where the looks of most were riveted, and strayed toward a particular lodge, that was, however, in no manner distinguished from those around it, except in the peculiar care that had been taken to protect it against the assaults of the weather.

At length one of those low murmurs, that are so apt to disturb a multitude, was heard, and the whole nation arose to their feet by a common impulse. At that instant the door of the lodge in question opened and three men, issuing from it, slowly approached the place of consultation. They were all aged, even beyond that period to which the oldest present had reached but one in the center, who leaned on his companions for support, had numbered a number of years to which the human race is seldom permitted to attain. His frame, which had once been tall and erect, like the cedar, was now bending under the pressure of more than a century. The elastic, light step of an Indian was gone, and in its place, he was compelled to toil his tardy way over the ground, inch by inch. His dark, wrinkled countenance was in singular and wild contrast with the long white locks which floated on his shoulders, in such thickness, as to announce that generations had probably passed away since they had last been shorn.

The dress of this patriarch for such, considering his vast age, in conjunction with his affinity and influence with his people, he might very properly be termed was rich and imposing, though strictly after the simple fashions of the tribe. His robe was of the finest skins, which had been deprived of their fur, in order to admit of a hieroglyphical representation of various deeds in arms, done in former ages. His bosom was loaded with medals, some in massive silver, and one or two even in gold, the gifts of various Christian potentates during the long period of his life. He also wore armlets, and cinctures above the ankles, of the latter precious metal. His head, on the whole of which the hair had been permitted to grow, the pursuits of war having so long been abandoned, was encircled by a sort of plated diadem, which, in its turn, bore lesser and more glittering ornaments, that sparkled amid the glossy hues of three drooping ostrich feathers, dyed a deep black, in touching contrast to the color of his snow-white locks. His tomahawk was nearly hidden in silver and the handle of his knife shone like a horn of solid gold.

So soon as the first hum of emotion and pleasure, which the sudden appearance of this venerated individual created, had a little subsided, the name of "Tamenund" was whispered from mouth to mouth. Magua had often heard the fame of this wise and just Delaware; a reputation that even proceeded so far as to bestow on him the rare gift of holding secret communion with the Great Spirit, and which has since transmitted his name, with some slight alteration, to the white usurpers of his ancient territory, as the imaginary tutelar saint[2] of a vast empire. The Huron chief, therefore, stepped eagerly out a little from the throng to a spot whence he might catch a nearer glimpse of the features of the man, whose decision was likely to produce so deep an influence on his own fortunes.

[2] The Americans sometimes called their tutelar saint Tamenay, a corruption of the name of the renowned chief here introduced. There are many traditions which speak of the character and power of Tamenund.

The eyes of the old man were closed, as though the organs were wearied with having so long witnessed the selfish workings of the human passions. The color of his skin differed from that of most around him, being richer and darker, the latter having been produced by certain delicate and mazy lines of complicated and yet beautiful figures, which had been traced over most of his person by the operation of tattooing. Notwithstanding the position of the Huron, he passed the observant and silent Magua without notice, and leaning on his two venerable supporters proceeded to the high place of the multitude, where he seated himself in the center of his nation, with the dignity of a monarch and the air of a father.

Nothing could surpass the reverence and affection with which this unexpected visit from one who belongs rather to another world than to this, was received by his people. After a suitable and decent pause, the principal chiefs arose, and, approaching the patriarch, they placed his hands reverently on their heads, seeming to entreat a blessing. The younger men were content with touching his robe, or even drawing nigh his person, in order to breathe in the atmosphere of one so aged, so just, and so valiant. None but the most distinguished among the youthful warriors even presumed so far as to perform the latter ceremony, the great mass of the multitude deeming it a sufficient happiness to look upon a form so deeply venerated, and so well beloved. When these acts of affection and respect were performed, the chiefs drew back again to their several places, and silence reigned in the whole encampment.

After a short delay, a few of the young men, to whom instructions had been whispered by one of the aged attendants of Tamenund, arose, left the crowd, and entered the lodge which has already been noted as the object of so much attention throughout that morning. In a few minutes they reappeared, escorting the individuals who had caused all these solemn preparations toward the seat of judgment. The crowd opened in a lane; and when the party had re-entered, it closed in again, forming a large and dense belt of human bodies, arranged in an open circle.

CHAPTER XXIX.

"The assembly seated, rising o'er the rest,
Achilles thus the king of men addressed."
—Pope's Illiad

Cora stood foremost among the prisoners, entwining her arms in those of Alice, in the tenderness of sisterly love. Notwithstanding the fearful and menacing array of savages on every side of her, no apprehension on her own account could prevent the nobler-minded maiden from keeping her eyes fastened on the pale and anxious features of the trembling Alice. Close at their side stood Heyward, with an interest in both, that, at such a moment of intense uncertainty, scarcely knew a preponderance in favor of her whom he most loved. Hawkeye had placed himself a little in the rear, with a deference to the superior rank of his companions, that no similarity in the state of their present fortunes could induce him to forget. Uncas was not there.

When perfect silence was again restored and after the usual long, impressive pause, one of the two aged chiefs who sat at the side of the patriarch arose, and demanded aloud, in very intelligible English:

"Which of my prisoners is La Longue Carabine?"

Neither Duncan nor the scout answered. The former, however, glanced his eyes around the dark and silent assembly, and recoiled a pace, when they fell on the malignant visage of Magua. He saw, at once, that this wily savage had some secret agency in their present arraignment before the nation and determined to throw every possible impediment in the way of the execution of his sinister plans. He had witnessed one instance of the summary punishments of the Indians, and now dreaded that his companion was to be selected for a second. In this dilemma, with little or no time for reflection, he suddenly determined to cloak his invaluable friend, at any or every hazard to himself. Before he had time, however, to speak, the question was repeated in a louder voice, and with a clearer utterance.

"Give us arms," the young man haughtily replied, "and place us in yonder woods. Our deeds shall speak for us!"

"This is the warrior whose name has filled our ears!" returned the chief, regarding Heyward with that sort of curious interest which seems inseparable from man, when first beholding one of his fellows to whom merit or accident, virtue, or crime, has given notoriety. "What has brought the white man into the camp of the Delawares?"

"My necessities. I come for food, shelter, and friends."

"It cannot be. The woods are full of game. The head of a warrior needs no other shelter than a sky without clouds; and the Delawares are the enemies, and not the friends of the Yengeese. Go, the mouth has spoken, while the heart said nothing."

Duncan, a little at a loss in what manner to proceed, remained silent but the scout, who had listened attentively to all that passed, now advanced steadily to the front.

"That I did not answer to the call for La Longue Carabine, was not owing either to shame or fear," he said, "for neither one nor the other is the gift of an honest man. But I do not admit the right of the Mingoes to bestow a name on one whose friends have been mindful of his gifts, in this particular; especially as their title is a lie, 'killdeer' being a grooved barrel and no carabyne. I am the man, however, that got the name of Nathaniel from my kin; the compliment of Hawkeye from the Delawares, who live on their own river; and whom the Iroquois have presumed to style the 'Long Rifle', without any warranty from him who is most concerned in the matter."

The eyes of all present, which had hitherto been gravely scanning the person of Duncan, were now turned, on the instant, toward the upright iron frame of this new pretender to the distinguished appellation. It was in no degree remarkable that there should be found two who were willing to claim so great an honor, for impostors, though rare, were not unknown among the natives; but it was altogether material to the just and severe intentions of the Delawares, that there should be no mistake in the matter. Some of their old men consulted together in private and then as it would seem, they determined to interrogate their visitor on the subject.

"My brother has said that a snake crept into my camp," said the chief to Magua; "which is he?"

The Huron pointed to the scout.

"Will a wise Delaware believe the barking of a wolf?" exclaimed Duncan, still more confirmed in the evil intentions of his ancient enemy: "a dog never lies, but when was a wolf known to speak the truth?"

The eyes of Magua flashed fire but suddenly recollecting the necessity of maintaining his presence of mind, he turned away in silent disdain, well assured that the sagacity of the Indians would not fail to extract the real merits of the point in controversy. He was not deceived; for, after another short consultation, the wary Delaware turned to him again, and expressed the determination of the chiefs, though in the most considerate language.

"My brother has been called a liar," he said, "and his friends are angry. They will show that he has spoken the truth. Give my prisoners guns and let them prove which is the man."

Magua affected to consider the expedient, which he well knew proceeded from distrust of himself, as a compliment and made a gesture of acquiescence, well content that his veracity should be supported by so skillful a marksman as the scout. The weapons were instantly placed in the hands of the friendly opponents, and they were bid to fire, over the heads of the seated multitude, at an earthen vessel, which lay, by accident, on a stump, some fifty yards from the place where they stood.

Heyward smiled to himself at the idea of a competition with the scout, though he determined to persevere in the deception, until apprised of the real designs of Magua.

Raising his rifle with the utmost care and renewing his aim three several times, he fired. The bullet cut the wood within a few inches of the vessel and a general exclamation of satisfaction announced that the shot was considered a proof of great skill in the use of a weapon. Even Hawkeye nodded his head, as if he would say, it was better than he expected. But, instead of manifesting an intention to contend with the successful marksman, he stood leaning on his rifle for more than a minute, like a man who was completely buried in thought. From this reverie, he was, however, awakened by one of the young Indians who had furnished the arms and who now touched his shoulder, saying in exceedingly broken English:

"Can the pale face beat it?"

"Yes, Huron!" exclaimed the scout, raising the short rifle in his right hand, and shaking it at Magua, with as much apparent ease as if it were a reed; "yes, Huron, I could strike you now, and no power on earth could prevent the deed! The soaring hawk is not more certain of the dove than I am this moment of you, did I choose to send a bullet to your heart! Why should I not? Why! because the gifts of my color forbid it, and I might draw down evil on tender and innocent heads. If you know such a being as God, thank Him, therefore, in your inward soul; for you have reason!"

The flushed countenance, angry eye and swelling figure of the scout, produced a sensation of secret awe in all that heard him. The Delawares held their breath in expectation; but Magua himself, even while he distrusted the forbearance of his enemy, remained immovable and calm, where he stood wedged in by the crowd, as one who grew to the spot.

"Beat it," repeated the young Delaware at the elbow of the scout.

"Beat what, fool! what?" exclaimed Hawkeye, still flourishing the weapon angrily above his head, though his eye no longer sought the person of Magua.

"If the white man is the warrior he pretends," said the aged chief, "let him strike nigher to the mark."

The scout laughed aloud, a noise that produced the startling effect of an unnatural sound on Heyward; then dropping the piece, heavily, into his extended left hand, it was discharged, apparently by the shock, driving the fragments of the vessel into the air, and scattering them on every side. Almost at the same instant, the rattling sound of the rifle was heard, as he suffered it to fall, contemptuously, to the earth.

The first impression of so strange a scene was engrossing admiration. Then a low, but increasing murmur, ran through the multitude, and finally swelled into sounds that denoted a lively opposition in the sentiments of the spectators. While some openly testified their satisfaction at so unexampled dexterity, by far the larger portion of the tribe were inclined to believe the success of the shot was the result of accident. Heyward was not slow to confirm an opinion that was so favorable to his own pretensions.

"It was chance!" he exclaimed; "none can shoot without an aim!"

"Chance!" echoed the excited woodsman, who was now stubbornly bent on maintaining his identity at every hazard, and on whom the secret hints of Heyward to acquiesce in the deception were entirely lost. "Does yonder lying Huron, too, think it chance? Give him another gun, and place us face to face, without cover or dodge, and let Providence, and our own eyes, decide the matter atween us! I do not make the offer, to you, major; for our blood is of a color, and we serve the same master."

"That the Huron is a liar, is very evident," returned Heyward, coolly; "you have yourself heard him assert you to be La Longue Carabine."

It were impossible to say what violent assertion the stubborn Hawkeye would have next made, in his headlong wish to vindicate his identity, had not the aged Delaware once more interposed.

"The hawk which comes from the clouds can return when he will," he said; "give them the guns."

This time the scout seized the rifle with avidity; nor had Magua, though he watched the movements of the marksman with jealous eyes, any further cause for apprehension.

"Now let it be proved, in the face of this tribe of Delawares, which is the better man," cried the scout, tapping the butt of his piece with that finger which had pulled so many fatal triggers.

"You see that gourd hanging against yonder tree, major; if you are a marksman fit for the borders, let me see you break its shell!"

Duncan noted the object and prepared himself to renew the trial. The gourd was one of the usual little vessels used by the Indians, and it was suspended from a dead branch of a small pine, by a thong of deerskin, at the full distance of a hundred yards. So strangely compounded is the feeling of self-love, that the young soldier, while he knew the utter worthlessness of the suffrages of his savage umpires, forgot the sudden motives of the contest in a wish to excel. It had been seen, already, that his skill was far from being contemptible, and he now resolved to put forth its nicest qualities.

Had his life depended on the issue, the aim of Duncan could not have been more deliberate or guarded. He fired; and three or four young Indians, who sprang forward at the report, announced with a shout, that the ball was in the tree, a very little on one side of the proper object. The warriors uttered a common ejaculation of pleasure, and then turned their eyes, inquiringly, on the movements of his rival.

"It may do for the Royal Americans!" said Hawkeye, laughing once more in his own silent, heartfelt manner; "but had my gun often turned so much from the true line, many a marten, whose skin is now in a lady's muff, would still be in the woods; ay, and many a bloody Mingo, who has departed to his final account, would be acting his deviltries at this very day, atween the provinces. I hope the squaw who owns the gourd has more of them in her wigwam, for this will never hold water again!"

The scout had shaken his priming and cocked his piece, while speaking; and, as he ended, he threw back a foot, and slowly raised the muzzle from the earth: the motion was steady, uniform, and in one direction. When on a perfect level, it remained for a single moment, without tremor or variation, as though both man and rifle were carved in stone. During that stationary instant, it poured forth its contents, in a bright, glancing sheet of flame. Again, the young Indians bounded forward; but their hurried search and disappointed looks announced that no traces of the bullet were to be seen.

"Go!" said the old chief to the scout, in a tone of strong disgust; "thou art a wolf in the skin of a dog. I will talk to the 'Long Rifle' of the Yengeese."

"Ah! had I that piece which furnished the name you use, I would obligate myself to cut the thong and drop the gourd without breaking it!" returned Hawkeye, perfectly undisturbed by the other's manner. "Fools, if you would find the bullet of a sharpshooter in these woods, you must look in the object, and not around it!"

The Indian youths instantly comprehended his meaning for this time he spoke in the Delaware tongue and tearing the gourd from the tree, they held it on high with an exulting shout, displaying a hole in its bottom, which had been cut by the bullet, after passing through the usual orifice in the center of its upper side. At this unexpected exhibition, a loud and vehement expression of pleasure burst from the mouth of every warrior present. It decided the question, and effectually established Hawkeye in the possession of his dangerous reputation. Those curious and admiring eyes which had been turned again on Heyward, were finally directed to the weather-beaten form of the scout, who immediately became the principal object of attention to the simple and unsophisticated beings by whom he was surrounded. When the sudden and noisy commotion had a little subsided, the aged chief resumed his examination.

"Why did you wish to stop my ears?" he said, addressing Duncan; "are the Delawares fools that they could not know the young panther from the cat?"

"They will yet find the Huron a singing-bird," said Duncan, endeavoring to adopt the figurative language of the natives.

"It is good. We will know who can shut the ears of men. Brother," added the chief turning his eyes on Magua, "the Delawares listen."

Thus singled, and directly called on to declare his object, the Huron arose and advancing with great deliberation and dignity into the very center of the circle, where he stood confronted by the prisoners, he placed himself in an attitude to speak. Before opening his mouth, however, he bent his eyes slowly along the whole living boundary of earnest faces, as if to temper his expressions to the capacities of his audience. On Hawkeye he cast a glance of respectful enmity; on Duncan, a look of inextinguishable hatred; the shrinking figure of Alice he scarcely deigned to notice; but when his glance met the firm, commanding, and yet lovely form of Cora, his eye lingered a moment, with an expression that it might have been difficult to define. Then, filled with his own dark intentions, he spoke in the language of the

Canadas, a tongue that he well knew was comprehended by most of his auditors.

"The Spirit that made men colored them differently," commenced the subtle Huron. "Some are blacker than the sluggish bear. These He said should be slaves; and He ordered them to work forever, like the beaver. You may hear them groan, when the south wind blows, louder than the lowing buffaloes, along the shores of the great salt lake, where the big canoes come and go with them in droves. Some He made with faces paler than the ermine of the forests and these He ordered to be traders, dogs to their women and wolves to their slaves. He gave this people the nature of the pigeon; wings that never tire; young, more plentiful than the leaves on the trees, and appetites to devour the earth. He gave them tongues like the false call of the wildcat; hearts like rabbits; the cunning of the hog (but none of the fox), and arms longer than the legs of the moose. With his tongue he stops the ears of the Indians; his heart teaches him to pay warriors to fight his battles; his cunning tells him how to get together the goods of the earth; and his arms enclose the land from the shores of the salt-water to the islands of the great lake. His gluttony makes him sick. God gave him enough, and yet he wants all. Such are the pale faces.

"Some the Great Spirit made with skins brighter and redder than yonder sun," continued Magua, pointing impressively upward to the lurid luminary, which was struggling through the misty atmosphere of the horizon; "and these did He fashion to His own mind. He gave them this island as He had made it, covered with trees, and filled with game. The wind made their clearings; the sun and rain ripened their fruits; and the snows came to tell them to be thankful. What need had they of roads to journey by! They saw through the hills! When the beavers worked, they lay in the shade, and looked on. The winds cooled them in summer; in winter, skins kept them warm. If they fought among themselves, it was to prove that they were men. They were brave; they were just; they were happy."

Here the speaker paused, and again looked around him to discover if his legend had touched the sympathies of his listeners. He met everywhere, with eyes riveted on his own, heads erect, and nostrils expanded, as if each individual present felt himself able and willing, singly, to redress the wrongs of his race.

"If the Great Spirit gave different tongues to his red children," he continued, in a low, still melancholy voice, "it was that all animals might understand them. Some He placed among the snows, with their cousin, the bear. Some he placed near the setting sun, on the road to the happy hunting grounds. Some on the lands around the great fresh waters; but to His greatest, and most beloved, He gave the sands of the salt lake. Do my brothers know the name of this favored people?"

"It was the Lenape!" exclaimed twenty eager voices in a breath.

"It was the Lenni Lenape," returned Magua, affecting to bend his head in reverence to their former greatness. "It was the tribes of the Lenape! The sun rose from water that was salt, and set in water that was sweet, and never hid himself from their eyes. But why should I, a Huron of the woods, tell a wise people their own traditions? Why remind them of their injuries; their ancient greatness; their deeds; their glory; their happiness; their losses; their defeats; their misery? Is there not one among them who has seen it all, and who knows it to be true? I have done. My tongue is still for my heart is of lead. I listen."

As the voice of the speaker suddenly ceased, every face and all eyes turned, by a common movement, toward the venerable Tamenund. From the moment that he took his seat, until the present instant, the lips of the patriarch had not severed, and scarcely a sign of life had escaped him. He sat bent in feebleness, and apparently unconscious of the presence he was in, during the whole of that opening scene, in which the skill of the scout had been so clearly established. At the nicely graduated sound of Magua's voice, however, he betrayed some evidence of consciousness, and once or twice he even raised his head, as if to listen. But when the crafty Huron spoke of his nation by name, the eyelids of the old man raised themselves and he looked out upon the multitude with that sort of dull, unmeaning expression which might be supposed to belong to the countenance of a specter. Then he made an effort to rise and being upheld by his supporters, he gained his feet, in a posture commanding by its dignity, while he tottered with weakness.

"Who calls upon the children of the Lenape?" he said, in a deep, guttural voice, that was rendered awfully audible by the breathless silence of the multitude; "who speaks of things gone? Does not the egg become a worm, the worm a fly and perish? Why tell the Delawares of good that is past? Better thank the Manitou for that which remains."

"It is a Wyandot," said Magua, stepping nigher to the rude platform on which the other stood; "a friend of Tamenund."

"A friend!" repeated the sage, on whose brow a dark frown settled, imparting a portion of that severity which had rendered his eye so terrible in middle age. "Are the Mingoes rulers of the earth? What brings a Huron in here?"

"Justice. His prisoners are with his brothers, and he comes for his own."

Tamenund turned his head toward one of his supporters, and listened to the short explanation the man gave.

Then, facing the applicant, he regarded him a moment with deep attention; after which he said, in a low and reluctant voice:

"Justice is the law of the great Manitou. My children, give the stranger food. Then, Huron, take thine own and depart."

On the delivery of this solemn judgment, the patriarch seated himself, and closed his eyes again, as if better pleased with the images of his own ripened experience than with the visible objects of the world. Against such a decree there was no Delaware sufficiently hardy to murmur, much less oppose himself. The words were barely uttered when four or five of the younger warriors, stepping behind Heyward and the scout, passed thongs so dexterously and rapidly around their arms, as to hold them both in instant bondage. The former was too much engrossed with his precious and nearly insensible burden, to be aware of their intentions before they were executed; and the latter, who considered even the hostile tribes of the Delawares a superior race of beings, submitted without resistance. Perhaps, however, the manner of the scout would not have been so passive, had he fully comprehended the language in which the preceding dialogue had been conducted.

Magua cast a look of triumph around the whole assembly before he proceeded to the execution of his purpose. Perceiving that the men were unable to offer any resistance, he turned his looks on her he valued most. Cora met his gaze with an eye so calm and firm, that his resolution wavered. Then, recollecting his former artifice, he raised Alice from the arms of the warrior against whom she leaned, and beckoning Heyward to follow, he motioned for the encircling crowd to open. But Cora, instead of obeying the impulse he had expected, rushed to the feet of the patriarch, and, raising her voice, exclaimed aloud:

"Just and venerable Delaware, on thy wisdom and power we lean for mercy! Be deaf to yonder artful and remorseless monster, who poisons thy ears with falsehoods to feed his thirst for blood. Thou that hast lived long, and that hast seen the evil of the world, should know how to temper its calamities to the miserable."

The eyes of the old man opened heavily, and he once more looked upward at the multitude. As the piercing tones of the suppliant swelled on his ears, they moved slowly in the direction of her person, and finally settled there in a steady gaze. Cora had cast herself to her knees; and, with hands clenched in each other and pressed upon her bosom, she remained like a beauteous and breathing model of her sex, looking up in his faded but majestic countenance, with a species of holy reverence. Gradually the expression of Tamenund's features changed, and losing their vacancy in admiration, they lighted with a portion of that intelligence which a century before had been wonted to communicate his youthful fire to the extensive bands of the Delawares. Rising without assistance, and seemingly without an effort, he demanded, in a voice that startled its auditors by its firmness:

"What art thou?"

"A woman. One of a hated race, if thou wilt a Yengee. But one who has never harmed thee, and who cannot harm thy people, if she would, who asks for succor."

"Tell me, my children," continued the patriarch, hoarsely, motioning to those around him, though his eyes still dwelt upon the kneeling form of Cora, "where have the Delawares camped?"

"In the mountains of the Iroquois, beyond the clear springs of the Horican."

"Many parching summers are come and gone," continued the sage, "since I drank of the water of my own rivers. The children of Minquon[1] are the justest white men, but they were thirsty and they took it to themselves. Do they follow us so far?"

"We follow none, we covet nothing," answered Cora. "Captives against our wills, have we been brought amongst you, and we ask but permission to depart to our own in peace. Art thou not Tamenund... the father, the judge, I had almost said, the prophet of this people?"

"I am Tamenund of many days."

"'Tis now some seven years that one of thy people was at the mercy of a white chief on the borders of this province. He claimed to be of the blood of the good and just Tamenund. 'Go', said the white man, 'for thy parent's sake thou art free.' Dost thou remember the name of that English warrior?"

"I remember, that when a laughing boy," returned the patriarch, with the peculiar recollection of vast age, "I stood upon the sands of the seashore and saw a big canoe, with wings whiter than the swans, and wider than many eagles, come from the rising sun."

---

[1] William Penn was termed Minquon by the Delawares, and, as he never used violence or injustice in his dealings with them, his reputation for probity passed into a proverb. The American is justly proud of the origin of his nation, which is perhaps unequaled in the history of the world; but the Pennsylvanian and Jerseyman have more reason to value themselves in their ancestors than the natives of any other state, since no wrong was done the original owners of the soil.

"Nay, nay; I speak not of a time so very distant, but of favor shown to thy kindred by one of mine, within the memory of thy youngest warrior."

"Was it when the Yengeese and the Dutchmanne fought for the hunting-grounds of the Delawares? Then Tamenund was a chief, and first laid aside the bow for the lightning of the pale faces..."

"Not yet then," interrupted Cora, "by many ages; I speak of a thing of yesterday. Surely, surely, you forget it not."

"It was but yesterday," rejoined the aged man, with touching pathos, "that the children of the Lenape were masters of the world. The fishes of the salt lake, the birds, the beasts, and the Mengee of the woods, owned them for Sagamores."

Cora bowed her head in disappointment, and, for a bitter moment struggled with her chagrin. Then, elevating her rich features and beaming eyes, she continued, in tones scarcely less penetrating than the unearthly voice of the patriarch himself:

"Tell me, is Tamenund a father?"

The old man looked down upon her from his elevated stand, with a benignant smile on his wasted countenance, and then casting his eyes slowly over the whole assemblage, he answered:

"Of a nation."

"For myself I ask nothing. Like thee and thine, venerable chief," she continued, pressing her hands convulsively on her heart, and suffering her head to droop until her burning cheeks were nearly concealed in the maze of dark, glossy tresses that fell in disorder upon her shoulders, "the curse of my ancestors has fallen heavily on their child. But yonder is one who has never known the weight of Heaven's displeasure until now. She is the daughter of an old and failing man, whose days are near their close. She has many, very many, to love her, and delight in her; and she is too good, much too precious, to become the victim of that villain."

"I know that the pale faces are a proud and hungry race. I know that they claim not only to have the earth, but that the meanest of their color is better than the Sachems of the red man. The dogs and crows of their tribes," continued the earnest old chieftain, without heeding the wounded spirit of his listener, whose head was nearly crushed to the earth in shame, as he proceeded, "would bark and caw before they would take a woman to their wigwams whose blood was not of the color of snow. But let them not boast before the face of the Manitou too loud. They entered the land at the rising and may yet go off at the setting sun. I have often seen the locusts strip the leaves from the trees, but the season of blossoms has always come again."

"It is so," said Cora, drawing a long breath, as if reviving from a trance, raising her face, and shaking back her shining veil, with a kindling eye, that contradicted the death-like paleness of her countenance; "but why, it has not permitted us to inquire. There is yet one of thine own people who has not been brought before thee; before thou lettest the Huron depart in triumph, hear him speak."

Observing Tamenund to look about him doubtingly, one of his companions said:

"It is a snake, a red skin in the pay of the Yengeese. We keep him for the torture."

"Let him come," returned the sage.

Then Tamenund once more sank into his seat and a silence so deep prevailed while the young man prepared to obey his simple mandate, that the leaves, which fluttered in the draught of the light morning air, were distinctly heard rustling in the surrounding forest.

CHAPTER XXX.

"If you deny me, fie upon your law!
There is no force in the decrees of Venice:
I stand for judgment: answer, shall I, have it?"
—Merchant of Venice

The silence continued unbroken by human sounds for many anxious minutes. Then the waving multitude opened and shut again, and Uncas stood in the living circle. All those eyes, which had been curiously studying the lineaments of the sage, as the source of their own intelligence, turned on the instant and were now bent in secret admiration on the erect, agile, and faultless person of the captive. But neither the presence in which he found himself, nor the exclusive attention that he attracted, in any manner disturbed the self-possession of the young Mohican. He cast a deliberate and observing look on every side of him, meeting the settled expression of hostility that lowered in the visages of the chiefs with the same calmness as the curious gaze of the attentive children. But when, last in this haughty scrutiny, the person of Tamenund came under his glance, his eye became fixed, as though all other objects were already forgotten. Then, advancing with a slow and noiseless step up the area, he placed himself immediately before the footstool of the sage. Here he stood unnoted, though keenly observant himself, until one of the chiefs apprised the latter of his presence.

"With what tongue does the prisoner speak to the Manitou?" demanded the patriarch, without unclosing his eyes.

"With what tongue does the prisoner speak to the Manitou?"

"Like his fathers," Uncas replied, "with the tongue of a Delaware."

At this sudden and unexpected annunciation, a low, fierce yell ran through the multitude, that might not inaptly be compared to the growl of the lion, as his choler is first awakened, a fearful omen of the weight of his future anger. The effect was equally strong on the sage, though differently exhibited. He passed a hand before his eyes, as if to exclude the least evidence of so shameful a spectacle, while he repeated, in his low, guttural tones, the words he had just heard.

"A Delaware! I have lived to see the tribes of the Lenape driven from their council-fires, and scattered, like broken herds of deer, among the hills of the Iroquois! I have seen the hatchets of a strong people sweep woods from the valleys, that the winds of heaven have spared! The beasts that run on the mountains, and the birds that fly above the trees, have I seen living in the wigwams of men; but never before have I found a Delaware so base as to creep, like a poisonous serpent, into the camps of his nation."

"The singing-birds have opened their bills," returned Uncas, in the softest notes of his own musical voice; "and Tamenund has heard their song."

The sage started, and bent his head aside, as if to catch the fleeting sounds of some passing melody.

"Does Tamenund dream!" he exclaimed. "What voice is at his ear! Have the winters gone backward! Will summer come again to the children of the Lenape!"

A solemn and respectful silence succeeded this incoherent burst from the lips of the Delaware prophet. His people readily constructed his unintelligible language into one of those mysterious conferences he was believed to hold so frequently with a superior intelligence, and they awaited the issue of the revelation in awe. After a patient pause, however, one of the aged men, perceiving that the sage had lost the recollection of the subject before them, ventured to remind him again of the presence of the prisoner.

"The false Delaware trembles lest he should hear the words of Tamenund," he said. "'Tis a hound that howls, when the Yengeese show him a trail."

"And ye," returned Uncas, looking sternly around him, "are dogs that whine, when the Frenchman casts ye the offals of his deer!"

Twenty knives gleamed in the air, and as many warriors sprang to their feet, at this biting, and perhaps merited retort but a motion from one of the chiefs suppressed the outbreaking of their tempers and restored the appearance of quiet. The task might probably have been more difficult, had not a movement made by Tamenund indicated that he was again about to speak.

"Delaware!" resumed the sage, "little art thou worthy of thy name. My people have not seen a bright sun in many winters and the warrior who deserts his tribe when hid in clouds is doubly a traitor. The law of the Manitou is just. It is so; while the rivers run and the mountains stand, while the blossoms come and go on the trees, it must be so. He is thine, my children; deal justly by him."

Not a limb was moved, nor was a breath drawn louder and longer than common, until the closing syllable of this final decree had passed the lips of Tamenund. Then a cry of vengeance burst at once, as it might be, from the united lips of the nation, a frightful augury of their ruthless intentions. In the midst of these prolonged and savage yells, a chief proclaimed, in a high voice, that the captive was condemned to endure the dreadful trial of torture by fire. The circle broke its order and screams of delight mingled with the bustle and tumult of preparation. Heyward struggled madly with his captors; the anxious eye of Hawkeye began to look around him, with an expression of peculiar earnestness; and Cora again threw herself at the feet of the patriarch, once more a suppliant for mercy.

Throughout the whole of these trying moments, Uncas had alone preserved his serenity. He looked on the preparations with a steady eye and when the tormentors came to seize him, he met them with a firm and upright attitude. One among them, if possible, more fierce and savage than his fellows, seized the hunting-shirt of the young warrior, and at a single effort tore it from his body. Then, with a yell of frantic pleasure, he leaped toward his unresisting victim and prepared to lead him to the stake. But, at that moment, when he appeared most a stranger to the feelings of humanity, the purpose of the savage was arrested as suddenly as if a supernatural agency had interposed in the behalf of Uncas. The eyeballs of the Delaware seemed to start from their sockets; his mouth opened and his whole form became frozen in an attitude of amazement. Raising his hand with a slow and regulated motion, he pointed with a finger to the bosom of the captive. His companions crowded about him in wonder and every eye was like his own, fastened intently on the figure of a small tortoise, beautifully tattooed on the breast of the prisoner, in a bright blue tint.

For a single instant Uncas enjoyed his triumph, smiling calmly on the scene. Then motioning the crowd away with a high and haughty sweep of his arm, he advanced in front of the nation with the air of a king and spoke in a voice louder than the murmur of admiration that ran through the multitude.

"Men of the Lenni Lenape!" he said, "my race upholds the earth! Your feeble tribe stands on my shell! What fire that a Delaware can light would burn the child of my fathers," he added, pointing proudly to the simple blazonry on his skin; "the blood that came from such a stock would smother your flames! My race is the grandfather of nations!"

"Who art thou?" demanded Tamenund, rising at the startling tones he heard, more than at any meaning conveyed by the language of the prisoner.

"Uncas, the son of Chingachgook," answered the captive modestly, turning from the nation, and bending his head in reverence to the other's character and years; "a son of the great Unamis."[1]

[1] Turtle.

"The hour of Tamenund is nigh!" exclaimed the sage; "the day is come, at last, to the night! I thank the Manitou, that one is here to fill my place at the council-fire. Uncas, the child of Uncas, is found! Let the eyes of a dying eagle gaze on the rising sun."

The youth stepped lightly, but proudly on the platform, where he became visible to the whole agitated and wondering multitude. Tamenund held him long at the length of his arm and read every turn in the fine lineaments of his countenance, with the untiring gaze of one who recalled days of happiness.

"Is Tamenund a boy?" at length the bewildered prophet exclaimed. "Have I dreamed of so many snows that my people were scattered like floating sands of Yengeese, more plenty than the leaves on the trees! The arrow of Tamenund would not frighten the fawn; his arm is withered like the branch of a dead oak; the snail would be swifter in the race; yet is Uncas before him as they went to battle against the pale faces! Uncas, the panther of his tribe, the eldest son of the Lenape, the wisest Sagamore of the Mohicans! Tell me, ye Delawares, has Tamenund been a sleeper for a hundred winters?"

The calm and deep silence which succeeded these words sufficiently announced the awful reverence with which his people received the communication of the patriarch. None dared to answer, though all listened in breathless expectation of what might follow. Uncas, however, looking in his face with the fondness and veneration of a favored child, presumed on his own high and acknowledged rank, to reply.

"Four warriors of his race have lived and died," he said, "since the friend of Tamenund led his people in battle. The blood of the turtle has been in many chiefs, but all have gone back into the earth from whence they came, except Chingachgook and his son."

"It is true...it is true," returned the sage, a flash of recollection destroying all his pleasing fancies, and restoring him at once to a consciousness of the true history of his nation. "Our wise men have often said that two warriors of the unchanged race were in the hills of the Yengeese; why have their seats at the council-fires of the Delawares been so long empty?"

At these words the young man raised his head, which he had still kept bowed a little, in reverence; and lifting his voice so as to be heard by the multitude, as if to explain at once and forever the policy of his family, he said aloud:

"Once we slept where we could hear the salt lake speak in its anger. Then we were rulers and Sagamores over the land. But when a pale face was seen on every brook, we followed the deer back to the river of our nation. The Delawares were gone. Few warriors of them all stayed to drink of the stream they loved. Then said my fathers, 'Here will we hunt. The waters of the river go into the salt lake. If we go toward the setting sun, we shall find streams that run into the great lakes of sweet water; there would a Mohican die, like fishes of the sea, in the clear springs. When the Manitou is ready and shall say "Come," we will follow the river to the sea, and take our own again.' Such, Delawares, is the belief of the children of the Turtle. Our eyes are on the rising and not toward the setting sun. We know whence he comes, but we know not whither he goes. It is enough."

The men of the Lenape listened to his words with all the respect that superstition could lend, finding a secret charm even in the figurative language with which the young Sagamore imparted his ideas. Uncas himself watched the effect of his brief explanation with intelligent eyes, and gradually dropped the air of authority he had assumed, as he perceived that his auditors were content. Then, permitting his looks to wander over the silent throng that crowded around the elevated seat of Tamenund, he first perceived Hawkeye in his bonds. Stepping eagerly from his stand, he made way for himself to the side of his friend and cutting his thongs with a quick and angry stroke of his own knife, he motioned to the crowd to divide. The Indians silently obeyed and once more they stood ranged in their circle, as before his appearance among them. Uncas took the scout by the hand and led him to the feet of the patriarch.

"Father," he said, "look at this pale face; a just man, and the friend of the Delawares."

"Is he a son of Minquon?"

"Not so; a warrior known to the Yengeese and feared by the Maquas."

"What name has he gained by his deeds?"

"We call him Hawkeye," Uncas replied, using the Delaware phrase; "for his sight never fails. The Mingoes know him better by the death he gives their warriors; with them he is 'The Long Rifle'."

"La Longue Carabine!" exclaimed Tamenund, opening his eyes, and regarding the scout sternly. "My son has not done well to call him friend."

"I call him so who proves himself such," returned the young chief, with great calmness, but with a steady mien. "If Uncas is welcome among the Delawares, then is Hawkeye with his friends."

"The pale face has slain my young men; his name is great for the blows he has struck the Lenape."

"If a Mingo has whispered that much in the ear of the Delaware, he has only shown that he is a singing-bird," said the scout, who now believed that it was time to vindicate himself from such offensive charges, and who spoke as the man he addressed, modifying his Indian figures, however, with his own peculiar notions. "That I have slain the Maquas I am not the man to deny, even at their own council-fires; but that, knowingly, my hand has never harmed a Delaware, is opposed to the reason of my gifts, which is friendly to them, and all that belongs to their nation."

A low exclamation of applause passed among the warriors who exchanged looks with each other like men that first began to perceive their error.

"Where is the Huron?" demanded Tamenund. "Has he stopped my ears?"

Magua, whose feelings during that scene in which Uncas had

triumphed may be much better imagined than described, answered to the call by stepping boldly in front of the patriarch.

"The just Tamenund," he said, "will not keep what a Huron has lent."

"Tell me, son of my brother," returned the sage, avoiding the dark countenance of Le Subtil, and turning gladly to the more ingenuous features of Uncas, "has the stranger a conqueror's right over you?"

"He has none. The panther may get into snares set by the women; but he is strong and knows how to leap through them."

"La Longue Carabine?"

"Laughs at the Mingoes. Go, Huron, ask your squaws the color of a bear."

"The stranger and white maiden that come into my camp together?"

"Should journey on an open path."

"And the woman that Huron left with my warriors?"

Uncas made no reply.

"And the woman that the Mingo has brought into my camp?" repeated Tamenund, gravely.

"She is mine," cried Magua, shaking his hand in triumph at Uncas. "Mohican, you know that she is mine."

"My son is silent," said Tamenund, endeavoring to read the expression of the face that the youth turned from him in sorrow.

"It is so," was the low answer.

A short and impressive pause succeeded, during which it was very apparent with what reluctance the multitude admitted the justice of the Mingo's claim. At length the sage, on whom alone the decision depended, said, in a firm voice:

"Huron, depart."

"As he came, just Tamenund," demanded the wily Magua, "or with hands filled with the faith of the Delawares? The wigwam of Le Renard Subtil is empty. Make him strong with his own."

The aged man mused with himself for a time; and then, bending his head toward one of his venerable companions, he asked:

"Are my ears open?"

"It is true."

"Is this Mingo a chief?"

"The first in his nation."

"Girl, what wouldst thou? A great warrior takes thee to wife. Go! thy race will not end."

"Better, a thousand times, it should," exclaimed the horror-struck Cora, "than meet with such a degradation!"

"Huron, her mind is in the tents of her fathers. An unwilling maiden makes an unhappy wigwam."

"She speaks with the tongue of her people," returned Magua, regarding his victim with a look of bitter irony.

"She is of a race of traders and will bargain for a bright look. Let Tamenund speak the words."

"Take you the wampum, and our love."

"Nothing hence but what Magua brought hither."

"Then depart with thine own. The Great Manitou forbids that a Delaware should be unjust."

Magua advanced and seized his captive strongly by the arm; the Delawares fell back, in silence and Cora, as if conscious that remonstrance would be useless, prepared to submit to her fate without resistance.

"Hold, hold!" cried Duncan, springing forward; "Huron, have mercy! her ransom shall make thee richer than any of thy people were ever yet known to be."

"Magua is a red-skin; he wants not the beads of the pale faces."

"Gold, silver, powder, lead all that a warrior needs shall be in thy wigwam; all that becomes the greatest chief."

"Le Subtil is very strong," cried Magua, violently shaking the hand which grasped the unresisting arm of Cora; "he has his revenge!"

"Mighty ruler of Providence!" exclaimed Heyward, clasping his hands together in agony, "can this be suffered! To you, just Tamenund, I appeal for mercy."

"The words of the Delaware are said," returned the sage, closing his eyes, and dropping back into his seat, alike wearied with his mental and his bodily exertion. "Men speak not twice."

"That a chief should not misspend his time in unsaying what has once been spoken is wise and reasonable," said Hawkeye, motioning to Duncan to be silent; "but it is also prudent in every warrior to consider well before he strikes his tomahawk into the head of his prisoner. Huron, I love you not; nor can I say that any Mingo has ever received much favor at my hands. It is fair to conclude that, if this war does not soon end, many more of your warriors will meet me in the woods. Put it to your judgment, then, whether you would prefer taking such a prisoner as that into your encampment, or one like myself, who am a man that it would greatly rejoice your nation to see with naked hands."

"Will 'The Long Rifle' give his life for the woman?" demanded Magua, hesitatingly; for he had already made a motion toward quitting the place with his victim.

"No, no; I have not said so much as that," returned Hawkeye, drawing back with suitable discretion, when he noted the eagerness with which Magua listened to his proposal. "It would be an unequal exchange, to give a warrior, in the prime of his age and usefulness, for the best woman on the frontiers. I might consent to go into winter quarters, now at least six weeks afore the leaves will turn on condition you will release the maiden."

Magua shook his head and made an impatient sign for the crowd to open.

"Well, then," added the scout, with the musing air of a man who had not half made up his mind; "I will throw 'killdeer' into the bargain. Take the word of an experienced hunter, the piece has not its equal atween the provinces."

Magua still disdained to reply, continuing his efforts to disperse the crowd.

"Perhaps," added the scout, losing his dissembled coolness exactly in proportion as the other manifested an indifference to the exchange, "if I should condition to teach your young men the real virtue of the weapon, it would smooth the little differences in our judgments."

Le Renard fiercely ordered the Delawares, who still lingered in an impenetrable belt around him, in hopes he would listen to the amicable proposal, to open his path, threatening, by the glance of his eye, another appeal to the infallible justice of their "prophet."

"What is ordered must sooner or later arrive," continued Hawkeye, turning with a sad and humbled look to Uncas. "The varlet knows his advantage and will keep it! God bless you, boy; you have found friends among your natural kin, and I hope they will prove as true as some you have met who had no Indian cross. As for me, sooner or later, I must die; it is, therefore, fortunate there are but few to make my death-howl. After all, it is likely the imps would have managed to master my scalp, so a day or two will make no great difference in the everlasting reckoning of time. God bless you," added the rugged woodsman, bending his head aside, and then instantly changing its direction again, with a wistful look toward the youth; "I loved both you and your father, Uncas, though our skins are not altogether of a color and our gifts are somewhat different. Tell the Sagamore I never lost sight of him in my greatest trouble and, as for you, think of me sometimes when on a lucky trail, and depend on it, boy, whether there be one heaven or two, there is a path in the other world by which honest men may come together again. You'll find the rifle in the place we hid it; take it and keep it for my sake and harkee, lad, as your natural gifts don't deny you the use of vengeance, use it a little freely on the Mingoes; it may unburden griefs at my loss, and ease your mind. Huron, I accept your offer; release the woman. I am your prisoner!"

A suppressed, but still distinct murmur of approbation ran through the crowd at this generous proposition; even the fiercest among the Delaware warriors manifesting pleasure at the manliness of the intended sacrifice. Magua paused, and for an anxious moment, it might be said, he doubted; then, casting his eyes on Cora, with an expression in which ferocity and admiration were strangely mingled, his purpose became fixed forever.

He intimated his contempt of the offer with a backward motion of his head, and said, in a steady and settled voice:

"Le Renard Subtil is a great chief; he has but one mind. Come," he added, laying his hand too familiarly on the shoulder of his captive to urge her onward; "a Huron is no tattler; we will go."

The maiden drew back in lofty womanly reserve, and her dark eye kindled, while the rich blood shot, like the passing brightness of the sun, into her very temples, at the indignity.

"I am your prisoner, and, at a fitting time shall be ready to follow, even to my death. But violence is unnecessary," she coldly said; and immediately turning to Hawkeye, added: "Generous hunter! from my soul I thank you. Your offer is vain, neither could it be accepted but still you may serve me, even more than in your own noble intention. Look at that drooping humbled child! Abandon her not until you leave her in the habitations of civilized men. I will not say," wringing the hard hand of the scout, "that her father will reward you for such as you are above the rewards of men but he will thank you and bless you. And, believe me, the blessing of a just and aged man has virtue in the sight of Heaven. Would to God I could hear one word from his lips at this awful moment!" Her voice became choked, and, for an instant, she was silent; then, advancing a step nigher to Duncan, who was supporting her unconscious sister, she continued, in more subdued tones, but in which feeling, and the habits of her sex maintained a fearful struggle: "I need not tell you to cherish the treasure you will possess. You love her, Heyward; that would conceal a thousand faults, though she had them. She is kind, gentle, sweet, good, as mortal may be. There is not a blemish in mind or person at which the proudest of you all would sicken. She is fair oh! how surpassingly fair!" laying her own beautiful, but less brilliant, hand in melancholy affection on the alabaster forehead of Alice and parting the golden hair which clustered about her brows; "and yet her soul is pure and spotless as her skin! I could say much more, perhaps, than cooler reason would approve but I will spare you and myself" Her voice became inaudible, and her face was bent over the form of her sister. After a long and burning kiss, she arose and with features of the hue of death but without even a tear in her feverish eye, she turned away, and added, to the savage, with all her former elevation of manner: "Now, sir, if it be your pleasure, I will follow."

"Ay, go," cried Duncan, placing Alice in the arms of an Indian girl; "go, Magua, go. These Delawares have their laws, which forbid them to detain you but I...I have no such obligation. Go, malignant monster... why do you delay?"

It would be difficult to describe the expression with which Magua listened to this threat to follow. There was at first a fierce and manifest display of joy and then it was instantly subdued in a look of cunning coldness.

"The words are open," he was content with answering, "'The Open Hand' can come."

"Hold," cried Hawkeye, seizing Duncan by the arm, and detaining him by violence; "you know not the craft of the imp. He would lead you to an amusement, and your death..."

"Huron," interrupted Uncas, who submissive to the stern customs of his people, had been an attentive and grave listener to all that passed; "Huron, the justice of the Delawares comes from the Manitou. Look at the sun. He is now in the upper branches of the hemlock. Your path is short and open. When he is seen above the trees, there will be men on your trail."

"I hear a crow!" exclaimed Magua, with a taunting laugh. "Go!" he added, shaking his hand at the crowd, which had slowly opened to admit his passage. "Where are the petticoats of the Delawares! Let them send their arrows and their guns to the Wyandots; they shall have venison to eat, and corn to hoe. Dogs, rabbits, thieves...I spit on you!"

His parting gibes were listened to in a dead, boding silence, and, with these biting words in his mouth, the triumphant Magua passed unmolested into the forest, followed by his passive captive, and protected by the inviolable laws of Indian hospitality.

CHAPTER XXXI.

"Flue.—Kill the poys and the luggage! 'Tis expressly against the law of arms; 'tis as arrant a piece of knavery, mark you now, as can be offered in the 'orld."

—King Henry V.

So long as their enemy and his victim continued in sight, the multitude remained motionless as beings charmed to the place by some power that was friendly to the Huron but the instant he disappeared, it became tossed and agitated by fierce and powerful passion. Uncas maintained his elevated stand, keeping his eyes on the form of Cora, until the colors of her dress were blended with the foliage of the forest; when he descended, and, moving silently through the throng, he disappeared in that lodge from which he had so recently issued. A few of the graver and more attentive warriors, who caught the gleams of anger that shot from the eyes of the young chief in passing, followed him to the place he had selected for his meditations. After which, Tamenund and Alice were removed, and the women and children were ordered to disperse. During the momentous hour that succeeded, the encampment resembled a hive of troubled bees, who only awaited the appearance and example of their leader to take some distant and momentous flight.

A young warrior at length issued from the lodge of Uncas and moving deliberately, with a sort of grave march, toward a dwarf pine that grew in the crevices of the rocky terrace, he tore the bark from its body, and then turned whence he came without speaking. He was soon followed by another, who stripped the sapling of its branches, leaving it a naked and blazed[1] trunk. A third colored the post with stripes of a dark red paint; all which indications of a hostile design in the leaders of the nation were received by the men without in a gloomy and ominous silence. Finally, the Mohican himself reappeared, divested of all his attire, except his girdle and leggings, and with one-half of his fine features hid under a cloud of threatening black.

Uncas moved with a slow and dignified tread toward the post, which he immediately commenced encircling with a measured step, not unlike an ancient dance, raising his voice, at the same time, in the wild and irregular chant of his war song. The notes were in the extremes of human sounds; being sometimes melancholy and exquisitely plaintive, even rivaling the melody of birds and then, by sudden and startling transitions, causing the auditors to tremble by their depth and energy. The words were few and often repeated, proceeding gradually from a sort of invocation, or hymn, to the Deity, to an intimation of the warrior's object, and terminating as they commenced with an acknowledgment of his own dependence on the Great Spirit. If it were possible to translate the comprehensive and melodious language in which he spoke, the ode might read something like the following: "Manitou! Manitou! Manitou! Thou art great, thou art good, thou art wise: Manitou! Manitou! Thou art just. In the heavens, in the clouds, oh, I see many spots many dark, many red: In the heavens, oh, I see many clouds."

"In the woods, in the air, oh, I hear the whoop, the long yell, and the cry: In the woods, oh, I hear the loud whoop!"

"Manitou! Manitou! Manitou! I am weak...thou art strong; I am slow; Manitou! Manitou! Give me aid."

---

[1] A tree which has been partially or entirely stripped of its bark is said, in the language of the country, to be "blazed." The term is strictly English, for a horse is said to be blazed when it has a white mark.

At the end of what might be called each verse he made a pause, by raising a note louder and longer than common, that was peculiarly suited to the sentiment just expressed. The first close was solemn and intended to convey the idea of veneration; the second descriptive, bordering on the alarming; and the third was the well-known and terrific war-whoop, which burst from the lips of the young warrior, like a combination of all the frightful sounds of battle. The last was like the first, humble and imploring. Three times did he repeat this song, and as often did he encircle the post in his dance.

At the close of the first turn, a grave and highly esteemed chief of the Lenape followed his example, singing words of his own, however, to music of a similar character. Warrior after warrior enlisted in the dance, until all of any renown and authority were numbered in its mazes. The spectacle now became wildly terrific; the fierce-looking and menacing visages of the chiefs receiving additional power from the appalling strains in which they mingled their guttural tones. Just then Uncas struck his tomahawk deep into the post, and raised his voice in a shout, which might be termed his own battle cry. The act announced that he had assumed the chief authority in the intended expedition.

It was a signal that awakened all the slumbering passions of the nation. A hundred youths, who had hitherto been restrained by the diffidence of their years, rushed in a frantic body on the fancied emblem of their enemy, and severed it asunder, splinter by splinter, until nothing remained of the trunk but its roots in the earth. During this moment of tumult, the most ruthless deeds of war were performed on the fragments of the tree, with as much apparent ferocity as if they were the living victims of their cruelty. Some were scalped; some received the keen and trembling axe and others suffered by thrusts from the fatal knife. In short, the manifestations of zeal and fierce delight were so great and unequivocal, that the expedition was declared to be a war of the nation.

The instant Uncas had struck the blow, he moved out of the circle, and cast his eyes up to the sun, which was just gaining the point, when the truce with Magua was to end. The fact was soon announced by a significant gesture, accompanied by a corresponding cry; and the whole of the excited multitude abandoned their mimic warfare, with shrill yells of pleasure, to prepare for the more hazardous experiment of the reality.

The whole face of the encampment was instantly changed. The warriors, who were already armed and painted, became as still as if they were incapable of any uncommon burst of emotion. On the other hand, the women broke out of the lodges, with the songs of joy and those of lamentation so strangely mixed that it might have been difficult to have said which passion preponderated. None, however, was idle. Some bore their choicest articles, others their young and some their aged and infirm, into the forest, which spread itself like a verdant carpet of bright green against the side of the mountain. Thither Tamenund also retired, with calm composure, after a short and touching interview with Uncas; from whom the sage separated with the reluctance that a parent would quit a long lost and just recovered child. In the meantime, Duncan saw Alice to a place of safety and then sought the scout, with a countenance that denoted how eagerly he also panted for the approaching contest.

But Hawkeye was too much accustomed to the war song and the enlistments of the natives, to betray any interest in the passing scene. He merely cast an occasional look at the number and quality of the warriors, who, from time to time, signified their readiness to accompany Uncas to the field. In this particular he was soon satisfied; for, as has been already seen, the power of the young chief quickly embraced every fighting man in the nation. After this material point was so satisfactorily decided, he dispatched an Indian boy in quest of "killdeer" and the rifle of Uncas, to the place where they had deposited their weapons on approaching the camp of the Delawares; a measure of double policy, inasmuch as it protected the arms from their own fate, if detained as prisoners, and gave them the advantage of appearing among the strangers rather as sufferers than as men provided with means of defense and subsistence. In selecting another to perform the office of reclaiming his highly prized rifle, the scout had lost sight of none of his habitual caution. He knew that Magua had not come unattended, and he also knew that Huron spies watched the movements of their new enemies, along the whole boundary of the woods. It would, therefore, have been fatal to himself to have attempted the experiment; a warrior would have fared no better; but the danger of a boy would not be likely to commence until after his object was discovered. When Heyward joined him, the scout was coolly awaiting the result of this experiment.

The boy, who had been well instructed, and was sufficiently crafty, proceeded, with a bosom that was swelling with the pride of such a confidence, and all the hopes of young ambition, carelessly across the clearing to the wood, which he entered at a point at some little distance from the place where the guns were secreted. The instant, however, he was concealed by the foliage of the bushes, his dusky form was to be seen gliding, like that of a serpent, toward the desired treasure. He was successful; and in another moment he appeared flying across the narrow opening that skirted the base of the terrace on which the village stood, with the velocity of an arrow, and bearing a prize in each hand. He had actually gained the crags, and was leaping up their sides with incredible activity, when a shot from the woods showed how accurate had been the judgment of the scout. The boy answered it with a feeble but contemptuous shout; and immediately a second bullet was sent after him from another part of the cover. At the next instant he appeared on the level above, elevating his guns in triumph, while he moved with the air of a conqueror toward the renowned hunter who had honored him by so glorious a commission.

Notwithstanding the lively interest Hawkeye had taken in the fate of his messenger, he received "killdeer" with a satisfaction that, momentarily, drove all other recollections from his mind. After examining the piece with an intelligent eye and opening and shutting the pan some ten or fifteen times and trying sundry other equally important experiments on the lock, he turned to the boy and demanded with great manifestations of kindness, if he was hurt. The urchin looked proudly up in his face but made no reply.

"Ah! I see, lad, the knaves have barked your arm!" added the scout, taking up the limb of the patient sufferer, across which a deep flesh wound had been made by one of the bullets; "but a little bruised alder will act like a charm. In the meantime, I will wrap it in a badge of wampum! You have commenced the business of a warrior early, my brave boy, and are likely to bear a plenty of honorable scars to your grave. I know many young men that have taken scalps who cannot show such a mark as this. Go!" having bound up the arm; "you will be a chief!"

The lad departed, prouder of his flowing blood than the vainest courtier could be of his blushing ribbon and stalked among the fellows of his age, an object of general admiration and envy.

But, in a moment of so many serious and important duties, this single act of juvenile fortitude did not attract the general notice and commendation it would have received under milder auspices. It had, however, served to apprise the Delawares of the position and the intentions of their enemies. Accordingly, a party of adventurers, better suited to the task than the weak though spirited boy was ordered to dislodge the skulkers. The duty was soon performed; for most of the Hurons retired of themselves when they found they had been discovered. The Delawares followed to a sufficient distance from their own encampment, and then halted for orders, apprehensive of being led into an ambush. As both parties secreted themselves, the woods were again as still and quiet as a mild summer morning and deep solitude could render them.

The calm but still impatient Uncas now collected his chiefs and divided his power. He presented Hawkeye as a warrior, often tried, and always found deserving of confidence. When he found his friend met with a favorable reception, he bestowed on him the command of twenty men, like himself, active, skillful, and resolute. He gave the Delawares to understand the rank of Heyward among the troops of the Yengeese, and then tendered to him a trust of equal authority. But Duncan declined the charge, professing his readiness to serve as a volunteer by the side of the scout. After this disposition, the young Mohican appointed various native chiefs to fill the different situations of responsibility, and, the time pressing, he gave forth the word to march. He was cheerfully, but silently obeyed by more than two hundred men.

Their entrance into the forest was perfectly unmolested; nor did they encounter any living objects that could either give the alarm, or furnish the intelligence they needed, until they came upon the lairs of their own scouts. Here a halt was ordered, and the chiefs were assembled to hold a "whispering council."

At this meeting divers' plans of operation were suggested, though none of a character to meet the wishes of their ardent leader. Had Uncas followed the promptings of his own inclinations, he would have led his followers to the charge without a moment's delay and put the conflict to the hazard of an instant issue, but such a course would have been in opposition to all the received practices and opinions of his countrymen. He was, therefore, fain to adopt a caution that in the present temper of his mind he execrated, and to listen to advice at which his fiery spirit chafed, under the vivid recollection of Cora's danger and Magua's insolence.

After an unsatisfactory conference of many minutes, a solitary individual was seen advancing from the side of the enemy, with such apparent haste, as to induce the belief he might be a messenger charged with pacific overtures. When within a hundred yards, however, of the cover behind which the Delaware council had assembled, the stranger hesitated, appeared uncertain what course to take, and finally halted. All eyes were turned now on Uncas, as if seeking directions how to proceed.

"Hawkeye," said the young chief, in a low voice, "he must never speak to the Hurons again."

"His time has come," said the laconic scout, thrusting the long barrel of his rifle through the leaves, and taking his deliberate and fatal aim. But, instead of pulling the trigger, he lowered the muzzle again, and indulged himself in a fit of his peculiar mirth. "I took the imp for a Mingo, as I'm a miserable sinner!" he said; "but when my eye ranged along his ribs for a place to get the bullet in, would you think it, Uncas I saw the musician's blower and so, after all, it is the man they call Gamut, whose death can profit no one and whose life, if this tongue can do anything but sing, may be made serviceable to our own ends. If sounds have not lost their virtue, I'll soon have a discourse with the honest fellow and that in a voice he'll find more agreeable than the speech of 'killdeer'."

So, saying, Hawkeye laid aside his rifle; and, crawling through the bushes until within hearing of David, he attempted to repeat the musical effort, which had conducted himself, with so much safety and eclat, through the Huron encampment. The exquisite organs of Gamut could not readily be deceived (and, to say the truth, it would have been difficult for any other than Hawkeye to produce a similar noise), and, consequently, having once before heard the sounds, he now knew whence they proceeded. The poor fellow appeared relieved from a state of great embarrassment for pursuing the direction of the voice, a task that to him was not much less arduous that it would have been to have gone up in the face of a battery, he soon discovered the hidden songster.

"I wonder what the Hurons will think of that!" said the scout, laughing, as he took his companion by the arm, and urged him toward the rear. "If the knaves lie within earshot, they will say there are two non-composers instead of one! But here we are safe," he added, pointing to Uncas and his associates. "Now give us the history of the Mingo inventions in natural English and without any ups and downs of voice."

David gazed about him, at the fierce and wild-looking chiefs, in mute wonder; but assured by the presence of faces that he knew, he soon rallied his faculties so far as to make an intelligent reply.

"The heathen are abroad in goodly numbers," said David; "and, I fear, with evil intent. There has been much howling and ungodly revelry, together with such sounds as it is profanity to utter, in their habitations within the past hour, so much so, in truth, that I have fled to the Delawares in search of peace."

"Your ears might not have profited much by the exchange, had you been quicker of foot," returned the scout a little dryly. "But let that be as it may; where are the Hurons?"

"They lie hid in the forest, between this spot and their village in such force, that prudence would teach you instantly to return."

Uncas cast a glance along the range of trees which concealed his own band and mentioned the name of:

"Magua?"

"Is among them. He brought in the maiden that had sojourned with the Delawares; and, leaving her in the cave, has put himself, like a raging wolf, at the head of his savages. I know not what has troubled his spirit so greatly!"

"He has left her, you say, in the cave!" interrupted Heyward; "'tis well that we know its situation! May not something be done for her instant relief?"

Uncas looked earnestly at the scout, before he asked:

"What says Hawkeye?"

"Give me twenty rifles and I will turn to the right, along the stream and passing by the huts of the beaver, will join the Sagamore and the colonel. You shall then hear the whoop from that quarter; with this wind one may easily send it a mile. Then, Uncas, do you drive in the front; when they come within range of our pieces, we will give them a blow that, I pledge the good name of an old frontiersman, shall make their line bend like an ashen bow. After which, we will carry the village and take the woman from the cave; when the affair may be finished with the tribe, according to a white man's battle, by a blow and a victory or in the Indian fashion, with dodge and cover. There may be no great learning, major, in this plan but with courage and patience it can all be done."

"I like it very much," cried Duncan, who saw that the release of Cora was the primary object in the mind of the scout; "I like it much. Let it be instantly attempted."

After a short conference, the plan was matured, and rendered more intelligible to the several parties; the different signals were appointed and the chiefs separated, each to his allotted station.

CHAPTER XXXII.

"But plagues shall spread, and funeral fires increase,
Till the great king, without a ransom paid,
To her own Chrysa send the black-eyed maid."
—Pope.

During the time Uncas was making this disposition of his forces, the woods were as still, and, with the exception of those who had met in council, apparently as much untenanted as when they came fresh from the hands of their Almighty Creator. The eye could range, in every direction, through the long and shadowed vistas of the trees; but nowhere was any object to be seen that did not properly belong to the peaceful and slumbering scenery.

Here and there a bird was heard fluttering among the branches of the beeches, and occasionally a squirrel dropped a nut, drawing the startled looks of the party for a moment to the place but the instant the casual interruption ceased, the passing air was heard murmuring above their heads, along that verdant and undulating surface of forest, which spread itself unbroken, unless by stream or lake, over such a vast region of country. Across the tract of wilderness which lay between the Delawares and the village of their enemies, it seemed as if the foot of man had never trodden, so breathing and deep was the silence in which it lay. But Hawkeye, whose duty led him foremost in the adventure, knew the character of those with whom he was about to contend too well to trust the treacherous quiet.

When he saw his little band collected, the scout threw "killdeer" into the hollow of his arm, and making a silent signal that he would be followed, he led them many rods toward the rear, into the bed of a little brook which they had crossed in advancing. Here he halted, and after waiting for the whole of his grave and attentive warriors to close about him, he spoke in Delaware, demanding:

"Do any of my young men know whither this run will lead us?"

A Delaware stretched forth a hand, with the two fingers separated, and indicating the manner in which they were joined at the root, he answered:

"Before the sun could go his own length, the little water will be in the big." Then he added, pointing in the direction of the place he mentioned, "the two make enough for the beavers."

"I thought as much," returned the scout, glancing his eye upward at the opening in the tree-tops, "from the course it takes, and the bearings of the mountains. Men, we will keep within the cover of its banks till we scent the Hurons."

His companions gave the usual brief exclamation of assent, but, perceiving that their leader was about to lead the way in person, one or two made signs that all was not as it should be. Hawkeye, who comprehended their meaning glances, turned, and perceived that his party had been followed thus far by the singing-master.

"Do you know, friend," asked the scout, gravely, and perhaps with a little of the pride of conscious deserving in his manner, "that this is a band of rangers chosen for the most desperate service and put under the command of one who, though another might say it with a better face, will not be apt to leave them idle. It may not be five, it cannot be thirty minutes, before we tread on the body of a Huron, living or dead."

"Though not admonished of your intentions in words," returned David, whose face was a little flushed and whose ordinarily quiet and unmeaning eyes glimmered with an expression of unusual fire, "your men have reminded me of the children of Jacob going out to battle against the Shechemites, for wickedly aspiring to wedlock with a woman of a race that was favored of the Lord. Now, I have journeyed far, and sojourned much in good and evil with the maiden ye seek and though not a man of war, with my loins girded and my sword sharpened, yet would I gladly strike a blow in her behalf."

The scout hesitated, as if weighing the chances of such a strange enlistment in his mind before he answered:

"You know not the use of any weapon. You carry no rifle and believe me, what the Mingoes take they will freely give again."

"Though not a vaunting and bloodily disposed Goliath," returned David, drawing a sling from beneath his parti-colored and uncouth attire, "I have not forgotten the example of the Jewish boy. With this ancient instrument of war have I practiced much in my youth and peradventure the skill has not entirely departed from me."

"Ay!" said Hawkeye, considering the deer-skin thong and apron, with a cold and discouraging eye; "the thing might do its work among arrows, or even knives but these Mengwe have been furnished by the Frenchers with a good, grooved barrel a man. However, it seems to be your gift to go unharmed amid fire; and as you have hitherto been favored major, you have left your rifle at a cock; a single shot before the time would be just twenty scalps lost to no purpose... singer, you can follow; we may find use for you in the shouting's."

"I thank you, friend," returned David, supplying himself, like his royal namesake, from among the pebbles of the brook; "though not given to the desire to kill, had you sent me away my spirit would have been troubled."

"Remember," added the scout, tapping his own head significantly on that spot where Gamut was yet sore, "we come to fight, and not to musickate. Until the general whoop is given, nothing speaks but the rifle."

David nodded, as much to signify his acquiescence with the terms; and then Hawkeye, casting another observant glance over his followers made the signal to proceed.

Their route lay, for the distance of a mile, along the bed of the watercourse. Though protected from any great danger of observation by the precipitous banks, and the thick shrubbery which skirted the stream, no precaution known to an Indian attack was neglected. A warrior rather crawled than walked on each flank so as to catch occasional glimpses into the forest; and every few minutes the band came to a halt and listened for hostile sounds, with an acuteness of organs that would be scarcely conceivable to a man in a less natural state. Their march was, however, unmolested, and they reached the point where the lesser stream was lost in the greater, without the smallest evidence that their progress had been noted. Here the scout again halted, to consult the signs of the forest.

"We are likely to have a good day for a fight," he said, in English, addressing Heyward and glancing his eyes upward at the clouds, which began to move in broad sheets across the firmament; "a bright sun and a glittering barrel are no friends to true sight. Everything is favorable; they have the wind, which will bring down their noises and their smoke, too, no little matter in itself whereas, with us it will be first a shot and then a clear view. But here is an end to our cover; the beavers have had the range of this stream for hundreds of years and what atween their food and their dams, there is, as you see, many a girdled stub, but few living trees."

Hawkeye had, in truth, in these few words, given no bad description of the prospect that now lay in their front. The brook was irregular in its width, sometimes shooting through narrow fissures in the rocks, and at others spreading over acres of bottom land, forming little areas that might be termed ponds. Everywhere along its bands were the moldering relics of dead trees in all the stages of decay, from those that groaned on their tottering trunks to such as had recently been robbed of those rugged coats that so mysteriously contain their principle of life. A few long, low, and moss-covered piles were scattered among them, like the memorials of a former and long-departed generation.

All these minute particulars were noted by the scout, with a gravity and interest that they probably had never before attracted. He knew that the Huron encampment lay a short half mile up the brook; and, with the characteristic anxiety of one who dreaded a hidden danger, he was greatly troubled at not finding the smallest trace of the presence of his enemy. Once or twice, he felt induced to give the order for a rush and to attempt the village by surprise, but his experience quickly admonished him of the danger of so useless an experiment. Then he listened intently, and with painful uncertainty, for the sounds of hostility in the quarter where Uncas was left but nothing was audible except the sighing of the wind, that began to sweep over the bosom of the forest in gusts which threatened a tempest. At length, yielding rather to his unusual impatience than taking counsel from his knowledge, he determined to bring matters to an issue, by unmasking his force, and proceeding cautiously, but steadily, up the stream.

The scout had stood, while making his observations, sheltered by a brake, and his companions still lay in the bed of the ravine, through which the smaller stream debouched but on hearing his low, though intelligible, signal the whole party stole up the bank, like so many dark specters, and silently arranged themselves around him. Pointing in the direction he wished to proceed, Hawkeye advanced, the band breaking off in single files, and following so accurately in his footsteps, as to leave it, if we except Heyward and David, the trail of but a single man.

The party was, however, scarcely uncovered before a volley from a dozen rifles was heard in their rear and a Delaware leaping high into the air, like a wounded deer, fell at his whole length, dead.

"Ah, I feared some deviltry like this!" exclaimed the scout, in English, adding, with the quickness of thought, in his adopted tongue: "To cover, men, and charge!"

The band dispersed at the word, and before Heyward had well recovered from his surprise, he found himself standing alone with David. Luckily the Hurons had already fallen back, and he was safe from their fire. But this state of things was evidently to be of short continuance for the scout set the example of pressing on their retreat, by discharging his rifle and darting from tree to tree as his enemy slowly yielded ground.

It would seem that the assault had been made by a very small party of the Hurons, which, however, continued to increase in numbers, as it retired on its friends, until the return fire was very nearly, if not quite, equal to that maintained by the advancing Delawares. Heyward threw himself among the combatants, and imitating the necessary caution of his companions, he made quick discharges with his own rifle. The contest now grew warm and stationary. Few were injured, as both parties kept their bodies as much protected as possible by the trees; never, indeed, exposing any part of their persons except in the act of taking aim. But the chances were gradually growing unfavorable to Hawkeye and his band. The quick-sighted scout perceived his danger without knowing how to remedy it. He saw it was more dangerous to retreat than to maintain his ground: while he found his enemy throwing out men on his flank, which rendered the task of keeping themselves covered so very difficult to the Delawares, as nearly to silence their fire. At this embarrassing moment, when they began to think the whole of the hostile tribe was gradually encircling them, they heard the yell of combatants and the rattling of arms echoing under the arches of the wood at the place where Uncas was posted, a bottom which, in a manner, lay beneath the ground on which Hawkeye and his party were contending.

The effects of this attack were instantaneous, and to the scout and his friends greatly relieving. It would seem that, while his own surprise had been anticipated and had consequently failed, the enemy, in their turn, having been deceived in its object and in his numbers, had left too small a force to resist the impetuous onset of the young Mohican. This fact was doubly apparent, by the rapid manner in which the battle in the forest rolled upward toward the village, and by an instant falling off in the number of their assailants, who rushed to assist in maintaining the front, and, as it now proved to be, the principal point of defense.

Animating his followers by his voice, and his own example, Hawkeye then gave the word to bear down upon their foes. The charge, in that rude species of warfare, consisted merely in pushing from cover to cover, nigher to the enemy; and in this maneuver he was instantly and successfully obeyed. The Hurons were compelled to withdraw, and the scene of the contest rapidly changed from the more open ground, on which it had commenced, to a spot where the assailed found a thicket to rest upon. Here the struggle was protracted, arduous and seemingly of doubtful issue; the Delawares, though none of them fell, beginning to bleed freely, in consequence of the disadvantage at which they were held.

In this crisis, Hawkeye found means to get behind the same tree as that which served for a cover to Heyward; most of his own combatants being within call, a little on his right, where they maintained rapid, though fruitless, discharges on their sheltered enemies.

"You are a young man, major," said the scout, dropping the butt of "killdeer" to the earth, and leaning on the barrel, a little fatigued with his previous industry; "and it may be your gift to lead armies, at some future day, again these imps, the Mingoes. You may here see the philosophy of an Indian fight. It consists mainly in ready hand, a quick eye, and a good cover. Now, if you had a company of the Royal Americans here, in what manner would you set them to work in this business?"

"The bayonet would make a road."

"Ay, there is white reason in what you say but a man must ask himself, in this wilderness, how many lives he can spare. No...horse[1]," continued the scout, shaking his head, like one who mused; "horse, I am ashamed to say must sooner or later decide these scrimmages. The brutes are better than men and to horse must we come at last. Put a shodden hoof on the moccasin of a red-skin and if his rifle be once emptied, he will never stop to load it again."

"This is a subject that might better be discussed at another time," returned Heyward; "shall we charge?"

"I see no contradiction to the gifts of any man in passing his breathing spells in useful reflections," the scout replied. "As to rush, I little relish such a measure; for a scalp or two must be thrown away in the attempt. And yet," he added, bending his head aside, to catch the sounds of the distant combat, "if we are to be of use to Uncas, these knaves in our front must be got rid of."

Then, turning with a prompt and decided air, he called aloud to his Indians, in their own language. His words were answered by a shout; and, at a given signal, each warrior made a swift movement around his particular tree. The sight of so many dark bodies, glancing before their eyes at the same instant, drew a hasty and consequently an ineffectual fire from the Hurons. Without stopping to breathe, the Delawares leaped in long bounds toward the wood, like so many panthers springing upon their prey. Hawkeye was in front, brandishing his terrible rifle and animating his followers by his example. A few of the older and more cunning Hurons, who had not been deceived by the artifice which had been practiced drawing their fire, now

[1] The American forest admits of the passage of horses, there being little underbrush, and few tangled brakes. The plan of Hawkeye is the one which has always proved the most successful in the battles between the whites and the Indians. Wayne, in his celebrated campaign on the Miami, received the fire of his enemies in line; and then causing his dragoons to wheel round his flanks, the Indians were driven from their covers before they had time to load. One of the most conspicuous of the chiefs who fought in the battle of Miami assured the writer, that the red men could not fight the warriors with "long knives and leather stockings"; meaning the dragoons with their sabers and boots.

made a close and deadly discharge of their pieces and justified the apprehensions of the scout by felling three of his foremost warriors. But the shock was insufficient to repel the impetus of the charge. The Delawares broke into the cover with the ferocity of their natures and swept away every trace of resistance by the fury of the onset.

The combat endured only for an instant, hand to hand, and then the assailed yielded ground rapidly, until they reached the opposite margin of the thicket, where they clung to the cover, with the sort of obstinacy that is so often witnessed in hunted brutes. At this critical moment, when the success of the struggle was again becoming doubtful, the crack of a rifle was heard behind the Hurons, and a bullet came whizzing from among some beaver lodges, which were situated in the clearing, in their rear, and was followed by the fierce and appalling yell of the war-whoop.

"There speaks the Sagamore!" shouted Hawkeye, answering the cry with his own stentorian voice; "we have them now in face and back!"

The effect on the Hurons was instantaneous. Discouraged by an assault from a quarter that left them no opportunity for cover, the warriors uttered a common yell of disappointment, and breaking off in a body, they spread themselves across the opening, heedless of every consideration but flight. Many fell, in making the experiment, under the bullets and the blows of the pursuing Delawares.

We shall not pause to detail the meeting between the scout and Chingachgook, or the more touching interview that Duncan held with Munro. A few brief and hurried words served to explain the state of things to both parties; and then Hawkeye, pointing out the Sagamore to his band, resigned the chief authority into the hands of the Mohican chief. Chingachgook assumed the station to which his birth and experience gave him so distinguished a claim, with the grave dignity that always gives force to the mandates of a native warrior. Following the footsteps of the scout, he led the party back through the thicket, his men scalping the fallen Hurons and secreting the bodies of their own dead as they proceeded, until they gained a point where the former was content to make a halt.

The warriors, who had breathed themselves freely in the preceding struggle, were now posted on a bit of level ground, sprinkled with trees in sufficient numbers to conceal them. The land fell away rather precipitately in front, and beneath their eyes stretched, for several miles, a narrow, dark, and wooded vale. It was through this dense and dark forest that Uncas was still contending with the main body of the Hurons.

The Mohican and his friends advanced to the brow of the hill, and listened, with practiced ears, to the sounds of the combat. A few birds hovered over the leafy bosom of the valley, frightened from their secluded nests and here and there a light vapory cloud, which seemed already blending with the atmosphere, arose above the trees, and indicated some spot where the struggle had been fierce and stationary.

"The fight is coming up the ascent," said Duncan, pointing in the direction of a new explosion of firearms; "we are too much in the center of their line to be effective."

"They will incline into the hollow, where the cover is thicker," said the scout, "and that will leave us well on their flank. Go, Sagamore; you will hardly be in time to give the whoop, and lead on the young men. I will fight this scrimmage with warriors of my own color. You know me, Mohican; not a Huron of them all shall cross the swell, into your rear, without the notice of 'killdeer'."

The Indian chief paused another moment to consider the signs of the contest, which was now rolling rapidly up the ascent, a certain evidence that the Delawares triumphed; nor did he actually quit the place until admonished of the proximity of his friends, as well as enemies, by the bullets of the former, which began to patter among the dried leaves on the ground, like the bits of falling hail which precede the bursting of the tempest. Hawkeye and his three companions withdrew a few paces to a shelter, and awaited the issue with calmness that nothing but great practice could impart in such a scene.

It was not long before the reports of the rifles began to lose the echoes of the woods, and to sound like weapons discharged in the open air. Then a warrior appeared, here and there, driven to the skirts of the forest, and rallying as he entered the clearing, as at the place where the final stand was to be made. These were soon joined by others, until a long line of swarthy figures was to be seen clinging to the cover with the obstinacy of desperation. Heyward began to grow impatient and turned his eyes anxiously in the direction of Chingachgook. The chief was seated on a rock, with nothing visible but his calm visage, considering the spectacle with an eye as deliberate as if he were posted there merely to view the struggle.

"The time has come for the Delaware to strike!" said Duncan.

"Not so, not so," returned the scout; "when he scents his friends, he will let them know that he is here. See, see; the knaves are getting in that clump of pines, like bees settling after their flight. By the Lord, a squaw might put a bullet into the center of such a knot of dark skins!"

At that instant the whoop was given, and a dozen Hurons fell by a discharge from Chingachgook and his band. The shout that followed was answered by a single war-cry from the forest, and a yell passed through the air that sounded as if a thousand throats were united in a common effort. The Hurons staggered, deserting the center of their line, and Uncas issued from the forest through the opening they left, at the head of a hundred warriors.

Waving his hands right and left, the young chief pointed out the enemy to his followers, who separated in pursuit. The war now divided, both wings of the broken Hurons seeking protection in the woods again, hotly pressed by the victorious warriors of the Lenape. A minute might have passed, but the sounds were already receding in different directions, and gradually losing their distinctness beneath the echoing arches of the woods. One little knot of Hurons, however, had disdained to seek a cover, and were retiring, like lions at bay, slowly and sullenly up the acclivity which Chingachgook and his band had just deserted, to mingle more closely in the fray. Magua was conspicuous in this party, both by his fierce and savage mien, and by the air of haughty authority he yet maintained.

In his eagerness to expedite the pursuit, Uncas had left himself nearly alone; but the moment his eye caught the figure of Le Subtil, every other consideration was forgotten. Raising his cry of battle, which recalled some six or seven warriors, and reckless of the disparity of their numbers, he rushed upon his enemy. Le Renard, who watched the movement, paused to receive him with secret joy. But at the moment when he thought the rashness of his impetuous young assailant had left him at his mercy, another shout was given, and La Longue Carabine was seen rushing to the rescue, attended by all his white associates. The Huron instantly turned and commenced a rapid retreat up the ascent.

There was no time for greetings or congratulations; for Uncas, though unconscious of the presence of his friends, continued the pursuit with the velocity of the wind. In vain Hawkeye called to him to respect the covers; the young Mohican braved the dangerous fire of his enemies, and soon compelled them to a flight as swift as his own headlong speed. It was fortunate that the race was of short continuance, and that the white men were much favored by their position, or the Delaware would soon have outstripped all his companions and fallen a victim to his own temerity. But ere such a calamity could happen, the pursuers and pursued entered the Wyandot village, within striking distance of each other.

Excited by the presence of their dwellings, and tired of the chase, the Hurons now made a stand, and fought around their council-lodge with the fury of despair. The onset and the issue were like the passage and destruction of a whirlwind. The tomahawk of Uncas, the blows of Hawkeye, and even the still nervous arm of Munro were all busy for that passing moment, and the ground was quickly strewed with their enemies. Still Magua, though daring and much exposed, escaped from every effort against his life, with that sort of fabled protection that was made to overlook the fortunes of favored heroes in the legends of ancient poetry. Raising a yell that spoke volumes of anger and disappointment, the subtle chief, when he saw his comrades fallen, darted away from the place, attended by his two only surviving friends, leaving the Delawares engaged in stripping the dead of the bloody trophies of their victory.

But Uncas, who had vainly sought him in the melee, bounded forward in pursuit; Hawkeye, Heyward and David still pressing on his footsteps. The utmost that the scout could effect, was to keep the muzzle of his rifle a little in advance of his friend, to whom, however, it answered every purpose of a charmed shield. Once Magua appeared disposed to make another and a final effort to revenge his losses; but, abandoning his intention as soon as demonstrated, he leaped into a thicket of bushes, through which he was followed by his enemies and suddenly entered the mouth of the cave already known to the reader. Hawkeye, who had only forborne to fire in tenderness to Uncas, raised a shout of success, and proclaimed aloud that now they were certain of their game. The pursuers dashed into the long and narrow entrance, in time to catch a glimpse of the retreating forms of the Hurons. Their passage through the natural galleries and subterraneous apartments of the cavern was preceded by the shrieks and cries of hundreds of women and children. The place, seen by its dim and uncertain light, appeared like the shades of the infernal regions, across which unhappy ghosts and savage demons were flitting in multitudes.

Still Uncas kept his eye on Magua, as if life to him possessed but a single object. Heyward and the scout still pressed on his rear, actuated, though possibly in a less degree, by a common feeling. But their way was becoming intricate, in those dark and gloomy passages and the glimpses of the retiring warriors less distinct and frequent; and for a moment the trace was believed to be lost, when a white robe was seen fluttering in the further extremity of a passage that seemed to lead up the mountain.

"'Tis Cora!" exclaimed Heyward, in a voice in which horror and delight were wildly mingled.

"Cora! Cora!" echoed Uncas, bounding forward like a deer.

"'Tis the maiden!" shouted the scout. "Courage, lady; we come! we come!"

The chase was renewed with a diligence rendered tenfold encouraging by this glimpse of the captive. But the way was rugged, broken, and in spots nearly impassable. Uncas abandoned his rifle and leaped forward with headlong precipitation. Heyward rashly imitated his example, though both were, a moment afterward, admonished of his madness by hearing the bellowing of a piece, that the Hurons found time to discharge down the passage in the rocks, the bullet from which even gave the young Mohican a slight wound.

"We must close!" said the scout, passing his friends by a desperate leap; "the knaves will pick us all off at this distance; and see, they hold the maiden so as to shield themselves!"

Though his words were unheeded, or rather unheard, his example was followed by his companions, who, by incredible exertions, got near enough to the fugitives to perceive that Cora was borne along between the two warriors while Magua prescribed the direction and manner of their flight. At this moment the forms of all four were strongly drawn against an opening in the sky, and they disappeared. Nearly frantic with disappointment, Uncas and Heyward increased efforts that already seemed superhuman, and they issued from the cavern on the side of the mountain, in time to note the route of the pursued. The course lay up the ascent, and still continued hazardous and laborious.

Encumbered by his rifle and perhaps not sustained by so deep an interest in the captive as his companions, the scout suffered the latter to precede him a little, Uncas, in his turn, taking the lead of Heyward. In this manner, rocks, precipices, and difficulties were surmounted in an incredibly short space, that at another time and under other circumstances, would have been deemed almost insuperable. But the impetuous young men were rewarded by finding that, encumbered with Cora, the Hurons were losing ground in the race.

"Stay, dog of the Wyandots!" exclaimed Uncas, shaking his bright tomahawk at Magua; "a Delaware girl calls stay!"

"I will go no further!" cried Cora, stopping unexpectedly on a ledge of rock, that overhung a deep precipice, at no great distance from the summit of the mountain. "Kill me if thou wilt, detestable Huron; I will go no further."

The supporters of the maiden raised their ready tomahawks with the impious joy that fiends are thought to take in mischief, but Magua stayed the uplifted arms. The Huron chief, after casting the weapons he had wrested from his companions over the rock, drew his knife and turned to his captive, with a look in which conflicting passions fiercely contended.

"Woman," he said, "chose; the wigwam or the knife of Le Subtil!"

Cora regarded him not, but dropping on her knees, she raised her eyes and stretched her arms toward heaven, saying in a meek and yet confiding voice:

"I am thine; do with me as thou seest best!"

"Woman," repeated Magua, hoarsely, and endeavoring in vain to catch a glance from her serene and beaming eye, "choose!"

But Cora neither heard nor heeded his demand. The form of the Huron trembled in every fibre and he raised his arm on high but dropped it again with a bewildered air, like one who doubted. Once more he struggled with himself and lifted the keen weapon again; but just then a piercing cry was heard above them, and Uncas appeared, leaping frantically, from a fearful height, upon the ledge. Magua recoiled a step and one of his assistants, profiting by the chance, sheathed his own knife in the bosom of Cora.

The Huron sprang like a tiger on his offending and already retreating country man, but the falling form of Uncas separated the unnatural combatants. Diverted from his object by this interruption, and maddened by the murder he had just witnessed, Magua buried his weapon in the back of the prostrate Delaware, uttering an unearthly shout as he committed the dastardly deed. But Uncas arose from the blow, as the wounded panther turns upon his foe, and struck the murderer of Cora to his feet, by an effort in which the last of his failing strength was expended. Then, with a stern and steady look, he turned to Le Subtil and indicated by the expression of his eye all that he would do had not the power deserted him. The latter seized the nerveless arm of the unresisting Delaware and passed his knife into his bosom three several times, before his victim, still keeping his gaze riveted on his enemy, with a look of inextinguishable scorn, fell dead at his feet.

"Mercy! mercy! Huron," cried Heyward, from above, in tones nearly choked by horror; "give mercy, and thou shalt receive from it!"

Whirling the bloody knife up at the imploring youth, the victorious Magua uttered a cry so fierce, so wild, and yet so joyous, that it conveyed the sounds of savage triumph to the ears of those who fought in the valley, a thousand feet below. He was answered by a burst from the lips of the scout, whose tall person was just then seen moving swiftly toward him, along those dangerous crags, with steps as bold and reckless as if he possessed the power to move in air. But when the hunter reached the scene of the ruthless massacre, the ledge was tenanted only by the dead.

His keen eye took a single look at the victims, and then shot its glances over the difficulties of the ascent in his front. A form stood at the brow of the mountain, on the very edge of the giddy height, with uplifted arms, in an awful attitude of menace. Without stopping to consider his person, the rifle of Hawkeye was raised; but a rock, which fell on the head of one of the fugitives below, exposed the indignant and glowing countenance of the honest Gamut. Then Magua issued from a crevice, and, stepping with calm indifference over the body of the last of his associates, he leaped a wide fissure, and ascended the rocks at a point where the arm of David could not reach him. A single bound would carry him to the brow of the precipice and assure his safety. Before taking the leap, however, the Huron paused, and shaking his hand at the scout, he shouted:

"The pale faces are dogs! the Delawares women! Magua leaves them on the rocks, for the crows!"

Laughing hoarsely, he made a desperate leap, and fell short of his mark, though his hands grasped a shrub on the verge of the height. The form of Hawkeye had crouched like a beast about to take its spring, and his frame trembled so violently with eagerness that the muzzle of the half-raised rifle played like a leaf fluttering in the wind. Without exhausting himself with fruitless efforts, the cunning Magua suffered his body to drop to the length of his arms and found a fragment for his feet to rest on. Then, summoning all his powers, he renewed the attempt and so far, succeeded to draw his knees on the edge of the mountain. It was now, when the body of his enemy was most collected together, that the agitated weapon of the scout was drawn to his shoulder. The surrounding rocks themselves were not steadier than the piece became, for the single instant that it poured out its contents. The arms of the Huron relaxed, and his body fell back a little, while his knees still kept their position. Turning a relentless look on his enemy, he shook a hand in grim defiance. But his hold loosened, and his dark person was seen cutting the air with its head downward, for a fleeting instant, until it glided past the fringe of shrubbery which clung to the mountain, in its rapid flight to destruction.

CHAPTER XXXIII.

"They fought, like brave men, long and well,
They piled that ground with Moslem slain,
They conquered but Bozzaris fell,
Bleeding at every vein.
His few surviving comrades saw
His smile when rang their loud hurrah,
And the red field was won;
Then saw in death his eyelids close
Calmly, as to a night's repose,
Like flowers at set of sun."
—Halleck.

The sun found Lenape, on the succeeding day, a nation of mourners. The sounds of the battle were over, and they had fed fat their ancient grudge, and had avenged their recent quarrel with the Mengwe, by the destruction of a whole community. The black and murky atmosphere that floated around the spot where the Hurons had encamped, sufficiently announced of itself, the fate of that wandering tribe; while hundreds of ravens, that struggled above the summits of the mountains, or swept, in noisy flocks, across the wide ranges of the woods, furnished a frightful direction to the scene of the combat. In short, any eye at all practiced in the signs of a frontier warfare might easily have traced all that unerring evidence of the ruthless results which attend an Indian vengeance.

Still, the sun rose on the Lenape a nation of mourners. No shouts of success, no songs of triumph, were heard, in rejoicings for their victory. The latest straggler had returned from his fell employment, only to strip himself of the terrific emblems of his bloody calling, and to join in the lamentations of his countrymen, as a stricken people. Pride and exultation were supplanted by humility, and the fiercest of human passions was already succeeded by the most profound and unequivocal demonstrations of grief.

The lodges were deserted; but a broad belt of earnest faces encircled a spot in their vicinity, whither everything possessing life had repaired, and where all were now collected, in deep and awful silence. Though beings of every rank and age, of both sexes, and of all pursuits, had united to form this breathing wall of bodies, they were influenced by a single emotion. Each eye was riveted on the center of that ring, which contained the objects of so much and of so common an interest.

Six Delaware girls, with their long, dark, flowing tresses falling loosely across their bosoms, stood apart, and only gave proof of their existence as they occasionally strewed sweet-scented herbs and forest flowers on a litter of fragrant plants that, under a pall of Indian robes, supported all that now remained of the ardent, high-souled, and generous Cora. Her form was concealed in many wrappers of the same simple manufacture, and her face was shut forever from the gaze of men. At her feet was seated the desolate Munro. His aged head was bowed nearly to the earth, in compelled submission to the stroke of Providence; but a hidden anguish struggled about his furrowed brow, that was only partially concealed by the careless locks of gray that had fallen, neglected, on his temples. Gamut stood at his side, his meek head bared to the rays of the sun, while his eyes, wandering and concerned, seemed to be equally divided between that little volume, which contained so many quaint but holy maxims, and the being in whose behalf his soul yearned to administer consolation. Heyward was also nigh, supporting himself against a tree, and endeavoring to keep down those sudden risings of sorrow that it required his utmost manhood to subdue.

But sad and melancholy as this group may easily be imagined, it was far less touching than another, that occupied the opposite space of the same area. Seated, as in life, with his form and limbs arranged in grave and decent composure, Uncas appeared, arrayed in the most gorgeous ornaments that the wealth of the tribe could furnish. Rich plumes nodded above his head; wampum, gorgets, bracelets, and medals, adorned his person in profusion; though his dull eye and vacant lineaments too strongly contradicted the idle tale of pride they would convey.

Directly in front of the corpse Chingachgook was placed, without arms, paint, or adornment of any sort, except the bright blue blazonry of his race, that was indelibly impressed on his naked bosom. During the long period that the tribe had thus been collected, the Mohican warrior had kept a steady, anxious look on the cold and senseless countenance of his son. So riveted and intense had been that gaze, and so changeless his attitude, that a stranger might not have told the living from the dead, but for the occasional gleaming's of a troubled spirit, that shot athwart the dark visage of one, and the deathlike calm that had forever settled on the lineaments of the other. The scout was hard by, leaning in a pensive posture on his own fatal and avenging weapon; while Tamenund, supported by the elders of his nation, occupied a high place at hand, whence he might look down on the mute and sorrowful assemblage of his people.

Just within the inner edge of the circle stood a soldier, in the military attire of a strange nation; and without it was his warhorse, in the center of a collection of mounted domestics, seemingly in readiness to undertake some distant journey. The vestments of the stranger announced him to be one who held a responsible situation near the person of the captain of the Canadas; and who, as it would now seem, finding his errand of peace frustrated by the fierce impetuosity of his allies, was content to become a silent and sad spectator of the fruits of a contest that he had arrived too late to anticipate.

The day was drawing to the close of its first quarter, and yet had the multitude maintained its breathing stillness since its dawn.

No sound louder than a stifled sob had been heard among them, nor had even a limb been moved throughout that long and painful period, except to perform the simple and touching offerings that were made, from time to time, in commemoration of the dead. The patience and forbearance of Indian fortitude could alone support such an appearance of abstraction, as seemed now to have turned each dark and motionless figure into stone.

At length, the sage of the Delawares stretched forth an arm, and leaning on the shoulders of his attendants, he arose with an air as feeble as if another age had already intervened between the man who had met his nation the preceding day and him who now tottered on his elevated stand.

"Men of the Lenape!" he said, in low, hollow tones, that sounded like a voice charged with some prophetic mission: "the face of the Manitou is behind a cloud! His eye is turned from you; His ears are shut; His tongue gives no answer. You see him not; yet His judgments are before you. Let your hearts be open and your spirits tell no lie. Men of the Lenape! the face of the Manitou is behind a cloud."

As this simple and yet terrible annunciation stole on the ears of the multitude, a stillness as deep and awful succeeded as if the venerated spirit they worshiped had uttered the words without the aid of human organs; and even the inanimate Uncas appeared a being of life, compared with the humbled and submissive throng by whom he was surrounded. As the immediate effect, however, gradually passed away, a low murmur of voices commenced a sort of chant in honor of the dead. The sounds were those of females and were thrillingly soft and wailing. The words were connected by no regular continuation, but as one ceased another took up the eulogy, or lamentation, whichever it might be called and gave vent to her emotions in such language as was suggested by her feelings and the occasion. At intervals the speaker was interrupted by general and loud bursts of sorrow, during which the girls around the bier of Cora plucked the plants and flowers blindly from her body, as if bewildered with grief. But, in the milder moments of their plaint, these emblems of purity and sweetness were cast back to their places, with every sign of tenderness and regret. Though rendered less connected by many and general interruptions and outbreaking's, a translation of their language would have contained a regular descant, which, in substance, might have proved to possess a train of consecutive ideas.

A girl, selected for the task by her rank and qualifications, commenced by modest allusions to the qualities of the deceased warrior, embellishing her expressions with those oriental images that the Indians have probably brought with them from the extremes of the other continent, and which form of themselves a link to connect the ancient histories of the two worlds. She called him the "panther of his tribe"; and described him as one whose moccasin left no trail on the dews, whose bound was like the leap of a young fawn; whose eye was brighter than a star in the dark night and whose voice, in battle, was loud as the thunder of the Manitou. She reminded him of the mother who bore him and dwelt forcibly on the happiness she must feel in possessing such a son. She bade him tell her, when they met in the world of spirits, that the Delaware girls had shed tears above the grave of her child and had called her blessed.

Then, they who succeeded, changing their tones to a milder and still more tender strain, alluded, with the delicacy and sensitiveness of women, to the stranger maiden, who had left the upper earth at a time so near his own departure, as to render the will of the Great Spirit too manifest to be disregarded. They admonished him to be kind to her, and to have consideration for her ignorance of those arts which were so necessary to the comfort of a warrior like himself. They dwelled upon her matchless beauty, and on her noble resolution, without the taint of envy, and as angels may be thought to delight in a superior excellence; adding, that these endowments should prove more than equivalent for any little imperfection in her education.

After which, others again, in due succession, spoke to the maiden herself, in the low, soft language of tenderness and love. They exhorted her to be of cheerful mind, and to fear nothing for her future welfare. A hunter would be her companion, who knew how to provide for her smallest wants; and a warrior was at her side who was able to protect he against every danger. They promised that her path should be pleasant, and her burden light. They cautioned her against unavailing regrets for the friends of her youth, and the scenes where her father had dwelt; assuring her that the "blessed hunting grounds of the Lenape," contained vales as pleasant, streams as pure; and flowers as sweet, as the "heaven of the pale faces." They advised her to be attentive to the wants of her companion, and never to forget the distinction which the Manitou had so wisely established between them. Then, in a wild burst of their chant they sang with united voices the temper of the Mohican's mind. They pronounced him noble, manly, and generous; all that became a warrior and all that a maid might love. Clothing their ideas in the most remote and subtle images, they betrayed, that, in the short period of their intercourse, they had discovered, with the intuitive perception of their sex, the truant disposition of his inclinations. The Delaware girls had found no favor in his eyes! He was of a race that had once been lords on the shores of the salt lake, and his wishes had led him back to a people who dwelt about the graves of his fathers. Why should not such a predilection be encouraged! That she was of a blood purer and richer than the rest of her nation, any eye might have seen; that she was equal to the dangers and daring of a life in the woods, her conduct had proved; and now, they added, the "wise one of the earths" had transplanted her to a place where she would find congenial spirits and might be forever happy.

Then, with another transition in voice and subject, allusions were made to the virgin who wept in the adjacent lodge. They compared her to flakes of snow; as pure, as white, as brilliant, and as liable to melt in the fierce heats of summer or congeal in the frosts of winter. They doubted not that she was lovely in the eyes of the young chief, whose skin and whose sorrow seemed so like her own; but though far from expressing such a preference, it was evident they deemed her less excellent than the maid they mourned. Still, they denied her no need her rare charms might properly claim. Her ringlets were compared to the exuberant tendrils of the vine, her eye to the blue vault of heavens, and the most spotless cloud, with its glowing flush of the sun, was admitted being less attractive than her bloom.

During these and similar songs nothing was audible but the murmurs of the music; relieved, as it was, or rather rendered terrible, by those occasional bursts of grief which might be called its choruses. The Delawares themselves listened like charmed men; and it was very apparent, by the variations of their speaking countenances, how deep and true was their sympathy. Even David was not reluctant to lend his ears to the tones of voices so sweet; and long ere the chant was ended, his gaze announced that his soul was enthralled.

The scout, to whom alone, of all the white men, the words were intelligible, suffered himself to be a little aroused from his meditative posture, and bent his face aside, to catch their meaning, as the girls proceeded. But when they spoke of the future prospects of Cora and Uncas, he shook his head, like one who knew the error of their simple creed, and resuming his reclining attitude, he maintained it until the ceremony, if that might be called a ceremony, in which feeling was so deeply imbued, was finished. Happily, for the self-command of both Heyward and Munro, they knew not the meaning of the wild sounds they heard.

Chingachgook was a solitary exception to the interest manifested by the native part of the audience. His look never changed throughout the whole of the scene, nor did a muscle move in his rigid countenance, even at the wildest or the most pathetic parts of the lamentation. The cold and senseless remains of his son was all to him, and every other sense but that of sight seemed frozen, in order that his eyes might take their final gaze at those lineaments he had so long loved, and which were now about to be closed forever from his view.

In this stage of the obsequies, a warrior much renowned for deed in arms, and more especially for services in the recent combat, a man of stern and grave demeanor, advanced slowly from the crowd, and placed himself nigh the person of the dead.

"Why hast thou left us, pride of the Wapanachki?" he said, addressing himself to the dull ears of Uncas, as if the empty clay retained the faculties of the animated man; "thy time has been like that of the sun when in the trees; thy glory brighter than his light at noonday. Thou art gone, youthful warrior, but a hundred Wyandots are clearing the briers from thy path to the world of the spirits. Who that saw thee in battle would believe that thou couldst die? Who before thee has ever shown Uttawa the way into the fight? Thy feet were like the wings of eagles; thine arm heavier than falling branches from the pine and thy voice like the Manitou when He speaks in the clouds. The tongue of Uttawa is weak," he added, looking about him with a melancholy gaze, "and his heart exceeding heavy. Pride of the Wapanachki, why hast thou left us?"

He was succeeded by others, in due order, until most of the high and gifted men of the nation had sung or spoken their tribute of praise over the manes of the deceased chief. When each had ended, another deep and breathing silence reigned in all the place.

Then a low, deep sound was heard, like the suppressed accompaniment of distant music, rising just high enough on the air to be audible and yet so indistinctly, as to leave its character, and the place whence it proceeded, alike matters of conjecture. It was, however, succeeded by another and another strain, each in a higher key, until they grew on the ear, first in long drawn and often repeated interjections and finally in words. The lips of Chingachgook had so far parted, as to announce that it was the monody of the father. Though not an eye was turned toward him; nor the smallest sign of impatience exhibited, it was apparent, by the manner in which the multitude elevated their heads to listen, that they drank in the sounds with an intenseness of attention, that none but Tamenund himself had ever before commanded. But they listened in vain. The strains rose just so loud as to become intelligible and then grew fainter and more trembling, until they finally sank on the ear, as if borne away by a passing breath of wind. The lips of the Sagamore closed and he remained silent in his seat, looking with his riveted eye and motionless form, like some creature that had been turned from the Almighty hand with the form but without the spirit of a man. The Delawares who knew by these symptoms that the mind of their friend was not prepared for so mighty an effort of fortitude, relaxed in their attention; and, with an innate delicacy, seemed to bestow all their thoughts on the obsequies of the stranger maiden.

A signal was given, by one of the elder chiefs, to the women who crowded that part of the circle near which the body of Cora lay. Obedient to the sign, the girls raised the bier to the elevation of their heads, and advanced with slow and regulated steps, chanting, as they proceeded, another wailing song in praise of the deceased. Gamut, who had been a close observer of rites he deemed so heathenish, now bent his head over the shoulder of the unconscious father, whispering:

"They move with the remains of thy child; shall we not follow, and see them interred with Christian burial?"

Munro started, as if the last trumpet had sounded in his ear, and bestowing one anxious and hurried glance around him, he arose and followed in the simple train, with the mien of a soldier but bearing the full burden of a parent's suffering. His friends pressed around him with a sorrow that was too strong to be termed sympathy even the young Frenchman joining in the procession, with the air of a man who was sensibly touched at the early and melancholy fate of one so lovely. But when the last and humblest female of the tribe had joined in the wild and yet ordered array, the men of the Lenape contracted their circle, and formed again around the person of Uncas, as silent, as grave, and as motionless as before.

The place which had been chosen for the grave of Cora was a little knoll, where a cluster of young and healthful pines had taken root, forming of themselves a melancholy and appropriate shade over the spot. On reaching it the girls deposited their burden, and continued for many minutes waiting, with characteristic patience, and native timidity, for some evidence that they whose feelings were most concerned were content with the arrangement. At length the scout, who alone understood their habits, said, in their own language:

"My daughters have done well; the white men thank them."

Satisfied with this testimony in their favor, the girls proceeded to deposit the body in a shell, ingeniously, and not inelegantly, fabricated of the bark of the birch; after which they lowered it into its dark and final abode. The ceremony of covering the remains, and concealing the marks of the fresh earth, by leaves and other natural and customary objects, was conducted with the same simple and silent forms. But when the labors of the kind beings who had performed these sad and friendly offices were so far completed, they hesitated, in a way to show that they knew not how much further they might proceed. It was in this stage of the rites that the scout again addressed them:

"My young women have done enough," he said: "the spirit of the pale face has no need of food or raiment, their gifts being according to the heaven of their color. I see," he added, glancing an eye at David, who was preparing his book in a manner that indicated an intention to lead the way in sacred song, "that one who better knows the Christian fashions is about to speak."

The females stood modestly aside, and, from having been the

principal actors in the scene, they now became the meek and attentive observers of that which followed. During the time David occupied in pouring out the pious feelings of his spirit in this manner, not a sign of surprise, nor a look of impatience, escaped them. They listened like those who knew the meaning of the strange words, and appeared as if they felt the mingled emotions of sorrow, hope, and resignation, they were intended to convey.

Excited by the scene he had just witnessed, and perhaps influenced by his own secret emotions, the master of song exceeded his usual efforts. His full rich voice was not found to suffer by a comparison with the soft tones of the girls and his more modulated strains possessed, at least for the ears of those to whom they were peculiarly addressed, the additional power of intelligence. He ended the anthem, as he had commenced it, in the midst of a grave and solemn stillness.

When, however, the closing cadence had fallen on the ears of his auditors, the secret, timorous glances of the eyes, and the general and yet subdued movement of the assemblage, betrayed that something was expected from the father of the deceased. Munro seemed sensible that the time was come for him to exert what is, perhaps, the greatest effort of which human nature is capable. He bared his gray locks, and looked around the timid and quiet throng by which he was encircled, with a firm and collected countenance. Then, motioning with his hand for the scout to listen, he said:

"Say to these kind and gentle females, that a heart-broken and failing man returns them his thanks. Tell them, that the Being we all worship, under different names, will be mindful of their charity; and that the time shall not be distant when we may assemble around His throne without distinction of sex, or rank, or color."

The scout listened to the tremulous voice in which the veteran delivered these words, and shook his head slowly when they were ended, as one who doubted their efficacy.

"To tell them this," he said, "would be to tell them that the snows come not in the winter, or that the sun shines fiercest when the trees are stripped of their leaves."

Then turning to the women, he made such a communication of the other's gratitude as he deemed most suited to the capacities of his listeners. The head of Munro had already sunk upon his chest, and he was again fast relapsing into melancholy, when the young Frenchman before named ventured to touch him lightly on the elbow. As soon as he had gained the attention of the mourning old man, he pointed toward a group of young Indians, who approached with a light but closely covered litter and then pointed upward toward the sun.

"I understand you, sir," returned Munro, with a voice of forced firmness; "I understand you. It is the will of Heaven, and I submit. Cora, my child! if the prayers of a heart-broken father could avail thee now, how blessed shouldst thou be! Come, gentlemen," he added, looking about him with an air of lofty composure, though the anguish that quivered in his faded countenance was far too powerful to be concealed, "our duty here is ended; let us depart."

Heyward gladly obeyed a summons that took them from a spot where, each instant, he felt his self-control was about to desert him. While his companions were mounting, however, he found time to press the hand of the scout, and to repeat the terms of an engagement they had made to meet again within the posts of the British army. Then, gladly throwing himself into the saddle, he spurred his charger to the side of the litter, whence low and stifled sobs alone announced the presence of Alice. In this manner, the head of Munro again drooping on his bosom, with Heyward and David following in sorrowing silence, and attended by the aide of Montcalm with his guard, all the white men, with the exception of Hawkeye, passed from before the eyes of the Delawares, and were buried in the vast forests of that region.

But the tie which, through their common calamity, had united the feelings of these simple dwellers in the woods with the strangers who had thus transiently visited them, was not so easily broken. Years passed away before the traditionary tale of the white maiden, and of the young warrior of the Mohicans ceased to beguile the long nights and tedious marches, or to animate their youthful and brave with a desire for vengeance. Neither were the secondary actors in these momentous incidents forgotten. Through the medium of the scout, who served for years afterward as a link between them and civilized life, they learned, in answer to their inquiries, that the "Gray Head" was speedily gathered to his fathers, borne down, as was erroneously believed, by his military misfortunes; and that the "Open Hand" had conveyed his surviving daughter far into the settlements of the pale faces, where her tears had at last ceased to flow and had been succeeded by the bright smiles which were better suited to her joyous nature.

But these were events of a time later than that which concerns our tale. Deserted by all of his color, Hawkeye returned to the spot where his sympathies led him, with a force that no ideal bond of union could destroy. He was just in time to catch a parting look of the features of Uncas, whom the Delawares were already inclosing in his last vestment of skins. They paused to permit the longing and lingering gaze of the sturdy woodsman, and when it was ended, the body was enveloped, never to be unclosed again. Then came a procession like the other, and the whole nation was collected about the temporary grave of the chief temporary, because it was proper that, at some future day, his bones should rest among those of his own people.

The movement, like the feeling, had been simultaneous and general. The same grave expression of grief, the same rigid silence, and the same deference to the principal mourner, were observed around the place of interment as have been already described. The body was deposited in an attitude of repose, facing the rising sun, with the implements of war and of the chase at hand, in readiness for the final journey. An opening was left in the shell, by which it was protected from the soil, for the spirit to communicate with its earthly tenement, when necessary; and the whole was concealed from the instinct and protected from the ravages of the beasts of prey, with an ingenuity peculiar to the natives. The manual rites then ceased and all present reverted to the more spiritual part of the ceremonies.

Chingachgook became once more the object of the common attention. He had not yet spoken, and something consolatory and instructive was expected from so renowned a chief on an occasion of such interest. Conscious of the wishes of the people, the stern and self-restrained warrior raised his face, which had latterly been buried in his robe, and looked about him with a steady eye. His firmly compressed and expressive lips then severed, and for the first time during the long ceremonies his voice was distinctly audible. "Why do my brothers mourn?" he said, regarding the dark race of dejected warriors by whom he was environed; "why do my daughters weep? that a young man has gone to the happy hunting-grounds; that a chief has filled his time with honor? He was good; he was dutiful; he was brave. Who can deny it? The Manitou had need of such a warrior, and He has called him away. As for me, the son, and the father of Uncas, I am a blazed pine, in a clearing of pale faces. My race has gone from the shores of the salt lake and the hills of the Delawares. But who can say that the serpent of his tribe has forgotten his wisdom? I am alone..."

"No, no," cried Hawkeye, who had been gazing with a yearning look at the rigid features of his friend, with something like his own self-command, but whose philosophy could endure no longer; "no, Sagamore, not alone. The gifts of our colors may be different, but God has so placed us as to journey in the same path. I have no kin, and I may also say, like you, no people. He was your son, and a red skin by nature; and it may be that your blood was nearer but if ever I forget the lad who has so often found at my side in war, and slept at my side in peace, may He who made us all, whatever may be our color or our gifts, forget me! The boy has left us for a time but, Sagamore, you are not alone."

Chingachgook grasped the hand that, in the warmth of feeling, the scout had stretched across the fresh earth, and in an attitude of friendship these two sturdy and intrepid woodsmen bowed their heads together, while scalding tears fell to their feet, watering the grave of Uncas like drops of falling rain.

In the midst of the awful stillness with which such a burst of feeling, coming as it did, from the two most renowned warriors of that region, was received, Tamenund lifted his voice to disperse the multitude.

"It is enough," he said. "Go, children of the Lenape, the anger of the Manitou is not done. Why should Tamenund stay? The pale faces are masters of the earth, and the time of the red men has not yet come again. My day has been too long. In the morning I saw the sons of Unamis happy and strong and yet, before the night has come, have I lived to see the last warrior of the wise race of the Mohicans."

LIST OF TITLES WITH ISBN NO.

ISBN	TITLE
9788194914129	1984
9789390575220	1984 & Animal Farm (2In1)
9789390575572	1984 & Animal Farm (2In1): The International Best-Selling Classics
9789390575848	35 Sonnets
9789390575329	A Clergyman's Daughter
9789390575923	A Study In Scarlet
9789390896097	A Tale Of Two Cities
9789390896837	Abide in Christ
9789390896202	Abraham Lincoln
9789390896912	Absolute Surrender
9789390896608	African American Classic Collection
9789390575305	Aldous Huxley: The Collected Works
9789390896141	An Autobiography of M. K. Gandhi
9789390575886	Animal Farm
9789390575619	Animal Farm & The Great Gatsby (2In1)
9789390575626	Animal Farm & We
9789390896158	Anna Karenina
9789390575534	Antic Hay
9789390896165	Antony & Cleopatra
9789390896172	As I Lay Dying
9789390896226	As You like it
9789390575671	At Your Command
9789390575350	Awakened Imagination
9789390575114	Be What You Wish
9789390896233	Believe In yourself
9789390896998	Best of Charles Darwin: The Origin of Species & Autobiography
9789390896684	Best Of Horror : Dracula And Frankenstein
9789390575503	Best Of Mark Twain (The Adventures of Tom Sawyer AND The Adventures of Huckleberry Finn)
9789390896769	Black History Collection
9789390575756	Brave New World, Animal Farm & 1984 (3in1)

9789390896240	Brother Karamzov
9789390575053	Bulleh Shah Poetry
9789390575725	Burmese Days
9789390896257	Bushido
9789390896066	Can't Hurt Me
9788194914112	Chanakya Neeti: With The Complete Sutras
9789390896042	Crime and Punishment
9789390575527	Crome Yellow
9789390575046	Down and Out in Paris and London
9789390896844	Dracula
9789390575442	Emersons Essays: The Complete First & Second Series (Self-Reliance & Other Essays)
9789390575749	Emma
9789390575817	Essential Tozer Collection - The Pursuit of God & The Purpose of Man
9789390896578	Fascism What It Is and How to Fight It
9789390575688	Feeling is the Secret
9789390575190	Five Lessons
9789390575954	Frankenstein
9789390575237	Franz Kafka: Collected Works
9789390575282	Franz Kafka: Short Stories
9789390575060	George Orwell Collected Works
9789390575077	George Orwell Essays
9789390575213	George Orwell Poems
9788194914150	Greatest Poetry Ever Written Vol 1
9788194914143	Greatest Poetry Ever Written Vol 1
9789390896301	Gulliver's Travel
9789390575961	Gunaho Ka Devta
9789390575893	H. P. Lovecraft Selected Stories Vol 1
9789390575978	H. P. Lovecraft Selected Stories Vol 2
9789390896059	Hamlet
9789390575022	His Last Bow: Some Reminiscences of Sherlock Holmes
9789390896134	History of Western Philosophy
9789390575121	Homage To Catalonia

9789390896219	How to develop self-confidence and Improve public Speaking
9789390896295	How to enjoy your life and your Job
9789390575633	How to own your own mind
9789390896318	How to read Human Nature
9789390896325	How to sell your way through the life
9789390896370	How to use the laws of mind
9789390896387	How to use the power of prayer
9789390896028	How to win friends & Influence People
9788194824176	How To Win Friends and Influence People
9789390896103	Humility The Beauty of Holiness
9789390896653	Imperialism the Highest Stage of Capitalism
9789390575084	In Our Time
9789390575169	In Our Time & Three Stories and Ten poems
9789390575145	James Allen: The Collected Works
9789390896189	Jesus Himself
9789390575480	Jo's Boys
9789390896394	Julius Caesar
9789390575404	Keep the Aspidistra Flying
9789390896400	Kidnapped
9789390896424	King Lear
9789390575824	Lady Susan
9789390896455	Law of Success
9789390896264	Lincoln The Unknown
9789390575565	Little Men
9789390575640	Little Women
9788194914174	Lost Horizon
9789390896462	Macbeth
9789390896929	Man Eaters of Kumaon
9789390896523	Man The Dwelling Place of God
9789390896349	Man The Dwelling Place of God
9789390575909	Mansfield Park
9788194914136	Manto Ki 25 Sarvshreshth Kahaniya
9789390896509	Marxism, Anarchism, Communism
9789390575664	Mathematical Principles of Natural Philosophy

9788194914198	Meditations
9789390575800	Mein Kampf
9789390575794	Memory How To Develop, Train, And Use It
9789390896486	Mind Power
9789390896585	Money
9789390575039	Mortal Coils
9789390575770	My Life and Work
9789390896035	Narrative of the Life of Frederick Douglass
9789390575152	Neville Goddard: The Collected Works
9789390575985	Northanger Abbey
9789390896530	Notes From Underground
9789390896547	Oliver Twist
9789390575459	On War
9789390575541	One, None and a Hundred Thousand
9789390896554	Othelo
9789390575435	Out Of This World
9789390575015	Persuasion
9789390575510	Prayer The Art Of Believing
9789390575091	Pride and Prejudice
9789390896561	Psychic Perception
9789390575381	Rabindranath Tagore - 5 Best Short Stories Vol 2
9789390575367	Rabindranath Tagore - Short Stories (Masters Collections Including The Childs Return)
9789390575374	Rabindranath Tagore 5 Best Short Stories Vol 1 (Including The Childs Return
9789390896622	Romeo & Juliet
9789390896127	Sanatana Dharma
9789390575596	Seedtime & Harvest
9789390896639	Selected Stories of Guy De Maupassant
9789390575206	Self-Reliance & Other Essays
9789390575176	Sense and Sensibility
9789390575299	Shyamchi Aai
9789390896738	Socialism Utopian and Scientific
9789390896646	Success Through a Positive Mental Attitude
9789390575428	The Adventures of Huckleberry Finn

9789390575183	The Adventures of Sherlock Holmes
9789390575343	The Adventures of Tom Sawyer
9789390896691	The Alchemy Of Happiness
9789390575862	The Art Of Public Speaking
9789390896288	The Autobiography Of Charles Darwin
9788194914181	The Best of Franz Kafka: The Metamorphosis & The Trial
9789390575008	The Call Of Cthulhu and Other Weird Tales
9789390575107	The Case-Book of Sherlock Holmes
9789390896110	The Castle Of Otranto
9789390896745	The Communist Manifesto
9789390575589	The Complete Fiction of H. P. Lovecraft
9789390575497	The Complete Works of Florence Scovel Shinn
9789390896820	The Conquest of Breard
9789390896813	The Diary of a Young Girl
9789390896332	The Diary of a Young Girl The Definitive Edition of the Worlds Most Famous Diary
9789390575701	The Great Gatsby, Animal Farm & 1984 (3In1)
9789390575312	The Greatest Works Of George Orwell (5 Books) Including 1984 & Non-Fiction
9789390575992	The Hound of Baskervilles
9789390896707	The Idiot
9789390896714	The Invisible Man
9789390575657	The Knowledge of the holy
9789390575558	The Law & the Promise
9789390896721	The Law Of Attraction
9789390896776	The Leader in you
9789390896363	The Life of Christ
9789390896196	The Man-Eating Leopard of Rudraprayag
9789390896783	The Master Key to Riches
9789390575268	The Memoirs Of Sherlock Holmes
9789390896479	The Midsummer Night's Dream
9789390575466	The Mill On The Floss
9789390896790	The Miracles of your mind
9789390896660	The Mutual Aid A Factor in Evolution
9789390896448	The Origin of Species

9789390896905	The Peter Kropotkin Anthology The Conquest of Bread & Mutual Aid A Factor of Evolution
9789390896806	The Picture of Dorian Gray
9789390896271	The Picture of Dorian Gray
9789390575275	The Power Of Awareness
9789390896356	The Power of Concentration
9788194824169	The Power of Positive Thinking
9789390575411	The Power of the Spoken Word
9788194914105	The Power Of Your Subconscious Mind
9789390896899	The Power of Your Subconscious Mind
9789390896417	The Principles of Communism
9789390575787	The Psychology Of Mans Possible Evolution
9789390896615	The Psychology of Salesmanship
9789390575732	The Pursuit of God
9789390575398	The Pursuit of Happiness
9789390896851	The Quick and Easy Way to effective Speaking
9789390575947	The Return Of Sherlock Holmes
9789390575138	The Road To Wigan Pier
9789390896981	The Root of the Righteous
9789390575855	The Science Of Being Well
9788194914167	The Science Of Getting Rich, The Science Of Being Great & The Science Of Being Well (3In1)
9789390896011	The Screwtape Letters
9789390896073	The Screwtape Letters
9789390575336	The Secret Door to Success
9789390575695	The Secret Of Imagining
9789390896868	The Secret Of Success
9789390896431	The Seven Last Words
9789390575930	The Sign of the Four
9789390896004	The Sonnets
9789390896516	The Souls of Black Folk
9789390896875	The Sound and The Fury
9789390575244	The State and Revolution
9789390896882	The Story of My Life
9789390896936	The Story Of Oriental Philosophy

9789390896752	The Strange Case of Dr. Jekyll and Mr. Hyde
9789390896943	The Tempest
9789390575916	The Valley Of Fear
9789390575879	The Wind in the willows
9789390896080	The Wind in the willows
9789390575763	Their eyes were watching gofd
9789390575831	Three Stories
9789390896950	Twelfth Night
9789390896592	Twelve Years a Slave
9789390896677	Up from Slavery
9789390896974	Value Price and Profit
9789390896967	Wake Up and Live
9789390896493	With Christ in the School of Prayer
9789390575602	Your Faith is Your Fortune
9789390575473	Your Infinite Power To Be Rich
9789390575251	Your Word is Your Wand
9789390575718	Youth
9789391316099	A Christmas Carol
9789391316105	A Doll's House
9789391316501	A Passage to India
9789391316709	A Portrait of the Artist as a Young Man
9789391316112	A Tale of Two Cities
9789391316747	A Tear and a Smile
9789391316167	Agnes Gray
9789391316174	Alice's Adventures in Wonderland
9789391316136	Anandamath
9789391316181	Anne Of Green Gables
9789391316754	Anthem
9789391316198	Around The World in 80 Days
9789391316013	As A Man Thinketh
9789391316242	Autobiography of a Yogi
9789391316266	Beyond Good and Evil
9789391316761	Bleak House
9789391316778	Chitra, a Play in One Act
9789391316310	David Copperfield

9789391316075	Demian
9789391316785	Dubliners
9789391316051	Favourite Tales from the Arabian Nights
9789391316235	Gitanjali
9789391316068	Gravity
9789391316150	Great Speeches of Abraham Lincoln
9789391316662	Guerilla Warfare
9789391316839	Kim
9789391316822	Mother
9789391316211	My Childhood
9789391316846	Nationalism
9789391316327	Oliver Twist
9789391316853	Pygmalion
9789391316334	Relativity: The Special and the General Theory
9789391316389	Scientific Healing Affirmation
9789391316341	Sons and Lovers
9789391316587	Tales from India
9789391316372	Tess of The D'Urbervilles
9789391316396	The Awakening and Selected Stories
9789391316402	The Bhagvad Gita
9789391316303	The Book of Enoch
9789391316228	The Canterville Ghost
9789391316907	The Dynamic Laws of Prosperity
9789391316006	The Great Gatsby
9789391316860	The Hungry Stones and Other Stories
9789391316433	The Idiot
9789391316440	The Importance of Being Earnest
9789391316297	The Light of Asia
9789391316914	The Madman His Parables and Poems
9789391316457	The Odyssey
9789391316921	The Picture of Dorian Gray
9789391316464	The Prince
9789391316938	The Prophet
9789391316945	The Republic
9789391316518	The Scarlet Letter

9789391316143	The Seven Laws of Teaching
9789391316525	The Story of My Experiments with Truth
9789391316532	The Tales of the Mother Goose
9789391316549	The Thirty Nine Steps
9789391316594	The Time Machine
9789391316600	The Turn of the Screw
9789391316983	The Upanishads
9789391316617	The Yellow Wallpaper
9789391316426	The Yoga Sutras of Patanjali
9789391316990	Ulysses
9789391316624	Utopia
9789391316679	Vanity Fair
9789391316020	What Is To Be Done
9789391316686	Within A Budding Grove
9789391316693	Women in Love